Sign up for our newsletter to hear
about new and upcoming releases.

www.ylva-publishing.com

OTHER BOOKS BY ANDREA BRAMHALL

Rock and a Hard Place
Just My Luck

Norfolk Coast Investigation Story
Collide-O-Scope
Under Parr
The Last First Time

ANDREA BRAMHALL

LOST FOR WORDS

DEDICATION

For Grandad
Harold Bramhall
3.10.1929–27.2.2018
There were so many times you left us all lost for words, Grandad.

ACKNOWLEDGEMENTS

Thank you to the team at Ylva—Astrid, Daniela, Michelle. Your help, encouragement, and support through all my writing endeavours is truly appreciated.

My lovely beta readers, Louise and Wendy, your help made this book much better and funnier than it would have been otherwise.

To all my family—without you, there would be little inspiration for all the funny moments in this book. Faye, I particularly owe the potpourri moment to you.

And lastly, to all of you who have taken the time to pick this book up and read it. Thank you for your support. Enjoy!

CHAPTER 1

"I have a confession to make."

Sasha Adams sighed inwardly, straightened her back, and spun to face her best friend. Bobbi Johnson's confessions ranged from eating the last chocolate biscuit when Sasha was PMSing to... Well, just about anything was possible.

"All right. Will we need bail money?"

"Erm...not this time."

"Spade to bury the body?"

Bobbi's dark-skinned face cracked into a wide smile, her coal-dark eyes twinkling with amusement. "Possibly. When you kill me." The relaxed afro curls in her short Mohawk flopped a little as she shuffled from side to side, and Sasha could see a sheen of sweat on her upper lip.

Sasha rolled her hand to hurry Bobbi along. It had been a long day at work, her feet were killing her, and all she wanted was to get home. The Serenity Spa was a luxurious, opulent place to work, but Sasha wanted nothing more than to kick off her shoes, put up her feet, and finish up the new project she was working on.

Bobbi sucked in a big breath and started, "I may or may not have accidentally—remember that part, it was totally accidental—but I may have introduced your mother to a new form of baking. Possibly."

Sasha frowned. "You've been baking with my mother?"

"Accidentally."

"How does one 'accidentally' bake? And with my mother? And what do you mean 'a new form'?"

"It's a long story."

Sasha blinked, then pointed to the corridor. "My last massage's done. You?"

Bobbi nodded.

"Then I guess you can tell me all about this long story while you give me a lift home."

She seemed to consider this a moment, then nodded. "You probably can't kill me while I'm behind the wheel. At least not without killing yourself too. Sounds like a plan."

They collected their things from the deserted staff room before they climbed into Bobbi's old red Astra. Well, red except for the blue door on the passenger side she got from a scrapyard after an incident with a skip and a vicious badger. But that was another long story.

Sasha waited until they'd pulled out of the car park, glad she didn't have to wait for the bus this evening as the drizzle covered the windscreen. She turned in her seat to watch Bobbi's face. The orange-tinted light of Manchester city after dark was more than enough to see her friend clearly.

"I'm ready for your confession, my child," she said, doing her best impression of a priest.

Bobbi snickered but began, "So, erm, you know the other night when you had a killer headache and went to bed early?"

"Which night? You have tea with us nearly every night, and I've had a couple of migraines recently."

"Two nights ago, we were having tea with your mum. Migraine from hell hit you."

"Okay, the scene is set."

"So your mum was having some of her pains, you know? The ones from her prosthetic."

Sasha nodded provisionally, wondering in another part of her brain if her mum had caused herself some new blisters on her stump. You'd think that nearly five years after a bone-cancer scare, with a leg amputation to show for it, Fleur would have learnt to let people take care of her more. It wasn't as if the myriad of phantom pains she suffered weren't consistent reminders to take it easy. "Get to the confession, Bobbi."

"Well, she was taking her medicine."

Sasha lifted her eyebrows. "Which medicine?"

"The one the doctor prescribed."

"The doctor's prescribed her with a range of 'medicines', honey. Which one are we talking about here?"

"She was smoking a joint."

"I hope you went in the conservatory with her. She's stinking the house out with all the pot she's smoking now."

"You've noticed, huh?"

"Noticed?"

"How much she's smoking lately?"

"Well, yeah. It's hard to miss when I walk out of the house smelling like a pothead all the time," Sasha commented. "Why?"

"Just wondered if it meant she was getting more pain than usual. That's all."

"She hasn't mentioned it particularly. I think she's just enjoying her official hippie status. She thinks she's back at Woodstock or something."

"Woodstock?"

"Apparently."

"Your mum went to Woodstock? *The* Woodstock?"

"So she tells me."

"Seriously?"

Sasha shrugged.

"How did I not know this? Tell me all about it. Now."

"No, you're still telling me about my mother and you baking."

Bobbi cast her a glance, then turned back to the road. "Fine, but later you're telling me about your supercool mother and Woodstock."

Sasha rolled her hand again.

"Well, she was coughing every time she tried to take a drag. So I asked her why she didn't stop smoking the stuff. She said she couldn't if she wanted to get any sleep that night, and I might have possibly mentioned, in passing, very, very briefly, that she could always take it a different way. One that wouldn't be so hard on her lungs all the time."

"You taught my mother how to make space cakes." It wasn't a question. It didn't need to be.

"It was an accident."

"That's not an accident, Bobbi. An accident is where you trip, fall off the kerb, and sprain your ankle. Or where you drop a glass when you're washing up because your hands are wet and soapy. Those things are accidents. Taking my mum into the kitchen, showing her how to make hash cakes, and no doubt helping her polish off some of those hash cakes, that's not an accident. See the difference?"

Bobbi nodded like a chastised child and mumbled an apology under her breath.

Sasha chuckled at the look of contrition.

"You gonna kill me now?"

"Nah."

Bobbi looked at her hopefully. "Really?"

"Really."

"I won't teach her anything else—"

"Honey, I hate to burst your little bubble here, but I'm pretty sure my mother has made hash cakes before. I'm *very* sure she's eaten them before. And if she hadn't been stoned already, your little 'accidental' divulgence would not have been anything new to her at all."

Bobbi eyed her sceptically from the corner of her eye. "I don't know. She seemed—"

"Woodstock," Sasha replied in a sing-song voice and tried to supress a grin when Bobbi nodded and wrinkled her nose.

"There are pictures of me as a five-year-old at Glastonbury with her in 1978."

Bobbi nodded again.

"There's not an awful lot left to teach her, hon."

"Fair point," Bobbi conceded. "I'll ask her for lessons in the leading-folk-astray category of life."

"Now you're learning, young grasshopper." They drove in silence for a few minutes until they tuned right into Sasha's road.

"Sasha?"

"Yeah?"

"Your mum's awesome."

Sasha rested her head back against the headrest, a grin spreading across her lips.

"You know that, right?"

"Yeah," she said quietly. "I do."

Bobbi parked up outside the house Sasha shared with her mum. One of many on a street filled with long lines of Victorian houses, each one joined to the next. Each one made of red brick that had long since faded to dirty. Paint colours were the only real distinction from one house or street to the next; graffiti acted like the territory lines for gangs of youths, and the paint on each front door was chipped and scarred.

Sasha liked to think theirs was fairing a little better than average. And the planters in the front yard were neat and weeded. The stone topper on the wall was painted too, and the bins were upright and not covered in graffiti. The window at the front had a net curtain stretched across it. A black cat sat on the windowsill staring out at them, green eyes watching them with bored disdain.

"Sasha?"

"Yeah?"

"Did she really go to Woodstock?"

Sasha pointed to the door. "Come on. We'll have some tea and you can ask her for the details yourself."

"Cool." Bobbi tugged her keys out of the ignition.

"But if she tries to tell you that I'm the secret love child of Jimi Hendrix...she's talking out of her arse."

Bobbi tutted. "Even I'd know that."

Sasha slid the strap of her handbag over her shoulder and glanced at her hand. Yup, her milky-white skin would definitely give that one away.

"You can't even play the guitar."

Sasha strode into the kitchen and popped an arm around her mother's shoulders, kissing her on the cheek as Fleur stirred a pan on the stove.

"Hey, sweetheart," Fleur said, not taking her eyes off the pan. "How was work today?"

"Same old, same old. Massages, manicures, facials, aching feet." Serenity Spa might be a luxury spa, but it was still a spa. She pointed to the pan. "Is there enough for one extra?"

Fleur smiled. "Of course. Hey, Bobbi."

"Hey, Mrs A." Bobbi stepped up and kissed Fleur's other cheek. "Thanks."

"You're welcome."

"How was your day, Mum?" Sasha dropped heavily into a chair and toed off her shoes. She groaned with pleasure as she wiggled her toes in contentment.

"Same old, same old," Fleur said, reiterating Sasha's well-used phrase. "Wine, girls?"

Sasha shook her head. "I think I'll just have a cuppa." She stood to put the kettle on to boil. "Bobbi?"

"Please."

"Mum?"

Fleur lifted the crystal necklace from her neck, pointed to two, seemingly random, spots on the counter, and hung the chain over it. Sasha resisted the urge to roll her eyes as Fleur closed hers, connected to her "higher spirit", then swayed back and forth for a moment before opening her eyes and giving a little nod.

"Yes, but I'll do it," Fleur said. "You've both been working all day."

"It's fine, Mum. I'm already up." Sasha filled the kettle and flipped the switch, eyeing her mother critically. "You okay? You look tired."

"You'll look tired too when you get to my age." Fleur tossed her shoulder-length grey hair over her shoulder with an exaggerated flounce. "In fact, there were several years where I don't recall sleeping at all. Must be catching up with me now. Now pass me the plates."

Sasha did as she asked, then finished making the tea while Fleur doled out generous helpings of pasta for Bobbi and Sasha, and a smaller one for herself.

"You're not eating much," Sasha commented, pointing to her mother's plate, then examining her fork with mock wariness. "Poison?"

Fleur tittered. "Too slow. Besides, what would I do with your bodies?"

They all laughed.

"Oo, that reminds me," Bobbi said, looking at Sasha. "IKEA tomorrow? I need a new mattress; the spring stuck in my back for the past six months actually broke free of the fabric last night." She pointed to her eye for effect. "I nearly lost this. You're off tomorrow, right?"

"No, I'm working half-day in the morning."

"I can pick you up when you finish. Go straight over to the shop then."

Sasha shrugged. "Sure. My last client is at twelve, so I should be out just after one."

"I'll be in the car park."

"Bobbi?" Fleur said.

"Yeah?"

"Why did my mentioning hiding your bodies remind you of IKEA?"

Bobbi shrugged. "Innovative storage solutions?"

Sasha and Fleur looked at each other. *What exactly do you say to that?*

Fleur cleared her throat after a few minutes of silence. "So, Bobbi, tell me what you've been up to."

"Me?" Bobbi squeaked.

"Yes, you."

"Why me?"

"Because I'm a boring old lady who needs to live vicariously through you youngsters."

Sasha almost spit out the mouthful of tea she'd just taken at her mother's bold-faced lie. "Mum, you have more going on in your life than we do. Yoga, Pilates, bowling." She pointed to the crystal hanging from a chain around her neck. "Wasn't it your meditation group meeting today?"

Fleur waved her fork in the air. "Life-Changes Dedication class, yes."

Sasha did roll her eyes this time. Bobbi bit her lip.

"Don't look at me like that, Sasha. Just because you don't have any faith doesn't mean you get to scoff at those who do believe in something greater than themselves."

"I wasn't scoffing." *Much.*

Fleur gave her *The Look.* The look only a mother can give her child. No matter how old you got, *The Look* would always make you break out into a case of guilt—even if you hadn't done anything wrong. *The Look* would always make you give up your wildest deeds and deepest secrets. *The Look* should be outlawed under the Geneva Convention. *The Look* should be a war crime.

Sasha cleared her throat and said quietly, "Sorry. How was your class?"

"It went very well, thank you." Fleur turned rather prim and proper, looking down her nose a little at Sasha. Sasha and Bobbi turned back to their plates, but Sasha pushed the food around for a few moments before taking a bite. "The spirits are pointing me in a very definite direction for one of my little projects."

"Oh." Sasha swallowed. "Which project is that?"

11

"Project Comp," she said with a wink at Bobbi.

Bobbi's eyes widened and she stared down at her plate, shovelling more pasta into her mouth.

Sasha frowned. "And what's Project Comp all about, then?"

"None of your business."

"Oo, a secret mission." Sasha grinned. "Will you tell me if I guess correctly?"

Fleur hooted, and Bobbi blanched. "Since there is no way in hell you'll ever guess this, I can agree to those terms."

Sasha narrowed her eyes. "You don't think I can guess your secret?"

"Not a chance, sweetheart."

"Hm…*Comp*?"

"Yes, Project Comp."

"Comp as in competition?"

"That was obvious, darling." Fleur lifted one eyebrow. "You'll never get beyond there."

"You've entered a baking competition and plan to wow the ladies of the WI with your new hash cakes?"

Fleur tipped her head back and chortled. "No, but what a wonderful idea. It's been some time since those old biddies let their hair down a bit."

Sasha looked around for inspiration. Nip, the black cat with stunning green eyes and an attitude from hell, sauntered through the kitchen doorway, hopped up on to Fleur's lap, and proceeded to pull a pasta shell off Fleur's plate, then batted it across the table until it was out of reach.

"You've entered Nip into a prettiest-pussy competition?" she guessed with a snigger.

Bobbi spat her tea across the table, earning her a disgusted look from both Fleur and Nip.

Fleur tutted. "It's no wonder neither of you have had sex in years." She chucked the cat under the chin, and Sasha avoided eye contact with Bobbi. Poor Bobbi thought she hid her feelings well. Sasha didn't agree, but for the sake of their friendship she ignored the longing looks. She couldn't help that she wasn't attracted to Bobbi like that. She was a friend, almost a sister with how close they were. There could never be anything else between them, despite what Bobbi so obviously wanted.

"You certainly are a pretty pussycat," Fleur continued with a stroke over Nip's head, "but no, that's not my project. That would be far too easy. This one is the first step in my greatest challenge yet."

"Talking a big game there, Mum. You sure you can back it up?"

Fleur smiled a little Mona Lisa smile. "Like I said, the spirits are on my side with this one. Everything is already in motion." She reached over and patted Sasha's cheek. "I can't lose."

Sasha squinted. "You've definitely entered your hash cakes in the WI baking competition."

Sasha closed the door to her bedroom and glanced at the clock. Eleven o'clock. She needed to be up at six thirty so she'd have time to get ready and make it for the seven twenty-five bus. If she didn't, she'd never get into work by eight. She should really get ready for bed and try to get some sleep. But exhaustion and she were becoming long-time companions, it would seem. She sighed heavily and resigned herself to another sleepless night as a need even more pressing urged her to her desk rather than her bed.

Powering up her laptop, she cracked her knuckles, twisted her head from side to side, listening for the satisfying crunch as her vertebrae realigned themselves, and then opened up the document she'd been working on. She quickly scanned the last page she'd written, re-familiarising herself with where she was, then let her fingers find the keys. Dialogue, scene descriptions, actions, and the final act of the script began to take shape beneath her fingers.

This one was a little different to her previous scripts. A murder mystery set against the sometimes bleak and sometimes stunning landscape of the Norfolk Coast. Sasha pictured each scene, watched through her mind's eye as her heroine approached the villain, weapon raised, ready to strike.

Sasha was captivated by these characters. In them she could see so much potential. She hadn't finished the first script, and already she could picture the second and the third. Maybe more.

She smiled as she concluded the last action scene and moved to the more sedate ending to the story. A hospital room, perhaps? Yes, a hospital.

Was it strange that her world felt more complete when she could escape to her fictional realm? Was it wrong that the words, the characters called to her and kept her awake when little in her actual life could do the same? The stories she created fulfilled her in a way her job could never compete with: giving a massage to some hairy-backed bloke or creating a narrative where she could see her wildest dreams and deepest fascinations played out and explored. It wasn't even a real choice.

Sasha needed her escape, her release. Her fictional friends kept her company when others could not, offered her a way to vent her frustrations, to weep the pain and fear away with. They allowed her to be herself with in a way she could not be with anyone else.

There was no judgement, no fear, and no consequences in her make-believe world. There were no pressures, no responsibilities, no ties.

As her characters kissed passionately and promised to return for another book, Sasha felt free.

CHAPTER 2

Jac Kensington ran her fingers through her hair and propped her head in the other hand. She glanced around the glass-topped conference table in the company headquarters. Mags French and Sophie Angel were scanning spreadsheets or reviewing contracts as they waited for her to finish her phone call.

She ended it and cleared her throat, "Okay, ladies, I hereby call this board meeting of Kefran Media Limited to attention."

Sophie rolled her eyes and flicked her gaze to Jac. "Just because you're the major shareholder doesn't mean I'm going to let you hijack this meeting like you did last year. This might be an annual scriptwriting competition, and our decision deadline might be looming, but the three of us will make this decision together. Then we can call it quits for the night."

Jac tapped her pocket, checking for her packet of cigarettes before remembering she'd quit. Again. She waved her hand at the scripts in front of them. "Fine, let's get this sorted so I can go home. I've got a really good bottle of vodka waiting for me."

"You shouldn't drink alone." Mags frowned at her. "It's not a good sign." She pushed her fingers through her short bob, frowning a little when her arm seemed to want to continue after her hair had run out. Still getting used to the new shorter hairstyle and colour on her long-time friend, Jac grinned as Mags pushed her horn-rimmed glasses up her nose.

"Vanessa will be there to share it with me." *Possibly.* Jac didn't really want to think about the odds that her girlfriend of the last eighteen months would actually be at home waiting for her when she finally left the office. But she certainly wasn't prepared to put money on it, a fact that must have shown on her face as Sophie snorted at her. "Fine," Jac said with a sigh, "then I'll go to a bar and get drunk before I go home. Happy?"

Sophie and Mags both shrugged unhappily before Sophie folded back the pages on one of the scripts, her long blond hair falling over her shoulders, blue eyes watching her, worry adding to the creases there, creases they were all beginning to notice at the corners of their own eyes.

"If you do," said Sophie, "at least have some crisps or pork scratchings to soak it up, then. It'll help with the hangover."

Jac cast her what she hoped was a withering look but said, "Fine," as she stared at Mags. "You start. Favourite and why?"

Sliding her glasses up her nose, Mags launched into a hearty speech supporting Jac's least-favourite script, but she made some good points. It was lighter and had a frivolous subject at the heart of it, so it would probably do quite well.

"Yeah, yeah," Sophie said. "It'll do okay and then fade into the background with all the other forgettable films we see produced." She waved the other script in front of them both. "This one has some funny moments in it. It's a romance, but, damn it, it's got a soul too. It has a meaning at its core, values that offer a moral to the story, rather than just some empty laughs that will be forgotten as soon as the credits roll."

Jac nodded—all points she'd noticed about *Nightingale* too.

"It has a bite to it, and it's so, I don't know, *relevant*. Maybe that's the right word. The cultural issues that we face today. Women's rights, human rights, religious differences—"

"That's where I have a problem with it," Mags said. "We could end up staring down the barrel of huge religious backlash as a result. If we got any of the religious elements wrong or out of context, we could be in real trouble. I don't know about you, but I don't fancy getting on the wrong side of all this."

Jac understood Mag's point of view. The script was culturally and religiously sensitive—a Muslim girl and a Christian girl falling in love with each other. Arranged marriages. The views of other religions and cultures on homosexuality and marriage. Honour killing. Sharia law. The rights of women in Muslim countries… Sensitive was an understatement. Yet this script handled it well. They could fact-check all the relevant points. They could get an expert on board to consult with.

"Yeah, but aren't you sick of just creating fluff films, Mags?" Sophie asked. "When we started this company, it was with the idea that the three of us could make a difference. Could use our skills and talents to really do some good. I know we had good reasons to move into the popular films, the romcoms. If we hadn't, we wouldn't be able to tackle the odd film that means something. Something like this is why we made those. Seventy-five percent market pleasers, twenty-five percent soul redeemers, remember?"

Jac nodded in acknowledgement as Mags slumped back in her chair a little. Sophie was right. That was exactly what they'd always planned to do. It just hadn't really happened yet.

"But we've always wanted to find the film that could do both, the one we could make ends meet with and yet was also important." Sophie waved the sheaf of papers she was holding in her hand. "*This* could really do that. The writer hasn't slammed Islam. She's pointed out cultural differences, but in a lot of ways she's also pointed out similarities between Middle Eastern and Western cultures, and the hypocrisy of people who commit the same abuses they condemn others for, by calling them something different." She dropped the script back on the table. "Domestic violence and crimes of passion are no different to honour killing, they just have a different name."

"We punish those crimes—" Mags began.

"Ladies, I think we can leave the social debate out of this. Between these two scripts, I think it's clear that *Nightingale* is the superior piece of work. Agreed?" Jac waited until both Sophie and Mags nodded. "Good. Our decision has to be whether or not we are comfortable going with the heavy subject matter that is a potentially risky prospect or sticking to the romcom that we know will do okay."

Sophie folded her arms over her chest and slumped back in her seat. "You know how I feel. I think this film is a must."

Jac turned to Mags. "Are you truly uncomfortable or just playing devil's advocate?"

"A little of both. I do think we need to be careful. But I do agree that Sophie has some good points." She grinned. "And I don't think it would be that big of a risk either. I think the marketplace is crying out for something like this. No one's been brave enough so far to do it."

"I agree," Jac said. "It has all the elements of a classic film: a great premise, great action, hot love scenes, and a few great monologues for the actresses to really sink their teeth into."

"And she's a local girl," Sophie added. She took a quick, excited-sounding breath before she launched into her next point. "It's set in Manchester, so we'll have all our assets and resources on hand to work this. No location issues to drive up production costs and make logistics a nightmare. We can all effectively work from home base. After all, it's not like we'd be able to go to Pakistan to film, so we would be looking at CGI for those scenes. We've got the best tech here in all of Europe."

"Another good point." Basing themselves at MediaCityUK—the most sophisticated HD production facility in Europe—in Salford Quays, rather than trying to find office and studio space in London, had been a decision they'd deliberated many times when they started their company, but it was one they hadn't lived to regret. It had, however, meant that Jac had worked on location for extended periods on more than one occasion, and one day soon she would again. But not this time. This time they could all work together from start to finish. It had been a while since they'd had a project like this. She'd have fun directing it, a fact that always showed through positively in the end product.

Really, she was finding fewer and fewer reasons to say no to this script.

"Okay." Jac held up her hand, a sheaf of pages wedged in her grasp, curling about her fist. "We're going with this one. *Nightingale* by Sasha Adams."

Sophie did a little dance in her chair until the top button on her blouse popped open. Jac and Mags stared, then burst out laughing, pointing like schoolchildren. Sophie rolled her eyes and quickly refastened it.

"Want me to contact the winner?" Sophie asked.

Jac shook her head as she glanced at her watch. "It's after ten. Too late to call now. I'll do it tomorrow and set up a meeting with her to start the paperwork and get the ball rolling."

"Gotcha."

Sophie and Mags collected their things and stood. Sophie looked Jac up and down, her expression softening, switching from driven business executive to concerned best friend in an instant. "You sure you're going to be okay?"

Jac gave her a small smile, then deliberately tried to broaden it. "Go on, I'm fine."

Sophie squeezed Jac's shoulder as she passed behind her chair on her way out of the conference room, then planted a kiss atop her head. "You know where I am if you want to talk."

"I do, thanks." She patted Sophie's hand. "Now go and get out of here before your wife comes looking for you." She threw her a practiced cheeky wink as the door closed behind Sophie and Mags, but not before she caught the look that flashed between the two of them. *Dubious* would be a generous word for it. The silence settled around her and she patted her pocket again, checking for her cigarettes. "Fuck." She sighed and picked up the screenplay they'd just decided to make a film and started reading again.

"Third read and it still has me vacillating between wanting to laugh and cry." She shook her head. "That's a good sign."

The beauty of living in an apartment in Salford Quays was that Jac's commute was less than five minutes. On foot. Thank God, because her leather jacket did bugger all to keep out the chill, or the rain, as she made her way down Broadway to the apartment block, fishing in her pockets for the fob that would let her into the building.

Cursing to herself, she checked the pockets on her messenger-style laptop case, chuckling when she found the fob and her keys in the main compartment. She'd slid them in with her MacBook when she was packing up. *Getting forgetful in your old age, Jac. Better watch that.*

She held up the fob to the outer door and pushed it wide, then hit the Call button between the two lifts. She spun the small bunch of keys around her finger by the metal loop that held them together, catching them in her palm every once in a while. When she realised what she was doing, Jac frowned. Yet another fidgeting habit to add to all the rest since giving up the evil tobacco.

She hated smoking. Hated the way the smoke clung to her and the way her body craved the nicotine. She hated how her fingers itched to hold one of the little sticks, hated her dependency on something—anything—that wasn't her alone. But she hated the process of quitting anything even more.

The fact she wasn't always driven purely by her own will... Well, that was not something she ever wanted to admit, not even to herself.

The lift alert chimed, and she stepped inside. Pizza? Curry? Chinese? She hopped back and forth between her dinner options before deciding it was likely to be a beans-on-toast night before falling into bed, ready to start again the next day. She was looking forward to talking to Sasha Adams. The woman could write, and if even half of that came across in her personality, she was going to be fun to talk to.

The doors opened at the penthouse floor and the spacious hallway that led to the four-bedroom apartment she called home. Jac spun her keys one last time and crossed the highly polished wooden floor to her door. It swung open, and she stepped inside, pleased the lights were on. Vanessa was home. Maybe they'd order a curry after all.

"Hey, Vee. Where are you?" Jac tossed her keys onto the table next to the coat rack, dropped her bag onto a chair, and hung her jacket on the peg. She ran her fingers through her hair, straightening the asymmetrical style so it hung over her right eye. Vanessa had told her how she loved the way it fell across her face like this. Made her look mysterious and sexy, she'd said. Granted, it had been a while since she'd said that. But she had said it. Once.

Across the apartment, the door to their bedroom opened and Vanessa walked out, pulling a rolling suitcase behind her. Her long red hair cascaded down her back like a wave of burnished copper, glinting in the light as she glided across the floor, heels clicking on the solid oak. Her blue eyes flashed with annoyance.

"I didn't expect you home so early."

Ah. So that's the way it's going to be. "Sorry to interrupt your plans." Jac didn't feign ignorance as to what was going on. Nor did she have any inclination to ask the obvious question. "Were you planning to leave a note, or was I going to find out when I reported you missing to the police?"

Vanessa held up the envelope Jac hadn't noticed she was holding. She didn't cross the room to give it to her. Instead, Vanessa leant over with an arm outstretched and let it plummet onto the coffee table. "I'm not that callous."

Jac disagreed, but it didn't really matter now.

"We had a good run, but we want different things, Jac."

Despite her earlier resolve, Jac managed to bite back any questions before they escaped her lips. They'd spent eighteen months as a couple, twelve of those living together in this apartment. At least a few of those months had been good. *But this isn't a surprise*, she told herself. It was never going to be.

"Maybe it's the age difference, but I'm not ready to just be at home all the time. I want to have fun," Vanessa said needlessly into the silence.

The twenty-five-year age gap wasn't really the issue at all. She wanted to scoff at that. And that Jac had only been looking for a beautiful distraction from the loneliness she didn't want to look at or analyse any more closely than she did her need for a cigarette. Both impulses made her fidgety and crave something to do with her hands.

"Aren't you going to say something?"

Jac's chuckle was absolutely without mirth. "What do you want me to say? Would you like me to ask who it is that's offered you a better part than I would?"

Vanessa slammed balled hands to her hips and squinted at Jac. The look formed hard lines on her face that suddenly made her look considerably older than her twenty-five years. It wasn't flattering.

"No?" Jac asked into the silence Vanessa left. "Would you like me to offer you a part in the new film I'm making? Lead role? Biggest part of your life? That's what you want, isn't it?" *That was all you ever wanted, wasn't it? When will I learn? That's all I've ever been for any of them.*

"I knew you didn't care." She grasped the handle of her suitcase. "You're not even putting up a fight for me."

Was she right? Was there no true sentiment behind the time they'd spent together? Jac shook her head. No, she wasn't that callous. "I cared for you, Vee. I truly did. And you're right, we had some good times, but we both know it hasn't been right for a while now." She smiled sadly. "I'm glad we can be honest about this."

Jac didn't want a fight. She didn't want to argue. If this was the path they were walking, then she just wanted it done with. And she didn't want to create any hard feelings. There was no need for that. Besides, Jac wasn't convinced that either of them felt enough for what they had to really cause either of them much in the way of hurt. That in itself said everything Jac needed to know. She stepped into the room properly and held her hands out to Vanessa.

"You're a wonderful young woman, Vee, and I wish you all the luck in the world going forward." She took Vanessa's face in her hands and placed a soft kiss to her forehead. "I'm sorry this didn't work out, but you're right to move on. We both deserve to be happy."

Vanessa's hands touched hers as she pulled back and looked into Jac's eyes. For a second, Jac saw the sparkle in her eyes that had attracted her to Vanessa in the first place, a sparkle she had mistaken for a depth Vanessa didn't truly possess and could adopt for only so long, like any other role she played.

Jac closed her eyes and touched her forehead to Vanessa's.

"Be happy, Vee."

Vanessa let a tear roll down her cheek as she pressed her keys into Jac's hand, squeezed, and walked away. Jac smirked. Vanessa could have her dramatic parting scene. She wouldn't even look back at her. Sure this would be aggrandised in the retelling to make it sound like the parting of two soulmates divided across a wasteland of broken promises and shattered dreams, but Jac found she didn't care. She focused on the wheels of the suitcase running and clicking across the floor and then the sound of the door opening, then closing with a tinny metallic *click*.

She fidgeted with the keys in her hand, spinning them around her finger, over and over again, just as her mind played over the conversation. She tossed her keys onto the coffee table and picked up Vanessa's envelope. As soon as she opened it, she saw how short and to the point the note was. That, too, told her everything she needed to know.

> *I'm sorry, but this isn't working for me anymore. Good luck and goodbye.*
> *V*

> *"We want different things, Jac."*

Jac looked about the empty flat; the sound of a boiler cycling on as the heating kicked in hummed in the background. The only break in the silence. Maybe she was right. Maybe Jac did want something different in her life. *Only question is…I don't know what the hell that is…well, not outside of work, anyway.*

CHAPTER 3

"I HAVE A CONFESSION TO make."

Sasha sighed inwardly, plastered on a smile and turned to face Bobbi, who stood with her hands stuffed into the pocket of her oversized hoodie, and her usually mischievous gaze glued to the floor.

"Another one? Already?"

Bobbi nodded.

"Need me to drive a getaway car?"

"You can't drive."

"Good point. I'd be useless at that, but I can ride a mean scooter."

"You've never ridden a scooter."

"'Course I have."

"Have not."

"I rode one to school every day in junior one. Ask Mum."

Bobbi sputtered, "I—I didn't mean a push scooter when you were six, you numpty."

Shrugging, Sasha said, "Yeah, but I did." She bumped Bobbi with her shoulder. "Come on, then. Out with your big confession."

"I sent your screenplay off to a competition I saw on Facebook and you made the finalist list, the winners are drawn by the end of the week, and you might be a winner, and the producer loved it," Bobbi said without taking a breath, and without looking up. As they stood in the middle of IKEA, her coal-black eyes flitting to Sasha's face before sinking to the lino-covered walkway again. She looked much younger than her forty-two years, and Sasha almost felt sorry for the discomfort she clearly felt.

Almost.

"What?"

Bobbi's throat worked in a heavy swallow, and her gaze slowly rose to meet Sasha's from under those long eyelashes. Her brown cheeks had paled, taking on a grey tinge Sasha hadn't seen on her before, and she tugged on her top from inside the kangaroo pocket. She took a deep, visible breath and started again. "I said, I entered you into a screenplay competition I saw on Facebook, and they like it." She shrugged one shoulder. "If you win, they're gonna make your script into a film."

"Fuck off!" Sasha blurted out, unable to stop herself. She clapped her hand over her mouth.

Bobbi's eyes widened, and the corners of her mouth twitched almost into a smile. Almost.

Sasha glanced around, noting a mother hurrying her child away from Sasha and her filthy mouth with a withering look. "Sorry," Sasha said and grabbed hold of Bobbi's arm, dragging her past the display of a ridiculously small model studio apartment with some admittedly clever storage solutions Sasha promised to revisit later. Some may just be big enough to hide a body Bobbi's size. She was only five-foot-nothing and skinny, and Sasha was pretty sure that if she was angry enough, she could fold her friend up like a paper doll.

Sasha found a deserted corner between two displays and shoved Bobbi in ahead of her, rose to her full five-foot-five inches in height, planted her hands on her hips, and stared menacingly. At least she hoped it was menacingly. Because Sasha was well aware that she was more the cuddly maternal type than the ferocious-warrior kind of woman.

But Bobbi gulped and looked suitably terrified. *Good.*

"They really like—"

Sasha held up a hand. "Start at the beginning. Which screenplay? What possessed you to think it was a good idea? And…and…and *what the hell?*"

Bobbi tucked her hands back into her pocket and sighed. "Right, so, that screenplay you let me read. The one about the girls at the music college, one of them was Muslim, the arranged-marriage one. You remember giving me that to read?"

Sasha waited. Toe tapping. Bobbi gulped again and glanced over Sasha's shoulder.

"Well, anyway, I thought it was so cool. I mean, so much better than loads of the lesbian films, well, than a lot of the *straight* films out there at the moment too. It was sweet and funny and sexy and, like, so relevant, it really should be made into a film, Sash. I told you that I thought it was awesome."

It was difficult to maintain the scowl under praise, but Sasha felt she did an admirable job. It had Bobbi looking at her feet again.

"Anyway, I saw this link being shared around on Facebook, it was a competition for writers to submit a screenplay they wrote for a chance at exposure, and the winner gets to talk to some big producer about the chance to make their screenplay into a film."

"How do you know this is legitimate and not some sort of scam? Did you have to pay money to enter this competition?"

"Just a nominal entry fee. And I looked up the company and the producer. It was legit, Sash. I swear. This producer's done some really cool stuff."

"Who is it?"

"Jac Kensington. She produced that one we watched last year. What was it called again? The one with the woman who was getting married and fell for the florist doing her bouquet. You know the one I mean, right?"

"*Bloomin' Perfect?*"

"That's the one. She did that one. It's her company, and it all looks totally legit, so I sent it to her."

"And she likes it?" Sasha was stunned. Her hands dropped from her hips.

"She loves it." Bobbi's excitement was palpable now that the fear of imminent death no longer tempered it. "She sent an email when the finalists were announced. I'll show it to you when we get out of here."

"Why didn't you tell me?" Sasha pointed her finger in Bobbi's face as the numb feeling gave way to something else, something not nearly so comfortable. Something a little like panic. She wasn't cut out for something like this. She wrote her little screenplays as a way to vent about her very normal, rather boring life, not to get to the finals list of a competition. Not to have a producer "love" her story.

She latched on to uncomfortable and ran with it, morphing her fear into anger…sort of. "Or better yet, why didn't you ask me? Point it out and let me decide for myself if I wanted to enter something like this? Why go behind my back like this?"

Bobbi took hold of her hands and squeezed them lightly. "Because you wouldn't have done it, Sash."

"You don't know that."

"Yeah, I do. So do you." She wiggled Sasha's hands. "You'd tell yourself it wasn't good enough, or that even if it was, you couldn't possibly enter, just in case you did win, because you couldn't possibly go anywhere."

"Well I can't—"

"Like Longsight is the place to be."

"My mum needs me."

Bobbi's eyes twinkled. "Who do you think paid the entrance fee?"

Sasha took a step back. "What?"

"Your mum was the one who paid for you to enter the competition."

Competition. Wait. Comp. *Project Comp.* Shit.

"Why would she do that? She needs me."

"You should probably ask her that."

"Oh, believe me, I will."

"But, you know, maybe she thinks it's time you, I don't know, moved out, or maybe *moved on* is a better way to put it. I mean, you're what, forty-five now? That's like—"

Sasha held up her hand again, and Bobbi cut herself off like she'd hit a brick wall. "Listen, Bobbi, I moved *back* in with my mother five years ago when she was battling cancer and needed help. Before that I was perfectly happy in my own place, thank you very much. I'm not some loser who's never cut the apron strings. Mum's still recovering. She still needs help."

Bobbi shrugged, clearly deciding not to pursue it any further.

Narrowing her eyes, Sasha had prepared herself for the next round when a vibration from her pocket drew Sasha's attention. She pulled out her phone, looked at the Unknown Number ID, and shifted it to voicemail. She wasn't in the mood for cold-callers today. "Come on," she said with a heavy sigh as she flicked her long hair over her shoulder. "You said you needed a new mattress." She backed out of the corner and headed towards the bedroom displays, Bobbi playing shadow behind her. "You can tell me the rest as we go around this bloody maze."

"The rest" turned out to be light on the details and heavy on the excitement until Sasha had a headache and Bobbi's new mattress was on the trolley ready to be loaded into the back of Bobbi's car. The rain had started while they'd been in the store, sometime during all three hours of looking, trying out, relooking, retesting, and then finally queuing up to buy said mattress. The grey clouds that had loomed earlier over Ashton-under-Lyne were now spitting their heavy load with a vengeance.

Bobbi grabbed the handles of the cart, towed it through the doors, and out to the car park while Sasha stood looking out, wishing they'd thought ahead to park under the covered section. Or that she'd thought to bring an umbrella.

Grateful she at least had a hood on her coat, she pulled her long hair into a bunch at the back of her head, twisted and tucked it into the collar, then flipped up the hood on her jacket.

A torrent of tiny pencils rained down on her head, past her face, and clattered to the ground with a tinkle and a splash.

Bobbi spun around, eyes and mouth making perfect circles, hands flapping before she started to yank the trolley behind her, gathering some speed. Her loud announcement was already trailing off into the distance she put between them.

"I have a littler confession to make!"

Bobbi looked at her sheepishly. "I'm really sorry, Sasha," she said as she turned off the main road. "I just get a bit bored and I can't help myself."

After a moment's thought, Sasha shook her head. She'd been on the receiving end of more than one of Bobbi's boredom-related incidents over the ten years they'd been friends. This was another she'd probably laugh at before long.

"Forget it, bitch. I'm saving up all these incidents for one hell of a revenge attack."

Bobbi grinned. "Oh, I look forward to that. See you at work tomorrow."

"Yup." Sasha tugged her coat tighter around her and stuffed her hands deep into her pockets as she climbed out of Bobbi's car. She waved as it retreated into the distance.

Sasha pulled her keys from her pocket and opened the door to the house. A cloud of smoke greeted her, and the combined odours of lavender, sage, and pot assaulted her nostrils. Holistic therapies, indeed. Sasha half expected to one day walk into their house and find her mother dealing her wares to the teenagers who hung around on the corner.

"I don't want to know."

She closed her eyes and seriously debated heading down to the pub for the night. But then decided against it. She had work in the morning, and working through the munchies after getting inadvertently stoned due to her mother's tinkering was better than trying to give a dozen massages, pedicures, or facials with a hangover.

"Mum?" She waved her hand in front of her face and made her way to the living room, opening windows as she went, hoping no one was driving by who might be interested in the pungent plume venting into the cold, dank evening. While it was perfectly legal for her mother to use the stuff, going through the rigmarole of explaining it to a new batch of coppers every time was…frustrating? Annoying? Time-consuming? All of the above? "You promised you'd only smoke in the conservatory! The whole house stinks now!"

"Oh, don't be such a fun-sponge. Here, have a puff on this."

Fleur was draped across the sofa in a sea of tie-dyed taffeta and chiffon. Her shoulder-length grey locks were tied back with a bandana of every colour under the sun. She looked like she belonged at Woodstock. Sasha sniffed. She smelled like she belonged at Woodstock, except for the cat that lay cradled along one arm while her mother stroked its back and it flicked its tail in Sasha's direction. Nip's green eyes stared malevolently, and Sasha wasn't sure if it was as stoned as her mother or plotting the interloper's death. Either was entirely possible, and it gave Fleur a decidedly Doctor Evil edge to her hippie chic.

Sasha waved the roach away. "Fun-sponge?"

"Yes, you know? A bore, dear." She pulled another drag off her spliff. "I'm up with the kids," she murmured around the smoke she'd inhaled, letting it seep out of the corner of her mouth in a way that always reminded Sasha of Frenchy from *Grease* trying to teach Sandy how to smoke.

Sasha wrinkled her nose. "I think you mean 'down with the kids', Mum. And, no, you're not."

Fleur shrugged, exhaled, and eyed her up and down before motioning Sasha to bend towards her. When they were eye to eye, she reached over and pulled a pencil out of her hair. "What happened to you?"

"Bobbi."

Fleur cracked a sloppy grin. "About time you got yourself a little lesbi-action there." She elbowed Sasha in the ribs. "Not gonna ask about the pencil. There are some things a mother does not need to know."

Sasha tutted, grabbed the pencil from her fingers, and tossed it onto the coffee table as she stood up straight. "That's just so wrong. You're my mother, and Bobbi's my friend."

"All the better. You're still young, and you're letting that thing heal itself closed like a pierced ear." Fleur waved her hand in the direction of Sasha's crotch. "It's not like I don't know what sex is, dear. How'd you think you got here? Your father and I, well, he used to do this thing with his tong—"

"Stop! Stop. Just...stop."

Fleur snickered somewhat evilly despite the obvious lethargy and said, "Rowr," while holding out her bony hand like she was clawing at something. The whole visual was just too...disturbing.

"Ew. So not going to happen. And please, don't ever make that noise again."

"Fun-sponge."

"So it would seem." She opened another window and handed her mother a blanket for the moment she would inevitably complain about the cold. She fetched two glasses of water and a jumbo-sized bag of crisps from the kitchen, then plopped down on the sofa next to her mum. Just far enough away to be out of Nip's reach, should she decide to attack. Not that it looked like the feline could be bothered...but Sasha had learnt to be cautious over the years. "Mum, why didn't you tell me?"

"Well, dear, I thought even you could tell that Bobbi wanted a little of your lady-loving."

Sasha rolled her eyes. "Bobbi told me all about Project Comp."

"That girl can't keep a secret to save her life."

"No, she can't. So, come on, why didn't you tell me you wanted me out of your hair?"

"I don't. I want you to let yours down a bit, honey." She reached across the back of the sofa and ran her fingers through Sasha's locks. "So soft." She twirled the strands around her fingers the way Sasha remembered her doing when she was a child. "And still lovely and dark. You can barely see those few grey ones scattered about."

"Love you too, Mother," Sasha said through gritted teeth. She wasn't particularly vain, but she didn't need to be reminded that she wasn't getting any younger either.

"Oh, pish. You're a beautiful, vibrant, young woman, and I want you to have a life."

"I do have a life. A very full one, as it so happens."

"You go to work, you come home, you cook, you clean, you tidy up after me, and you lock yourself away in that room of yours. That's not a life. That's servitude."

"Stop it. It's no different to what you did for me when I was a kid. Why did you do all that if not to get payback now?" Sasha grinned.

"I did that because I'm your mother and I love you."

"Well, I'm your daughter and I love you. What's the difference?"

"A mother's job is to always look after her children. Always. A daughter's is to grow up and live her own life."

"Why do you have to make it sound like I'm a middle-aged loser still living with you because I haven't got anything else, haven't done anything else? I have lived on my own. I have lived with a woman other than you. I've done that. I have a good job, a lot of great friends. I came back here to help you. To spend time with you. I'm happy here with you."

"Bullshit."

"Excuse me?"

Fleur waved her hand, disturbing Nip, who meowed angrily and jumped out of Fleur's embrace. Arching her back, she offered Sasha a hiss for good measure, then curled herself up onto the crisp packet, making good and sure she crushed anything left inside.

"Yes, I know all that, and, believe me, I'm very grateful you did come back. I love having you here with me. But you aren't happy. You're content. You're settled. But you're not happy. You're working in a job that, well... Frankly, you could do better."

"What's wrong with being a massage therapist?"

"Nothing. Nothing at all. But you don't want to be a massage therapist. You want to be a scriptwriter, or whatever they call it. You want to write films and plays and all that stuff."

"It's not as easy as that. You have to find the right people. You have to know the right people."

"Which is why I paid that entry fee when Bobbi asked me about it. I asked the crystals, and they were very clear in their directions, honey. Very clear."

Sasha fought not to roll her eyes again. Her mother's devotion to crystals and seeking guidance from her higher self was just…great. Really. Really great. Just as long as she kept it out of Sasha's life.

"They clearly told me that this was a turning point in your life. A pivotal moment, where all your hopes and dreams could come to fruition or all my fears and worries would. All I had to do was lead you to the path, and your higher self will do the rest. You're alone, and unhappy, and you shouldn't be." She linked her fingers with Sasha's. "You don't need to be."

"Mum, even if that was the case—which I'm not saying it is—but even so, it's not that easy."

"You let the crystals take care of all that, honey." She patted Sasha's hand and leant her head back against the sofa. "Let the crystals take care of everything."

"Crystals don't hold the meaning to life, Mother. And they certainly don't hold the answer to every question I have." She didn't mean for it to come out as snippy as it did, but…well…it did.

Fleur turned to look at her, for once, her expression completely serious, her eyes clear of the usual pot or pain haze, and her hands steady as she lifted them to cradle Sasha's cheeks. "No, I don't suppose they do." She stroked her thumb over her jaw, then let it fall and took hold of Sasha's hand. "Do you remember when you were little and I used to read to you every night before you went to sleep?"

Frowning, Sasha said, "Of course. But what—"

"Do you remember what your favourite story was?"

Sasha smiled at the memory of those idyllic childhood moments curled into her mother's side, where words met dreams and fuelled her imagination for a lifetime. "*Peter Pan*."

Fleur patted her hand. "Do you remember why?"

"You mean beyond it being a fabulous story that has layers and layers of meaning that still resonate for me today as an adult?"

Fleur snorted. "Yes, beyond that."

"Okay," Sasha said, drawing the word out. "There were two lines in it that were amazing to me when I was a little girl. So many of the stories were

31

about girls who were princesses being saved by the handsome prince, or they were just sidekicks. But in *Peter Pan*, it always felt more like Wendy was the one who could save Peter. And it was almost like Peter knew it. There were lines that reflected that and stuck with me, like the bit where Peter says, 'Wendy, one girl is more use than twenty boys' and 'it's wonderful what clever girls can do'."

"Yes." Fleur looked her directly in the eye. "It is, isn't it?"

"Mum," Sasha said. Admittedly, it came out with more of a whine than she'd intended. "This isn't a book or a film. It's real life."

"Do you want to know what my favourite line is?"

"What?"

"'Keep adventuring and stay not a grown-up.'"

"Sounds about right," Sasha said with a chuckle.

"That doesn't mean I'm not right, though." Fleur closed her eyes, a smile pulling at her lips as sleep claimed her.

Sasha sighed and covered her with the thick woollen blanket, knowing she'd sleep for several hours. She squinted at her mother's face, wondering at her colouring. The hue seemed a little off, a little yellow. *Must be a trick of the light.* She pressed a kiss to the top of her head and whispered the words Fleur had whispered to her almost every night of her childhood: "So come with me where dreams are born and time is never planned. Just think of happy things, and your heart will fly on wings in Never Never Land."

Nip took advantage of the lull in conversation and curled up against Fleur's stomach, purring as she watched Sasha head for the door. Her eyes clearly told Sasha she'd won the battle for Fleur's affections. Again.

"Yeah, yeah," Sasha murmured and pulled the door closed behind her. She went to her bedroom and pulled her copy of *Peter Pan* from the shelf on her way to bed. The pages were loose in the spine, the corners dog-eared, and the pages shiny from where her fingers had run across them so many times. She pulled a blanket around her shoulders, slumping back against the headboard and opening to the first page.

"All children, except one, grow up," she read aloud, sighed, and snuggled deeper into her pillows.

CHAPTER 4

"Oh, yeah. Right *there*." The soft voice was muffled by the padded surface of the table as Sasha glided her hands over oiled skin before digging in again with the heel of her palm. "Oh God, that feels so good."

"You've got knots all over the place, Mrs West."

"I know. Thank God you've got magic hands."

It wasn't the first time she'd heard that compliment at work. "Thank you. Let's hope they're up to this task." She felt the tell-tale ping of a corded muscle under her fingers and worked it like a guitar string until it was loose and supple and Mrs West was practically snoring on the table. Usually Sasha used the quiet time with her clients to daydream up new ideas for scripts, to develop her characters or a line of dialogue that was bothering her. Today she was focused on Bobbi's confession and her mother's sincere words. Was she really using her mother as an excuse to stop herself from living life? Was her life really as empty an existence as she and Bobbi seemed to think it was?

So it had been a number of years since she'd split up with Pam. But damn it, she'd been busy the past five years. Her mother's fight against cancer, the rehab, the adjustments, the crystals, the weed…it all took time to work through and find solutions. All of that was true. All of it had been important. Her mother was seventy-five years old and in remission from cancer…Sasha didn't want to contemplate the future too much, but she wanted to have plenty of memories of her mum when the day came and she wasn't around to make any new ones with her. Was that so wrong?

Or was that simply being too pessimistic? She sighed heavily and Mrs West snored as Sasha made one final sweeping pass over her back and tugged the towel up to cover her shoulders. She bent down to the woman's ear and whispered, "Take your time, Mrs West, and get dressed when you're ready. I'll wait for you outside."

The woman smacked her lips. "Thank you," she said, her voice husky with sleep and lassitude.

Sasha smiled and slipped from the room, crossing to the staff room to wash her hands and forearms before Mrs West would even be off the table. The quiet hallway and plush surroundings of the salon oozed opulence, and Sasha reflected for the thousandth time how the odour of money practically hung in the air. The Serenity Spa Salon offered individual treatments as well as spa breaks—be those for the day or longer. Customers paid a lot of money to feel like they were far away from the cares and worries of the often high-powered professions they temporarily escaped under Sasha's skilful hands. When she'd first started working there, the surroundings—the incredible indulgence—had made her uncomfortable. As had the attitudes of some of the clients; money didn't seem to buy a person manners or a personality as far as Sasha could tell. But fortunately there were enough lovely clients to make up for the few ingrates who crossed Sasha's path. The service industry was the service industry after all, and into every life a few arseholes must fall.

The door opened, and Sasha smiled at the tiny woman almost hidden inside the thick terry cloth towel issued to all guests for their treatments. She held out her arm. "If you'll follow me to the chill-out room, I'll get you something to drink while you relax and recuperate, Mrs West."

She beamed up at her dreamily. "Thanks."

"Welcome."

When Sasha had her situated on a day bed—bundled up in a cosy blanket with water in hand—she stepped back into the hallway. Brushing her hand across the wall's slate façade, Sasha enjoyed the rough texture for a moment before she caught sight of Bobbi backing out of a treatment room, hands held up in supplication, eyes wide. A sputtering, angry woman was coming after her.

"I'm sorry. I'll see if there's another therapist available for your treatment, Ms Polyakov. I'm very sorry," Bobbi said softly.

"Get out. I want proper therapist. My boyfriend is paying good money to you people," she said with a sneer, her voice heavily accented with what sounded like Russian inflections, as she looked Bobbi up and down. "You will not do."

Bobbi cast her gaze down, and Sasha knew she was biting her tongue. What the hell was this woman's problem? Bobbi was one of the most experienced technicians working at the salon. She was well trained, professional, and polite.

Sasha stepped towards them. "May I ask what the problem is?"

The small, skinny blond looked Sasha up and down, and her frown shifted into a smile. "Finally. You will do." She clicked her fingers and went back into the room, turning her back on Sasha and Bobbi.

Sasha looked at Bobbi, the *what the fuck?* question in the air between them.

"Ms Polyakov is the girlfriend of the new star Man City striker and will be coming here for her treatments from now on. Big money, high profile," Bobbi whispered.

In other words, what the bitch wants, the bitch gets.

"And?"

"Seems the Russian princess has a problem with the way I look."

"Huh?"

"She doesn't care for my tan."

"Seriously?"

Bobbi nodded. "Among other things she pointed out, but yeah. That one stuck out for some reason."

"Racist bitch," Sasha whispered. "I'll get Maria. She can get rid of her."

Bobbi shook her head. "She won't."

Sasha pointed to the sign over the door that warned customers they were expected to treat staff members respectfully and would be asked to leave in the event of abuse, bullying, or the like. "We have a policy. Maria has to stick by it. She has to stick by you."

"She already told me this woman has booked in for her hen-party spa weekend with twenty-five other women, as well as her wedding day treatments, and has talked half the other WAGS to switch to coming here. It's too much business for her to throw her out for this."

"WAGS?"

Bobbi stared at her incredulously. "Seriously, Sasha?"

"What? How am I supposed to know what that means?"

35

Shaking her head, Bobbi said, "WAGS as in wives and girlfriends." She waited expectantly. Sasha was none the wiser and Bobbi glared at her. "The wives and girlfriends of the footballers."

"Oh, right. Yeah. I see what you mean." She didn't but who the hell cared.

"Will you take her for me?" Bobbi asked, putting her hand on Sasha's arm.

"You want *me* to go in there and do her treatment?"

Bobbi nodded.

"I can't, hon. I've got a mani-pedi booked in."

"I'll take that for you. I'll talk to the girls on reception and switch what we need to. I'll take care of it all."

"Bobbi, let me talk to Maria—"

"Will you be long?" the woman shouted from inside the room. "I don't have all day."

"Please," Bobbi pleaded. "I know you want to stand up for me, and, believe me, I appreciate it. But Maria can't afford to turn her away. I get it. I don't like it, but I get it. She's one person who could put this place out of business in a month; then we're all fucked rather than me just being really, really fucked off."

"How are you even this calm? Why aren't you raging and demanding that her racist arse be dumped on the street?"

Bobbi grinned evilly. "Because she's here for her first ever Brazilian."

"The boyfriend's request?"

Bobbi nodded, and Sasha felt her own evil grin tug at her lips.

"Hey, you, I ask you question?" The woman was shouting already as she opened the door and stepped into the hallway again.

Sasha raised one eyebrow in question and Bobbi nodded. "I'm sorry, Ms Polyakov. I just have to make a few arrangements to accommodate your request of a change of technician. Please just give me a couple of minutes, and I'll be right with you."

The woman looked Sasha up and down and grasped her chin in her hand, turning her face from side to side like Sasha was a prize poodle she was judging. "You could have been model if you weren't so short." She turned Sasha's face to the side again, then picked up a lock of Sasha's long dark hair. "Perhaps hair modelling. Or the eyes. And that husky voice. Like, what was her name? The singer…you know." She broke into a very, very, *very* bad rendition of "I Need a Hero" by Bonnie Tyler.

Bobbi supplied the name, and Polyakov scowled before turning her attention back to Sasha. "Yes, like Bonnie Tyler. You could do voice-over work." She waved her hand. "It is better than this place, that is for sure. I know people. I will make calls. You will be grateful."

I don't fucking think so!

"Thank you, but I can't accept something like that." She waved her hand back at the room. "While you wait, if you could get undressed and lie down on the bed, there is a blanket to cover yourself. I will be as quick as I can." She offered what she hoped was a smile rather than a snarl.

"Fine. But every minute will reduce the tip I shall be leaving, so be quick about it."

Okay, so she's clearly pissed that I didn't fall over myself at the chance to become Britain's next aging model. Boohoo. Sasha murmured her acknowledgement at the woman and closed the door behind her. "Last chance, hon," she whispered to Bobbi, who was still standing there, watching the whole interaction blankly. "You sure you don't want me to bring in Maria?"

"Nah. I just wish I could be a fly on the wall. She's so gonna cry."

Sasha didn't usually enjoy these treatments. She didn't enjoy inflicting pain—even on a voluntary basis—to people. It was the main reason she was rarely assigned to do wax treatments, any wax treatments. So her skills were a little rusty in this department, but Polyakov had demanded her. She was a racist and was treating everyone like shit. She was a bitch.

Sasha checked the clock on the wall.

"Time for a coffee after this?" Sasha asked quietly, tipping her head towards the staff room.

Bobbi frowned. "No idea. I'll let you know what the changes to the schedule are after we finish the next clients."

"Oh, okay."

"Look, Sash, I know I said it yesterday, but I just wanted to say it again. I'm sorry, okay? I didn't mean to…well…I didn't think it would really upset you so much to enter you into that stupid competition. I thought you'd be stoked to make the finalist list. I really did. I thought it was awesome, I mean, they had literally thousands of entries, and yours is like in the top five."

"I am happy about that. You're right; it is an achievement to be proud of. I'm not upset about that."

"Then what's the problem?"

"Because it's my life to make decisions about. Not yours, and not my mother's."

"But it was just a competition. They take what you've done and make it into a film. It's cool. You'll get to go to the pictures with me and see your film. I mean, how fucking awesome will that be. I'll buy you the DVD for Christmas, then we can watch it anytime we want. Honestly, Sash, it'll be great."

Sasha hung her head. Bobbi was never going to get it. She just didn't see the problem. "Never mind."

Bobbi beamed. "I should run now, I've gotta get to your mani-pedi, and you've got a stripping to attend to." And then she was gone. At least she looked cheered up, Sasha decided.

She stepped back into her treatment room. Polyakov was playing on her phone, naked from the waist down, with the hairiest snatch Sasha had seen in a long time staring back at her. *Someone took the half-a-centimetre-or-more rule of waxing and ran with it. This is not going to make this less painful.*

Sasha checked that her tools were laid out and close to hand and that the wax pot was up to temperature and then pulled on a pair of latex gloves.

"Okay, Ms Polyakov. You might want to put your phone away now, and we'll begin."

The woman grunted and lifted the phone a little higher. "Just do your job and get on with it."

Sasha ground her teeth and took a deep breath. "Very well, I need you to spread your legs. Heels up to your bottom, and let your knees fall open." She picked up a spatula and dipped it in the wax. *Brace yourself...I'm going in!*

"I saw her limping out the door," Bobbi said as she wandered back into the treatment room. "You didn't kick her, did you?"

"Didn't have to." Sasha gathered the towels that covered the treatment table and stuffed them into the laundry hamper, nodding to the countertop. "Thought you might get a little sense of justice if you saw that."

Bobbi approached the work surface, then stared back at Sasha, agape. Sasha shook out a new set of towels and quickly made up the room again.

"I haven't heard screaming like that since I was in training."

"I'm not surprised." Bobbi leant over the specimen.

Sasha sniggered. "I think someone might have told her it had to be half a meter long before it could be waxed."

"I could use that under my coffee table, I need a new rug."

"Well, that could be your trophy rug. Instead of a bearskin rug—"

"I could have a racist-skin rug." Bobbi lifted a spatula out of a jar and prodded at it like it might be alive before shuffling it into the bin.

"Good riddance."

"Yup." Bobbi shivered. "Listen, thanks again for that and for wanting to stand up for me."

"You don't need to thank me for that. That's what any decent human being should do."

Bobbi shrugged and stared at her adoringly. "But *they* didn't—you did." She stepped up to Sasha and wrapped her arms around her. Sasha didn't hesitate to return the hug Bobbi so obviously needed. She could see the tears shimmering in her eyes.

"She's not worth it." She ran her hands up and down Bobbi's back, trying to soothe her, to offer all the support she could.

"I know," Bobbi whispered.

Sasha gave her a little longer, then slowly pulled away. "Drinks tonight?"

Taking a deep breath, Bobbi shook her head. "Thanks, but no. I'm trying out a new Zumba class."

"Zumba, hey?" Sasha asked, eyebrows raised.

"Yup." Bobbi squared a little, put her arms out like she was grabbing something in front of her chest, and started to gyrate. "Gonna get my Zumba on." She gyrated and wiggled as she left the room, looking like she was having some sort of fit.

"You want me to call an ambulance for you?"

Bobbi offered her a rather rude hand gesture and gyrated away.

"There might be a cream you could use?" She chuckled and finished setting up the room for the next client.

The 192 was as crowded as it ever was at rush hour. In other words, the bus was packed. Hard-working folk at the end of a long day were standing cheek by jowl in the aisle, shuffling and leaning over those in seats whenever someone wanted to get off—or another body tried to get on. Sasha was lucky enough, if you could call it that, to have got a seat for the duration. What wasn't so lucky was the bloke hovering over her, obviously trying to look down her cleavage. *I'm wearing a bloody uniform. I don't have cleavage right now!*

There were still a good few minutes until her stop, but it was the next one. Time to start her shuffle to the front. She pushed the bell and made to stand. Mr Hover didn't make it easy for her to get to her feet, clearly hoping for a brush-by as she scooted around him and bumped into the woman in front. Sasha touched her shoulder and motioned to the seat she'd just vacated. The woman smiled gratefully, and Sasha started moving down the aisle.

The ringing phone grabbed Sasha's attention. She pulled it out of her pocket. Unknown number. Again. She sighed and answered the call.

"Hello," she said into the phone.

There was a pause before a voice said, "Hello, is this"—the woman on the other end cleared her throat—"I'm sorry, is this Sasha Adams?"

Sasha sighed. "Look, I'm sorry, I don't have any outstanding PPI's, I wasn't in an accident that you can claim injuries for me, and I don't need any solar panels on my roof, thanks. If I do, I'll call you. Please, can you take me off your call list."

There was a short, sharp laugh down the line.

"You're funny. My name's Jac Kensington, and I swear I have nothing to do with PPI's, insurance, or solar panels. I tried to call you yesterday actually, but it went to voicemail, and I didn't want to do this with a message."

"Wait? Did you say Jac Kensington?"

"Yes."

"Like the producer—" Sasha looked around at the faces now turned towards her. She lowered her voice and whispered, "Like the producer and director, Jac Kensington?"

"Yes," Jac said, copying her lowered tone. "Why are we whispering?"

Sasha's knees weakened. She grasped one of the overhead straps to steady herself and looked at the phone in her hand.

"Hello? Hello? Are you still there?"

Sasha shook her head and put the phone back to her ear. "Yes, sorry, just…caught me by surprise. And I'm whispering because I'm on the bus."

"Oh, right. Sorry about that, but hopefully this is a good-news call. Would you rather I call back later?"

Only one reason Jac Kensington could be calling her number. "No, no, it's fine. Is this about the screenplay?"

"Yes, it is."

"Okay." Sasha steeled herself and turned her back on a woman staring up at her, mouth hanging open to show several missing teeth. *If I can't see them, they can't hear me. That's a fact, right?*

"I, well, I think… I'd like to meet with you at your earliest convenience to discuss the production of *Nightingale*."

"Production?"

"Yes. You've won the competition, and my company, Kefran Media Limited, would like to discuss the rights to the screenplay with a view to making it into a film."

"A film?"

Jac laughed. "Yes, that was the competition. I realise this must be a bit of a surprise. That's why I was hoping to meet with you; then we don't have to go through everything over the phone. You live in Manchester, is that right?"

"Yes." The bus pulled to a stop and Sasha fought her way to the front and stepped off. Two other people bustled passed her, hurrying to wherever. Sasha couldn't have cared less right then. She pointed herself towards home and let her feet take her while she continued to listen.

"What are the chances of getting you to come and meet with me?"

Sasha's mind was racing. Spinning around in excited circles, like a puppy chasing its tail… Wait, that wasn't a great analogy. "When? I have work, so I'd need to arrange things."

"Of course. I can make myself available pretty much any day. One of the perks of being the boss. So why don't you let me know when is good for you, and I'll take care of the rest. How's that?"

Sasha nodded, then remembered that Jac couldn't see her. "That sounds great. My next day off is Wednesday. Would that be okay?" She heard rustling, like paper being shifted around.

"Looks fine to me. I'll check the diary, and I can email you the details. I have an email address of…" There was a cough. "Bangablebabe75 at Hottermail dot com. Is that right?"

Bangable? Bobbi, what were you thinking? "Good God, no." Her voice was too loud and caused a couple of the lads hanging around on the corner to turn towards her. The tough-looking one, Dante, tipped his head towards her as he hitched up his tracksuit bottoms so the crotch hung at mid-thigh instead of by his knees. The peak of his baseball cap sat over his left ear, and a thick rope of what was probably gold plate hung around his neck. She nodded back. No need to be rude to one of Mum's friends. She was pretty sure it was Dante who made sure she never got hassled by any of the other lads on the corners.

"That's the address the submission was sent from."

"My friend submitted the screenplay as a surprise, would you believe?"

"Oh."

"Exactly."

"Well, that's…unexpected."

"I'm sorry, is it a problem?"

"Well, I guess not, if you're on board with the terms and conditions of the competition."

"Well, you see, I've literally only just found out. Yesterday afternoon, actually, while Bobbi and I were shopping in IKEA, of all places, and I've been at work all day today, so I haven't even had a chance to look at those."

"Oh."

"I'm sorry."

"No need to be. By the sound of it, it's not your fault."

"No, but I don't like to mess people around either." She rubbed at her eyes with her free hand, trying to dispel her frustration. "Look, I understand if you want to go with a different option, but if you can email me over the rules, or whatever it is you need me to look at, I can do it this evening and get straight back to you. I promise I won't keep you waiting."

The line was quiet for a moment before Jac said, "Tell me one thing."

"Sure."

"Do you want to see your screenplay made into a film?"

Sasha paused for a moment. Did she? She wasn't as naive as Bobbi was. She didn't for a moment believe that this didn't have the potential to change her life in ways she couldn't even comprehend yet. The film might be a flop. A complete and utter failure. Or it could be a hit, and she'd manage to sell other scripts. Right now, she could live in her head as the biggest undiscovered talent the UK had never seen—sod it, the world. But the moment Bobbi had sent that script in...

Someone had seen her work now. Someone had *read* her work. Yeah, they'd liked it. So much so that they wanted to give it a shot. But that didn't mean everyone would. Even good movies got withering reviews all the time. She was putting herself out there where the potential for ridicule, criticism, and failure were very real possibilities. And it was her name on that script.

But was this fear she felt reason enough not to try?

Maybe Bobbi was right. Maybe she did need to take more chances.

Sasha took a deep breath and made the decision she hoped she wouldn't regret. "Of course."

"Great. Then I'll email you everything you need."

"But—"

"Sasha. May I call you Sasha?"

"Yes, of course."

"Well, Sasha, your screenplay is great. One of the best I've seen on my desk ever. I'm excited about this project, and I think it'll make one hell of a film. Your characters are fully rounded, they have pathos and pain, offset by a little humour. The situation is real, one we've seen played out in the news over and over again, and I can feel the humanity behind it. We can work out the details if I know we both want to make this into a great film. So, do we?"

Sasha's ego practically purred under Jac's effusive compliments. Yes, her mum and Bobbi had liked her scripts, but this was Jac fricking Kensington telling her it was good. No, not good, *great*. She'd specifically used that word.

Well? What the hell can I say to that? "Yes. Yes I do."

CHAPTER 5

THE DAY WAS GETTING AWAY from her, but there was still an endless pile of paper on Jac's desk. She groaned and caught sight of the Post-it note on the corner of her computer screen.

"Fuck." As promised, she sent all the information to the email address Sasha had given her last night. Then she clicked a few more buttons, tapped a few keys, and waited for the searches to come back. Sasha Adams, with her unexpected disclosure and her sultry voice had kept Jac up thinking way too late last night. God, that voice. Jac had found it hard to focus on the words Sasha had been saying as the hairs on the back of her neck had stood on end. Her insides had melted like chocolate.

She shivered and twitched in her seat. *Focus, woman. You've got work to do.*

But it wasn't work that was waiting for her on her computer. It was her search results. And there wasn't a lot there. There was, however, Sasha's Facebook page.

"I shouldn't do this," Jac whispered to herself. "This is so not right." Her hand hovered over the mouse. "I mean, I'd hate it if someone was checking up on me." She grasped the mouse and moved it so the cursor hovered over the cross in the corner, ready to close the window and the results. "But it's Facebook. That's like putting something on a banner and waving it along the M1. It's a public space. Everyone knows that. If you don't want people to find it, you don't put it on there. Or you only make it available to people you want to see it. If this stuff is accessible to anyone, she's not hiding it."

But then Jac slapped her hand to her forehead.

"I shouldn't be doing this." She tipped her head side to side, going over the debate like she was watching a tennis match. "Do we always check out new employees?" Jac asked herself. "Why, yes, Jac. Yes, we do." She smiled and moved the cursor again. "But we usually do that by getting references and interviewing the person, not Facebook stalking." After a long silence, she scoffed at herself aloud. "This is hardly stalking. I merely typed in her name to an Internet search engine. Looking for…information. Newspaper reports of criminal activity, that sort of thing."

Jac dropped her forehead to her desk and banged it. Several times.

"Sod it. I'm not stalking, merely making myself as informed as possible. I mean, it'd be nice to know who I'm looking for when I go to meet her, right? That's not creepy in the slightest. She could be doing the same thing with me, after all. And there are tons of pictures of me out there for her to find. I mean someone conscientious going for an interview would research the company and, if possible, the person they're interviewing with, right?"

Jac nodded. "Yeah. And Sasha is probably the conscientious type. I mean, the amount of research that's evident in her script shows that. So this is just levelling the playing field."

Finally satisfied with her logic, Jac clicked and scooted through the pictures that popped up, trying to find one tagged as Sasha. There were lots of pictures of a rather grumpy-looking cat with big green eyes and an attitude, given the captions underneath them. Even more of an elderly lady in funky tie-dye skirts and Bohemian-style tops. In some photos, she was in a wheelchair, others on crutches, and others with a walking stick. Then, finally, triumphantly holding a prosthetic leg aloft and balancing on one leg.

Jac carried on scanning through the pictures, but there was nothing tagged as Sasha, and she closed the page with a disappointed grunt. She scowled at the screen before dropping her head onto the desk.

"What are you doing?" she berated herself. "So the woman had a nice voice. Big deal. You'll meet her in two days. Why—"

"Why are you talking to yourself?"

Jac straightened in her chair and stared up at Mags's head peering at her around the edge of her door. A frown marred the seemingly disembodied head, and she squinted at Jac through the thick glasses perched on her nose.

"'Cos I don't answer myself back."

"Sure sign of craziness right there."

"Yeah, yeah. What do you want?" Jac sighed wearily. "My crazy arse is knackered, so if you're planning to dump any more shit from the paper fairy on my desk you can just go and shovel it somewhere else."

"No, Julie ordered me to invite you for dinner tonight. For some reason, she likes you and wants to make sure you don't die of scurvy."

"Scurvy?"

"I may have mentioned your dinner plans of crisps, pork scratchings, and vodka from the other night."

"Thanks, pal."

Mags smiled, pushed open the door, and walked into the room. She leaned on the back of the chair across Jac's desk. "So, dinner?"

"Why the hell not?"

"A ringing endorsement. I'll lie and tell Julie you were much more enthusiastic, so play along later."

Jac offered a mock salute and turned back to her computer screen.

"What were you talking to yourself about before?"

"Nothing," Jac said with a shake of her head.

"If you don't tell me, I'll get Julie to ask later."

"That's just cruel."

Mags grinned unrepentantly. "I know. The woman is merciless in the hunt for information."

"It's called gossip, Mags. Gossip. Need me to spell it for you?"

"Nope, I'm good with that, thanks. So…?" She spread her hands out and beckoned with her fingers.

"Nothing, I was just looking for a little background info on the writer I'm meeting with on Wednesday."

"The competition winner?"

"Yeah."

"And?"

"And nothing. I can't really find anything."

Mags came around the back of her desk and hovered behind her chair. "Where've you looked?"

"Just Google. That brought up a Facebook page."

She gave a scan of the results. As their resident tech whizz, Mags was always their go-to girl when it came to things like this. "Okay, I'll do a search for you and send you the results in an hour or so. Anything specific you want me to look for?"

Jac shook her head.

"Why're we looking?"

"Just because I'm meeting her on Wednesday."

"Hm. Not buying. You usually have me do searches and references and such *after* your initial meeting."

Jac coughed and pretended to study her desk as Mags crossed the room again and turned to grin at her when she reached the door.

"You're squirming in your chair."

"I am not."

Mags guffawed. "You so are."

"Not."

"Child."

Jac stared at her open-mouthed before crying at her, "I am not!"

"You so are."

Throwing her best scowl at her friend and turning to her computer, Jac ignored her as she murmured, "Not."

Mags rapped her knuckles on the doorframe, then crossed her arms over her chest. "Okay, let's test my powers of deduction here." She tapped her chin thoughtfully. "You were supposed to call our mystery writer last night to give her the good news and set up a meeting. So I'm taking it I was a positive conversation?"

Jac nodded, and turned to stare at her computer.

"Okay, so you talked to her. Just a phone conversation, right? Not a Skype or FaceTime?"

"Just a phone call."

Mags's smirk grew. "Okay, and now you're squirming in your chair like you did when we went to that Bonnie Tyler concert back in the day. God, I can still hear you going on and on about what that voice did to you. Oh, and Elkie Brooks too. You squirm every time her songs come on the radio. It's practically chair dancing what you do when 'Pearl's a Singer' comes on. We never went to see her in concert, though."

"She's got a new album out," Jac supplied. "She'll probably be doing some gigs. Maybe we could—" She caught herself when she saw how wide Mags's grin was. *Shit.*

"Uh-huh. So one new-writer conversation, one squirming Jac trying to find 'information' about her."

Jac hated when Mags did that finger-quote-marks-in-the-air thing. Hated it. She always looked so fucking smug. She ground her teeth.

"So I'm going to go with a voice like Elkie Brooks for one hundred?"

Jac groaned. *Why the hell do these two have to know me so well?* "More like Elkie Brooks dipped in honey."

Mags's jaw sagged a little before she started laughing. "Boy, are you in trouble, then. Need a chaperone for this meeting? You'd probably promise her the company if her voice is that good."

"Funny. Now get out of my office. I've got work to do." She shooed her away.

"Sure you do. Dinner's at six. Don't be late." Mags rounded the door and called behind her, "I'll forward you a picture as soon as I find one."

"Bitch," Jac muttered under her breath, then reached for her earbuds and selected an old favourite to help her get her head back in the game. The beat kicked up, and the whiskey-soaked tones began asking for a good man while Jac drummed on her desk. "Ah, Bonnie, Bonnie, Bonnie, you're asking the wrong question, love." She smashed the air cymbal with imaginary drumsticks. "If you want a real hero, you need to ask where have all the good *women* gone."

CHAPTER 6

Jac waited outside Velvet for Sasha Adams to arrive. She'd eaten and drunk in the restaurant-cum-bar many times over the years. It was one of her favourite places to go in Manchester's Gay Village. The food was good, the atmosphere relaxed, and the art on the bare brick walls was often incredible. She'd even bought a few pieces for the office and for her apartment from there over the years. Jac's particular favourite was a metal sculpture of a woman's body in repose—her weight leaning back on her hands, her knees half bent, and her head tilted back with an expression of pleasure. She almost wanted to fan her own face as she thought about it.

Mags had done a good job of finding information about the woman she was to meet, including several options for women who could be Sasha; but on this point, she couldn't be certain. There was no image on the net that screamed, "This is her, oi, Jac, this one!" with a big red arrow pointing at her. Instead there were pictures of the elderly lady in tie-dye, a tiny black woman with a Mohawk, a black cat in various poses, and a few others Jac was almost certain were Sasha's friends or acquaintances…but not the woman herself. The mystery only added to the excitement.

She just hoped she hadn't built up this meeting too much in her mind. God, the poor woman had a lot to live up to right now. She patted her pocket in search of her cigarettes.

"For fuck's sake, how long before I get a hold of that habit?"

She stuffed her hands in her pockets and scanned the foot traffic as she waited. She glanced up at the rapidly greying sky and was beginning to think her idea of waiting here might have been a bad one. It was going to pour down any second. She stepped inside the doorway, swerving to avoid four guys coming up the steps from the downstairs restaurant as she checked the clock.

"It's okay, it's only just time now. She's not late or standing you up, Jac. Chill."

She swallowed back nervousness and stepped outside again just in time to see a woman trying to avoid the guys before staring at the building like it was suddenly on fire.

"Are you okay?" Jac asked softly. The woman looked like she was about to run, and Jac was pretty sure that wouldn't end well, given the heels she was wearing.

"Oh, no. I mean yes, I'm fine, thank you."

That voice. Elkie Brooks dipped in honey wasn't even close. The husky tone, the subtle vibrato that shook even in speech, made Jac's insides quiver. It was Sasha. Jac would recognise that voice anywhere. She'd been dreaming about it for days. Her breath caught in her throat as she wrapped her fingers around the woman's arm to stop her leaving, because oh. My. God.

Sasha Adams was a knockout. Long dark hair, verging on black, hung down her back, slipping over one shoulder as she moved. Jac guessed her height at around five-foot-five, as even in the three-inch heels, she was still considerably shorter than her own six foot. But, my, what she was packing into those five feet and five inches was making Jac drool. Beneath the dark-grey skirt suit, Jac could see she was barely disguising curves that would make Jessica Rabbit weep. When their gazes met, Jac felt like she was falling into eyes as deep and rich as melted chocolate.

"Ms Adams?"

She nodded, and placed her hand on top of Jac's, still wrapped around her forearm. She squeezed a little, a subtle reminder that she was touching and she shouldn't. But Jac could feel the tremble in those long fingers. Nerves? Or a simple reaction to being touched by a stranger?

"Sorry, forgive me. I'm Jaclyn Kensington. Please call me Jac."

Sasha didn't move or say anything, and Jac couldn't help herself. She knew she was moving, but she felt unable to control or stop herself as she lifted Sasha's hand to her lips and kissed it.

What the fuck? This is a business lunch, not a pickup bar. Tone it down, idiot, before she slaps you.

She glanced at Sasha's face in time to see her lick her lips, an unconscious gesture, no doubt, but a telling one. Jac grinned, relieved she didn't seem to be in trouble for her display. She waved one arm towards the building behind them.

"Shall we?"

Sasha nodded again and allowed Jac to tuck her hand into the crook of her elbow as she led the way through the doors and down the stairs into the restaurant.

After the hostess had them seated and they perused the menu, Jac noticed Sasha biting her lip and fidgeting. She had yet to say another word.

Jac gave her what she hoped was a reassuring smile and spoke softly, "You okay?"

Sasha glanced up, eyes wide and apprehensive, but she slowly drew in a deep breath that made her shoulders climb towards her ears. She let it out and said, "I'm sorry. I'm not used to all this, and it's making me even more nervous than I was to begin with, and I really don't know how to start with all the questions I have about the paperwork you sent me, and I don't know how to do this. I don't. Oh God, now I'm waffling, I'm sorry, I'm going to shut up now, and you can just let me know what I'm supposed to do." She cast her gaze back to her menu.

Jac chuckled softly, partly to break the tension and partly to try to distract herself. Sasha's voice was so much better in person than it had been over the phone. Jac was pretty damn sure she could listen to Sasha read the phone book and still fall for that voice. *What? Shit. Not helping.*

"Hey, don't worry. No need to be nervous, Sasha."

Sasha looked at her sceptically. It brought a grudging smile to Jac's face. "Okay, whether you need to be nervous or not, you are. So how about this? We table the discussions about the script and the paperwork until later. Right now, let's just have lunch and talk."

"I don't want to take up your time. I'm sure you've got better things to do with your day than waste a business lunch with me and then still have the work to do later."

Jac shook her head. While Sasha's statement wasn't untrue, she was honest enough with herself to acknowledge that she didn't care. She'd work until midnight after Sasha was gone if she had to. She wanted to spend this time talking with her. And justifying it was easy enough.

"Getting to know you is important. I need to know if we can work together or not in order to inform some of the decisions we make about this project going forward. If we can, then working with you to make any changes we might want or need to the script will be easy. If we can't, and I'll have to find another writer to work with, it's always better to know that sooner rather than later."

Sasha's brow furrowed. "Are there a lot of changes you want to make?"

Jac had expected the question. "Some. There always are. Does that bother you?"

"I guess it depends on what the changes are and if it makes the script better. If it does, then, no, it won't bother me. If it doesn't, then I guess I'd need to understand why it had to be changed before I could decide how I felt about it."

Jac smiled. *Perfect. A writer who wants to learn. Not like the last one. Damn, no script is ever perfect. None. But Sandra Pain-in-the-Arse Larson sure thought hers was.* Even if giving the script to a writer who wasn't invested in it like Sasha was would be immeasurably easier to get the changes she wanted, having Sasha make them would undoubtedly make them more authentic, more heartfelt, and therefore more meaningful in the long-term. Having Sasha on board throughout the project would make a better film. Jac was already sure of that.

The waiter arrived, and they quickly placed their orders before he took the menus from them.

"Well, okay, then. We can talk about all that after lunch, but, right now, why don't you tell a little bit about yourself?" Jac asked.

Sasha grimaced. "What would you like to know?"

"Let's start with what you do for a living."

"I'm a massage therapst, but I also do other beauty treatments."

"In Manchester?"

Sasha nodded. "Yes, the Serenity Spa Salon, it's on—"

"Deansgate, I know the place. Do you live alone?"

Sasha shook her head, and Jac's stomach dropped. *Should've known a woman like you would be taken—*

"I'm almost ashamed to admit I live with my mother." She laughed. "I moved back in with her a few years ago. She had some health issues and needed extra care." She shrugged. "It's taken a long time to get to a place where she feels she can be alone again." She picked up her water glass and sipped. "Though I'm not sure I've reached the point where I think she can be alone again yet."

"Ah," Jac murmured, and a smile tugged at the corner of her lips. The pictures of the woman in tie-dye with the prosthetic leg now made sense. "I'm sorry to hear that." Sasha frowned and Jac clarified. "About her health issues, I mean."

"Oh, thanks."

"So how did you start writing screenplays?"

Sasha bit her lip, seemingly unsure about sharing her story.

"Oh, you can't give me that look and not share. Come on." She wiggled a finger beckoningly. "Spill it, Adams."

Sasha let out a full throaty laugh that Jac felt all the way down to her toes, and her eyes sparkled with mischief.

"All right, but you can't get pissed off, then."

"Now I'm really intrigued."

"I'd been watching a run of romance films, and I felt like they were each getting worse. They weren't, it was just that they were each following the same formula. I was getting bored, so I stopped watching them. But I couldn't get it out of my head that there should be something more available…something not necessarily better, but different. Another option. I mean, surely not every single lesbian in the world only likes the A-B-C formulaic romance, right?"

Jac nodded but let her continue.

"So I decided to entertain myself one winter by seeing if I could come up with anything different." She sipped her water again. "It was the winter when I was taking Mum to and fro to the hospital, there was a ton of waiting time while she was having treatments, and all she really seemed to do was sleep. So I dusted off my old laptop and picked the last film I'd watched with a couple of friends. I picked it apart and decided where it could have been tweaked to make it different and in my opinion better. And I do stress that it is only my opinion."

"What film did you choose?"

Sasha grimaced and squinted as she said, "*When Lightning Strikes.*"

"My *When Lightning Strikes*?" Jac cocked her head to the side and Sasha nodded. "Really?"

She nodded again and whispered, "Sorry. It wasn't the worst one I watched. In fact, it wasn't all that bad, really. It's just, like I said, I'd watched a run, and they all followed the same formula, and I was bored with it. I wanted something different." She glanced down. "Sorry."

"Don't be. I didn't write it." She offered a cocky little grin. "I just couldn't work with the original writer on the changes it needed, so we had to use a staff writer. It turned out pretty well, but I'd love to see what you'd have done with the script."

"Really?"

"God, yes. We knew when we were filming that it was missing something. We just couldn't put our fingers on it at the time."

"We?"

"Yes, Kefran Media Limited is made up of myself, Mags French, and Sophie Angel. We knew it needed something else, but none of us are writers and we couldn't make our ideas work with the budget or time we had left at the end of the day. It would have meant adding scenes, perhaps a car chase, or a new character."

Sasha laughed again. "You're pulling my leg."

"Only about the car chase."

"Well, you didn't need to do all that. You had all the elements in the story already. You just needed some extra dialogue in a few scenes, and an exaggeration on one of the peripheral characters to add tension."

"Will you let me see it?"

Sasha bit her lip, clearly hesitant, but damn if that didn't make Jac shiver.

"Please? I'd really like to see how we could've improved it. And stay on budget."

"Okay. I'll email it to you." She held up a finger. "But be gentle. It was my first attempt."

Somehow, Jac didn't think she'd need to be gentle on Sasha's early work, but she promised anyway. "You have my word."

"What about you?"

"What about me?"

"How did you get into film production?"

"Long story short, it's what I always wanted to do. Well, to be honest, I wanted to be an actress first. Stage more than screen. But when I got to uni and discovered the real magic happened behind the scenes, I got hooked. Sophie and I met there, and we forged ahead. I was always interested in the camerawork, directing where to place them, how to get the shots we needed for this scene or that. How to create more atmosphere in a particular setting and so on. Sophie was always better with sound, music, and talking to the divas." Jac laughed. "We made quite a pair but we needed a third to assist with the computer editing. That's where Mags came in. We each went out and honed our skills when we graduated but we were the best of friends and kept coming back to the idea of doing what we loved together, making our own films." She sighed heavily. "It took a long time, but we finally got there when Sophie was sent the script for *When Lightning Strikes*. The writer was an old friend of hers from uni. We bought the script and the rest, as they say, is history."

"Wow, impressive."

Jac shook her head. "No, we all just knew what we wanted and decided to take a chance and go for it. Sophie says we hung our stall on faith, trust, and a little bit of pixie dust."

"A fan of *Peter Pan*?"

Jac tipped her head to one side and took another drink. "Something like that," she said, then pointed her glass at Sasha. "But it's not that much different from you writing your scripts and being here now. Taking a chance and chasing the dream."

"Except I didn't. Bobbi sent that script in without telling me."

"I don't agree. You still came here today. You're here now. Yes, this Bobby sent the script in and pointed you in this direction, but he didn't force you to come here today, did he?"

"It's *she*, and, no, Bobbi didn't force me to come and meet you."

"Oh, sorry. So is Bobbi your…girlfriend?"

Sasha laughed again and waved her hand in front of her. "No, no," she said when she stopped laughing. "Bobbi is a friend. She's a pain in the arse most of the time, but a lovable one. She's just a very good friend, though."

"Ah." They ate quietly when their meals arrived, seemingly content to exchange small talk over duck ravioli and caramelised celeriac soup. When the mains were set down, Jac stared at Sasha as she savoured the first bite of her lamb rump, her tongue quickly licking at a drop of gravy on her lip.

Jac swallowed and tightened her grip on her knife and fork. She cleared her throat. "Good?"

"You have no idea." Slowly, she scooped up another forkful and extended it to Jac. "Here, try a bite. It's amazing."

Jac took the morsel, letting Sasha's fork caress her tongue. Their gazes locked, and Sasha froze, her fork still between Jac's lips. Her jaw slackened and her eyes widened.

"I'm so sorry," she whispered. "I didn't even think."

Jac wrapped her hand around Sasha's, pulled the fork from her mouth, and swallowed. "Don't be, you're right. That was delicious. Would you like to try some of the veal?" She pointed to her own plate, trying to inject some normalcy between them again and ignoring the way the muscles in her abdomen had clenched at the erotically charged moment. Jac scooped up a generous forkful from her plate and held it as though she was going to feed it to Sasha.

"No, thank you. I'm sorry, but I don't eat veal."

Jac put the fork on her plate. "I'm sorry if I've offended you."

Sasha waved a hand in front of her. "No, no, it's just a personal thing. I've thought many times about becoming a veggie, but I can't quite bring myself to do it. But there are some things I just can't bring myself to put in my mouth." She swallowed and looked at Jac with a sheepish expression. "My foot, however, I manage to insert quite regularly."

Jac chuckled. "I'm sure that's not true." She waved the waiter over, intent on getting him to take away the plate. "Hi, can you swap this for another of the lamb, please?" she asked when he arrived at their table. She lifted her napkin from her lap and dabbed at her mouth.

"Certainly." He turned to Sasha. "Would you like me to get you a fresh plate at the same time?"

"No!" Sasha looked stunned and pointed to the plate in his hand. "Put that back down." She looked at Jac. "Sending it back is just wasteful. I don't have an issue with you eating it. What good would it do to waste the food now?"

Jac cocked her head to the side but motioned for the waiter to put the plate back down and leave them alone again. *Fabulous. Now she thinks you're wasteful as well as callous.*

"I'm sorry," Sasha said. "See what I mean about this foot-in-mouth disease I have?" She exhaled heavily and leant back in her chair. "Sorry for ruining our lunch."

"You haven't." *I seem to be doing a great job of that myself today.*

"But—"

"Truly." Jac smiled and hoped it conveyed her genuine happiness at meeting Sasha, despite the awkward moments that had just passed. "I can't remember the last time I actually enjoyed myself quite so much meeting someone new." She lifted her fork and grinned at Sasha. "It's certainly a lunch I'll never forget. Now finish your lamb while I tuck in over here. We've got a lot of things to discuss this afternoon."

Like the next time I can see you, for a start.

The offices of Kefran Media were sleek, modern, and clean. And situated in Quay House, the home to MediaCity and the heart of all things TV in Manchester. All smooth lines, glass tabletops, and tablets stuck to people's hands. Sasha found herself a little disappointed. She'd almost wanted to see lots of old books and piles of scripts on the edges of every desk, with their corners yellowed and curling with age. Instead, she was greeted by a perky receptionist whose teeth were amazingly white when she beamed and offered to get them coffee. Jac agreed for them both and directed her to bring it to the conference room.

Jac had no sooner ushered Sasha into a chair near the head of the room when a blonde stuck her head around the door, smiled, then walked in with her hand extended.

"Hi, I'm Sophie Angel. One of Jac's business partners."

Sasha stood and took her hand. "Sasha Adams."

"I know. Love your screenplay. I can't wait to see it on screen."

Sasha grinned back at her. Sophie's enthusiasm was infectious. "Me too."

"Can I get you anything? Coffee?"

"Already on the way," Jac said from her seat at the end of the conference table.

"Great, then I'll leave you two to chat," Sophie said and backed out of the door. "I'll catch up with you before you go, but I have a conference call in two minutes regarding the financing of the project. Mags is in there with me," she told Jac.

"Perfect. See you in a bit." A different woman entered with a tray of coffee, milk, and sugar and set it on the table with a huge smile for Jac. "Thanks," Jac said, her gaze not drifting from Sasha. "So where would you like to start?" she asked when the door closed behind the young woman.

"Can we start with the changes you'd like to make to the screenplay?"

"Sure." Jac stood and placed a hand on Sasha's shoulder as she walked behind her chair. "Let me just go grab my copy and I'll show you. Won't be a second." She pointed to the tray. "Why don't you pour while I run to my office?" Then she was gone.

And Sasha's shoulder burned from the gentle pressure of Jac's hand. Her scent lingered in the air. The earthy aroma of sandalwood and the spicy perfume of cinnamon clung to the fabric of her jacket. It made her tongue tingle with the desire to taste those flavours on Jac's skin.

Wow, okay there, Sash, that was…unexpected. She fanned her face, then reached out with shaking hands to pour two cups of dark, richly scented coffee. She added a little milk to her own and sipped gingerly while she waited and tried to ignore the way Jac affected her, what with her tall, lean body beneath the expensive business suit and the lilac tie. Her silver-grey hair, cropped close to the head on the left and worn almost to shoulder length across the centre and right-hand side gave her the air of both experience and having not lost her edge. Plump, full lips smiled at her and Sasha stared up into the most arresting eyes she had ever seen. Grey like the gathering storm clouds overhead, flecked with hints of blue and green around the irises. *God, I could get lost in those eyes.*

She turned her head slightly when she heard the door open behind her, but Jac's hand was on her shoulder again as she dropped a sheaf of pages onto the table in front of her. She couldn't focus on the pages as that scent filled her nostrils again.

Jac slid into her own chair and reached for her coffee cup. She sipped the un-doctored brew. "Just the way I like it."

Sasha filed that tidbit away for future reference, swallowed hard, and forced herself to pick up the bound pages of her screenplay. Marks had been made in the margins in red pen. Not many, but enough to get her thinking about the story and take her mind off Jac.

Slowly, she began to relax, and talking to Jac about the project became easier. She found she could see exactly where Jac was trying to direct the characters to grow, and how she could push them even further.

"I can make these changes, Jac, but if I do, I see further potential to develop them. Do you have a problem with that?"

"Will it add any further scenes?"

"No."

"Any car chases?" She tapped her fingers against her cup in a descending pattern, index to pinkie, one after the other. It was almost hypnotic. But it was her grin that truly captivated Sasha. The mischief and warmth was even more intoxicating than those eyes.

Sasha laughed and shook her head. "No, and no new characters either. Just a touch more dialogue here and there."

"Then I look forward to reading what you suggest." Jac's smile was warm and genuine and it made Sasha's stomach flip.

"When do you need the changes?"

"As soon as you can, really. Dock 10 has a window of time open in the studio in about two months time. We can get the bulk of recording done then, and then shoot the location scenes at the end. If you can get me the changes in the next week or two, then I can get casting on it, then get the cast learning their lines."

"A couple of months?"

"Yes." Jac touched Sasha's hand. "I also wanted to talk to you about that. I usually have the writer on set while filming so we can make any changes required as we go. Sometimes what we see on the page just doesn't come across on screen and we need to tweak things. I think we're pretty much on the same page, and that you and I will work well together on this project. Am I right?"

Sasha nodded, not sure where Jac was leading with this.

"So I'd need you on set while we're filming. You'd watch it all with me and make those changes as needed. Would that be okay?"

"Wow, I... Well, I wasn't expecting that."

Jac grinned. "I'm sorry to have blindsided you, then, but it's a really important part of the process, and trying to do that from a distance just doesn't work for me."

"How long will filming take?"

"If we manage to stay on schedule, then it should take around five or six weeks."

Six weeks? So many questions flew through Sasha's mind that she was unable to grasp a hold of any one of them.

Jac carried on. "The money isn't great, I know that, but it's pretty decent for a first-time screenplay." She pushed a piece of paper towards Sasha, and Sasha felt like she was floating away from her body, watching the scene in slow motion.

Not great? It was more than Sasha made in a year…make that two. But what about her job? With two years' salary coming to her in one clump, did she care? Nope. Not a damn bit.

"There can be long hours. Some days we might start at eight, earlier if there's a reason to, and it might be midnight before we wrap for the day."

Mum. Yes, she'd told Sasha to get her arse in gear that morning and not come back until she had this all sewn up. But that didn't mean Sasha could effectively leave her mum to fend for herself for six weeks while she worked those kinds of hours!

"I need to—" Sasha bit off what she was about to say. She didn't need to talk to her mum. Fleur had been clear. Crystal clear. She wanted Sasha to jump on this opportunity. She wanted her to grab it with both hands and run. Fleur had told her as much on Sunday evening. She'd pretty much told her the same thing this morning when Sasha had been walking out the door. Her mother wasn't a child, and as much as Sasha felt wrong about leaving Fleur to it, she was capable of looking after herself. It wasn't Sasha's place to mother her. Fleur had made it brutally clear that she didn't want that. So why was she even thinking about putting Jac on hold? Why was she even contemplating holding back on this?

Jac's smile seemed to fade a little, and her fingers stopped their drumming. She clearly sensed Sasha's indecision. She offered, "If it helps you make a decision, I'd really like to look at other stuff you've written, Sasha. I'd like to work with you on other projects, if this is anything to go by, and given how productive our discussion today has been, I think we'll work really well together." Jac's expression was open, candid, and sincere, and Sasha couldn't help but smile back.

"Really?"

"Oh God, yes."

Sasha looked down at the script in her hands. *Sasha Adams, scriptwriter.* It had a ring to it. *Sasha Adams, writer.* She liked that.

Nightingale, *a film by Sasha Adams.* She rolled it around in her mind. *I really like that.*

She licked her lips, tugged the bottom one between her teeth as she rolled the phrase around in her head once more. Sasha Adams, writer.

She held out her hand to Jac, lifted her head, and steadily met Jac's gaze. "Let's do this."

Jac's grin was huge—like cheek-cracking huge—as she pumped Sasha's hand up and down over and over. She was talking, babbling about things Sasha couldn't hear over her internal voice shouting and whooping at her while dancing around the disco Sasha's head had turned into.

I'm doing this. I'm really doing this.

CHAPTER 7

THE BUS RIDE HOME WAS uneventful, and Sasha sat staring unseeingly out of the window, the day's events running through her mind even as she tried to make notes of all that had happened and every word Jac had said.

The details of financing the project were intricate, and more than a few had gone over her head, but one thing was clear: Jac knew what she was doing. And Jac wanted her on the project, in just a couple of months.

Then there was the money. It wasn't going to make her a lady of leisure for the rest of her life, but still. It was more than a little surreal.

Sasha's head was buzzing, and every vibration drew her back to thoughts of Jac, and that cocky, sexy haircut that made Sasha's fingers itch to explore. She wanted to run them across those shorn locks before twisting into the longer tresses that hung enticingly over her right ear. The long glances and accidental brushes of Jac's hand against her own as she'd pointed things out to her throughout the course of the afternoon had left Sasha longing for…more. A lot more. As had Jac's quick wit, her cheeky grin, and the intelligence that had shone through those piercing grey eyes.

Heat burnt Sasha's cheeks, and she placed her cool hand against her burning skin. It had been a long, long time since she'd reacted so strongly to another woman. And never so quickly. Was that why the passion hadn't lasted with her previous partners? Because they'd all been friends before they'd become anything more? Sure, she'd respected them, loved them, even. But had she truly lusted for either Claire or Pam? With either of them, when had she'd stared out of window and wondered what they were doing right then, or tried to find the exact right word to describe the colour of their eyes? When had she ever tried to label the notes of their perfumes?

"I feel like a teenager with a crush," she mouthed and watched her light puff of breath fog on the glass. "And in a couple of months, I'll be working with her every day." She let her head fall onto the cold glass.

When she finally got home, she was more than a little worried to see her mother stumbling through the house as Nip wound herself around Fleur's legs and her crutch. By this time, she was normally asleep after spending the evening in the conservatory getting stoned. She looked unsteady.

"Mum? Are you okay?"

"Of course. I just woke up. Nip and I had a little nap on the couch."

Sasha noted her mother's glassy-eyed gaze and her direction of travel. She quickly wrapped her hand around her elbow, offering support to the bathroom.

After Fleur finished up and was settled back on the sofa, cuppa in hand, she said, "Chop-chop, then. Let's hear all about it."

Sasha sighed, sipped her brew, and then started to tell her mother everything. Well…except for how sexy Jac was and how big a crush she was currently fighting for the woman.

"So you're going to be on the set? For the whole filming?" Fleur asked.

"I—I, well, I agreed to do it."

Fleur beamed. "Excellent."

Sasha didn't say anything. It *was* excellent, but she was still concerned for Fleur. Was she really okay? The lines around her mother's eyes seemed deeper lately. Every time she asked, Fleur merely said she was tired, or stoned. She probably was and Sasha was driving herself crazy for no reason. Fleur went to all her appointments, all her check-ups. Her mother didn't seem to worry at all about her health, so why should Sasha?

"What's this?" Fleur wiggled a finger in front of Sasha's face. "It's not excellent?"

Sasha shrugged one shoulder.

"I know that look. Tell me."

"Part of me is still not sure I should do it."

"Why ever not?"

Sasha sighed. "Jac said there would be a lot of long hours. I won't be around to help you. I don't want anything to happen to you while I'm at work."

Fleur slapped her arm.

"Ow."

"I'm a grown woman, and, more importantly, so are you. Don't think I didn't see that twinkle in your eye when you talked about this Jac woman. I might be stoned, but I'm not dead. Besides, something could happen just as easily while you're at work now as it could if you were working on the film. You're making excuses, and not even very good ones. I can cope on my own. So you don't have to worry about that."

"Mum—" Sasha started to tell Fleur she was winding her up, but Fleur was just getting started.

"No. Enough. I'll kick you out if I have to. You need to follow your dreams, Sasha. I'm not always going to be here—"

"Don't say that."

"It's the truth, honey. We both know that. I'm not saying I'm going anywhere right this second, but I'm seventy-five years old. I'm almost an old woman, and I can be honest, some days I'm even starting to feel a little over sixty." She sniggered, and Sasha couldn't stop herself from laughing. "I've got a lot of good years under my belt, as well as a few tough ones. I've seen as much of the world as I want to see. I've raised a wonderful daughter, and there is truly only one thing left I want before I can go and see your father again."

Tears welled in Sasha's eyes. "What?"

"To see you happy." She squeezed Sasha's knee. "That's all I want now."

Sasha sniffed and took the handkerchief Fleur held out for her.

"I only ever loved your father, and God could that man drive me bloody potty sometimes. But I loved him with everything that was in me, and he loved me the same. We completed each other. I want that for you, Sasha. I want to know you're taken care of before...well, you know."

"Do we have to be so morbid?"

"Not at all. As long as you agree to do this. Besides, Bobbi was telling me about this website thingy called Tinder, and I think I might find myself a new chappie on there. Having you at home so much would put a crimp in my style."

"Oh God, don't even joke about it."

"What? I can catch me a fella if I want one."

"I meant about you going on Tinder."

"Why?"

"You'd need a smartphone to access the app."

"Why do I have to get a smartphone? I'd rather just have a normal one. I don't need all those gizmos and wotsits."

"And this is why it's not a good idea."

Fleur looked at her and pulled a face like she was sucking a lemon. "Fine, I'll do it the old-fashioned way."

"What's that?"

"I'll get myself down to the bowling club."

Sasha snorted.

"That's better. So when are you going to tell this woman you'll take her up on this offer?"

"I already did. I told you that. I just...well..."

"You're scared."

Sasha nodded.

"Of failing? Or succeeding?"

"Maybe a bit of both." She laughed sadly. "This will change things."

"Good. Things have needed to change for quite some time, my darling girl."

"Doesn't mean it doesn't make me uncomfortable."

Fleur slapped her on the arm.

"Ow." Sasha rubbed the spot. "What was that for?"

"For getting so maudlin and letting me waffle on with all that sentimental crap when all you really need is a good old-fashioned kick up the arse."

"You saying you didn't mean it? Please say you didn't mean the Tinder bit."

"Just for that, I'm going to get Bobbi to hook me on."

"It's hook me *up*, and I'm gonna tell her not to."

"Pft, that girl knows what's good for her, so she damn well will hook me *up*." Fleur pointed her nose in the air. Snooty. Clearly impressed with herself and her correct use of slang. "So, what are you going to do about work? I think you should tell 'em where to stick it."

"Not sure that should be my first option, Mum, but I'll keep it in mind. I was thinking I might ask for unpaid leave."

Fleur rolled her eyes. "Just quit. That'll give you more incentive to make this work."

"And what if it doesn't? There are thousands, probably millions, of writers out there who are waiting tables to pay the bills. I've got a decent job. Quitting that to go running after a hope and a prayer isn't a very smart idea. I'm forty-five years old, Mum. I need to be more sensible than that." But even as she said it, she remembered Jac and how she and her friends had thrown everything into making their dreams a reality. Now they were living it. Could she be as brave? Or was it reckless?

"Pish. If it doesn't work out, you come back and get another job rubbing naked strangers' backs. There's plenty of folk out there go in for that. You'll have no problem finding a job when you want one. Besides, we've got this house, it's all paid for, and there's a bit put aside. We'll not want for out, honey. So put your big-girls pants on and bloody well resign."

Could she? Was it truly as easy as that? Roll the dice and let the chips fall where they may? *Since when did I get so bloody clichéd?*

"I'll think about it."

Fleur tutted and lifted her crystal necklace from over her head. "What's to think about?" She held the crystal over the plate of brownies on the coffee table, shut her eyes, and let it swing as she mumbled something Sasha couldn't make out. A smile spread over her lips and she reached out for the chosen cake slice without opening her eyes. After she took a huge bite, she moaned. "These are getting better and better, if I do say so myself."

"New recipe?"

"Yes, young Dante on the corner gave me a top tip this morning."

"Oh yeah. What's that?" *Don't burn your space cakes?*

"I can't tell you, dear. He told me in confidence."

Sasha looked up at the ceiling and wondered how many slices Fleur had eaten already. "Since when are you on first-name terms with the local drug dealer, anyway?"

"Dante's a nice boy. He helped me with my bags a few days ago when I went shopping. We were out of margarine."

"Why didn't you ask me to get it on the way home?"

"Because I wanted to get the next batch in. I'm finding these cakes are working better for me than the smoking right now."

Sasha shook her head. "Fine. So he carried your bags for you?"

"Yes."

"And you started swapping recipes?"

"Yes."

"You realise that if I wrote this shit, no one would believe me."

"Speaking of writing shit, go and write your resignation."

Sasha smiled. She could feel it stretching across her lips at the thought of why that was even a possibility. Sasha Adams, writer.

"And then make me a sandwich. I'm getting hungry and I should make the most of you waiting on me hand and foot for as long as I can, now. Right?"

Sasha nodded and hoisted herself off the couch. She'd do the sandwich first, then attend to her career alterations. "What do you want on it?"

"Spam and mustard."

She shuddered. Sasha hated the gelatinous tinned meat, but Fleur was a long-time fan, and she wasn't going to change her now. "Right," she said around a sigh.

"With cheese and onion crisps on it too."

Revolting. But Sasha threw her a mock salute before escaping to the kitchen.

CHAPTER 8

"So how'd it go?" Bobbi asked when Sasha entered the staff room and switched the kettle on to boil.

She shrugged and emptied her cuppa-soup sachet into a mug, stifling a yawn as she did. "Good."

Bobbi frowned. "You look tired."

"I couldn't sleep last night. Too many things running through my mind."

"Like?"

She shrugged again and poured the boiled water into the mug and stirred as she made her way over to the comfy-ish chairs scattered about the room. "Trying to decide whether or not to thank you for starting off this whole chance-of-a-lifetime thing or not."

Bobbi laughed. "What's to decide? You just said it was the chance of a lifetime."

Sasha threw her head back and laughed too. "You're right." She wrapped her arms around Bobbi and squeezed until Bobbi groaned and let out a strangled breath.

"Need air," she gurgled.

"Thank you." She kissed the top of Bobbi's head and let go.

"You're welcome."

Sasha reached into the pocket of her tunic and showed Bobbi the envelope.

"What's that?" Bobbi asked.

"My resignation."

"You're quitting?" Bobbi's eyes widened as she stared at her, slack-jawed.

Sasha nodded, then shrugged. "Yeah, I-I think I have to."

"But why?"

"Because they want me to work on the set with them while they make the film. To do any rewrites and stuff that comes up."

"But that doesn't mean you have to quit. What will you do when the film's done?"

"I'll get another job or maybe…I don't. Maybe I'll have another script to sell then. I'm not sure."

"But-but that means we won't work together every day?"

"Well, no. But we'll still see each other all the time, Bobbi. You're my best friend. Nothing's going to change that."

"Right." Bobbi's shocked expression clouded and shifted to a frown, and Sasha wasn't sure what expression passed over Bobbi's face before she tossed the magazine she'd been reading on the coffee table and scurried out of the room, mumbling about getting back to work.

"Well," Sasha said to herself, "that wasn't the reaction I expected." She looked at the envelope in her hand. She still had a couple of appointments booked in before she finished for the day, but she had twenty minutes until the next one. "Now's as good a time as any, I suppose." She stalked out of the staff room and didn't stop walking until she was standing in front of the door with a placard saying, *Maria Carter, Owner*.

"Come in," the voice on the other side of the door called when Sasha knocked. As soon as she was inside, she slid into the seat opposite Maria.

"Maria, I've—"

The woman silenced her with a look and folded her arms across her chest. "A little birdie, who shall remain nameless, spent all of yesterday telling anyone and everyone how amazing this screenplay written by her best friend is. Won some big competition, gonna be a film, *yada, yada, yada*. On and on and on. All bloody day. So much so, I made her email it to me."

"You did?"

Maria held up the tablet in her hand. "Not quite finished yet, but I figured if I was going to lose one of my best staff members, I should at least have an idea why."

"You like it?" Maria had always seemed so standoffish, aloof even. So much so that Sasha hadn't even been sure she knew the names of the people who worked for her. The idea she was reading Sasha's story felt strange. Exciting. But strange.

"I do. So I'm going to make this easy on you."

Not sure where this was going, Sasha cocked her head to the side and waited.

"Sasha, you're fired."

Sasha stared at her, well aware she was impersonating some sort of fish, her mouth opening and closing, attempting to form words she couldn't seem to force past her lips.

Maria's grin was smug, maybe even a little cocky.

"Wh-what?" Sasha finally managed to sputter.

"You're fired."

"You're sacking me?"

Maria grinned evilly. "Yeah. I'm going to consider it my claim to fame when you're collecting your Oscar. I want a mention in the thank-you speech, by the way, and if you feel like crying when you mention my name, I'd be most grateful."

"You're firing me?"

"Yes, we've covered that already."

"But I was going to resign."

Maria waved her hand. "Don't want that."

"I was going to give you like a month's notice. Maybe even six weeks to find a replacement." She held out her carefully worded resignation letter for Maria to take.

Maria snorted and waved it away. "This is Manchester and we're an upscale spa. I've got CVs coming out of my ears. I'll have a new you in here tomorrow."

Sasha felt more than a little affronted. "Gee, thanks."

"You're going to have to grow some thicker skin than that, love." Maria chortled. "The critics will be a lot meaner, I'm sure."

Sasha had to acknowledge she was probably right. Still… "You're really sacking me?"

"Yup, told you, my claim to fame."

Sasha stared, slack-jawed and still in shock. She stuffed the envelope back into her pocket. "Do you want me to leave now?"

"End of the day will do, dear."

Sasha nodded, still feeling a little numb. *So this is what a push feels like*, she thought. *Not sure I like it.* Then she pictured her next boss—her new boss. Jac Kensington. She pictured walking into the suite of offices at MediaCity, sitting behind a desk—her desk. She could see that name plate on it. Sasha Adams, Writer. This was happening. It was really happening.

"I think I'll get Bobbi to organise your leaving party to start after the last appointment tonight." Maria shook her head. "On second thought, I'll do it myself. I want to be able to listen to the music and drink Prosecco, not some sort of alcoholic pop." She stood and walked across the room, putting her hand on Sasha's shoulder leading her out of the office. "I'm really happy for you, Sasha. You deserve this. So grab hold and enjoy." She squeezed Sasha's shoulder, then closed the door.

"Well," she said, staring into the hallway, "doesn't look like I have much of a choice now." She held up an imaginary glass, toasting her imaginary future. "Second star on the right, and straight on till morning."

CHAPTER 9

JAC CLICKED ON HER EMAIL icon and held her breath when she saw a message from Sasha waiting for her. She opened it and quickly scanned the contents. A smile spread across her face, then she went back and read the missive thoroughly.

Dear Jac,

Please find attached the signed contract. I've put the physical copy in the post for you too.

You should also find attached a first draft with the changes you requested for the screenplay. Is that what you're looking for?

Kind regards,
Sasha Adams

Jac pumped her fist in front above the keyboard and hit the Reply icon.

Sasha,

Great to hear from you, and thanks for the contract. Good thinking about the physical copy too. I'll review those changes and get back to you on them.

I'll be in touch soon.

Jac

She shrugged as she hit Reply again. Sasha's immediate response of gratitude made Jac smile. She opened the file and scanned the changes Sasha had made. Subtle in some places, broad in others, and totally in line with everything Jac had asked…plus the little something extra Sasha had hinted at. Jac was pleased, very pleased. Sasha was a gifted writer. The other works she'd sent to Jac were more than enough to convince Jac that Sasha could have a future as a screenwriter if she wanted to pursue it beyond this project—and she truly hoped she did.

Jac leant back in her chair and looked across her office and out through the glass half-wall. She'd worked with many writers over the years, both through Kefran and in her previous incarnation at the BBC as a producer and director. Few of them had had the innate flair and natural ability Sasha seemed to have and brought so effortlessly to the page.

Jac hoped it translated as well to the screen. It should do. And would do. She was determined to make sure of it.

She went back to her computer and again checked through the dates again where they could get access to the studio space operated and managed by Dock 10. It was amazing to think that ten years ago when they moved in down the hall, MediaCity had been a rundown old warehouse, and now they were going to have access to Europe's most technologically advanced HD studios, the heart of broadcasting across the country, the home to *Coronation Street* and *Blue Peter*.

The thousands of exciting people working here on a daily basis, and the many thousands more contracted on revolving project-by-project work, made the pace hectic, but all of the energy in this place every day never failed to go straight to her bloodstream, and Jac loved it; she hoped Sasha would too.

Sophie opened the door and dropped a folder on her desk.

"Thank you, paper fairy, for shitting on my desk. What's this?" She flipped open the file. A photo of a pretty young woman stared up at her.

"Headshots of all the actors I've shortlisted to audition for the MCs. I need your choices soon so I can get them on board and work out logistics for the final round of auditions."

"Okay. I'll get them to you by the end of the day." Jac closed the file and sat back in her chair again.

"What's up with you? You looked lost in thought when I came in."

"Just thinking about when we moved into the offices here."

"Yeah, we'd have never got this space without your connections. Life at Beeb was good to you."

Jac agreed. "But I think we'd have probably still got the space here. They needed us as much as we needed them in the beginning."

"Maybe, but not now." Sophie looked around. "Now it's something else."

"Hm."

"Hm, what?"

"Oh, nothing."

"Christ, Pan-pan, some days it's like pulling teeth to get even a hint of conversation out of you. Spit it out."

"I'm going to invite Sasha for a tour around when it's time to check out the sets."

"Okay."

Jac bit her lip.

"What's up?" Sophie asked. "You're all frowny."

She felt unsure of herself, and the feeling was…unsettling, to say the least. She was never unsure of herself. Not when it came to work stuff. Not when it came to beautiful women. But when it came to Sasha, something was throwing her off her game, making her question herself. "Do you think she'd, I don't know, find it interesting or useful to see it?"

Sophie smirked.

"What?"

"Nothing." Sophie held up her hands. "Ask her. The worst she can say is no."

"Hm. Do you have a date when the mock-up sets will be ready to check out?"

"I think it'll be about two more weeks yet, just before we're ready to start rehearsals. You know how this works. Need me to get the projected date off my computer?"

"Please. Then I'll see what I can set up with Sasha. I think she needs to see it all if she's going to be working here. Maybe…I don't know. Have you had a chance to look at those other scripts she sent me?"

"Not yet. I was planning to take a look over the weekend."

"Okay, well, when you see how good they are, you'll see what I mean. It'd be great if she'd work with us on more projects. She's got it. I mean she's really got it."

Sophie nodded and scrambled to her feet. "Right, well, I'll email you the date and get to reading, then." She waved her hand as she exited, closing the door behind her.

Jac opened her email program and drafted her message.

Sasha,

The changes look great. But I also wanted to see if you were up for a tour of MediaCity and a look at the mock-ups for the sets for Nightingale? Would that be something you'd be interested in?

Jac

Jac opened the file to look at the casting choices she had the final say on. She looked at the first headshot—too harsh for the vulnerable Muslim girl. She turned it face down. The second looked too old. The character was in her early twenties, and the woman she was looking at seemed to be in her late thirties. She hated watching films where they cast thirty-year-olds as schoolgirls. Just wrong. She patted her pocket for her cigarette packet and remembered again that she'd quit.

"This damn habit is getting old—fast," she grumbled, then grinned when her computer pinged and an email dropped into her inbox.

Jac,

Would love to see the place and the sets. Wow! Yes, please. Just let me know when, and I'll see you then.

Really glad you liked the changes. That's a huge weight off my mind.

Sasha

Jac grinned as she fired off a quick response to Sasha and then began to close her computer down. *It's a work meeting, that's all*, she thought over and over. It didn't seem to be helping too much, though. She couldn't help but feel excited she'd be seeing Sasha again soon. They were going to spend lots of time working together. And while Jac knew it wasn't the case, she felt she already knew Sasha pretty well. She'd gotten to know her through her writing. And she couldn't wait to see how much of what she'd figured out of the woman behind the words was actually true.

It's a work meeting. That's all.

CHAPTER 10

Sᴀsʜᴀ ᴛᴀᴘᴘᴇᴅ ᴀᴡᴀʏ ᴀᴛ ʜᴇʀ laptop, then dabbed her index fingers under each eye to wipe away the tears before they fell. She changed one last comma to a full stop, clicked Save, sniffed, and closed the document. Done. The changes Jac wanted to the script were finished. The last of the character treatments were completed, scene descriptions were finalised. As far as Sasha could tell, her job was concluded—until they all got on set, at least, and could see what was or wasn't working.

All she had to do now was make sure everything was as easy as possible for her mum while she was out for hours and hours at a time. She ran through the list she'd made of alterations she wanted to make to the house: just a few extra grab rails here and there that would make it easier for Fleur to move around on her own. She'd have to remember to ask Bobbi to give her a hand putting those up next time she spoke to her.

The wheelchair in the corner caught her eye, and she added more to her list—oil the axel, make sure the tyres were pumped up, and check the brakes. Not that Fleur used the thing all that often, just on occasion, though come to think of it, she'd been using it a fair bit lately. She added another note: *check Mum's stump for blisters*, the usual reason she resorted to the chair.

Sasha twisted her head from side to side, trying to loosen her shoulders, and decided a quick bathroom stop and a cuppa were in order. She tutted when she spotted that the loo roll was empty and grabbed a fresh one to change it, kicking the pedal of the small bin to deposit the old cardboard tube. A flicker of something catching the light drew her attention to the contents inside.

A thin strip of plastic, about three inches, with what looked like metal or copper at each end, a blue band in the middle, and white chevrons. The tip was stained red. *Is that blood, or some sort of reactive agent?*

She bent down and picked the strip out of the almost-empty bin. It looked like a of medical test strip of some sort. She shrugged. She knew that her mother had to give samples when she went for her appointments to test her kidney functions. Probably just had something to do with that.

Shaking her head, she'd headed into the kitchen to make a brew when she caught sight of Bobbi waving at her from the kitchen window. With a hand to her chest, Sasha opened the back door. "You scared the crap out of me."

"Sorry." Bobbi closed it behind her and shrugged out of her coat. "When no one answered the front door, I was a bit worried. I thought you might be out, and I wanted to check your mum was okay."

"You knocked at the front?"

"Yup."

"Sorry, I didn't hear you."

"'S okay."

"Wait, the gate at the end of the ginnel's locked. How did you even get around the back?"

Bobbi held up one arm and showed off a rip in her coat. "Yeah, that gate's a bitch to climb, but I've got skills. Like I said, I would've gone, but I was worried about your mum."

"Thanks, Bobbi. I really appreciate you looking out for her." She didn't mention that she was pretty sure Bobbi and her mum often got high together and so it wasn't a purely altruistic motive on Bobbi's part. Still, it was kinda self-interestedly sweet. "Mum's already gone to bed. She said she was tired tonight. Coffee?"

Bobbi nodded. "Please. Kinda early for your mum, huh? I mean, it's only just nine o'clock."

"Yeah, but I heard the TV on when I was up there a little while ago, so she's probably not asleep. She's been giving me some space to finish the script changes the last few days." Sasha shrugged. "Plus, she had a couple of brownies after dinner. She was pretty mellow, so she might just be sleeping them off."

Bobbi grinned. "Your mum is so freakin' cool, Sash. There's a better chance of me Zumba dancing with a great white shark than getting my mother stoned."

She had a laugh at the imagery as she made their drinks and put one on the table as Bobbi sat down. Taking a seat, she blew across the top of her drink before she took a sip of the scalding, bitter liquid and sighed with contentment.

"Haven't seen you for a few days." Bobbi's tone was carefully neutral, but the fact she wouldn't meet Sasha's eyes when she said it spoke volumes.

"I've been here, Bobbi. Why didn't you come around for tea like normal?"

"I didn't want to disturb if you were in the middle of something important. You said you had stuff to do."

"Bobbi, hon, you're important to me. Our friendship is the most important thing to me. Just because I've got this great new opportunity that doesn't change. I told you that."

Bobbi shrugged half-heartedly.

"Besides, I just finished them and sent them off to Jac. She'll let me know if I need to do anything else once she's had a look, I'm sure. Celebrate with me."

Bobbi's face split into an eager grin. "Cool. So…*Friends* fest?"

"You read my mind."

Bobbi held up her hand, fist balled, and looked at Sasha expectantly.

"I'm not some sort of gangsta rapper," Sasha said and folded her arms. "You can have a high five, but that's my token gesture to cool."

"That's not even a token towards cool, Sash. Even your mum fist-bumps."

"My mum's cool. I'm not."

"Alas 'tis true." She stood and headed for the front room. "I'll set up the DVD."

"And I'll get the popcorn."

Deep into the third episode, Bobbi and Sasha were sprawled across the sofa, the empty bowl of popcorn between them and fresh mugs of tea in their hands when Bobbi asked, "Are you excited?"

"About the film stuff?"

Bobbi nodded.

"Yeah. I mean I get scared sometimes too. Worried I guess."

"About what?"

"What if no one goes to see it when it's done? What if I can't really do this and they're only making the film because they're obligated to because of the competition—"

"They wouldn't have picked it as the winner if that was the case."

"I didn't say it was logical. You asked what I was scared of." She shrugged.

"Is that all?"

Sasha shrugged again.

"Come on, Sash. You can tell me."

Of course she could, but her worries and concerns were all about her own fears. She knew that. "I guess I've always been cautious. And this running after dreams seems so rash and so not me. Yes, it's exciting. It's overwhelmingly exciting in so many ways. I want to run through the house screaming and shouting half the time, and then I get this fear that I can't really do this after all. That it's some big wind up, and someone's going to jump out of a cupboard any second and tell me this was one great big elaborate set-up. But the logical side of me knows that's stupid. I do. But that almost makes it even more difficult to get my head around."

"Glass-half-empty kinda girl, hey?"

Sasha snorted a quick laugh. "I like to think of myself as a realist, not a pessimist. And the reality is that, yes, this script is being made into a film. But that doesn't mean anything else I've written or will write will be. This could be the only thing I ever produce that's good enough." She squeezed the mug, hoping to steal some of the warmth from it as her hands seemed to cool around it as she spoke. "This could be two months of excitement that have cost me my job and that's it. All for nothing, really."

"Bloody hell, you are a pessimist. So what if nothing else gets made into a film? This one is. You'll be able to point to that for the rest of your life and say, 'See? I fucking did that. I'm that good. Me. Sasha Adams. My name's right there in the credits.' Who cares about the Spa when you can have that?"

"I do. Because the credits of one film won't feed me for the rest of my life."

"You need to learn to live in the moment, Sash," Bobbi said with a groan.

Sasha lifted her eyebrows at Bobbi. "Perhaps you need to learn to plan for the future."

"Your mum was right."

"About what?" Sasha asked, a frown tightening her forehead.

"She said you'd waste the opportunity."

"Waste it? How am I wasting it? I've agreed to go and work with the production company to make the film. I've sent them other examples of my work to see if anything else is good enough. I'm trying to—"

"But have you taken a moment to enjoy any part of it?"

The image of Jac holding her arm outside Velvet danced across the back of her eyelids and she swallowed thickly. She thought of the way her heart raced when Jac had complimented her. The way her palms got a little tacky when she read Jac's comments on her script, and the little emoticons she used, the little jokes Sasha was beginning to anticipate in Jac's emails. And for a second she wondered if she was excited about this opportunity for what it was or because of the time it afforded her with Jac. "Of course I have," she managed to mumble.

"Really?"

"Yes, really."

"When?"

When Jac pulled open the door for me and her hand rested at the bottom of my back. "Lots of times."

"Be specific."

The way Jac's eyes sparkled when we talked, but mostly when she laughed. Bloody hell, I've only met the woman once. Get a grip! "I can't think off the top of my head."

"Then you've proven my point, or rather your mum's point."

Sasha flicked her gaze around the room, trying to think of anything she could say that would shut Bobbi up without giving the pair of them more ammunition to give her grief about later. But anything pertaining to Jac would only lead to more grief. Sasha was excited about it all. She truly was. But yes, the cautious part of her was worried too. Wasn't that natural? And no, if she was honest, she wasn't worried about her job at Serenity. As everyone had pointed out, she could pick up another job like that tomorrow if she had to. Besides, she had other skills that made her employable. It wasn't that. It was the thought of failing. The idea that her writing wasn't good enough to achieve what Jac wanted it to. It was the idea of failing in front of Jac that truly scared her. Of failing Jac. After all, Jac was tying her reputation to Sasha's in this endeavour. Was her work—was she—really good enough to do this?

Bobbi was still staring at her, still waiting for an answer Sasha wasn't sure she could give. When her gaze fell on her laptop, she blurted out, "The writing. I've loved every single moment when I've been writing. I've learnt so much already over the past couple of weeks that I can see how much I've grown as a writer." *Perfect.*

"You loved that before." Bobbi rolled her eyes. "That isn't new, and while it may constitute growth as a writer, it doesn't constitute growth as a person."

"Whoa. Where's this all coming from?"

"I've been reading your scripts."

Sasha cocked her head to one side.

"Maybe you should try reading what you write sometime."

"You mean my natural pessimism doesn't taint it all?"

"Shockingly, no." She grinned.

"Good to know."

"Look," Bobbi began, "I'm not trying to tell you what to do; I like my head attached to my shoulders. But if it were me stepping into a whole new world where no one knows me, even if it was just for a little while, I might be tempted to let loose a bit. Maybe try a few things I don't have the chance to try in everyday life."

"Like what, Bobbi?"

Bobbi cleared her throat. "Like maybe, I don't know, maybe going out with someone or something."

A grin tugged at the corners of her mouth and Sasha couldn't help herself. "Are you suggesting I find myself a quick shag?"

Bobbi's face flushed, turning her dark skin even darker. "I—no—I didn't—I'm not…" She rubbed her hand over her face. "I wasn't meaning it quite so bluntly, but you're, you know…and you should, you know, if, well, you know, you want to."

Sasha almost took pity on her. Almost. "Has my mother been telling you I'm the oldest virgin in Manchester or something?" She had to bite her lip at the horrified look on Bobbi's face.

"Wha—no— She never even—and if she had, I wouldn't believe that. You're too... *you know*, for that to be true."

"Too what, Bobbi? Old?"

"No! Too gorgeous."

Sasha sat back in her chair. *Okay, maybe I've pushed this a little too far.* She opened her mouth to stop Bobbi from saying anything else she might regret later, but Bobbi had worked up a full head of steam now.

"You're beautiful, Sasha, and you deserve to find a woman who can show you that. Who can love you and make you happy. You deserve that." She swallowed and reached for Sasha's hands. "You're my best friend, and all I want is for you to be happy."

"I am happy."

Bobbi shook her head. "No, you're not. You're, well, it's like you're treading water. Waiting. Just waiting for that next thing to happen. Waiting for the next person to fall into your life. The next adventure to find you. But it won't, Sash. It won't come to you. You have to go out there and find them. There's too much of you in here"—she tapped Sasha's head—"that you won't ever let any of us see, because you think it'll blow our tiny minds." She smiled again, sadder this time. "And you're probably right." She clasped Sasha's hands in hers once more. "But that doesn't mean there isn't a person out there who can handle you. All of you. Because there is so much more in there to come out. Maybe this film stuff won't work out, maybe it will. But if you don't give it a shot, if you don't give *you* a shot to come out of your shell, you'll never know." She lifted Sasha's hand to her lips and placed a gentle kiss against her knuckles. "Time to stop treading water."

"What if I can't swim?"

"Then I'll come and save you." She glanced around the living room they were sitting in. "Bring you back to this little pond and never suggest you take off the arm bands ever again. But if you don't try, Sash, if you don't give it a real try, you'll regret it. You know you will."

Sasha swallowed the lump in her throat. "Since when did you get to be so wise?"

"I already told you, since I started reading your scripts." She squeezed her hand once more and then let go. "They're how I really got to know you, Sasha. The real you. You have a talent and a passion that's amazing."

"Bobbi, what if I can't—"

"You can. You really can. So go out there and be fabulous. Show me that dreams really do come true."

"You make it sound so simple."

"Sometimes I think it can be." She drained her mug and put it back on the coffee table and stood, then slipped into her coat again. She leant down and kissed Sasha's cheek. "Just don't forget who your friends are."

"Never."

"Good. Bye, then, Sasha," she whispered and then left, quietly closing the door behind her.

In words and action, Bobbi had shown Sasha exactly what she'd been talking about, and Sasha couldn't help but admire her. In the same situation, would she have been as selfless? She'd like to think so. But could she be as brave?

She pictured Jac, the floppy hair, the grey eyes, the charming smile, and that delicious wit.

Could she be brave? She'd like to think so.

CHAPTER 11

PILES OF PAPER WERE STACKED around her desk, emails sat in her inbox awaiting her attention, but Jac couldn't concentrate on the work. Instead, she flicked her pen between her middle and index fingers, then stared at her hand. *Exactly how I used to flick ash off the end of a fag. Bloody hell.* The craving only added to her frustrations.

Jac picked up the handset for the phone at the corner of her desk and punched the speed dial to Sophie's office before jamming it between her chin and shoulder as she continued to type. The ringing in her ear was annoying. Especially on rings eight, nine, and ten. It bounced as she threw it back into the cradle, jumping out and landing on her desk, spinning around the cord. In some absurd portion of her mind, it looked like a plastic fish. She sighed heavily and put it back with more care, deciding another email was probably the better way to go. Less chance of an argument.

The door to her office swung open, and Mags leant against the frame, arms folded over her chest, ankles crossed. "You know it's almost six, right? Time to knock off for the day."

Jac shook her head. "Can't. Too much to do. I need to get the contracts out to the actors we cast this morning. Speaking of, is Sophie still pissed at me?"

"Uh-huh," Mags hummed.

"Shit." It wasn't often they disagreed, especially not on casting decisions, but Sophie had been dead set against the actress she and Mags had felt was right for the role of Charlie. Apparently, something about her was "off". The "debate" had become heated, and in the end Sophie had stormed off. Not at all usual. They'd get over it. They always did. You don't remain friends for thirty years and not have the odd blow-up from time to time. "This project—"

"Will still be there in the morning." Mags strode into the room, rounded Jac's desk, and grabbed her hands. She pulled her away from the desk. "Come on. I'm calling this an intervention."

Jac slapped at her hands. "Call it what you like, I've got work to do." She turned her back on Mags, continually putting the back of her chair between the two of them as Mags kept trying to intervene. She would cave and leave soon.

"Fine."

Victory is mine.

"She's all yours," Mags shouted to the outer office.

Shit.

Sophie strode in, champagne flute in one hand, party hat in the other.

Double shit.

Sophie pressed the glass into Jac's hand, then strapped the gaudy purple party hat over her head, pinged the elastic strap under her chin just a little harder than necessary, then grabbed her hands and pulled. Mags's hands on the back of the chair prevented Jac from spinning away and out of reach again.

"I know that you know what date it is today, Jac McGrumpy, because you've typed it on every single one of those bloody emails you've been firing at me all day."

Double-dog shit.

"And I know you're good enough with numbers to have figured out what that means." Sophie tugged her out of her corner office and into the main space. The cubicles where the staff worked were strewn with streamers, balloons, and a banner. Oh yes, they'd even got a banner.

Sophie's lips were warm on her cheek, and Jac knew she'd have a lipstick mark there, a fire-engine-red one. "Happy fiftieth birthday, you old git."

It wasn't really her birthday. Jac had no idea when that was. No one did. Except the mother who had abandoned her. Instead, this was the anniversary of the day she was found. Doctors had estimated her to be more than a couple of days old, but probably less than a week. It was difficult for them to say, and there had been precious little for them to go on. No one ever came forward to claim her. It was just another thing she would never know about herself, one more thing she had no way of ever knowing. She hadn't even celebrated her birthday for much of her life. What's to celebrate about being abandoned anyway? It wasn't until Sophie came along and spun her negative thoughts around. They were celebrating Jac being found. Being saved. Being alive. And everything she had achieved all by herself ever since.

The woman was more like a sister to her, and the closest thing to family that Jac had ever known. "Bitch," Jac said with a grin.

"Back at ya, babe." After a quick squeeze of Jac's shoulders, Sophie pushed the glass towards her lips. "Drink up. It's part of your anti-aging regime now."

"What's that?"

"Pickling oneself in alcohol."

Jac sniggered but dutifully swallowed the champagne. Noting for a change that it actually was champagne and not Prosecco. Sophie's arm slid around her waist, while Mags wrapped one about Jac's shoulders from the other side.

"How does it feel?" Mags asked.

"Why? Worried you won't make it another month to yours?"

"Nah, wondering if I should start seeing a shrink now or wait till after the big day." They laughed together.

"I wouldn't worry about it, Mags," Sophie quipped. "You're too late. Start counselling for sixty in about, I don't know, two weeks' time should just about work for ya."

Mags feigned indignation. "Oh, the baby of the group has her claws out." She grabbed for Sophie's hand and held it up. "And what claws they are too. Lauren must walk with a permanent limp."

"Who says I use the *claws* on my lovely wife?" Sophie smirked and licked her lips suggestively. Jac snorted and almost spit out her drink while Mags blushed fiercely.

Clapping Mags on the shoulder, Jac said, "You should've learnt that lesson by now, mate."

"Yeah, yeah." She swallowed the last of her drink and held up her glass. "Refill, ladies… Oh, and Soph?"

"Funny," Sophie deadpanned, "but yes." She held out her glass for Mags to take, then curled her fingers into Jac's. "Come on, old lady, go mingle before we have to get you back to the nursing home. Your staff wants to pick what's left of your brains before you retire."

"Yeah, right." Jac trailed behind her.

"Don't pout. I made them get you red-velvet cake."

Jac brightened at the mention of her favourite treat of the moment. "And Baileys cream?"

"Yes, though how you think that combination works together is beyond me."

"Have you tried it?"

"No. The smell of Baileys makes me want to jump in the canal."

"Drama queen."

Sophie appeared to weigh up the insult, then shrugged, as if content to accept the accolade. She handed Jac a plate and a jug with the cream in… just for her. "Don't say I never give you anything."

"I don't. You give me heartburn, palpitations, and an ulcer regularly."

Sophie backhanded her in the stomach and walked away as one of the staff members sidled up to Jac. "We're all heading out to Coyote's," Tanya said. "Want to join us?" Tanya was twenty-six, blond, slim, and working for them on reception…while trying to pick up jobs as an actress. Jac sighed inwardly but smiled widely at her.

"Thanks, Tanya. I'll have a think about it, but probably not. I've got an early start in the morning, and Sophie—the bitch—tells me that at my age I need all the beauty sleep I can get."

Tanya giggled and ran a hand down Jac's arm. "Well, if you change your mind, you know where to find me." She smiled coyly and wandered back over to her friends as Mags handed Jac a full glass, eyebrows raised in question.

"Don't go there. I said no."

"To getting older and wiser, then." Mags held up her glass.

Jac snorted but clinked her glass to Mags's before swallowing it in one. "Thirsty?"

"Something like that." She put her plate down on the table, the cake untouched. "Back in a minute." She held up the glass up indicate where she was going, but the open door to the balcony called her as she got closer to the drinks table. It was a no-brainer.

Jac stood on the balcony outside her office and stared out across the Manchester skyline. Lights twinkled in buildings towering over her head, and streetlights glittered three stories lower than where she stood. She fidgeted with her lighter, needing something to do with her hands but not having her usual cigarette to hand to meet the need.

"What're you doing out here?"

Jac turned to look over her shoulder at the sound of the familiar voice. Sophie grinned and shook her long blond hair over her shoulder before crossing the balcony and leaning on the rail next to Jac.

"Nothing much," she said with a smile.

"I should've guessed. How long's it been so far?" she asked, pointing at Jac's fidgeting hands.

"Couple of weeks." Jac tapped the lighter against the rail and spun it so it was upside down before tapping and spinning it again. "What're you doing out here?"

"Came to clear the air."

Jac waved her hand. "No need—"

"Yeah, there is. I shouldn't have stormed off like that."

"Everything okay?"

"Yeah, just…" Sophie sighed heavily. "Lauren's been on at me to go and see the doctor."

"You're ill? What's wrong?"

"Nothing." She reached out and grabbed Jac's hand. "Nothing unusual, anyway." She grimaced. "Irritability, hot flashes, weight gain. Ring a bell?"

Jac chuckled, then cut it off instantly as Sophie's eyes narrowed. She held up her hands in surrender. "Sorry." She turned back to look out across the skyline, tapping her fingers on the railing.

"She's suggested HRT. I don't know if I want to go down that route or just get it over with."

They'd had this discussion before, when Sophie's wife had started the change. Sophie hadn't liked the idea of Lauren going on the patches, but Lauren was now a dedicated devotee of the treatment. Sophie still wasn't convinced.

"Well, it's your body, Soph. You have to do what's right for you."

"True. What about you?"

"I don't think I've had any hot flashes yet."

"Funny. I've been worried about you. You haven't seemed yourself for a while."

"No need," Jac said with a soft smile. "I'm fine."

"Uh-huh. So, last time you quit smoking, your bad temper led to a broken camera."

Jac grunted her acknowledgement.

"The time before that it was that antique priceless vase Mags had inherited from her least-favourite aunt ever."

They both laughed at the memory of a drunken, stumbling night for them all that led to the fake Ming vase—that had always been passed off as the real thing—ending up in shards.

"I could go on."

"No need, babe. You've made your point."

"Good. So…broken anything yet?"

"Not much."

"Come on, what was it this time?" Sophie asked with a snigger tainting her voice. "That lead-crystal decanter Lauren insisted we get you last Christmas?"

Jac smiled sadly and shook her head. "I knew that wasn't your idea."

"True. My contribution was the whiskey you filled it with."

"Good call."

"I know you well, my friend. So come on. Tell Auntie Sophie all about it." She nudged Jac with her shoulder, then froze, a look of mock horror on her face. "Please, God, don't let it be another camera. The last one cost three grand to replace. Not to mention calming down the sound technician and the extra. Oh, and the frog." Sophie offered up her prayer to the heavens and interlocked her fingers in a mock imitation of a cherub.

"Funny." Jac scrubbed a hand over her face. "I smashed a couple of glasses."

"Uh-huh." Sophie shook her head. "Not buying it." She wiggled a finger in front of Jac's face. "This says you broke something bigger than a couple of glasses."

"I might have dropped a bottle of vodka."

"Might?"

Jac shrugged. "Nah."

"I'm not going anywhere, so you might as well tell me."

Taking her time, Jac stared out across the skyline again, then said with a sigh, "Fine. It seems I broke my relationship—"

"Shit." Sophie put her hand on Jac's arm. "Explains why she never answered my calls about this little soiree. You okay, Pan-pan?"

Jac shrugged and smirked a little at the old nickname Sophie liked to use when it was just the two of them. She had ever since she'd learnt of how and where Jac had been found. It was a gentle reminder of how Sophie accepted her without question or hesitation no matter how hard Jac had tried to keep her at arm's length. Sophie had told her that she would have been Jac's friend—her family of choice—no matter when they'd found each other; as children, adults, or into their dotage. She was there for Jac; always had been, always would be. She'd rotated through various permutations of Peter Pan over the years before landing on "Pan-pan". From Sophie's lips, it was like hearing, "I love you, I accept you, and I will never leave you". Being abandoned tended to give a child a fear of abandonment, a sense of unworthiness, and feelings of being unlovable, in a way that was hard to shake. Sophie, and eventually Mags too, had seen beyond her painful past and proven to her that there were people out the who cared for her. Deeply.

"Yeah, I'm fine."

"What happened?"

"Just one of those things." And it was. Jac knew that.

"I told you she wasn't right for you, babe. I mean how old was she?"

Jac looked at her hands and spun the lighter again as she mumbled, "Twenty-five."

Sophie chortled. "Good God, woman. You're fifty years old. Don't you think it's time to find someone who will do more than look good on your arm and make you feel like a stud until she kicks your arse to the kerb?"

"I know," she said under her breath.

"I mean, I know she was fucking hot, but seriously, Jac, did you ever actually talk to her?"

Jac opened her mouth to answer but Sophie just ploughed straight on.

"I tried once, when you brought her to the office party. I had a better conversation with the printer just afterwards. It's got that new interface that lets you command by voice. Awesome. Anyway, where was I?"

"Dissing my choice in girlfriends."

"*Girl* being the operative word there, babe. You need you a real woman. Someone who can excite you outside the bedroom as well as in it. A woman who can hold a conversation with you, who isn't using you for what you can do for her career, and who isn't looking to use you as a stepping stone to the next best thing that ever happened to her."

While Sophie wasn't telling Jac anything she didn't already know, she was pretty sure she didn't need to hear it put quite so…well. "Yeah, well I really appreciate you not saying I told you so, or anything like that. Good chat, Soph, made me feel tons better about everything."

Sophie snickered. "See, that's one of your best qualities, right there. You're funny. But I can guarantee that the women you've been dating for the last few years sure as shit never picked up on that."

Jac took a huge breath and let it out slowly. "I hear you, it's just…well, how many new forty-slash-fifty-something women do I get to meet? Add to that a brain, interested in women, single, and somewhat attractive."

Sophie nodded, but she carried on anyway. Jac needed to straighten some things out in her head, and she always did that best when she spoke. Usually with Sophie.

She shrugged. "I don't think it's too much to ask for, Soph, but it sure as hell feels like it."

"Forty-slash-fifty-something is a big jump from twenty-five. You sure you're ready for that, Pan-pan?" Jac just stared at her until she threw her head back and laughed. "Fine, fine. Point taken." She kicked one foot onto the bottom rail of the balcony and settled her arms across the top rail, leaning over in a mirror of Jac's own pose. "Maybe we need to get you on Tinder or something."

"Fuck off. I'm a little bit lonely, not desperate."

Sophie snickered along with her before they settled into a comfortable silence, both staring out at the orange-grey sky.

"When did she go?"

"Hmm. About three days after I stopped smoking."

"Why didn't you say anything?"

"Didn't want to feel like any more of a loser than I already do."

"You aren't." Sophie shook her head sadly.

Jac snorted derisively and refused to meet Sophie's gaze, even though she could feel it boring holes into the side of her head.

"Do you miss her?"

Jac closed her eyes and swallowed the wave of guilt that threatened her. The one she felt because she really didn't miss Vanessa at all. She didn't miss the woman, she just missed their being someone at home waiting for her. Someone on the other end of the phone for her to call and talk about her day, or just hear about hers. And that made her feel all the worse for it. They'd spent eighteen months together, and now Jac couldn't recall anything she'd truly miss about Vanessa.

"Let me guess," Sophie said softly.

"Do you have to?"

Sophie smiled sadly when Jac turned to look at her. "No, we both know the truth, babe. Question is, what are you going to do about it?"

Jac shrugged again. "What can I do? I can't magic women out of thin air." She tried not to picture Sasha Adams and her sultry voice, full curves, and smoky eyes that called to her. Again and again. She really did try. She failed. But she did try.

Sophie bumped her shoulder. "Oh, damn. That's why I've been hanging around you all these years."

"You don't get any funnier, you know?"

"How long have we been friends?"

"Thirty years."

"Right, and in that time, we've built an empire."

Jac grinned. They totally had. Their production company was going from strength to strength. New ways of financing projects, new distribution methods and outlets had allowed them to break into markets that hadn't even existed ten years ago. Now, they were successful, powerful women at the top of their game. And both Sophie and Mags had someone at home to share that with.

"And you have Lauren."

"I so do. And if I had to choose between the two—"

Jac held up her hands. "I know. Me and the company are both very grateful Lauren is very accommodating of all the late nights. Trust me, I know." She pulled Sophie into a hug. "I'm jealous as fuck, but I love you anyway."

Sophie chuckled and pulled out of Jac's arms. "You don't have to choose either. When the right woman comes along, she won't use you or make you choose. Maybe hold out for that for a while, rather than jumping on the next distraction that walks into your life."

"Easy for you to say. You've got a wife at home to help you out with those 'distractions'."

Sophie slapped her shoulder and said, "And on that note, I'm off home to wake up my wife and kiss her senseless."

"Tease."

"Only when she deserves it," she said, tossing her hair over her shoulder.

Jac laughed and listened to the door close behind her.

CHAPTER 12

"You really didn't need to do this, you know?" Sasha said as she met Jac at the gate. "I could have just got the bus into town and met you at the studio."

"Believe me, this is easier. They produce all these big shows there, so they're pretty strict on security there nowadays. If they saw you hanging around waiting for me, well, they might not have let you in."

"You two get in here. I've made coffee," Fleur shouted from the front door.

"That's my mother." Sasha put a hand on Jac's arm. "Whatever you do, if you want to be safe to drive away from here today, don't eat the cakes."

"What?" Jac asked in confusion. "Is she a bad cook?"

"Come on, it's getting cold," Fleur shouted again.

"Just trust me. I'll explain later. I think there's some beetroot or parsnip crisps about, if you want to nibble on something."

The idea of nibbling on something scattered Jac's thoughts in a decidedly different direction from cakes, especially when Sasha brushed her hair over her shoulders. Jac stared at the long neck and nibbleable earlobes that were now visible, and tripped on the step into the house.

Sasha caught her elbow to help steady her. "You okay?"

Jac nodded and murmured, "Sorry."

"If you're that dizzy now, you really must stay away from the cakes."

Jac shrugged at the earnest expression in Sasha's dark brown eyes. "You're the boss."

Sasha snorted. "Yeah, I wish."

"Is the coffee safe? I could do with a cup of that."

"Hopefully." Sasha led her into the house.

Jac sat on the sofa where Sasha pointed, her nostrils twitching at the scent in the air. Surely that wasn't the scent she thought it was. She glanced at Sasha. Was it?

"Is that...?"

Sasha blushed but didn't say anything. Well, well, well. Fleur bustled into the room, pushing a small hostess trolley with mugs, coffee, and fixings, and a huge plate of what looked like chocolate brownies on it. She transferred everything to the coffee table in the middle of the room and dropped heavily into a comfortable-looking armchair. The blanket that had been draped over the back of the chair dropped on top of Fleur's head. She shoved it back impatiently as Sasha sat forwards and poured the steaming brew into the crockery. She passed one to Jac and another to her mother before she sat back with her own.

"Have a cake, Jac," Fleur offered.

"She's driving, Mum."

"Pish." She reached forwards and held a purple-coloured crystal hanging on a long chain over the plate of brownies, a low droning hum passing her lips. A cat jumped up onto the coffee table and started to swipe at the dangling crystal. Sat on its back legs, front paws spread wide as it tried to catch...either Fleur's hand or the chain—Jac wasn't sure which— its huge green eyes looked crazed. She wasn't 100 percent sure, but one pupil may have been a little bigger than the other. The cat's dancing almost knocked over a bowl of shrivelled, twisted, purply-pink-and-beige...somethings. The beetroot and parsnip crisps?

"Oh God," Sasha murmured and squeezed her eyes shut.

"Nip, get out of it." Fleur pushed the black cat off the table and began her process again.

Jac watched in rapt fascination as Fleur let the stone swing over the plate with her eyes closed, her lips moving quickly in some sort of prayer or affirmation. Then she smiled and grabbed one of the squares that was half-hidden under the pile. Jac looked at Sasha for some sort of clue as to what it was all about, but she had her eyes squeezed shut, a knuckle between her teeth. Jac made a mental note to ask her about it later. It would surely make for an interesting conversation.

Sasha sighed and mumbled, "Back in a minute."

"So, Jac," Fleur began around a mouthful of brownie. "Help yourself to something to eat." She waved her hand at the table.

Jac eyed the brownies. They looked good, but Sasha's warning rang in her ears. She eyed the shrivelled bowl of dubious-looking crisps. Well, she liked beetroot. She liked parsnips. How bad could crisps made of root vegetables be? *Why do all these newfangled creations have to look like wood shavings and sawdust?* She decided not to think about it and picked one of the twisted beige slivers and lifted it to her mouth, bit down, and wondered at the odd taste.

It didn't taste anything like parsnip. There was a woody texture to it, certainly, but it almost smelled in her mouth rather than tasted. It smelled of lavender, not even remotely like a parsnip. *Was this one of those Heston Blumenthal wild-and-wacky ideas? Like eating an egg that tasted like chocolate…mess-with-your-mind kind of food?* And, oh my God, was it dry! Jac took a long drink of the scalding coffee in the hopes of ridding her mouth of both the lavender taste-slash-smell and all the bits that felt like wood chips on her tongue.

She plastered on a smile that was probably as shrivelled as the crisp she'd just eaten. "This is great, thanks." She sipped some more coffee. "Really great."

Fleur stared at her. Her hand frozen halfway to her mouth, brownie crumbling between her fingers. Sasha entered the room with a bowl in her hands.

"I thought I'd get you some of those crisps I mentioned, Jac." She looked between Jac and her mother. "What?"

Fleur waved her cake-wielding hand in Jac's direction. "Needn't have bothered, love. Your friend seems quite happy with my potpourri." She doubled over, laughing uncontrollably as she pointed and crumbled her treat on the floor. Sasha stared in horror at what Jac now realised was a bowl of scented wood shavings, then stared at the bowl of crisps in her hand. Then set about scooping up crumbs as the cat swooped in, trying to steal as much as she could.

It was almost eleven by the time they bid Fleur farewell and buckled up their seat belts.

"Are you ready for this?" Jac asked while Sasha waved at her mum.

"If you are."

Jac sniggered. "I was born ready." She pulled out of the driveway and edged onto the road. "Which way?"

Sasha smiled. "Second star on the right—"

"And straight on till morning."

"I hope for your sake we're there before then."

"Me too."

"I'm so sorry about my mother."

"It's fine."

"And the potpourri."

"Not quite so fine, but it's okay."

"Easy mistake, I suppose."

"Really?" Jac asked, still terribly embarrassed by the whole incident.

Sasha snorted and bit the inside of her lip for a good ten seconds before she managed to say quietly, "No, not really, but it seemed like the right thing to say."

"Thanks. Appreciate it," Jac deadpanned as she navigated the narrow streets until she got to the junction for the A6. "So, on that note, tell me about the baking and the crystals?"

When they arrived at the studio, it took almost ten minutes, the production of Sasha's passport, and several annoyed glances from Jac at the security guard before Sasha held a credit-card–sized square of plastic with her face emblazoned on it.

Peering over Sasha's shoulder, Jac read, "Sasha Adams. Writer, Kefran Media." She grinned. "How does that feel?"

"Surreal." Sasha's voice was lower and huskier than normal.

Jac grinned and took her elbow, gently leading her towards the lift. "Come on, let me show you around." She cleared her throat and affected a slightly high and nasal accent. "Welcome to the MediaCityUK tour, ladies and gentlemen, my name's Jac, and I do hope you'll enjoy yourselves today."

Sasha giggled and followed her into the lift.

"Where would you like to see first?" Jac whispered.

"Whatever you'd like to show me."

Jac resisted the immediate impulse to raise her eyebrows at Sasha, and closed her eyes instead. *Get a grip, Kensington.* "Okay." She opened her eyes and pushed the button to close the doors behind them. "Very well." She cleared her throat and began her tour spiel. "MediaCityUK is the most technically advanced HD production site in Europe. It truly is an amazing facility, and one we take advantage of whenever we can."

"How?"

"Well, Dock 10 is a company that operates and manages the facility. They can rent out whatever is needed for each production. So sometimes it's just the studio space. Other times they do post-production and content too. Depends on the project, who they're working with, and what each client is willing to pay for."

"And we're making my film here?"

Jac grinned. "We most definitely are."

The lift doors opened, and Jac led her through another set of doors. Sasha's jaw sagged.

"Dock 10 has seven HD studios, two audio studios—including one for the BBC Philharmonic—and all the facilities required to manage end-to-end digital workflows."

"Meaning?"

"Oh, right. CGI special effects and the like."

"Ah, I see." She looked around at the darkened studio, lit only in the middle of the space where there was a set. "Are those the chairs the judges use in *The Voice*?"

"Yup. They aren't filming on this stage at the moment, but it's set up for later this afternoon. One of the judges doesn't like to do early mornings."

"Oh my God. Seriously? I love that show. Will.I.Am is so…unique."

Jac grinned. "Seriously. Wanna go and sit in one?"

She hadn't even finished asking the question before Sasha hurried across the dark space and tossed herself into the end chair. "Oh, these are really comfy." She slouched back, and Jac caught the mischievous look in her eye under the set lights. She tossed her hair over her shoulders and hiked her feet onto the podium in front of her. She leant one elbow on the armrest and twirled the other hand in the air. "Sing for me, Jac. Let me see if you get the button push or get left hanging," Sasha said, affecting the attitude of one of the famous judges of the show.

Jac laughed. "I can't sing. Trust me."

"Aw, go on. Just a little bit." Jac shook her head and Sasha pouted. "You're no fun."

"Hey, I might make you a model if we get to the *Blue Peter* set in time."

Sasha relented and climbed off the throne-like chair. "Fair enough."

Jac glanced at her watch and caught Sasha's eye. "Come on, we'd best get a move on."

With one final glance around, Sasha stood and followed Jac out of the studio and down a series of twisting corridors. "How the hell did you manage to get space here for my little project?"

"Well, aside from renting the space we're going to use, I still have a lot of contacts from the days when I worked at the Beeb. I've helped them out more times over the years than they can count, so they let me know when last-minute slots are available; those tend to be a little cheaper, which makes budgeting easier. And that is always the biggest issue we have with small projects. That and the talent."

"When we just came into the office to talk about the script that time, I didn't realise we'd be filming here too. I honestly thought we'd be putting together bits of studding in an old warehouse or something. I wasn't expecting something so…"

"Slick?"

"Maybe." Sasha laughed, sounding a little embarrassed. "Not that you ever came across as anything less than professional. It's just I didn't expect—well, I didn't think I'd ever…"

"You didn't think your script, your work, would be good enough for something like this. Right?"

Sasha nodded.

"Well, believe me, it is. And so much more." Jac grinned and held out her hand. "Let me show you the rest, then we can go and take a look in the warehouse space where they're putting together the drafts of our sets."

The rest took three hours to look over. MediaCity was a sprawling complex of glass walls, office spaces, vast studios, famous sets, and more than a few famous faces. And Jac was enthralled by Sasha's reaction to each and every one. She could have spent the rest of the day showing her new things in the otherworldly place that was MediaCity, but there was still the jewel of their own sets to see. And Jac couldn't wait to see Sasha's reaction to her own imagination brought to life from the words she had printed on a page.

Jac was pretty happy. It had been a long day but a satisfactory one.

"Do you need to get home, or would you like to get something to eat?" she asked as they finally left the warehouse.

Sasha looked at her watch. "It's only seven, we could—"

A tune blared from Sasha's bag. It sounded like panpipes and... "Is that 'Puff the Magic Dragon'?"

"Seemed appropriate." Sasha held up her phone in front of her, inspecting it. "It's my mum. Do you mind?"

"Not at all."

"Hey, Mum."

She leant against the wall a little way off and tried not to listen in too much. But it was hard. It wasn't like there was a lot going on to distract her from Sasha's dulcet tones.

"No, we're still in Salford. It's been incredible. There's so much to see, and we just—"

Staring down at her fingernails, she noted she'd torn one at some point in the day.

"Jac and I were just discussing going to get something to eat, and then I was going to head home. Why?"

Jac tore off the rest of the nail with her teeth and grinned when she heard that Sasha was happy to join her for dinner. *Now, where to take her? Somewhere close by. Don't want to have to go too far, and I still need to take her home afterwards. Maybe Nando's?* Jac shook her head. *Nah, I can do better than that.*

"No, I don't know where you put the Vaseline. I didn't know you had Vaseline. The doctors said not to use that on the blisters from your prosthetic."

Jac scratched her head. *Maybe that Chinese place just down the road. They do a great crispy duck dish.*

"Okay, then you ask Mr Hunt if he's got any. But don't use it on those—"

She glanced over at Sasha, amused to see the blush colouring her cheeks.

"That's way more information than I needed, Mum, but I'm very glad to know you aren't lonely or anything while I'm out working."

Frowning, Jac held her hands up in question. Sasha shook her head and closed her eyes.

"No, I wasn't being sarcastic. I—" She lifted a hand like she was trying to stop Fleur from speaking. "Yes, I know you're my moth—" She leant forwards and banged her head against the wall. "You don't want me to come home tonight?" She pulled the phone away from her ear and stared at it like it was an alien. She shook her head and put it back to her ear, then listened for a few seconds before she said, "I know you don't have to answer to me. I wasn't saying—"

Jac bit her lip to stop herself from laughing.

"Yes, I realise that, Mother. I'm not totally stupid." She ran her fingers across her eyes, and pinched the bridge of her nose. "I truly have no idea if that would be better with or without your teeth in, and that really was more information than I ever needed to know." Sasha's head dropped forwards and she rested her chin in her hand. "Right, you go and answer the door, then. I'll call you in the morning."

Sasha swallowed heavily, her throat working as Jac continued to stare at her.

"Of course, not too early." She held the handset away from her ear. "Good chat, thanks for that, bye-bye, now." She shut it down and dropped it back into her bag. "Wish I'd never answered that call."

"What did she want the Vaseline for?"

"Mr Hunt."

"Yeah, I know she was going to ask him if he had any but... Oh!" Jac rolled her hands in front of her as Sasha grimaced. "For *Mr Hunt*." She winked suggestively. Sasha sighed and slunk back against the wall. "I didn't realise your mum had a boyfriend...or a man friend."

Sasha cleared her throat. "She didn't before I left the house this morning."

They looked at each other and burst out laughing, tears slipping down their cheeks. "You should really tell her water-based lubes are much better. They don't damage the condoms."

"I don't think she has to worry about condoms. It's not like she'll get pregnant." Sasha's shudder was unintentionally comical.

"STDs are still a thing to worry about. Chlamydia, HPV, herpes, HIV. I could go on."

"Oh God." Sasha groped in her bag for her phone. "I can't be taking my seventy-five-year-old mother to the scabs-and-crabs clinic cos she fancied a quickie." She punched a few buttons, then cursed. "Voicemail. Mum, it's me. Listen, make sure he uses protection…a condom…even when you take your teeth out. You don't know where he's been." She put her phone away again.

"So, what's better with or without teeth?"

"Fellatio."

Laughter bubbled up and escaped Jac's lips at the same time as a quiver rippled up her spine.

"Exactly." Sasha visibly shivered and wrapped her arms about her body. "I need a drink. And somewhere to stay tonight. Aren't parents supposed to tell their kids to make sure they come home at a reasonable hour?"

"I'm not sure that rule stands when you get past forty." Jac wiped at the tears rolling down her cheeks.

"Didn't you say there was a Premiere Inn in this complex?"

Jac shook her head.

"No? Is it a Holiday Inn?"

"No, I mean there is a Premiere Inn, but you're not staying there. I only live five minutes away, got plenty of space. You can stay with me."

"I can't put you to that trouble."

"It's no trouble. It saves me taking you home or having to worry about you not going home. Then I'll sleep better. You won't have to waste money on a hotel room so your mother can get laid—"

"That's just so wrong."

"Agreed. Usually it's the person getting laid that shells out for the hotel."

Sasha shook her head again and let her chin fall to her chest as she shook with what Jac hoped was laughter and not tears. "I'll let her know that for next time."

"Exactly. So, what do you say? Stay at my place?"

"Honestly, Jac, you've been so kind. I can't put you out like this."

"You aren't. Honest, it'll stop me worrying, and potentially laughing all night. Plus I can make sure you're not late for your first day in the morning, and if you have any issues with finding your way around this maze, I can be on hand to guide you through. You'd be doing me a favour, really."

Sasha chuckled and said sarcastically, "Well, when you put it like that, it certainly does seem like a sensible solution, but what about your partner? Surely she won't want me camping out at your place for the night. I don't even have a change of clothes with me. Bloody Mother."

"Partner?"

"Yes. I remember Sophie mentioning when we met that a girlfriend lives with you."

"Oh, well, Sophie has a big mouth and isn't afraid to use it. She also happened to be working with outdated intel at the time. I'd split up with Vanessa a few days before that. I just hadn't told Sophie and Mags then."

Sasha put her hand on Jac's arm. "I'm sorry to hear that." She squeezed gently. "Are you okay?"

"I'm fine. It wasn't a surprise. Well, maybe the timing of it was, but not the split. If that makes sense?"

Sasha nodded but didn't say anything, clearly content to let Jac talk if she wanted to.

"Just one of those things."

"Were you together long?"

"Eighteen months. So not really, no."

"Long enough when you love someone."

"If you love someone, yes, I guess it is."

"Ah," Sasha said softly. Knowingly.

"Yeah, *ah*," Jac mimicked.

"I'm still sorry. Even if you didn't love her, you must have cared to stay with her so long."

Jac nodded. She did care about Vanessa, and there was still the void that was her home without someone else there to help fill the space. Jac wasn't prepared to head down the road into maudlin tonight. "Yeah, well, the upside is no partner to object to you using the guest room."

"And I won't be in your way? Newly single and all that?" Sasha's voice was playful, and the timbre sent a shiver down Jac's spine.

"Ah, no. We've got a project to concentrate on and a lot of work to do. Newly-single–type distractions aren't on the horizon anytime soon. And certainly not for tonight."

Sasha looked sceptical.

"Besides, it'll be nice to have some company around the place."

Sasha cocked her head to one side and waited.

Jac pointed a finger at her in warning and said, "If you tell Sophie I said any of this…"

Crossing a finger over her heart, she held up three fingers in a facsimile salute. "Girl Scout's honour."

"You were a Girl Scout?"

Sasha rolled her eyes and wiggled her fingers to encourage Jac to get on with it.

"I hate to admit it, but it feels so empty that I hate going home right now." She crossed her arms over her chest. She didn't want to admit she'd stayed with Vanessa as long as she had just so she didn't have to be alone. Somehow, she didn't think she needed to say it. Sasha was an intelligent and insightful woman, and more than capable of reading between the lines.

"You sure you don't mind?"

For a moment, the only thing Jac was sure of was that she wanted Sasha in her home. Sure enough that she decided just to go with the feeling and not question it. She'd trusted her gut instinct more than once, and it had never steered her wrong. The only time she remembered life going all to shit was when she ignored it. "I'm positive."

Sasha stared at her for several long moments before she nodded and looked away again. She looked unaffected, but Jac felt naked, like she'd been stripped to her soul. A tremor swept the length of her spine, and the hairs on the back of her neck stood on end as though even they were reaching out towards Sasha. Jac was self-aware enough to admit her attraction to herself, and to acknowledge she was in big trouble right now.

"Do you have a washing machine?"

"Yes, why?"

"Well, if I'm going to be stuck in the same clothes tomorrow, I'd at least like to try and wash my shirt." She plucked at the red blouse and pencil-line black skirt she was wearing. "My mother has already traumatised me this evening, I'm not sure I can face a walk of shame that isn't even my own tomorrow. I mean, it's the first day in my new job!"

Jac took a moment to look her up and down. "I can't do much to help with the skirt; I don't own one. And I don't think my pants would fit you.

But I'm sure I can find a shirt in my wardrobe that would look okay for the day." Sure, Sasha had a much curvier body than she did, but her shoulders and back were much narrower, and added to the height difference, Jac was pretty sure she'd find something wearable.

Sasha eyed her sceptically.

"Might be a bit butcher than your normal style, but with the skirt, it should be okay."

"Seriously?" Sasha took in her body, and Jac could feel her eyes on her as if she were using her hands. "I'm not sure anything in your wardrobe would fit me."

Jac took hold of Sasha's hand and started to tug her out of the door. "Trust me, I won't let you make a fool of yourself in front of anyone tomorrow." She went through her wardrobe in her mind and settled on the white shirt with the pleated front. Add in the black braces bisecting the white shirt and clipped to Sasha's black skirt…yeah, she'd look hot. A flush swept her cheeks. Maybe with her hair piled on top of her head…and those glasses she kept in her handbag… Jac wanted to fan her face. Hot didn't even begin to cover the image in her head.

"You okay now?" Jac opened the door to her apartment and ushered Sasha inside. "Or are you still traumatised?"

"I think she's managed to traumatise me tonight for the rest of my natural life." Sasha stumbled past Jac and into the large living room. Then stopped in her tracks as Jac flicked on the lights. "Wow." Sasha stared. "This is your home?" she asked unnecessarily.

"Yeah." Jac looked about her and tried to see it from Sasha's point of view. The floor-to-ceiling windows along the two external walls of the room let in the light of the moon and the buildings across Salford Quays and Manchester, each twinkling in competition with the other to chase away the shadows of the night. The huge L-shaped sofa dominated the sunken floor space, strewn with cushions and throw rugs in an attempt to make it look homey and lived-in instead of the showpiece Jac often felt it was. It was so big that she and Vanessa had been able to lie out flat on it and still not be able to touch each other if they so wished…and that had seemed to be the case far more often than not.

The kitchen was at the opposite side of the open-plan living area, all highly polished white cupboards, stainless-steel appliances, and granite worktops. It was functional and modern and hardly ever used, so little used, in fact, that Jac wasn't actually sure which of the cupboard doors hid the dishwasher, though she could locate the fridge…and the wine cooler.

The two spaces were separated by the metal sculpture she'd purchased at Velvet three years ago, displayed on the five-foot-long plinth like an island with a sunbather upon it. But that wasn't what had drawn Sasha's attention.

Sasha dropped her bag where she stood and crossed the floor like she was being pulled by a magnet. The telescope the decorator had set up looked out the window, and Sasha's hand reverently stroked the length of it.

"I always wanted a telescope when I was a kid." She looked over at Jac. "May I?"

"Please," Jac said softly, watching as Sasha bent over to position herself and her skirt pulled taut across her backside. Jac licked her lips. *Stop it*, she admonished herself as Sasha adjusted the eyepiece and stared through the lens.

"It's beautiful," she whispered. "It's all so beautiful. How long have you lived here?"

"About five years now. It's a fairly new development, so I'm the only person to have owned this place."

"You're very lucky. This view is incredible."

Jac nodded as she continued to stare at Sasha. "Incredible," she echoed softly.

"Sorry, you must be exhausted." Sasha stood and held her hands out in question. "Where shall I park my stuff?"

"Follow me." Jac led her to the guest room, pointing out the en suite as they went while Sasha grabbed her bag from the floor where she'd dropped it. "We need to leave about eight to get to tomorrow's meeting in time. I've already messaged Sophie to bring coffee and croissants so we don't need to grab breakfast before we leave. Is that okay? Personally, the longer I can spend in bed in the morning, the better, but if you want, we can grab something on the way. I don't have too much in—"

Sasha held up a hand to stop her rambling. "Breakfast at work sounds great to me. Tomorrow is going to be a long enough day; no need to add to it by insisting on getting up for a healthy breakfast." She dropped her handbag on the bed and went to the bathroom to have a look around. "You have a gorgeous home."

"Thanks."

Sasha stared at her expectantly, but Jac wasn't sure what she was expecting. They'd had a wonderful day together, a lovely meal to finish off the evening, and had this been a date rather than time spent with a work colleague, Jac knew she'd be leading Sasha to that big bed behind her and would spend the night worshipping her body until they both passed out from exhaustion.

Sasha cleared her throat. "You mentioned something about a shirt for the morning. Maybe something to sleep in tonight?"

"Oh God, of course. Sorry." She slapped a hand to her forehead. "One minute." Jac ran from the room, straight-armed the door to her own open, and rummaged through her wardrobe until she found the shirt and braces. Then she pulled open a drawer in the chest and grabbed an oversized T-shirt and a pair of boxer shorts. She was back in Sasha's room—*Sasha's room?*—within two minutes.

"I wasn't sure what you'd sleep in, but I didn't think my pyjamas would work. I hope this is okay?"

"Well, well, well, this is a surprise, Ms Kensington." Sasha held up the T-shirt and grinned at Jac.

"What?" Jac frowned. "You don't like T-shirts?"

Sasha turned it around and showed her the character on the front. "I'd have guessed you as more of a Peter Pan…maybe even a Hook fan. But Tinkerbell? Really?"

Tinkerbell was winking at her from the front of the shirt—right over Sasha's breasts—and offering her the slogan of *All you need is faith, trust, and a little bit of pixie dust*. Jac laughed, and marvelled at just how much of that she was doing around Sasha.

"You're right. I don't think I've ever worn that. Sophie bought it for me as a gag gift one Christmas. That line's kind of our company motto."

"I remember you telling me that." She put the shirt on top of the comforter and unfolded the white shirt, then draped the suspenders over the shoulder of the hanger. She turned the shirt side to side, like she was unpicking the stitching and mentally resewing it again as she did. "Might be a little tight across the chest. The suspenders should detract from that a little." She nodded to herself, seemingly satisfied, but Jac was more than a little disappointed she wasn't trying it on. "This should be fine. Thank you."

"You're welcome." She stuffed her hands in her pockets to stop herself from reaching out to caress Sasha's cheek or pull her in for a kiss. She cleared her throat again. "I should let you go and get some sleep."

Sasha smiled. "Thanks, and goodnight." She leant forwards and placed a gentle kiss on Jac's cheek. "Thanks for letting me stay here. I know you could have done without the trauma too."

Jac grinned, her cheek burning with the imprint of Sasha's lips. "I can honestly say I've never enjoyed a trauma more." She grasped and squeezed Sasha's fingers before backing out of the door. "Goodnight, Sasha. See you in the morning."

CHAPTER 13

SASHA STARED INTO THE WARDROBE where she'd hung the borrowed shirt last night, wishing to God she had something of her own to wear instead. She felt woefully underprepared for the day ahead of her. She felt nervous and so out of place that she was sure, with every second that passed, she should never have picked up the phone to speak to Jac, never mind signed the bloody contract. What on earth had she been thinking? She looked at the door, ran her hand through her hair, and contemplated going to find Jac and tell her just that. That she was sorry to have messed her about, but she needed to get back home, to look after her mother. After the phone call, Jac surely wouldn't be surprised. Clearly her mother couldn't be trusted to her own devices.

She bowed her head. What was she saying? Her mother was a grown woman who was clearly set on having a good time. Maybe Sasha did need to take a leaf out of her mother's book. Well…sort of.

"So," Sasha said to herself as she plucked the hanger from the rail, "time to put on your big-girl pants and get on with it." She shimmied into her skirt and stepped into her mid-heeled shoes. She piled her hair on top of her head in a messy bun that she secured with the only item she could find in her bag—a pencil. She smoothed on lipstick, eyeliner, and a little mascara before a knock startled her.

"Sasha, are you almost ready?" Jac's voice was muffled by the door.

"Yep, I'll be right there." She pulled Jac's shirt up her arms. She'd been right about it being tight across the chest. She had to leave an additional two buttons undone or risk them taking out someone's eye throughout the day. That meant it was only fastened in line with her bra. She clipped the braces into place and tugged them over her shoulders. There was a vast amount of cleavage on display. More so than Sasha would consider appropriate for a working Monday, but she had to admit it wasn't an unattractive image that looked back at her. Kind of librarian chic.

"Sasha?"

"Coming now." She grabbed her bag on her way across the room, slipping it over her shoulder as she pulled the door open.

"Wow," Jac said with a smile from the other side. "Just...wow, that looks totally great on you."

Sasha's cheeks burned as she glanced down shyly. "Thanks."

Holding out her coat and her arm, Jac asked, "Shall we?"

"Such gallantry." Sasha wrapped the fingers of one hand around Jac's bicep and took her coat with the other. "Thank you."

Jac led her towards the door. "Are you ready for this?"

"Nope."

"Nervous?"

"Of course."

"Okay, remember something for me today."

Sasha waited a moment, then prompted, "And that would be?"

Jac pointed over her shoulder. "Above the door. Read what it says."

"'The moment you doubt whether you can fly, you cease forever to be able to do it,'" Sasha said. "Another *Peter Pan* quote? You'll have me thinking it's a favourite of yours or something."

"It is."

"Really?"

"Of course. I know, I know. It's a children's book, but there are reasons why some children's books are classics. There are layers of meaning we can only begin to fathom in them when we're grown up. We usually rediscover them and learn more from them when we start reading them to our kids, but I don't have the pleasure of reading them to my children, so I just have to read them for myself." She shrugged. Sasha squeezed the arm beneath her fingers.

"It's always been one of my favourite stories. I made my mum read it to me nearly every night when I was a child." She smiled, feeling more than a little shy herself. "I read it again just a few days ago."

Jac's grin was every bit as cheeky and heart-melting as she'd always imagined the boy Peter's had been, but Jac's grin made Sasha's heart skip and her belly tighten. "Good to know. So," she said and pointed to the door, "remember that if it weren't for you, none of us would be doing this at all, and don't doubt, not for a second, that you can fly."

"Even without the pixie dust?"

"Especially without the pixie dust." Jac opened the door and led her to the lift. "I've met your mother, after all."

"Funny."

"I thought so." The door opened and lowered them to the streets of Salford.

The room was already full when they arrived, and Sasha cursed herself for making them late until she glanced at the clock and saw they were still five minutes early. The aroma of coffee and sugar hung in the air, but was made to battle with the pungent scent of overpriced perfume and manly deodorant. Sasha quickly fixed coffee for herself and Jac and sat next to her, smiling as Sophie caught her eye and sat on her other side. She clasped her hand and squeezed her fingers together.

"Hey, girl. You okay?" She leant over and kissed Sasha's cheek. "Love this outfit, by the way. Very sexy."

"I'm good, and thanks." Sasha felt the heat in her cheeks. "You?"

"I'm good. Ready to get this project started, that's for sure. I hope you don't mind me saying so, but you look a little tired. Worry about this keeping you up?"

"A little, I think. But I never really sleep well in an unfamiliar bed. And after being banished from home last night, well, let's just say it was a late night."

"Okay, unfamiliar bed…I was about to congratulate you and ask for details, but banished… Now I'm truly curious. What do you mean?"

"Jac didn't tell you?"

"You slept with Jac?" Sophie stared at her, wide-eyed, incredulous…and maybe just a little disapprovingly.

"What? No. I meant she didn't tell you that my mother told me not to come home because she had a man staying with her. So I ended up staying in Jac's spare room."

"Oh, right." Sophie looked more than a little relieved, and Sasha snorted a laugh. "That was generous of her."

"Yeah, it really was. I was going to get a room at a hotel, but she wouldn't hear of it. And she helped take my mind off being pissed off with my mother."

"Fair enough. So how long has your mother been seeing this dude?"

Sasha glanced at her watch. "About fifteen, maybe sixteen hours now."

It was Sophie's turn to snort. But hers included the mouthful of coffee she'd just taken, and she put a hand to her nose. "Ouch." She cackled. "Enough said. I'll make sure the coffee keeps coming to get you through the day." She tipped her head to indicate something over her shoulder. Sasha followed the gesture. "Seems one of our leading ladies isn't too happy that the other leading lady got the bigger part."

"Is that normal?" Sasha asked as she looked them both over.

"No, and if she doesn't let it go once this starts, I'll sort it out, but it would be easier if they can do it themselves. At least then there won't be embarrassment to add to the mix of jealousy and drama."

Sasha sipped her coffee, holding the mug under her nose to offset the lingering scent of deodorant as one of the male actors pulled out a chair a little way down the table.

Sophie's nose wrinkled and she whispered, "Welcome to the glamorous world of the wannabe famous."

Sasha sniggered, content to sit between her new friends and wait for Jac to call the session to some sort of order.

"Back in a minute," Sophie whispered and indicated the door with *Ladies* written over it in bold script.

"No worries. You might want to check your"—she pointed at the coffee splatters down Sophie's chest—"while you're in there."

"Thanks," Sophie said with a glance down, a roll of her eyes, and a quick trot to the bathroom. The door had barely closed behind her when the seat beside Sasha was filled with the disgruntled blonde Sophie had pointed out a few minutes ago. She held out her hand with a smile so fake that Sasha could feel herself recoiling and had to catch herself.

"I'm Gemma Jackson."

Name's as fake as the smile, hon. Sasha took her hand and tried her own false smile. "Sasha Adams."

"Are you part of the production team?"

Sasha nodded. *The writer is part of the production team, right? Part of those who produce the thing the actors act in.*

"Good, I thought so, given your age and everything."

Bitch.

"So listen, I don't want to be rude to anyone or anything, but there's been a serious casting mistake here. Becca over there…" She pointed to a young woman who could be the embodiment of the female Middle Eastern lead Sasha had envisioned when writing the script. "Well, she's under the mistaken impression she's playing the lead character in this thing, but clearly it needs a, well, let's not beat around the bush. This script and this character needs a little…something, you get me, hon? So my skills and charisma are definitely needed to help it out." She flicked her blond hair over her shoulder, and her smile turned conspiratorial. "So I thought if you could just tell the director it was a typo or something, maybe pretend it was your mistake or something like that, then we could get this thing on track. Then when it's a roaring success, you can drop the bomb that you fixed this whole mistake and get the credit for it. I don't mind doing that for you." She offered Sasha a wink. "What do you say?"

Sasha wasn't sure which emotion would win out in the battle between insulted and incredulous. Did people like this really exist? Really? Could someone be this wrapped up in their own little world and still be able to function? Did her script really need so much help?

But Hazaar was a British Muslim. Gemma's blond hair and blue eyes made her the perfect counter to that, and they were fairly close to what Sasha had pictured on Charlie. While the film took its name from *Hazaar*, the Arabic word for nightingale, Charlie was in actual fact easily as big a part, possibly more so. So, no, switching them would not be possible. It simply wouldn't fit. Had this woman even bothered to read the damn script?

Or is she right? Does she have a point? Was her script so bad that this woman—with her fake smile and her fake name, and God knew what else fakeness—was good enough to make it better? Jesus, if that was the case, maybe she should have stayed back at home. *What am I doing here? I'm going to fuck everything up. I'll ruin Jac's company.*

The thoughts racing through her head paused when they hit that one. Jac wouldn't let someone ruin the company she'd spent years building. And even if she'd been inclined to throw someone a bone, Sophie wouldn't. They'd put their faith in her. Their trust. The words above Jac's door filled her mind's eye, and in the end insulted won out.

"Gemma? Is that what you said your name was?"

The woman…no, the girl, nodded.

"Well, I tell you what. Why don't you go back over there and take a look at the script you're holding again? Then remember I said my name is Sasha Adams." She pointed to the script in Gemma's hand and the seat across the room and hoped Gemma didn't notice how badly her hand was shaking as she quickly brought it back to the table. "Then take a look at the character descriptions. Then if you still want to discuss this crappy script and all the help it needs, come find me again."

Oh, that felt good. Sasha had to stop herself from smiling and hold on to the cold look she was trying to display.

Gemma huffed and drew herself up out of the seat with a grace Sasha knew she'd never possess. "Don't try to say I didn't offer you a chance, love. But I suppose there's a reason you're still behind the scenes and no one knows you at your age." She wiggled her fingers and crossed the room.

Sasha jumped when a hand touched her knee under the table, and she turned to see Jac grinning at her.

"Sorry, didn't mean to make you jump." She squeezed Sasha's knee gently, then let go. "But that was awesome, and if you turn around now, I think you'll see your little bomb go off."

Sasha glanced across the room and noticed Gemma's head snap up and her gaze lock on Sasha's. Her face paled. Sasha could clearly see the *oh shit* that went through her mind and smirked broadly as she waved her hand at Sophie's chair, inviting her back for the discussion, but Gemma tossed her head and turned away. Jac stifled a laugh as Sophie walked back to the table and caught Sasha's *never mind* gaze as she sat back down.

"What did I miss?" Sophie asked.

"Sasha sorting out our casting drama," Jac answered and grinned at Sasha. "I'll fill you in later." Jac cleared her throat. "Okay, people, let's get this show on the road!"

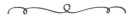

"I got Chinese food," Mags said as she dumped two plastic bags on the table they'd been sat around all day. At least now only the four of them remained. "I got a selection of stuff, so dig in and help yourselves."

Jac was the first to stand and start pulling out containers.

"I'll grab some plates." Sophie stood. "Don't eat all the prawn crackers before I get back." She pointed at Jac before she left.

"Yeah, yeah. You do something once on a bet and they make it haunt you forever." Jac held up plastic tubs to check contents. "What's your poison, Sasha?"

"What're the choices?"

"Looks like beef in black-bean sauce, sweet-and-sour chicken, duck in what?"

"Plum," Mags answered, plopping down heavily into her chair. "There's also pork chow mien, and prawn with cashew nuts for Madam out there. Don't touch that or she'll chop your fingers off."

"Good to know. Sweet and sour it is, then."

"There's rice and noodles too." Jac slid foil dishes across the wooden tabletop and grabbed a prawn cracker from the bag with a devilish grin.

"Rice is good, thanks."

Sophie came back in and passed out plates and cutlery as they all busied themselves with dishing out food. Sasha was starving. It had been a long day, and the croissants had long since left a hole in her appetite. Coffee alone was not enough to sustain her throughout a day, especially not one filled with angst in the form of a pouting Gemma Jackson.

"Okay, ladies," Jac said, "I think we need to make a quick decision on this one. We just about have time to find a replacement for Gemma, or we suck it up and see how it goes."

Swallowing, Sasha watched the faces of the other women around the table.

Sophie grinned evilly and opened her mouth, "I told—"

"You don't need to say it," Jac cut her off. "Yes, you said Gemma wasn't the right one for the part." She waved her hand in Mags's direction. "We were wrong, you were right. What are the chances of getting your pick on board now?

"Nada. She's already signed up for a theatre project as of two days ago. It's a years-long contract on a touring company. She's not ditching that for us."

"Damn it."

"You snooze, you lose."

"Yeah, yeah. So who else do we have?"

"There aren't a huge amount of options out there. You shot down the proper top candidate, and I can guarantee you won't want to go with option three." Sophie bit into a prawn and shuffled in her seat like she was dancing. "Gorgeous, thanks, Mags."

"Welcome."

"Why? Who was option three?"

Sophie took her time chewing through her bite of food before she replied. "Vanessa."

"Vanessa? As in my ex, Vanessa?"

Sophie nodded and carried on eating.

"Shit."

"Told you, you wouldn't like it."

Jac bent over the desk and bumped her forehead against the wooden surface. "Why do I get myself into these messes? Why? Why? Why?" She banged her head in time with each word.

"Well, I think it's called mixing business with pleasure," Mags said and forked rice into her mouth.

"Thank you for those words of wisdom, Yoda."

Mags shrugged, swallowed, and said, "We did warn you—"

"Many, many times," Sophie interjected.

"About picking up the talent," Mags finished.

"Fine. But we'd all agreed she'd become overexposed in our films. That's why we terminated her contract." She snorted a derisive laugh. "That's why she left me in the end, ladies. Now you want me to offer her another contract?"

Sophie and Mags looked at each other and shrugged.

"So it looks like we're stuck with Gemma."

"She's decent, Jac. She can play the role," Mags said.

"*Can* doesn't mean she will. I want them to put in the best performance they can, not just show up and say the lines," Jac said and crunched another cracker.

"I'll have a word," Sophie said. "Make sure she knows what's expected of her."

They'd made good progress with the tabletop rehearsal so far, but Gemma's lacklustre performance was making it a little difficult to see if everything was coming across exactly as Sasha had intended. She thought it did…but doubt niggled at the back of her mind.

"What do you think, Sash?" Sophie asked. "Is it what you expected so far?"

Sasha swallowed the forkful of rice she just taken and wiggled her hand from side to side. "Sort of. I'm not entirely sure what I was expecting to begin with, but this makes sense. Getting as much prepared ahead of going onto the sets saves time and, no doubt, money, right?"

"Absolutely. If we tried to do all the rehearsals on set, it would add weeks to the schedule, all of which would have to be paid for." She circled her head around to indicate the room they were in. "Using our own office space adds nothing to the overheads that we aren't already paying."

"Yeah, but did you enjoy it?" Mags asked. "It's exciting, right? Hearing them read out your words and bringing your characters to life?"

Sasha grinned. "I had to pinch myself I don't know how many times today to make myself believe I wasn't dreaming. It's still kind of surreal."

"Well, keep reminding yourself of that feeling when we've been on set for three weeks straight and Gemma's still turning in a performance like this one today." Jac stabbed a fork at her plate and looked at Sophie. "Let me have a talk with Vanessa and see if she's interested. We didn't really part on bad terms, and this would be a part she could sink her teeth into. Plus, she can sing. We wouldn't have to bring in a voice double for that audition scene at the beginning. That always makes the editing easier."

Sophie frowned. "Are you sure you want to do that, my dear Pan? You know she's likely to think it means you want her back, as in, you want *her* back?"

"Trust me, I'll be clear that's not going to happen, but if she can give me a more genuine performance than what Gemma was turning in, then I think it's worth talking to her at least."

"I'm sorry, but the character is a young twenty-something," Sasha said. "I'm not sure your ex would fit the role, and there is a lot that would have to be rewritten to fit an older woman. Jokes that just wouldn't work and so on. I'm sure we can do it, but do you want to go to all the trouble, rather than give Gemma a chance?"

Mags and Sophie were looking between Sasha and Jac with amused expressions. Jac was staring at her plate and refusing to look up, no matter how hard Sasha tried to catch her eye.

"Sorry, I didn't mean any offence—"

Mags and Sophie hooted as Jac's cheeks flamed red and she tossed a wadded-up napkin at Mags.

"I think I'm missing something." Sasha had clearly stuck her foot in it. What was this about?

"Jac didn't tell you Vanessa is twenty-five, did she, hon?" Sophie asked.

Sasha lifted her eyebrows and Jac's cheeks grew even redder. "Really?"

Jac cleared her throat and said, "Erm, yeah, she is, and no, it never came up in conversation."

"Sorry," Sasha said. "I shouldn't have made assumptions. I...well, I—" She shook her head. "You should do what you think is best."

Jac nodded and pulled her phone from her pocket. "I'll call her now. If she's coming on board, it'd better be sooner rather than later. She'll need to get her hair dyed, or sort out a good wig at least." She stepped out of the room.

Sasha wasn't sure why, but the idea of Jac with a woman so much younger made her heart clench uncomfortably. But why wouldn't Jac date a younger woman if she could? A young actress, who was no doubt stunning, and half her age? Jac was a gorgeous woman herself. Gorgeous, intelligent, funny... Why wouldn't she be with a beautiful, young actress?

Sasha swallowed another mouthful of food she was no longer hungry for.

CHAPTER 14

GEMMA JACKSON'S EXIT FROM KEFRAN Media Ltd the next morning was neither graceful nor quiet. The scathing looks she sent Sasha's way spelled out exactly where she felt her problems lay, and she wasn't shy in letting everyone know. Nor was she shy in letting her insults fly.

Mags sat next to Sasha in the conference room they'd used to break the news to Gemma and ran her fingers through her hair. "Well, if she thinks that's the way to make it in this business, she's got another thing coming, I can tell you that for damn sure."

"Oh, I don't know. You don't think she'd get an award for that performance?"

"Only if she was going for Banshee of the Year."

Sasha scanned the script in front of her, wanting to be prepared for the day ahead as much as she could. After several minutes of deep concentration, the sensation of someone bumping her elbow startled her. She looked up.

Mags nodded in the direction of the windows that lined the conference room.

A tall redhead glided down the hallway. Oversized sunglasses covered half of her face, and her lips shone with bright red lipstick.

"Vanessa Coyne."

"Jac's ex?"

"Yep." It hadn't been a question but Mags answered anyway. "Bitch."

Sasha sniggered. "Oh, don't sugarcoat it, Mags. Tell me how you really feel about her."

Mags cackled. "Fair enough. You'll see for yourself soon enough, anyway. She's a sleep-your-way-to-the-top kind of girl who no doubt thinks she's doing Jac a favour now being here, since she's moved on to bigger and better things after walking out on Jac. And by bigger and better things, I mean she's sleeping with a producer at the BBC who was rumoured to have got the green light to start casting for a sitcom starring Dawn French." She winked at Sasha. "But that's all hush-hush."

"Of course. Well, at least she's consistent."

"Oh yeah, she's consistent. And ambitious, and, like I said, a bitch."

"Got it."

"I always found it best to ignore her wherever possible and if not, smile and think pleasant thoughts until she goes away."

"Why is she a better option than Gemma again?"

"Vanessa is ambitious enough to perform no matter what's going on off-camera. She knows that at the end of the day, what the camera sees is what she'll be remembered for, and she will happily use any drama to enhance her performance."

"So she's actually pretty good at her job?"

"Unfortunately."

"Why 'unfortunately'?"

"Because women like her give the rest of us a bad name, and if she worked at it, she really could make it on her own. She doesn't need to give head to get ahead."

Sasha laughed. "Nice, I might have to borrow that line somewhere along the way."

"Feel free. I've got a ton of 'em." Mags waved a hand.

"Think she'll get the part she's after and ditch us?"

"What, the sitcom part?"

"Yeah."

"Nah. Dawn French turned it down, and it's already fallen through. Vanessa's bigger and better suddenly looked a whole lot smaller and shittier."

They stared at the door to Jac's office as Jac and Vanessa came out arm in arm, sunglasses sitting atop Vanessa's head as she clung to Jac's arm like an octopus, laughing at something and stroking her hand up and down Jac's bicep. Sasha gritted her teeth and tightened her grip on her pen.

"Looks like she's trying to rekindle the old flame," she remarked tightly and made a concerted effort to loosen her grip. *What the hell is wrong with me? What do I care if Jac gets back together with her ex?*

"Nah. If that's what Vanessa's after, she's got no chance. Once Jac's done, she's done. She's never gone back to anyone, especially when she wasn't the one walking away in the first place. She's not the type to forgive and forget like that. When Vanessa left, she was just going to walk out of the apartment while Jac was at work, leaving a little note. As far as Jac's concerned, that's abandonment, and she doesn't deal well with that. It's something that…well, it's something she can't forget, so if someone leaves her, she just walks and keeps on going."

The door opened and Jac walked in, Vanessa barely inches away. "Mags," she said and inclined her head.

"Jac. Vanessa, you're looking well."

Vanessa smiled. "Thanks. How're you doing, Mags?"

"I'm good." She stood. "But if you'll excuse me, I've got a lot of work to get on with."

"Thanks, Mags," Jac said as she passed her on the way to the door. "Vanessa, this is Sasha Adams, Sasha, Vanessa Coyne. She'll be taking Gemma's place and playing Charlie in *Nightingale*. Vee, Sasha is the writer who created this." Jac smiled brightly at Sasha as she spoke. "Without her, we wouldn't be here now."

Vanessa's smile faltered a moment as she watched Jac, but she held her hand out to Sasha and stepped forwards. "A pleasure to meet you. I read the script last night after I spoke to Jac. It's incredible. The mixture of humour and pathos is just, well, incredible. I'm looking forward to those action scenes towards the end too. That should be a lot of fun." She smiled warmly, and it was easy to see how much better for the role she'd be than Gemma had been. And just how perfect her teeth were. And her hair. And those blue eyes, smiling at her.

Sasha cleared her throat. "It's great to meet you too, Vanessa. Thanks for stepping in at such short notice. We really appreciate it."

"Oh, it was no trouble at all." She stood up straight and wrapped her hand around Jac's arm again. "I'd do anything to help out Jac here. She's just the best, isn't she?"

Smiling and nodding, Sasha said, "Absolutely."

Jac looked like she wanted to roll her eyes as Sasha just barely managed to keep a straight face. She noticed how Jac used Vanessa's own grip on her arm to edge her towards the door. "Sasha, the rest of the cast will be around the table in about five. See you there, okay?"

Sasha nodded and lifted a hand to them as Jac moved them out the door. The last thing Sasha heard as the door closed was, "Give it a rest, Vee."

Well, gorgeous didn't even begin to cover Jac's ex. Stunning. Yes, physically, she was stunning.

The dulcet tones of soul singer Anastacia telling the world she's "got another confession to make" erupted from Sasha's jacket pocket. She reached in and pulled it out, sliding her finger across the screen to answer as she did.

"I've got a confession to make," Bobbi said by way of greeting.

"Do you need bail money?"

"Not this time."

"An alibi?"

"Possibly…later."

"We were in the pub watching the football."

"Football season's over."

"Rerun?"

Bobbi chuckled. "Not likely."

"Better spill, then, my child. I've got rehearsals to get to in a couple of minutes. We don't have time for a full round of Hail Marys and prayers this time."

"You're always busy," Bobbi grumbled.

"And whose fault is that? I didn't send my script off to a competition, now did I?"

Bobbi sighed heavily. "Fine. So I might have, possibly, kind of walked out of my job."

"What!"

"Erm, yeah, maybe."

"Shit, Bobbi, what happened? You need that job. What're you going to do?"

"Which question do you want me to answer first?"

"Funny. Tell me what happened."

"Polyakov was in again. Facial and a mani-pedi."

"Okay."

"We were short-staffed because the girl Maria hired to replace you didn't turn up this morning."

"Right."

"So there was only me there to deal with the racist bitch."

"Uh-oh."

"She demanded you."

"And you told her I didn't work there anymore."

"Yup."

"And she was stuck with you?"

"Yup."

"Went over like a lead balloon?"

"Better. She demanded to see Maria."

"Fabulous."

"Maria tried to stick up for me, said I was her best worker and all that guff. She was actually really nice, but that woman is such a bitch, Sash. I couldn't just stand there and let her say that shit to me. Not again. It's not right."

"I know it's not, hon. So, what happened?"

"I just walked out."

"You just left?"

"Yeah."

"In the middle of the shift?"

"Erm…yeah."

"Bobbi! What about Maria? You left her in the lurch!"

"I know, but I couldn't take it anymore. I just couldn't."

Sasha could hear the tears in Bobbi's voice. "Shush, it's okay. I'll call Maria. I'm sure she'll understand."

"No, don't."

"But, Bobbi, you can't just leave it like this. You need that job. How're you going to pay your rent if you're not working?"

"I'll get another job."

"Not if you expect Maria to give you a reference after just walking out on her like that."

"You didn't hear what she was saying, Sash." Bobbi's voice was so quiet she almost couldn't hear her. Almost. But while the words were quiet, Bobbi's pain came through loud and clear.

"Maybe you should call her, then?"

"I can't. I don't want to go back there, Sash. It's not the same. It all feels wrong now."

"How do you mean? You loved that job. You loved working there."

"I loved working with you. The job's just a job. Something I have to do to pay the bills. I don't want to go back there."

"Oh, Bobbi. We knew things would have to change when I won this competition." A knock at the door caught her attention. She looked up to find Jac watching her from the doorway, eyebrows lifted in question. *Shit, I'm late.* She mouthed the word *sorry* to Jac and stood, grabbing her script and pen as she headed for the door. "Listen, Bobbi, I've got to get to rehearsals now. Can I give you a call on the way home tonight? We can come up with a plan then. Maybe you can come around and we can hash it all out over a *Friends* fest and popcorn. What do you say?" Sasha followed Jac down the corridor.

Bobbi was quiet for a moment. "Sure, I've missed…that."

"Okay, then, I'll call you on my way home tonight. Later, hon." She hung up and slid the phone back in her pocket. "I'm so sorry I'm late. That was Bobbi. She's had an awful day and just lost her job."

"Oh no, what happened?"

"She was being verbally abused by a customer—not the first time—and she'd just had enough. She walked out."

"What was the abuse about?"

"A racist customer didn't like the fact Bobbi's black."

"You're joking?"

"Nope. Wish I was."

"I can't say I blame her for walking, then."

"Nope. But that's not going to help her when her rent's due."

Jac held open a door for her, waving her through with a slight frown. "Is she a good worker?"

"Yes. She'd been there as long as I had. She was one of the best members of staff."

"Does she make a decent brew?"

"Her coffee's spot on; tea's good, if you like it builder style."

"Strong and hot?"

"That's the one. Why?"

"I might have a solution. I'll tell you about it when we break for lunch."

"Get your arse around to mine, I've got news," Sasha said into her phone as she stepped off the bus and turned up her road.

"Good news or bad news?" Bobbi asked.

"Good."

"On my way."

Sasha slid her phone in her pocket, waved to Dante, then looked away quickly with a shudder as he "adjusted" himself. She fished her house keys out of her bag. When she had opened the door, she shouted out, "Mum? I'm home."

"In the conservatory, dear."

Sasha sent up a silent prayer—for strength—hung up her coat and bag, then went to find her mother. A thick plume of pungent smoke escaped as she opened the door. She wafted her hand in front of her face and tried not to breathe too deeply. "I thought you weren't smoking as much?"

"Felt like it today." Fleur stared at her, glassy-eyed. "Problem?" she asked harshly.

Sasha shook her head. It was unusual for Fleur to snap. Especially when she was as stoned as she looked right now. Things not going well with Mr Hunt, maybe? Sasha thought about asking but decided against it. She already had far more information on the subject than she needed… wanted…could never remove from her brain. "Bobbi's coming around in a little bit. She had a bad day." She quickly filled Fleur in on Bobbi's news and asked, "Do you want anything to eat?"

"I'm not very hungry, dear."

"Okay." Sasha pulled the door open behind her.

"Maybe just a sandwich."

Sasha smiled. "What kind?"

"Spam and egg, I think."

"Fried egg?"

"Yes."

"Okay."

"And black pudding."

"All right."

"And a hash brown."

Sasha snorted. "Bacon?"

"Oo, yeah. And maybe some sausage too."

"One fry-up on the way."

She'd almost finished cooking an old-fashioned English fried breakfast for tea when Bobbi knocked on the door. "It's open," Sasha called out and spooned beans onto three plates. Bobbi never turned down food. "Mum, tea's ready."

Fleur shuffled out of the conservatory and hobbled into a chair at the table. She grinned at Bobbi. "Dude, heard you had a shit-kicker day." She held her fist out to Bobbi as she sat down heavily opposite Fleur, then bumped her fist.

"I feel like I've had the shit kicked out of me, that's for sure."

"Well, I'm going to make it better for you," Sasha said as she put down the plates, then added a plate to the middle filled with slices of buttered toast.

"You've got that racist bitch's address and a shovel handy?"

"Not that much better."

"You won the lottery and you're going to share?"

"Not that much better either."

Bobbi dipped a bit of sausage in her egg yolk and shrugged. "Buggered if I know, then."

"I've got you a new job. Starts tomorrow."

"I don't want to go back to Serenity. It's too—"

"You'll be working for Kefran Media as a runner. It's not a great job, but you'll be on set, doing whatever needs doing. Tomorrow I think Jac said you'd be helping with the final touches to the sets being built for the film."

Bobbi dropped her fork, spattering her "dip me in chocolate and throw me to the lesbians" hoodie with bean juice. "Shut the front door."

"Already closed, my friend."

"I'm gonna be working with you again?"

"Well, not exactly. But you'll be on the set. You'll have a job, but it'll be different from what I'm doing. I won't be able to hang around with you all the time like we used to, but—"

"The A-Team is back in business!" Bobbi fist-pumped like she'd just won Wimbledon, then pulled a version of Usain Bolt's signature move... while the strings of her hoodie dipped themselves through the bean juice.

Sasha leaned back in her chair and tossed a tea towel from over the handle of the oven at her. "Clean yourself up, Murdoch."

"Why do I have to be the crazy one? Why can't I be Face?"

Sasha looked at her mum. "Do you wanna take this one?"

"You see, dude, it's like this...," Fleur started, a huge grin spreading across her face.

CHAPTER 15

JAC LEANT ON THE DOOR frame to the office she'd had set up for Sasha and smiled. Sasha was frowning at her computer screen, seemingly oblivious to anyone else around her. It gave Jac time to study her while she waited to be noticed.

Sasha's hair was piled on top of her head in a messy bun with a pencil sticking out of the side, in what she was quickly coming to see as Sasha's signature hairdo. Jac wasn't sure if the pencil was holding her hair up or had merely been stuffed there for safekeeping. Not that it mattered; either way, it was just so perfectly Sasha. She tapped the end of a pen against her lips, occasionally pulling it away to scribble something on the pad beside her laptop. The black-rimmed glasses perched on her nose added to her studious expression and threw Jac into yet another series of sexy-librarian fantasies that had always been a not-so-guilty pleasure of hers.

Jac closed her eyes. It occurred to her why she'd decided to offer Bobbi a job and put Vanessa on the project while getting rid of Gemma. The answer was simple. Sasha was important to her. Bobbi was important to Sasha. Gemma was being mean to Sasha, and it had been within Jac's power to do something about all of that. It didn't matter that having Vanessa on set for the next two months would be uncomfortable for her. The situation would be easier for Sasha to have Gemma gone. So she was gone. Sasha would feel better having Bobbi here. So she was here.

But what did *that* mean? *Did* it mean anything? Other than she thought Sasha a good person who deserved someone making her happy?

The past week of rehearsals had gone well. Vanessa had fit in well with the rest of the cast, and she'd even been pretty well behaved with the crew.

Mostly. Bobbi was a different story, but one that could be dealt with. She just needed to temper her…enthusiasm a bit. Okay, a lot. But still, Jac could see her heart was in the right place. Mostly.

Jac sighed heavily, glad she'd already seen Vanessa leave for the day and she didn't have to face the prospect of turning a corner and running into her. She was debating the merits of carrying a mirror to look around corners for the foreseeable future—just in case—when Sasha looked up and offered her a beaming smile.

"Hey," she said.

"Hey," Jac replied, crossing her arms over her chest. "You ready to get out of here?"

"Has everyone gone already?" She closed the lid of her laptop and started packing her bag.

"Yup. Why? Do you need someone?" Like Bobbi, maybe? The woman had barely been in her new job for an hour before it had become clear that that she intended to do everything she could for Sasha. Regardless of what her job actually was. A production assistant was not Sasha's secretary or personal assistant or whatever Bobbi seemed to think she was. Jac held back the sigh that wanted to escape her lips for fear of the questions Sasha would ask as a result. Questions she didn't want to answer. Or really even think about, if she were totally honest. Sasha and Bobbi were friends. Good friends. Sasha had been clear about that. Jac just needed to talk to Sophie—again—about making it clear to Bobbi exactly what her role was. And to make sure she was doing it.

"No, just wondered how you shook Vanessa today."

Jac rolled her eyes. They were only a few days into working together, and Vanessa had already propositioned her. Several times. "I really couldn't have been more clear with her and she's seeing someone else. I don't know what's wrong with her."

"Maybe she's realised what she lost and is genuine that she wants you two to work it out."

"Do you really believe that?"

"Does it matter what I believe?"

Yes. "I value your opinion."

Sasha shrugged as she got to her feet. "I don't know her like you do."

"You know her enough."

Sasha sighed as Jac held the door open for her. "Thanks. Okay, well, I'm not convinced it's you she wants back as much as what you can do for her."

"Exactly." Jac held her arm out for Sasha and stifled the gasp when Sasha's fingers wrapped around her bicep. "I'm not interested in her, and I've told her that. It won't stop her from trying again, though, and there's nothing I can do until filming is done. I knew this would happen before I offered her the role."

"So why did you offer it to her?"

Because of you. "Because she was better for the role than Gemma. Because your film is more important than a couple of uncomfortable comments from Vanessa. Because it was the right thing to do, even if it wasn't the best thing for me."

"Ah, martyrdom." Sasha chuckled.

Jac couldn't help but laugh. "Yeah, I'm working towards my sainthood."

"Saint Jac." Sasha tapped her chin thoughtfully. "It has a ring to it."

"Yeah, yeah, mock me. You might as well join the ranks in giving me a hard time."

"Aw, are you feeling picked on?"

"Always," Jac said, throwing her lip out in a childish pout.

Sasha giggled and lightly slapped her arm. "Bet I can make it up to you?"

"Uh-huh. What do you plan to do? Make me a millionaire with a click of your fingers?"

"I was thinking dinner," Sasha said with a frown, "but if money's all you're after—"

"Dinner?"

Sasha nodded.

"With you?"

"Well, yes. I was thinking you could use a home-cooked meal. We've eaten together every night this week here in the office. Always takeaway. I'm not sure you know what a vegetable is."

"Oh, right. Dinner at home." Jac swallowed down disappointment. Sasha wasn't asking her out on a date, she was inviting her to her house, with her mother present. "That'd be great."

"What? You'd prefer someone else cook for you?"

"No," Jac said quickly as she started to realise the merit of a home-cooked meal...with Sasha, even with other people there. "You're cooking? Not your mum?"

"No, not my house. I was thinking more like I'd put that wasted kitchen of yours to good use for a change. I'm pretty sure you've never cooked anything but coffee in there."

"I refuse to say anything on the grounds that I may incriminate myself."

Sasha chuckled. "As I suspected. Well, is that all right with you? I mean, we could go to my house of course. But Mum said she was seeing Mr Hunt again today, so..." She shuddered.

"Ah, I see your game now. You want to bribe me for the use of my spare room again."

"Well, I couldn't honestly say it hadn't crossed my mind...like all day... but, no, I was going to cook for you, then leave you. Later. Much later. Like, well-after-my-mother-will-be-asleep later."

"You're more than welcome to stay, Sasha." *Anytime.*

"Well, we'll see. Now, since this meal is to soothe your wounded ego—"

"—while you hide from your mother."

"Maybe, but anyhow...what'll it be?"

"I don't know. Whatever you want to make. You're the cook."

"Hm, chef, actually."

"Really?"

"Yeah. I've had a few different jobs in the past. But that's a story for another time, so come on. What do you want?"

"Anything?"

"Well, it's almost six now, so it can't be slow-roasted pork or a mutton casserole; we wouldn't be eating until tomorrow if that were the case. But give me some ideas and I'll see what I can do."

"Okay, Chef, how about duck?"

"Duck's fine. What kind? Chinese style with plum sauce or a more traditional English style? Maybe with a blackberry sauce, mushrooms, potatoes, some celeriac?"

"Oh, that sounds good."

"Okay. Anything you don't like? Allergies?"

"I don't like bananas."

"Okay. They don't go very well with duck, so we're fairly safe there."

132

"Funny."

"I thought so. Dessert?"

"Erm, anything."

"Chocolate good for you?"

"Huh?"

"Are you okay with chocolate?"

"Is that a trick question?"

"No. What do you mean?"

"Have you ever met a woman who wasn't okay with chocolate?"

"One, yeah."

"Really?"

"Yes."

"Not a mythical creature? Not an allergy of some sort?"

Sasha laughed. "No, she really didn't like chocolate. She did like bananas, though."

"Freak."

"Probably should have told me all I needed to know, but hey-ho."

"Ah. An ex?"

"Yeah," Sasha said with a nod. "Long time ago."

"How long since you split?"

"Five years. Not long before Mum got sick actually."

"Can I ask what happened?"

"Not a lot to tell, really. We grew apart until one day I came home and she told me she was in love with someone else. And I realised I didn't care enough to feel anything more than kicked in the gut because this other woman was ten years younger than me." She laughed sadly. "Kinda said it all, really."

Jac glanced over as they reached the doors to the building and she led Sasha to her car. She kept it in the car park at work in case she had to run out for meetings and such. "I was right."

"About what?"

"She's a freak." Jac squeezed Sasha's hand and their gazes locked. Sasha's dark brown eyes were soft with unshed tears, and Jac didn't believe for a second that Sasha hadn't been more hurt by the idiot's affair. Sasha cared, and the pain was there to see. "Do you still love her?" she asked as she drove on to the street.

"God, no." Sasha's answer was immediate and unequivocal. "Like I said, it was the blow to my ego—"

"You don't need to do that. Not with me."

"Do what?"

"Downplay it. You loved her enough to be with her. That's more than a blow to the ego."

"All right, you want honest? Pam's affair cut deep. I'd thought we were settled. Yes, we got into a bit of a rut, and life seemed a bit, well, boring. But isn't that what happens to everyone every so often? Isn't that what grown-up relationships are when the drudgery of everyday life gets to you?"

"Not sure I can tell you." Jac shrugged. "I'm not sure I've ever had a grown-up relationship."

"But we'd had good times. Still had a laugh together. History. She and I built a home together. But then it wasn't enough for her. *I wasn't* enough for Pam."

Jac could see the battle inside Sasha. The battle for what she didn't know. "Do me a favour, okay?" She glanced away as the lights turned green and she turned into the car park at the supermarket.

"What's that?"

"Be honest with me. No hiding, no pretending. Just be yourself." Something told Jac she hadn't had that freedom in a long time, and she longed to give her the space to do so. To just be herself.

Sasha was quiet for a moment. "Will you do the same?"

Jac pondered the question while Sasha studied her intently with those coffee-dark eyes. Jac played through her head all the half-truths she'd already told Sasha and wondered how she would have reacted to full disclosure on each one.

Sasha licked her lips, then pulled the bottom one between her teeth as she waited. Jac's belly flipped with the desire to kiss her and pull that lip between her own teeth.

"Will you?" Sasha prompted.

"Okay," Jac said softly, almost too quiet to hear. *God help me.*

After a long moment, Sasha smiled and pointed out of the window. "Come on, then. I've seen the inside of your fridge. We definitely need a supermarket if I'm going to make you a duck dish."

What have I just agreed to? Jac wondered.

The shopping trip flew by. Sasha selected items quickly and paid for them before Jac got her credit card out, saying simply, "My treat." Jac or one of the others had paid for the takeaways every night of the week. This felt like she was getting off light.

When they were back in Jac's apartment and everything was unpacked, she quickly set about finely dicing vegetables, searing the duck breasts, and setting the sauce to reduce while Jac sat across the kitchen island.

"Okay, I have one rule for tonight." Jac held up a bottle of wine. "But, first, Merlot?"

"Yeah, that'll work well with the fruity sauce. In fact, hand it over when you've uncorked it. A splash in the sauce will add a nice bit of depth."

"*Oui*, Chef." Jac sniggered and uncorked the bottle, then let it breathe a moment before she poured two glasses and passed the bottle to Sasha. Sasha sniffed it, letting the bouquet tantalise her senses before adding a decent glug to the pan.

"So, what's your rule for the night?"

"No talk about work."

"None?"

"Nope."

"Why not?"

"Open and honest?"

"Of course."

"I want to get to know you, Sasha. Not the woman behind the laptop." She grinned that cocky grin that made Sasha's insides tighten. "I want to know what makes you tick."

She focused on checking the reduction of the sauce. "You do, huh?"

"Yup."

Mushrooms were added to a pan. "Okay. Fire away."

"Why did you stop being a chef?"

"That's easy. Unsociable hours coupled with crappy pay. I fell out of love with it, so I decided to try something else."

"And does being a massage therapist still tick all the boxes for you?"

Sasha snorted and sliced up some of the greens they'd bought. "It has more reasonable hours, and it's a lot quieter. Customers one-to-one and the pay is marginally better."

"And I'll bet some of those customers don't even speak, so you write in your head while you're pummelling the knots in their backs, right?"

"It's been known."

"Any other careers you've taken for a test drive?"

"Hm, I've tried a few different things, but they were more jobs to pay the bills than a career I was pursuing or training for."

"Stopgaps rather than destinations?"

"Exactly." She stirred the saucepan and quickly tasted it, adding a little salt from the pinch pot she'd set on the counter. "What about you? What did you do at the BBC?"

"I worked my way up to producing some documentaries and then some drama shows. Nothing major, but enough to serve as an apprenticeship of sorts, I guess."

"So it's what you've always wanted to do?"

"Yes, but we're straying dangerously close to the work topic now, so let's change that."

Sasha grinned. "Okay, then, I have a question for you."

"Uh-oh. Sounds serious." Jac sipped her wine, then put down the glass.

Shrugging, Sasha tossed the pan with mushrooms and *cavolo nero* sautéing in butter. "Never mind, then."

"No, no. We had a deal." She swirled the wine around in her glass. "Go on, hit me with it."

"I just wondered, why Vanessa? I mean, of course she's stunningly beautiful, but… I don't know. I guess I'm curious. Have all your girlfriends been a lot younger than you?"

Jac took a deep breath and blew it out slowly between pursed lips. "Open and honest, right?"

Sasha nodded and waited, tending her pans and checking the duck breast in the oven.

"Well the easy answer is as shallow as that. She's beautiful. I can't deny it, and the attention was flattering. I mean, I'm honest enough to admit that. Who wouldn't find it flattering when a woman half your age is throwing herself at you? And to answer the other question, yes. For, God, probably the last ten years or fifteen years—while we've been establishing the company—they've all been younger than me. And, yes, they've all been using me to some extent to try and further their careers. Either by a role I had to offer or by someone I could introduce them to."

"If you knew they were using you, why go along with it?"

"Because it was easy. For the most part it was fun, and it stopped me being lonely in a way I didn't have to commit too much of myself to while I was fully committed to making the company a success." She shrugged. "I used them every bit as much as they used me, I suppose." She pulled a face.

"What?"

"Makes me a bit of bitch really."

Sasha frowned and shook a pan. "Did you force anyone into your bed?"

"God, no."

"Did you make sleeping with you a condition of whatever role they were offered?"

"Before Vanessa I've never offered a role to a lover or an ex-lover."

"Did you pursue them or did they seek you out?"

"They sought me out."

"Then I think opportunist might be a better description to bitch."

Jac gurgled. "Gee, thanks."

"Sorry," Sasha said as she pulled plates out of the top oven and plated the food.

"What about you?"

"I've never slept with Vanessa."

"Funny," Jac said with a laugh. "I know that. Pam, was it?"

"Yeah, Pam."

"Was she older or younger?"

"Oh, right. Five years older."

"And other relationships?"

"Similar kind of thing, I suppose. Pam and Claire were both just a little older than me."

"Wow. So, long-term relationships all the way, hey?"

Sasha wanted to cringe. She really did sound boring. "Well, yeah." She scrunched up her nose and pushed a plate and cutlery across the island to Jac. "I was always looking for what my mum and dad had."

"Ah, perfect relationship set a high standard?"

She sat next to Jac and sliced into her duck breast, pleased with the perfectly cooked flesh that came away easily. "A little, I suppose, but it was more that they worked through their issues. They never hid the fact they had arguments or got pissed off with each other. But they never hid that they always made up afterwards and grew stronger from whatever it was. I think I was always looking for that in my partners."

She thought again about Pam. Had she ever really let Pam see all of her? No. Was that where they went wrong? They'd had never fought, but then Pam had let her hide in her books and never tried to bridge the gap. And Sasha had been more than content to carry on like that. Would things have worked out differently if Sasha had tried a little harder? If she'd opened herself up to Pam?

Maybe, maybe not. One thing she did know was that there was no going back, no do-over, no repeats. And she would have no more regrets.

"Well," Jac said, "looking for those kinds of relationships is not a bad thing."

"No, but it seems it was impossible to find."

"Was? You sound like you've given up looking."

Jac took a bite and hummed. Sasha could see the reflection of the flavours dancing over her palate so clearly on her face it was as though she'd spoken her pleasure aloud. "Oh my God, that is amazing." She pushed sauce over a mushroom and slid it into her mouth. "That sauce is just... Oh, I have no words."

"It's okay, then?"

Jac nodded and shovelled more into her mouth, waving her hands in front of her to stop conversation. Sasha chuckled and decided watching Jac eat was as enjoyable as the dish itself. *Had there been more customers like this, I might have just stayed at the whole cheffing game.*

When Jac finished the last bite, and crossed her cutlery on the plate, she leaned back on the high stool with a contented sigh. "That was amazing."

Sasha's cheeks warmed under the praise. "Better than potpourri?"

Jac groaned. "Did you have to remind me? I can still taste lavender on my tongue when I think about that." She shuddered, then swiped her finger through the last of the sauce on her plate and sucked the digit clean.

Swallowing down the surge of desire the act invoked, Sasha stood abruptly and gathered the plates, then stacked them in the dishwasher. She took refuge in pulling a tray from the fridge and sliding it into the oven, checking the timer as she closed the door.

"Eight minutes."

"Till what?" Jac asked, rubbing her stomach and sipping her wine.

"Chocolate."

"Cool. So, have you?"

"Sorry, what?"

"Given up?"

"Oh." She slid back into her seat and drank some more wine. "I'm not sure. I've been getting a lot of conflicting orders-slash-advice lately."

"You've lost me."

"Well, since I was pushed into the opportunity of a lifetime, I've been told to chase what I want, charge after my dreams, and have faith that all my hard work will pay off, while at the same time I'm being told I need to stop planning for the future and live in the moment. Not to worry about what tomorrow will bring and have some fun."

"Confusing."

"A little."

"And this confusion made you decide to give up looking for a partner?"

Sasha rested her head on one hand and glanced at Jac. "Maybe what I've given up is going into things with the same expectations as I always had before."

"How so?"

"Well, I guess I went on dates with the typical expectations. You know, 'get to a year and move in together, then that's it forever' kind of expectations."

"You gave it a year?"

"At least."

"A poor excuse for a lesbian."

"Oh yeah, and what's your timescale, Ms Stud?"

"Three to six months," Jac said quietly into her glass, making Sasha chuckle again. "And now you're open to what, a shorter timescale? No moving in together?"

"I don't know. Maybe just taking that living-in-the-moment piece of advice on this and seeing what happens. Not going into it with the expectation that one good date or one kiss will lead to forever. That it can be just that—a fun experience rather than an expectation."

"Can't it be both?"

"Not in my experience."

"That's sad."

Sasha glanced at the clock and went to remove their desserts from the oven. She sprinkled them with caster sugar and a dollop of whipped cream that she'd added sugar and vanilla to earlier before sliding one in front of Jac.

"Is this what I think it is?" Jac asked, rubbing her hands together like a giddy schoolgirl.

"Chocolate soufflé with Chantilly cream. Enjoy."

"Oh my God, I'm going to get fat if you keep cooking for me." She dipped her spoon into the treat and ate greedily. Sasha watched, letting the chocolate dissolve on her tongue—light and airy. The sweetness of the sugar offset the vanilla in the cream perfectly.

"I'm gonna get fat and I don't even care," Jac said before dropping into silence while she finished her dessert. When she finally dropped her spoon back to her bowl, she looked at Sasha and said, "Pam didn't even like this stuff?"

"Nope. Nada. Nothing chocolate whatsoever."

"She didn't deserve you."

Ducking her head, Sasha smiled shyly and pulled her lip between her teeth as she reached for Jac's bowl. Jac caught hold of her hand.

"Do you have any idea how much I want to kiss you right now?"

Sasha looked up. Jac's eyes were smoky, her pupils dilated, and her lips glistened in the light of the kitchen. Oh yes, Sasha had a pretty good idea how much Jac wanted to kiss her. Almost as much as Sasha wanted her to.

Pushing the crockery away from her, Sasha reached out to touch Jac's cheek. She ran her fingertips from the hairline at her temple to the edge of her jaw, just below her ear.

"Then why are you all the way over there?"

Inch by inch, Jac leant towards her. "I was waiting for an invitation."

Sasha slid the tip of her index finger along the underside of Jac's strong jawline to her chin and leant her weight on the forearm resting on the island unit. She licked her lips and watched Jac's pupils widen further. Her heart beat wildly, and part of her wished Jac would hurry up and get on with it while the other part exalted in the delicious anticipation. Her eyelids grew heavy and she knew her own gaze was as hooded with desire as Jac's was.

Trailing her fingertip down the length of Jac's neck until she got to the V at the base of her throat, she whispered, "Consider it sent."

Then Jac's lips were on hers; warm, wet, and wanting, tasting of chocolate and wine, which made them taste all the sweeter. Despite having expected the kiss, Sasha gasped at it, the passion and speed of it taking her by very pleasant surprise. Jac's tongue slid between Sasha's parted lips and inside, searching and exploring to her heart's content. Sasha was more than willing to oblige.

She wrapped her hand around Jac's neck, then up into her hair, indulging in the contrasting sensations of short-cropped hair prickling her palm one instant and silky-soft strands falling through her fingers the next. Wrapping her other arm around Jac's shoulders, Sasha shivered in delight. Jac's hands ran up her arms and slipped around her back, pulling her closer. The angle shifted, and Sasha realised Jac had climbed off her stool to position herself between Sasha's legs. She pulled her body closer.

Sasha tipped her head back to maintain the kiss, her mouth opening wider for Jac to plunder. And plunder she did. Her hands were in Sasha's hair, travelling the length of her back, caressing her throat, her cheeks, her jaw, and all the while her tongue sought to memorise every millimetre of Sasha's mouth. Her own tongue joined the dance, back and forth, until she whispered Jac's name on a breath.

Panting, Jac rested her forehead against Sasha's and wrapped her arms around her waist in a gentle hug.

Sasha leant into the embrace, snaking her arms around Jac's waist, eyes closed as she tried to absorb every sensation still flying through her.

"Wow," Jac whispered.

"Yeah." Sasha opened her eyes and was greeted by a shyly smiling Jac. Her cheeks were flushed, and her eyes shone with more than just desire.

"You okay?"

Sasha nodded.

"You sure?"

Sasha nodded again.

Jac's grin widened. "Can you speak?"

Sasha grinned too and shook her head.

"I've rendered you speechless."

"Hm, yeah, I'm lost for words."

"Ah, you found them again."

"Looks like it." She reached up to cup Jac's cheek, soft and gentle, and traced the contour of those high cheekbones. "I think I should say goodnight."

Jac's smile turned into a frown. "Really? It's still early."

"I know. But I think it's for the best." She stood, grateful her knees didn't give out.

"Are we…?"

Sasha waited but Jac didn't say anything. "Are we what?"

"Are we okay? Did I just ruin everything?"

"Not at all." Sasha smiled and placed a soft, chaste kiss to Jac's lips. "I'm working on that no-expectations thing, remember?"

"Oh, right." Jac's frown was still there.

Sasha smoothed away the crease between her brows. "I've never been the kind of woman to do more than kiss from the get-go, but I'm not sure how many more of those kisses I could take before I'd be willing to let you do just about anything to me, Jac Kensington."

Jac's smile slid slowly back into place. "Yeah?"

"Yeah, so, goodnight." She couldn't resist kissing those soft lips once more. "I'll see you in the morning."

"Goodnight, Sasha."

Glancing over her shoulder as she walked through the door, Sasha smiled at Jac as she leant against the island unit, hair all messy, shirt askew, a sloppy grin on her face. A sloppy grin that was tainted with Sasha's lipstick. *Grr, sometimes being a good girl is bloody torture.*

CHAPTER 16

Sasha watched as Jac drove away after dropping her home. The morning was bleak and wet, and a fog hung across the city, dampening everything it touched. Except Sasha's spirits. They were still soaring from the magical, wonderful, incredible experience of Jac's kiss.

No expectations, remember? Just enjoy it for what it was. Bliss.

She took a deep breath and hung her coat on the peg by the door, noting the man's tartan flat cap and heavy tweed coat next to her mum's. *A tartan flat cap? I didn't know Mr Hunt was Scottish.*

"Mum?"

Nip meowed at her from halfway up the stairs, her slanted green eyes watching her with intent. Sasha was just never sure if that intent was good or bad. Affection could sometimes take a dangerous turn with Nip. If she offered her belly for stroking, proceed with caution. She wasn't called Nip because of her fondness for catnip.

"Are you still waiting on breakfast?"

"Meow."

"I'll take that as a yes. Come on, then." Nip followed her into the kitchen, then wound herself around Sasha's legs as she filled the bowl with dry kibble, then emptied a pouch of gelatinous-covered chunks of what-might-be-meat on top—Nip's preferred presentation—and put it down on the floor for her. She crouched beside her and stroked her head while she ate, purring so loud she sounded like a small tractor engine humming away. "I wish you were always this easy to please, Nip. Now," she said, standing, "let's go see where our mother's at."

She looked up the stairs with trepidation, one hand on the bannister, one foot on the first step as she whispered to herself, "People have sex. They sleep in the same bed. And your mother's no different. She's a grown woman, and she's more than capable of making her own decisions about these things."

She took the second step and crossed herself. "Wait, which way round does that go again?" She closed her eyes and tried to picture it, but for some reason her mind had gone blank as she continued up the stairs.

"Oh, I remember that rhyme. How did it go again?" She cast her mind back for the childhood rhyme she and her friends had run around the playground chanting with their Catholic friends. "Erm, I think it was, 'spectacles, testicles, wallet, then watch'." She ran it through her mind a few times. "Yeah, that's it. But which side was the wallet, and which one was the watch?"

Unable to remember, she opted to go from left to right and hope God wasn't in one of his-slash-her moods today if she'd got it wrong.

She stepped onto the landing and froze.

"I think… Oh yeah, that's good." A man's voice drifted towards her from the partially open bedroom door at the end of the hallway.

Sasha screwed up her eyes and turned to start back down the stairs. Hopefully loud TV and lots of wine would help. "I'm not a prude," Sasha said to herself, "I just don't need to hear her doing that. I mean I never heard her and Dad going at it."

"Oh, that's definitely better without yer teeth in, lass."

The grunt that accompanied the sentence was enough to send Sasha running down the last steps.

"Must have been the other way around." She could hear the whimper in her own voice as she thought of her clearly fucked-up crossing herself. God must be pissed.

She grabbed her bag and coat and opened the door.

"That was too much for anyone to be subjected too." She shuddered and slipped into her coat as she made her way down the street to Bobbi's house, hoping she wasn't working. Thankfully, Bobbi's house was a house share and someone was always in, so at least she wouldn't be left out in the cold if Bobbi wasn't there. She checked her watch; it was only nine thirty in the morning. On a Saturday morning. Most of Bobbi's housemates would have been out the night before.

"Oh, well, I can knock loud. I'd rather piss off Bobbi's housemates than go back home right now."

She rounded the corner and spotted Bobbi as she was getting into her car.

"Bobbi! Hey, wait up!"

Bobbi leaned on the roof of her car. "Sorry, Sash, I'm on my way to Zumba class."

"On a Saturday morning?"

"I know, great. Right?"

"Right. I don't suppose I could get a ride with you, could I?"

"'Course. Jump in." Bobbi waited until they were on the A6 before asking, "You want me to drop you off somewhere?"

Sasha shook her head. "Nah, do you mind if I wait for you? I'll just get a coffee from the café or something."

"Nah, that's cool. How come you're not spending the day with your mum?"

She could feel her face contort.

"Uh-oh. You and Fleur are arguing again."

"No, she already has plans, that's all."

"Plans? Without you?"

"Yup. With Mr Hunt." Sasha shuddered again as the memory of those words echoed in her head.

"Who's Mr Hunt?"

"You remember the old guy that moved across the street from us a couple of years ago?"

"Erm…"

"Has the terrier that pees up your wheels."

"Oh yeah. Bastard."

"That's Mr Hunt."

"Okay. So, what're they doing? Why don't you just go with 'em?"

"Not going to happen. If they're looking for someone else to join them, I really don't want to know about it."

Bobbi looked confused as she merged into another lane, readying herself for the right turn across traffic.

"Well, I was ordered to stay out last night—for the second time—and this morning when I got home, there was moaning."

"Moaning?"

"And grunting."

"Grunting?"

"And a comparison between teeth and no teeth."

"No teeth?"

"Yes, and I think I need to bleach my brain."

"Because of teeth?"

"Fellatio, Bobbi. Keep up."

"I'm trying, but you're not making much sense."

"Don't make me say it any more clearly." Sasha watched Bobbi's face as she put together the pieces Sasha had laid out. Fleur. Mr Hunt. Moaning. Grunting. No teeth.

"Ew."

"Exactly."

"Why couldn't you have just said, 'Bobbi, trust me, you don't want to know?' I would have been cool with that explanation." She banged her hand to her head like she was trying to dislodge the image from her brain.

"No, you wouldn't."

"No, I wouldn't, but you could've tried."

"No, I couldn't."

Bobbi sighed and shook her head again and missed a gap in the traffic she would have been able to turn through. "Bitch."

"Not my fault."

They sat in silence while Bobbi waited for another gap. Sasha wrestled her mind onto a different topic and naturally landed on Jac and that perfect kiss. She could still feel the soft heat of Jac's lips on her own. Falling asleep last night had taken forever. All she'd been able to think about was Jac somewhere in the apartment sleeping. Did she sleep naked or was she wearing pyjamas? Should she take the opportunity and go find her? Clearly Jac would have been happy to continue where that kiss had left off.

Jac's shy demeanour when she'd poured coffee and handed her a plate of toast this morning had been a revelation. She'd expected Jac to be perhaps a little blasé about their kiss. Maybe even try for another, but no. Jac hadn't pushed it, and hadn't mentioned it, yet it had been acknowledged between them. The brush of Jac's fingers across the back of her hand when she'd taken the plate. The way she'd helped Sasha into her coat at the door. Even the brush of Jac's hand on her shoulder. All sweet, affectionate, and so damn endearing. If she wasn't careful, she'd be stepping firmly out of living-in-the-moment territory and straight into expectations.

When Bobbi parked, Sasha realised she'd managed to daydream her way through almost the whole twenty-minute drive to the leisure centre. "Sorry," she mumbled and climbed out of the car.

"It's all right." Bobbi locked it behind them, leading Sasha across the car park. "Come on, my class starts in ten minutes."

Sasha grinned. "Maybe I'll find a seat by the window and pull faces at you through the glass."

"Don't you dare."

"Why not? I need to have a little bit of fun today."

"If you do, I'll make you think about things that will scar you for the rest of your life."

"After this morning, you're too late."

"Wanna bet?"

Sasha planted her hands on her hips and lifted an eyebrow.

"Wonder how many of those little blue pills he has to take—"

Sticking her fingers in her ears, Sasha started singing, "La la la," as she ran through the door and away from Bobbi's evil laughter.

CHAPTER 17

THE SET WAS A TWO-SIDED representation of an auditorium, complete with a piano on the stage, hanging lights, and red-velvet–covered seats with their backs to the camera. Vanessa and Becca were on the stage, playing and replaying the scene so the cameras could get all the angles they needed for this first significant meeting between the two main characters. They needed shots of Becca at the piano and of Vanessa singing her heart out as she auditioned for a music professor in the audience. They weren't rolling the tape until the afternoon, but the camera guys were determined to know where everyone was to be positioned before they broke for lunch.

Jac was pleased with the attention to detail the set builders had gone to. It looked great and really captured the mixture of anxiety and hope that lingered in the air in every theatre Jac had ever set foot in.

She glanced over at Sasha and watched her scribbling some notes on her script, then pushing her hair behind her ear as she watched the actors on set, and then scribbling some more. Movement out of the corner of her eye drew her attention from Sasha to Bobbi as she wandered across the edge of the set, tripped over a power cable, and almost knocked over a fake wall. Jac rolled her eyes as one of the production assistants ran over to help her up and stabilise the wall before it toppled over and buried them both. Sasha seemed so lost in her notes that she didn't even look up at the commotion. Jac hoped she managed to hide the smirk she could feel tugging at her lips, and the distinct feeling she'd just won a point in a game she hadn't realised she was playing.

"Problem?" Jac asked, leaning close to her ear to make sure she got her attention.

"No, just a few notes where they might be able to put different emphasis to bring out some nuances when we start filming this afternoon."

Jac nodded, pleased that Sasha was being so diligent, and she wondered if her notes corresponded with Jac's own. "Can we get together at lunch and see if we're on the same page?"

"I'd like that." Sasha glanced up and smiled shyly.

Me too.

"Jac, I don't think this scene is working," Vanessa said from her position behind the desk on the set.

There was a mutiny afoot. "Here we go," Jac said to Sasha. "And why's that, Vanessa?"

Vanessa launched into her thoughts and motivations, and Jac found herself tuning out. The scene was working. Vanessa's ideas were simply over the top and too dramatic. But Jac had often found letting the actor try it one way, one time, was a quicker solution to ridding them of these interruptions and getting the actors to trust her vision for the project than to get into running battles with them every single day. So she let Vanessa try it her way and asked everyone for their feedback. The other actors, camera crew, sound techs, even the make-up and wardrobe gang, got to weigh in on it. Everyone agreed it was too much, and Vanessa's ideas were put away. Mutiny averted.

By the time lunch rolled around, Jac was more than ready for a break.

"Bitch," Sophie said as she slid sandwich bags across the conference table Jac, Sasha, Sophie, and Mags were now all seated around. The door was still open. Bobbi walked past the door…slowly. Once. Then again, slower. Sasha had her back to the door, and Jac knew they had things to discuss over lunch. Things that didn't involve the ever-present Bobbi and her cling-on tendencies. If it hadn't been getting in the way Jac could almost feel sorry for the woman. She was clearly not dealing with the changes in their friendship well, but she'd been the one to instigate it all. She'd been the one to enter Sasha in the competition—without her permission or knowledge—so what was with all this…clinging? Why couldn't she just grow up and get on with it?

Jac shrugged and tore open the bag to her new yorker club sandwich on rye. *My favourite.* "Someone was always going to try and make a power play. They always do. And as the newcomer who's supposedly dragged our arses out of the fire, it was always going to be Vanessa."

"I don't know how you do it," Mags said around a mouthful of her lunch. "The thought of working with any of my exes scares the living shit out of me. And let's not even think about how Julie would react."

"Well," Jac began, "Julie's always been a little on the, erm, possessive side. Hasn't she, hon?"

Mags wrinkled her nose. "It's all part of her fiery nature."

Sophie laughed. "Is that what you call it?" She turned to Sasha. "You'll meet Julie before long. She always turns up at some point early in the filming to make sure Mags isn't eyeing up any of the totty that's around."

"Totty?" Jac sniggered. "That's so degrading, Soph."

"Would you rather I call the girls you date eye candy instead?"

Mags cackled loudly. "One–nil." She scored a finger in the air and pointed to Sophie.

"I'd rather you call them women." She flashed a glance at Sasha to see how she was reacting to the conversation.

"I'm not sure they're old enough to be called women," Sophie said.

"Two–nil," Mags interjected.

Sasha was merely smiling softly as she ate, shaking her head a little as she watched the three of them bantering.

"Fine, whatever. Anyway, you said you had some notes on the script, Sasha."

With a nod, Sasha slid her copy across the desk to Jac. She covered her mouth with her hand as she finished the mouthful she was eating before reaching for her bottle of water and taking a sip.

"Not a lot, to be fair, just a few things. Mostly for Vanessa, actually. She was already going over the top before she tried her melodrama."

"Agreed." Jac glanced over the neat handwriting in the margins. "This is pretty much the same as what I had to feedback. Good." She nodded and smiled happily at Sasha as she slid the pages back to her. "Excellent."

Jac couldn't tear her gaze from Sasha. She wanted to reach across the table and kiss her again. Kiss her and not stop until Sasha was begging her for more. Sasha's cheeks were flushed, and the pink tinge to her olive complexion made her lips stand out more. Jac found herself licking her own lips as Sasha pulled that bottom lip between her teeth.

Somewhere in the room a phone rang and Mags said, "Sorry, need to take this or Julie'll be down here before we know it."

From somewhere, Jac managed to find the strength to look away from Sasha and sniggered at Mags scurrying out of the room, the soft "hey, babe" just barely audible as the door closed behind her. When Jac looked back, Sasha was bent over her script, seemingly determined not to look at Jac again. She quickly finished the last of her sandwich and stood.

"I could do with checking in with my mother. She had a doctor's appointment this morning."

"Everything okay?" Sophie asked.

"I think so. She just has to go for check-ups every so often because she's had cancer. Just to make sure everything's still as it should be."

"Well, give her my best, if you would. I've heard a lot about her, and I'm dying to meet her. She sounds like a real scream."

"That's one way to put it." She pushed open the door. "See you both back on set in a few."

Then she was gone.

And Sophie was staring right at her with that...that look on her face. The one that said, 'I know exactly what you're thinking, Jac Kensington, so don't even think about trying to lie to me.' That look.

"Something you want to tell me, Pan-pan?"

Want to tell you? "Nope?"

"Let me rephrase, then: what's going on between you and the lovely Sasha?"

Jac swallowed and twisted the napkin between her fingers. "Nothing's going on."

"Uh-huh."

"Really."

"Jac, I might be the baby of this particular trio, but I wasn't born yesterday. I saw those looks between the two of you. You're still blushing now. You, Jac Kensington, are blushing. You never blush. So spill."

Jac sat quietly, debating what to say.

"Did you sleep with her?"

Jac's head whipped up. "What? No."

Sophie's expression softened a little. "But you want to?"

"Have you seen her? Who wouldn't?"

Sophie folded her arms across her chest and waited.

Sneaky tactic. Sophie knew damn well Jac hated when she employed this particular method of interrogation. She sighed heavily. "Fine. Fine. We kissed after she made me dinner on Friday night, then she stayed at my place…"

"And?" Sophie asked.

"And what?"

"And what are you going to do now? When are you seeing her again?"

Jac glanced at the clock on the wall. "In about five minutes."

"No, outside of work. When are you taking her out?"

"I don't know. We haven't spoken about it or about anything, really. She said she didn't expect anything like that." And Jac still couldn't help but feel a little rejected.

"And you call yourself some sort of expert on women." Sophie shook her head.

"No, I never said that."

"Look, Casanova, it's simple. I don't know Sasha nearly as well as you do yet, but it's easy to see she's a grown-up. And I don't mean that in terms of age or anything like that. I mean she's a mature, responsible, sensible woman who isn't given to rash actions or flights of fancy. Am I right?"

"Yes," Jac agreed with a growl. *Damn it, why does Sophie always have to be right?*

"So she isn't like the kind of girls you've been used to over the past God knows how long. Right?"

"Yes," Jac said through gritted teeth. She couldn't deny her past, and she couldn't deny that Sasha was so different from them all.

"Do you remember what we talked about at your birthday party? The kind of woman you described?"

"Vaguely."

"I think it was a forty-slash-fifty-something woman with a brain, interested in women, single, and somewhat attractive." Sophie tapped her chin. "I think that was it. Sound about right?"

Sounded exactly right to Jac. "Maybe."

"Well, let me tell you that Sasha is all that and a hell of a lot more."

True.

"You want her, right?"

Jac nodded. There was no point denying it with Sophie.

"Are you sure you want to do this again?"

"Do what?"

"Repeat the same pattern."

"How am I repeating a pattern? You've just gone over all the ways Sasha's different from the women..." Sophie gave her the look again. "...okay, from the girls I usually get involved with. I'm breaking the pattern here."

"You work with her."

"Yes. So?"

"You worked with Vanessa."

Jac rolled her eyes. "And?"

"And while you didn't work with any of your other groupie girlfriends, you met them all through work."

"And?"

"And where did you meet Sasha again?"

Jac grinned. "At Velvet."

"Funny. You know what I mean. This is the pattern I'm talking about."

"Okay, okay. I know what you're saying, but this is different, Soph. I mean, she's different, and I'm different around her."

Sophie stared at her a for a long time. "Are you sure? She isn't like Vanessa. If this goes wrong, she won't work with you again. You were keen—"

"I'm still keen to work with her in the future. She's so talented, Soph. It would be an absolute crime not to work with her again. But I like her. I really like her." She swallowed hard, trying not to think about the feel of Sasha's lips against hers, the press of her body as she'd wrapped her arms about Sasha's shoulders. She failed. But she tried.

"On your head be it, then," Sophie said with a sigh.

Jac grinned.

"You know your usual tactics aren't going to work with her, right?"

"I don't have usual tactics."

"Sure you do. You wait for someone to approach you and throw themselves at you because they want something from you and are willing to prostitute themselves for it."

"Wow, that was cynical."

"Tell me I'm wrong."

"I can't. Doesn't mean I think 'prostituting themselves' is a bit harsh."

Sophie shrugged, totally unrepentantly. "If the whore fits."

"Again with the cynical."

"Sasha won't throw herself at you. She has too much self-respect to even contemplate sleeping her way to the top. And besides, you've already signed the contract with her."

"You know, you're a wonder for my ego."

"Grow up. She likes you. She wouldn't have kissed you if she didn't. So now all you've got to do is convince her you'd make the perfect partner for her."

"I think she already knows we'd be great together. That kiss was…well, I've never felt anything like it."

"Great. But I meant out of bed as well as in it. Sasha's the kind of woman who needs a partner, not just a good fuck."

Jac spluttered.

"And quite frankly, so do you."

"Thanks."

"Just telling it like it is. You've been getting laid forever, but you still haven't been happy."

"So what's your master plan?"

Sophie tutted. "Ask her out on a date, stupid."

"That's it? That's your master plan?"

"Yes."

"Just walk up to her and ask her on a date?"

"Yes."

Frowning, Jac said quietly, "I've never done that before."

"Seriously?" Sophie asked incredulously.

"Nope." Jac threaded her fingers together, wishing she had a cigarette to ease the edge to her nerves. "I mean, I've asked them out again, after the first one, but not for the first time."

Sophie lifted her eyebrows.

"Wow, I really did wait for women to throw themselves at me."

"Yup. Time to change tactics."

Jac's palms were sweating and her heart raced. Was this what she wanted? No, wrong question. She wanted it. She wanted Sasha, and not just for a moment. She wanted everything she'd seen Sophie and Lauren live over the past decade. She even sort of wanted what Mags and Julie had. Jac had never experienced jealousy, but when she thought of Sasha with her ex...her gut twisted uncomfortably and she recognised it for what it was. No, the question wasn't did she want this. What she needed to ask herself was, *am I ready for this?*

"I don't know if I can do this, Soph."

"Do what?" Sophie asked softly, empathy and compassion radiating in her eyes.

"How do I— I never worried if it didn't work out before. With Vanessa or any of the others, if it didn't work out, if they left, I knew I'd be okay. I knew."

Sophie reached for her hand. "And now?"

"It already feels different. I feel different."

"How?"

"For years I've watched you and Lauren, and I've wanted that. I've wanted what you two have. You complete each other."

Sophie smiled the smile she always did when she thought of her wife. It was soft and sweet, yet spoke of all the intimacies and secrets they shared.

"I want someone to look like that when they think about me," Jac whispered and pointed to Sophie's face. "I want to look like that when I think about someone else."

Sophie didn't play coy and ask what look she was talking about. Instead, she spoke just as softly as Jac had and said, "You've already started too, Pan-pan."

Jac's heart clenched as the words settled inside it. As the reality of what they meant cracked open like an egg and spilled its contents—messy, and fragile, but at its core life-giving. Nurturing. And fucking terrifying.

"I barely know her."

"Does that matter?"

Jac shook her head sadly. "I don't know if I can do it."

"What?"

She wasn't sure what she was striving for but couldn't seem to grasp. So she didn't say anything, letting the silence of the office wrap itself around them like a thick woollen blanket. As uncomfortable as it was comforting; itching at her skin even as it offered its protection.

"Trust," Sophie whispered into the quiet. It wasn't a question. It was simply a statement of fact. "You don't know how to trust."

And there it was. Right there. That one word that seemed so simple, so innocent, yet it had the power to hold everything together or destroy her completely.

"I understand, Jac. But you learnt to trust me. You learnt to trust Mags."

"I wasn't as broken then." Jac's voice cracked when she remembered those early days of their friendship. Days at university when they'd go out and get drunk and little by little she'd told them her story. The story of a child abandoned. A foundling. A sickly baby who had never been adopted. Grown up in an orphanage, never loved, never cherished, never trusted. And who had learnt only to trust that one day everyone inevitably walked away from her.

"I beg to differ, hon. I think you were more broken then. It was fresher. You were only just out of the orphanage, really. Now you know there are people out there who love you. You know you are lovable. Because I love you." Sophie tugged her into a tight hug. "I will always love you. No matter what." She kissed Jac's head. "You're my sister. My family. The family I chose all those years ago. And I will always be here for you. And those things you want, I want them for you too. We all do. Thirty years ago, you took a chance and let me and Mags into that beautiful heart of yours." She pulled back and put her hand over Jac's chest. "It paid off, right?"

Jac smiled and only realised tears were coursing down her cheeks when Sophie reached up to wipe them away.

"Yeah, can't get rid of you now."

Sophie winked. "Exactly." Sophie didn't break eye contact, letting her meaning truly sink in. And it did. If Jac wanted to find the love that Sophie and Lauren had, that Mags and Julie shared, she had to take another chance and be open to the possibility of it. She had to take the leap and trust herself to be vulnerable. To love if she wanted to be loved in return. She had to trust in Sasha.

Jac thought again of the look in Sasha's eye after that kiss, the way she'd moved around her kitchen, cooking for Jac, cleaning up afterwards, taking care of her. Jac couldn't remember the last time a lover or potential lover had tried to do that for her. And she wanted more of it. But more than that, she wanted to do that for Sasha too. And that was really new.

All she had to do was take a chance. *Faith, trust, and a little bit of pixie dust.*

"So how do I do this?"

Sophie laughed. "You walk up to her and ask her."

"Just like that?"

"Just like that."

Jac's hands shook at the mere thought of it. "What if she says no?"

"Then you wait a little bit, let her get to know you a bit more, then you ask her again. And again, and again, if you need to. What's the phrase? Faint heart never won fair lady?"

Jac nodded.

"Time to win your lady."

CHAPTER 18

SASHA LOOKED ACROSS THE TABLE to see Jac fiddling with her phone again even as she spoke to Vanessa and Becca about the scene they were about to do. She'd been on it all afternoon, and when she wasn't, she was distracted. But every time Sasha had asked what was wrong, she'd dismissed the question, declaring she was fine and that she was paying attention. She wasn't. On either score. And the blatant lie was pissing her off. If Jac didn't want to talk, all she had to do was say so. Not lie to her.

"Are you even listening to me?" Bobbi squatted beside the chair Sasha sat on as she watched the proceedings. The scowl marring Bobbi's forehead clearly told Sasha she was well aware of the answer to her own question.

"Sorry, Bobbi. I was miles away. What were you saying?"

"I was saying that I'm thinking of throwing a party round at mine on Friday." She pointed over her shoulder with her thumb. "You think this lot will be up for it?"

Sasha frowned a little at her. Bobbi was not usually one to throw parties at her home. Doing so in a shared place was often awkward, so she usually met up with people at the pub or club. "Are your housemates up for it?"

"If they're invited too, I'm sure they would be," Bobbi said as she shrugged. "I thought you could crash over at mine, then. Give your mum the house to herself."

Shuddering, Sasha gave an unenthusiastic nod of agreement. It might be nice to spend time with her new colleagues outside of the office-slash-set.

"Cool beans." Bobbi's grin was infectious. "And don't worry, I'll take care of everything." She gently squeezed Sasha's arm. "Later, gator."

Bobbi sauntered away just as Jac walked away from the conversation she was having with Vanessa and Becca and took her seat next to Sasha again.

"Everything okay?" Sasha asked.

"Yeah, yeah. Fine." Jac's voice was anything but convincing, and Sasha found herself even more annoyed. *If that's how it's going to be then, Jac. That's just fine.*

When Jac finally called an end to the day's rehearsal, Sasha jumped out of her seat and was out of the door before anyone could say anything to her. She walked quickly to the office Sophie had allotted her and slammed the door behind her. She needed to get her notes compiled and then she was out of here.

Sasha opened her laptop and set to work, pecking at the keys, and let the clatter of them soothe the anger that bubbled in her. Why couldn't Jac just say what was bothering her? Or at least that she didn't want to talk about it? Why lie and say she was okay? And why the hell was it bothering her so much? Jac was old enough to deal with her problems and frustrations on her own. She'd been doing it for some time, by all accounts. Sasha needed to stop stewing about it and just get on with her own shit.

She hadn't turned on the light to her office when she'd entered. The laptop screen and backlight keyboard were more than sufficient for her to get done what she needed. As a result, her darkened office gave her the perfect place to hide away while everyone passed by the glass wall, ignoring her seemingly empty office and continuing their business.

Jac was one of them. With Vanessa close behind her. Well, at one point she was, then she was practically climbing on her back, then grabbing her arm, her waist, anything she seemed able to get hold of. Jac was moving her arms quickly in a valiant effort to protect soft targets and grasp hold of the offending tentacle-like limbs. She couldn't hear what was said, but the look on Jac's face wasn't overly happy. Octo-Nessa's back was to Sasha, so she had no chance of knowing what was going through her mind. Well, other than the obvious.

Before she had time to think, Sasha was on her feet and opening the door. "Jac, we need to go over... Oh, sorry, Vanessa, I didn't see you there for a moment."

Vanessa stood up straighter and looked Sasha up and down before clearly dismissing her. She slid her hand up Jac's arm and curled it over her shoulder. Jac slinked away from her touch and towards Sasha's office.

"Sorry, Vanessa, Sasha and I have work to do. I'll see you tomorrow." Jac pushed Sasha gently back inside the office and closed the door behind her. "Thanks for the rescue," she said quietly.

"Welcome," Sasha whispered, her anger and frustration having melted when she'd seen Jac being pawed. "I wasn't sure if Octo-Nessa's tentacles had suckers to them, but I thought an interruption might give you the chance to escape."

"Octo-Nessa?"

"Yeah."

"Fitting."

"It was that or something to do with fungus because of the way she clings… I'm rambling now. Sorry. I'll be quiet."

Jac chuckled. "I think Octo-Nessa was for the best, then."

"Yeah." Sasha decided to take one last stab at getting Jac to open up to her. "Are you sure you're okay? You've been distracted all afternoon. I know we don't know each other all that well, but if something's wrong, I hope you know you can talk to me. I'd like to think we're friends and that you know I'll help if I can."

"I do know. And yes, I was distracted, but I am okay. I promise. I was just trying to figure out the best way to do something I've never done before."

"Oh, what's that? Something with the film?"

"No, not at all. Sasha, would you go on a date with me? I've been invited to the opening night of *Peter Pan* at the Opera House on Friday. I was hoping, well, I wondered if you'd accompany me?"

This is what had been distracting her all afternoon?

"A date?"

Jac nodded, face tilted towards the floor as she gazed at Sasha from underneath the fringe that hung over one eye. Sasha didn't even think. She brushed it back from her face, running her fingers through the soft strands and smiling gently into Jac's grey eyes.

"Yes, you, me, Peter, maybe dinner before."

"I'd love to."

Jac's grin was so wide Sasha was sure her cheeks must ache, but it didn't stop Jac taking hold of her hand, bringing it to her lips, and kissing it.

"Excellent."

Sasha swayed towards Jac, waiting for her to lean forwards and kiss her. God, how she wanted Jac to kiss her. Instead, Jac stepped back towards the door.

"I can't wait." Then Jac was out of the door and Sasha was left standing in the middle of her office, panting. Smiling. And contemplating her date with Jac Kensington in four days' time.

"A date." She touched the back of her hand, where it felt as though the imprint of Jac's lips were seared into her flesh. Sexy, hot Jac Kensington. "I need to go shopping." She grabbed her phone and hit Connect. "Bobbi, I need a shopping buddy."

"IKEA again?"

"Nope. Jac just asked me out on a date. I need something to wear to the theatre and maybe dinner too."

Bobbi was quiet for a few seconds, then she cleared her throat and said, "Cool beans. What're you going to see?"

"*Peter Pan.*"

Bobbi laughed. "Sounds fitting."

"What's that supposed to mean?" Sasha asked, a frown creasing her brow.

"Nothing," Bobbi said quickly. Too quickly. "Nothing at all. I guess we can go shopping on Saturday. Makes sense if you're staying at mine Friday night after the party."

"Party?"

"Yeah. We talked about it earlier, remember? Party at mine. Friday night. Asking the crew to come. You crashing at mine. Ring a bell?"

"Erm…yeah, yeah, it does now." Sasha smacked her palm against her forehead. *Shit. I totally forgot about that.*

"No need to sound so enthusiastic about it, Sash. I mean, I'm only your best friend. Throwing an epic party for the new crew."

This was not going to go over well. But Jac had tickets for the show. Opening night. Bobbi only mentioned this party idea a few hours ago. How much planning could she have already done for this impromptu get-together? "Yeah, listen, Bobbi, about that—"

"Oh no, I know that tone of voice."

"What tone of voice?"

"That one that says you're not coming to my epic party."

Sasha groaned. "I'm sorry, but the tickets Jac has are for Friday night. It's the opening performance."

"You're ditching me," Bobbi yelled incredulously.

"No, I'm not ditching you."

"Yes, you are. We had plans, now fancy knickers comes along, makes you a better offer, and you're dropping me like a fucking rock."

"It's not like that."

"I don't fucking believe this."

Bobbi, don't be like this. "Can't we do the party Saturday night instead?"

"I already spoke to all the crew and my housemates. Everyone knows it's Friday night."

Fuck. "Okay, but we've still got a few days to speak to everyone and let them know about a change in plans. I'll talk to everyone tomorrow."

"Yeah, don't worry about it. I think...I think I'll just stick with the plans I've already made."

"Bobbi, please—"

"No, you know what, Sasha? No. Just no. I've had enough. Since you started this new job, you never have time for me anymore. We work in the same fucking room, and we never talk. Production assistant isn't as fancy a title as director or producer, but you know what? I thought that kind of shit didn't matter to you. I thought you were better than that."

"You know that's not—"

"I'm not finished."

Sasha was shocked to silence at the venom in Bobbi's voice. She'd never heard Bobbi so upset, so angry. So she waited.

"I've been there for you every time you needed me. For years. When Pam ditched you, I was there for you. When your mum was ill, I was there for you. When you needed someone to talk to, to make you laugh, to hold you when you cried, it was always me. I was the one who was there for you. Now you've got your fancy new job and your fancy new friends, and I'm not good enough for you. I'm the one who gets kicked to the kerb."

"It's not like that, Bobbi. I'm sorry I've been busy with work. This is a huge opportunity for me. An opportunity that you gave me. And I'm sorry we haven't had as much time to spend together as we normally do, but this is all so different. And we're doing it together. Like you said, you're here with me every day, you're a part of the project too."

"I'm a glorified fucking tea boy!"

"That's not true—"

"No, you're right, it isn't. But that doesn't change anything else. I was there for you, Sasha, but that's not enough for you, is it? You have a good night with Jac and your kiddie play." Bobbi disconnected the call.

"Damn it." Sasha hit the Redial button, but the call went straight to voicemail. "Come on, Bobbi. Answer the damn phone." She hit Redial again. Then again. Bobbi didn't answer. Sasha was stuck. She didn't want to cancel the plans with Jac. It was opening night of *Peter Pan*. A first date with Jac. Despite being upset with herself for forgetting about Bobbi's party and the argument they'd just had, she couldn't stop the smile that spread across her lips at the thought of being on a date with Jac Kensington.

This was clearly about more than just one night of changing plans for Bobbi. Sasha tried to think back over the past few hectic weeks and remember what else Bobbi might have taken grievance with, but she was coming up blank. No, they hadn't had as much time to spend together, but it wasn't like she'd cancelled plans with Bobbi before. They never really made plans. They always just fell into doing whatever they did together. Bobbi would come around for tea and they'd watch TV or play Monopoly with Fleur—Fleur was always the cheating, swindling banker. She said she wanted the game to be as true to life as possible. Sasha couldn't remember the last time they'd had a game of Monopoly. Or the three of them had eaten tea together. Or watched TV.

"Shit. I've been such a bad friend."

Her annoyance flared. Yes, things had changed. But, damn it, Bobbi had started it all. Bobbi had entered her into the competition. Bobbi had encouraged her to pursue her dreams. Bobbi had even told her to pursue a little romance if that was what she wanted. And now she was pissed because Sasha was following her advice. Angry because she was grabbing these opportunities—every one of them—and running with them. Well, as her friend, shouldn't Bobbi be happy for her? Wasn't that what she'd do if the situation were reversed? Of course she would. But that meant ignoring the fact she'd ignored for the duration of their friendship. That Bobbi wanted more from Sasha than she was willing to give.

As much as Bobbi had wanted Sasha to be happy, Sasha knew that Bobbi had never truly prepared herself to see Sasha happy with someone other than her. Bobbi had as much as admitted it when she'd told Sasha how she expected them to enjoy seeing Sasha's triumph together. Bobbi had pictured it still as the two of them against the world.

Now there was Jac.

And Sasha wanted Jac in a way she'd never wanted Bobbi. And Bobbi knew it. She was jealous and trying to hold on to Sasha. That's what the party had been about. It was so obvious now. Why hadn't she seen it before? Why hadn't she realised it had been Bobbi's way of tugging her back into Bobbi's sphere? Simple. *I'm too tied up in this film and mooning over Jac.*

There was a simple solution to the problem. Tell Jac she couldn't go out with her on Friday. Go to the party and give Bobbi what she wanted. Simple. But in the end, would that solution really help Bobbi? Would it help her? It would upset Jac, that was for sure. She'd been so tentative in her invitation. So unsure of herself. She didn't want to do anything to disturb their budding relationship. She wanted that. But she wanted her friendship with Bobbi too. And the sooner Bobbi got used to the idea of Sasha with someone else, the sooner they could get their friendship back on an even keel. That was the only thing that made sense. Face the changes and find the new normal. This was always going to happen at some point...unless Sasha had stayed single for the rest of her life.

She groaned and flopped back in her chair, trying the phone one more time before giving up. "I'll talk to Bobbi tomorrow. Jac and I can go to the party after the play finishes."

The conversation didn't happen. Tuesday and Wednesday were a torrent of lingering looks, shy glances, and a desperate desire to get Jac alone, knowing that once she did, she wanted Jac to kiss her again, but equally uncertain if she was ready for it. If some of the looks Jac gave her were anything to go by, their next kiss was going to be something else. And Bobbi had been busy...no, the truth was she was ignoring Sasha. She was practically hiding. Sasha hadn't been able to talk to her to even say good morning since their aborted phone conversation. She hadn't responded to any of Sasha's messages or texts. Nothing. And by Thursday, Sasha was seriously pissed off. Christ, it was a genuine mistake. She hadn't booked the tickets. She hadn't made the schedule clash. But damn it, if it had been the other way around, Sasha knew damn well she'd be a lot more understanding. For God's sake, shit like this happened all the time. What was the big deal? All it would take was a few words to switch the party to the next night. It didn't need to be this big a drama. Not at all. She wanted her friend talking to her again and damn it, she needed a dress—something that was going to knock Jac's socks off—and she was running out of time.

In her distraction, she clattered one of the coffee mugs on the drainer in the staff room and managed to knock a glass to the floor. It shattered everywhere. "Shit." She bent down to start picking up the bigger shards.

"Here, let me help." Sophie bent down beside her, dustpan and brush in hand. "This'll do the trick."

Sasha smiled at her. "Thanks."

"You okay?" Sophie asked as she swept the slivers glinting in the light into the small pan.

"No. I need to go shopping, but I don't seem to have the time to do it and no one to go with me. Shopping alone is just so…meh."

"Shopping for…?"

"I need a dress for tomorrow night."

Sophie offered her a questioning look, and Sasha's cheeks heated.

"I'm going out with Jac."

"Who do you normally shop with?" Sophie asked, her lips spreading into a slow, satisfied smirk.

"Bobbi or my mum."

"And they can't this time because…?"

"Mum's busy with her new toy boy, and Bobbi's not speaking to me."

Sophie's eyebrows hiked up. "Right, well, then. You, me, this afternoon. Girly shopping trip! You've got so much gossip to tell me, it'll be awesome!"

"We can't this afternoon. We're still in rehearsals."

"Leave it to me. You just be ready to leave here when we break for lunch. We'll grab something to eat out after you've picked the perfect outfit."

"I don't want to let Jac down and leave all the work—"

"Seriously, Sasha, it'll be cool. You've been putting in way more hours at this stage than any other writer we've worked with. So, chill. We can take an afternoon off. In fact, let me see if I can book us in for facials later too."

"Might be a bit short notice."

"Leave it to me, honey. We're having a girls' day out!" Sophie clapped her hands together. "I can't remember the last time I had a girly pamper day! I can never get Mags or Jac to agree to a girly day out. Jac's pretty good when it comes to shopping, but mention a spa day and she starts to itch. Trying to get her to sit still for any length of time is a nightmare. As for Mags, she starts hyperventilating when you mention the word *shopping*. You should see her at Christmas. Before Amazon came along and saved her, she'd try to bribe me and Jac to do all her gift shopping for her."

"I can't imagine why." Sasha giggled and shook her head.

"I know, right? How on earth would their reputations survive?" She wrapped her arms around Sasha's back. "It's so good to have another woman around here to share these things with. One who enjoys the finer things in life. I mean, who doesn't enjoy a good pamper session, right?"

Sasha nodded and grinned. She couldn't imagine Jac in a spa with cucumber slices over her eyes, and mud pack on her face. No, that just wasn't Jac.

"Don't get me wrong, I love every little butchy bone in their bodies, but I miss having someone to talk about girly stuff with. And I can't wait to hear more about your mother and her toy boy. I'll even listen to your Bobbi troubles. Later." She squeezed one last time and was gone in the whirlwind of motion Sasha was quickly recognising as Sophie's trademark entrance and exit.

Well, this should be fun.

"Oh, hell no!" Sasha shouted out of the changing room. "I'm not wearing this, Sophie."

"Just try it on."

"There's nothing to try on. It's barely two scraps of fabric strategically placed." She turned the "dress" on the hanger. "Possibly strategically placed. I'm not going out to the theatre showing more than if I was wearing my underwear."

She pushed it through the curtain and into the waiting hand on the other side.

"Fine," Sophie sighed in resignation. "What else do you have in there?"

Sasha eyed the knee-length white fitted dress with capped sleeves, a plunging neckline, and no back. It was a beautiful dress. Not conservative, but just classy enough that she felt it was appropriate for the theatre and sexy enough for a date. She imagined walking up the steps to the theatre with Jac's hand on the small of her back—on the bare skin at the small of her back—and a delicious shiver raced up her spine.

"Just a sec. Last one."

Sasha quickly slipped into the dress, slid the zipper closed, and turned to get a look over her shoulder, eyeing herself critically. She'd lost weight over the past few years. A physically demanding job that didn't involve food being to hand at all times had certainly helped with that. The stress's impact on her loss of appetite hadn't hurt either. She'd been left with a lean but curvaceous body. Her skin was a little pale, but it was clear, and remarkably line-free. She ran a hand through her dark hair, checking around the temples and crown for those long, coarse, grey little bastards that kept sneaking in when she wasn't looking. They were well-hidden today, so all was well.

"Okay, let's see what her ladyship has to say about this one." Sophie, she'd found, didn't pull her punches when it came to frank—and brutal—honesty about the merits of any particular outfit. Sasha had a feeling that at someone else's expense, the commentary would be rather amusing, especially if you didn't like the person. However, directed at herself... Well, she knew if she found a dress Sophie was happy with, it was going to look bloody gorgeous.

"So? What do you think?" Sasha held her arms out slightly as she stepped out of the changing cubicle.

Sophie whistled. "Turn around."

Sasha did a little twirl, to another whistle, and bobbed a little curtsey as she faced front again.

"Perfect." Sophie stepped forwards and tugged a little on one sleeve, making it lay flatter against her skin. "Absolutely perfect."

"No disparaging comments at all?" Sasha asked, relieved beyond measure that they'd finally found one they were both happy with.

"Just that you're wearing it and not me." She winked. "Seriously, it looks stunning. Jac's going to fall over her tongue when she sees you tomorrow night."

"You think so?"

"I know so." She pushed Sasha into another turn. "Jesus Christ, I could almost go for you myself."

Sasha chuckled and gave her a push, then stepped back into the cubicle to change out of it. "I'm sure your wife would just love to hear you say that."

"She would if she were invited too."

Peeking her head around the curtain, Sasha said, "Ha-ha."

"Who said I was joking?" She winked again and leaned back against the wall.

"I know you're taking the piss, so you can stop trying to make me blush now."

"Why? It was working."

Sasha arched an eyebrow at her.

"Fine, fine." Sophie threw her hands up. "Tell me what's going on with Bobbi, then. She's certainly not seemed herself the last couple of days."

Sasha screwed up her face and sniffed. "She's pissed with me because I'm going out with Jac instead of going to her party on Friday night."

"She doesn't want you to get involved with Jac?"

"No, it's not that." *At least I hope it's not that.* "She'd already told me about the party before Jac asked me out. But I forgot about it, agreed to the date with Jac, and then when Bobbi reminded me, I suggested switching the party to Saturday instead of Friday so there wouldn't be a clash."

"So she thinks you've ditched her when something better came along."

Sasha groaned and reluctantly agreed. "Yeah, but I've been trying to talk to her since, to ask her about Jac and I coming to the party together after the play. You know, so I can do both things?"

"Something tells me that isn't what Bobbi wants either."

"No, probably not." *Change of subject. That's what's needed right now.* "Can I ask you a question?"

"Yes, Lauren would totally think—"

"No, silly. Why do you call Jac *Pan-pan*?"

"Ah. Well, it's a bit complicated, my lovely, and it's really her story to tell. It's something that goes back a long way. Why?"

"Just curious. Seems an unusual nickname."

"Well, Jac's a pretty unusual woman. Don't you think?"

Sasha nodded as "Puff the Magic Dragon" blared out of her bag, and Sophie's laughter grew as she fished it out and slid her finger across the screen to answer.

"Hey, Mum. What's up?"

"I need you to pick me up some stuff while you're out shopping."

"Okay, what do you need?" Sasha unzipped the dress with the phone wedged between her ear and shoulder.

"Hang on, let me read this out."

Paper rustled down the line. "You've got a list? Why don't you send me a text with it?"

"Right, I've got it now."

Clearly, she hadn't been listening to Sasha's end of the conversation.

"I need batteries, size CR2032."

"That's the wrong size for your hearing aid, Mum. I know which ones you need." She hung the dress back on the hanger and stepped into her jeans.

"They're not for my hearing aid, dear. I need CR2032. And I need four of them."

"Fine, what are they for, then?"

"None of your business."

Sasha rolled her eyes. "Anything else, Master?"

"Yes, I need a tin of that whipped cream. The squirty stuff in the can. You know the one I mean?"

"Yes. The stuff you said you'd never allow in your house? That stuff?"

"That's the one."

Sasha pulled her jumper over her head, then put the phone back to her ear. "Right, batteries and squirty cream. Anything else?"

"Nope." And then she was gone.

"Of course I don't mind being your slave, Mum. Love you too, Mum. See you soon, Mum." Sasha tossed the phone back in her bag and slung it over her shoulder, grabbed the dress on the hanger, and stepped out of the cubicle.

"I've always got tons of spare batteries for all sorts of things. What sort does she need?"

"CR2032."

"I think I have some back at the office. If memory serves, Mags uses them for her big calculator. Is your mum taking up algebra or something?"

"No idea. The last I knew, the only thing she'd taken up was Mr Hunt."

"Then that would negate the other use I know of for those particular sized batteries."

"I dread to ask, but I know you're gonna tell me anyway. I can see it in your eyes."

Sophie leaned close and whispered in her ear. "They operate my industrial-sized, battery-powered vibrator."

"I need to stop seeing these images in my head." Sasha slumped as she took another step. "You are an evil woman, Sophie Angel. Pure and sadistically evil."

"Hey, not my fault. I didn't ask you to buy me vibrator batteries. And what was the other thing again?"

Groaning, Sasha said, "Squirty cream."

Sophie stopped walking, then bent double with laughter. "Your mum's fucking awesome."

CHAPTER 19

JAC STRAIGHTENED HER TIE BEFORE she knocked on Sasha's door, glancing back over her shoulder to make sure the limousine she'd ordered for the evening hadn't disappeared. *Yeah, like limousines do, Jac. Fuck's sake, chill out, woman. You're behaving like you've never taken a woman out before. I'd give anything for a cigarette right about now. Well, maybe not anything but—*

The door opened and Jac was surprised when a guy with a shine bald head answered the door. He was fairly short, maybe five-foot-four, and had a considerable paunch. She'd never been great at guessing men's ages, but she'd put him at somewhere in his late fifties, maybe early sixties.

"Hello," he said cordially through a thick Yorkshire accent.

"Hi, I'm Jac. I'm here to pick up Sasha."

"Oh, right." He held out his hand to shake hers. "I'm Mike." He pointed over her shoulder. "Hunt. From across the road."

"Mike Hunt?" Jac asked, pronouncing the words very carefully.

"Aye, I'm a neighbour from across the road." He pointed again.

"You're Mike Hunt?" *That's got to be a joke. Who would call their kid Mike Hunt? If you're a bit sloppy pronouncing that H, you could be in big trouble.*

"That's right. Well, I say 'neighbour', but I'm more a friend of her mother's, truth be told." He nodded his shiny pate. "Yes, we're good friends, Fleur and I."

Jac nodded, mirroring his actions. *Okay.* Jac had no choice but to swallow the uncomfortable laughter bubbling in her stomach and run with it. *Thanks for the heads-up, Sasha.* "Nice to meet you," she said, shaking his soft hand. "Everyone needs good friends, Mr Hunt."

"Very true. So where are you and young Sasha off this evening, then?"

"To the Opera House."

He rubbed his hands together. "Lovely. That'll be right nice. What play are yer takin' 'er to see?"

"*Peter Pan.*"

"In't that a kiddie play?" he asked with a frown.

"It's a classic play." Sasha's throaty voice drew Jac's attention to the stairs. Her breath caught in her throat, and her brain short-circuited with far too many thoughts and feelings zipping through it. Her mouth had gone dry, and she wasn't sure if it was because her mouth was hanging open or simply because all the moisture in her body had fled to parts south of the border. Stunning didn't begin to describe the way Sasha looked. Her hair was coiled in a twist at the back of her head. Smoky eyes gave her a sultry look, highlighted by the deep wine-coloured lipstick, and the figure-hugging dress.

"My, my, my, don't you scrub up well, lass." Mr Hunt's slightly nasal voice cut through Jac's appraisal and her disjointed thoughts, and Jac wanted to slap him for the backhanded compliment.

"She always looks beautiful, Mr Hunt. Tonight she just happens to look even more so."

"Aye. That's what I said."

Fleur appeared out of the door to the living room and used a crutch to limp to Sasha. She looked quite unsteady, and her eyes watered as she held Sasha in her arms. "Have a wonderful time, darling."

"I will, Mum."

Fleur pulled back, looking into Sasha's eyes while she stroked her cheek. "Love you."

"I love you too."

Sasha's eyes were damp, glistening with unshed tears as she stepped away from Fleur and wrapped her hand around Jac's bicep, leaning over to kiss Jac's cheek. "Love the tux," she whispered. "Looks wonderful on you."

"Thank you." Jac beamed. "You really do look absolutely stunning, Sasha. Thank you," she said as she led her out of the house and into the waiting limousine.

"What for?"

"For agreeing to be my date for the evening." Jac handed her one of the glasses of champagne she'd had the driver prepare for them while she was waiting.

"Then shouldn't it be me thanking you?"

"For...?"

"For asking me."

Jac sipped her drink, settled back in her seat, and chuckled. "Something tells me we could be here all night at this rate."

"Hm. Probably."

"So let's agree we're both grateful and both happy to be here."

"Sound like a very good plan, Ms Kensington." She held up her glass for a toast. "To the night's adventure."

Jac touched her glass gently to Sasha's. "To all our adventures," she said and hoped Sasha understood every aspect of what she meant in those four words. The darkening look in her eyes told Jac she just very well might.

The touch of Jac's hand on the small of her back was even more delicious than Sasha had imagined it would be as she was ushered up another set of stairs and into one of the boxes to the right-hand side of the stage. The Corinthian column separated their box from the next, and the highly polished marble reflected the lights shining all around them. The huge cantilevered balconies were filling up around them. The sound of hushed voices and shuffling feet against the plush carpet grew despite the air of reverence in the grand old hall.

"What can I get you to drink?" Jac asked, her mouth close enough to Sasha's ear that her breath ruffled the tiny hairs on the back of Sasha's neck. Her hand was warm on Sasha's upper arm.

"You don't have to go back to the bar. It was bedlam down there."

"There's a smaller bar, just through those doors." Jac pointed over her shoulder. "It won't take long at all. Wine?"

"Hm, white, please."

"Sure, anything else?"

"No, thanks."

"Okay, I won't be a minute."

Sasha smiled and covered the hand on her arm with her own. "Better not be."

Jac's throat worked as she swallowed and almost tripped up over her chair while backing out of their booth.

Sasha had been to the theatre many times, but she'd never been seated in one of the boxes before. She'd always been in the cheapest seats she could find, way back in the nosebleed section, the ones where you couldn't really even tell if the actors had faces. Well, not without binoculars, anyway. So this was a real treat.

The theatre was an old one, opened originally in 1912, and holding seats for almost 2,000 people, for all but a five-year period from 1979 to 1984 when it was a bingo hall, it had been a fixture of Manchester's cultural scene. And the musicals it had staged were beyond magnificent. Chandeliers, carved friezes, and massive ionic columns held together a symmetrical auditorium that was truly a work of art.

How many times had she been there before? With her mum or Bobbi, even with Pam—once—watching one of the hundreds of shows she'd seen in the past. But she felt like she was seeing everything for the first time. Part of her wanted to send Bobbi a quick text, maybe a selfie of her with the stage behind her, but she couldn't do that. Yes, she'd fucked up, but Bobbi was taking this way too far. The punishment did not fit the crime, and Sasha was more than a little hurt. Bobbi was her best friend. Shouldn't she be happy Sasha was taking her advice, after all? Grabbing life by the scruff of the neck and taking a few chances? Getting out of her comfortable existence, just like Bobbi and her mother had been telling her to do? Everything had been great until she'd actually started doing that, doing what they told her she should do.

"Take the job, Sasha. Grab on to it." Then Bobbi walked out because she wasn't there anymore. Sasha wasn't stupid. She knew the real reason Bobbi didn't want to go back to Serenity—even if Bobbi didn't. She also knew the real reason behind Bobbi's reaction to this date. It wasn't just about her not being at Bobbi's party. It wasn't even about her being out with Jac. It was purely that she was out with someone—anyone—who wasn't Bobbi.

Sasha had known everything was going to change when she'd grabbed hold of this chance of a lifetime. And no matter how much or how often Sasha had told Bobbi that, Bobbi hadn't believed her. She hadn't comprehended just how much was going to be affected. Now Bobbi felt abandoned. And

Sasha was sickened by how much her friendship with Bobbi was suffering. Tomorrow, she promised herself, she'd get hold of Bobbi tomorrow and apologise again. Maybe go and help with the after-party cleanup. Surely that would get her off the hook and set things right again.

"One glass of white wine for you," Jac said as she entered their box again.

Sitting back in her chair, Sasha took the glass with a broad smile. "Thank you."

Jac sat beside her as the lights dimmed. The noise settled to silence as darkness crept through the grand hall. She shuffled her chair closer to Jac's until their shoulders were touching and she could feel the heat of Jac's body against hers. But it was Jac who took her hand and threaded their fingers together like they belonged together; palm to palm, fingers entwined, thumb brushing across the back of Sasha's hand. It was perfect. In the dim light of Emergency Exit signs and the twinkle of stage lights from behind the curtain across the old proscenium arch, Sasha lost herself in Jac's grey eyes as they reflected the stormy passions within. And in that instant, she knew she could spend forever figuring out each emotion as it flittered through Jac's mind.

No expectations, she reminded herself. *Just enjoy the moment, and let tomorrow take care of itself.*

The narrator's voice cut through the auditorium and drew their attention from each other and in to the stage. "All children, except one, grow up…"

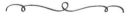

Jac almost stumbled down the steps towards the waiting limo, laughing, her hand still entwined with Sasha's as Jac helped her into the open door of the car. The one the driver was already holding open for them. Sasha didn't care; the gesture was sweet, and it meant she got to keep hold of Jac's hand. Something she wasn't planning on ever letting go of, if she had any say in the matter.

She laid her head back against the headrest and sighed, while Jac climbed in behind her—their fingers still entwined.

"Sasha?"

"Hm?" She turned her head and looked at Jac.

"I don't want to be presumptuous or anything, but I… Well, I don't want this evening to end." She swallowed and carried on. "Not yet, at least. Would you like to go for a drink before I take you home?"

Jac seemed as though she couldn't meet her eyes as she asked, and Sasha wasn't sure how forward she should be. She didn't want the evening to end either. At all. Was Jac on the same page? Would Jac be offended if she asked her to take her back to Jac's apartment instead of going for a drink somewhere? Would Jac think she was easy if she asked Jac to take her to bed? To kiss her, and hold her, and to make love to her? Did she care?

She rubbed her thumb across the back of Jac's hand and waited until Jac was looking at her. She could see it in Jac's eyes then. The desire. The longing. The want. Sasha saw it all and more.

Sasha leant forwards, brushed her lips across Jac's cheek, and whispered in her ear, "I don't want to go home tonight." She pulled back just enough to see Jac's eyes again. She trailed her finger down Jac's jaw, flicked her gaze to Jac's lips, and waited for her words to sink in.

It took longer than she'd expected. So much so that she was beginning to wonder if Jac was going to ignore them. She started to pull back slightly. "I'm sorry. Have I read this situation wrong?" Her voice was shaky, quiet, barely a whisper as it left her lips, but the words just wouldn't stop coming. "It wouldn't be the first time. There was a girl in college—Carla—the epitome of a baby butch, one fateful spin of a bottle, and probably the clumsiest kiss in the history of kisses. I mean it was all teeth and tongues. But it made everything so clear. It was girls for me all the way. Then the next day, when I was sober with a touch of a hangover. Okay, a lot of a hangover. Like enough to slay dragons. I told Carla how I felt. And she told me to fuck off, never darken her door again, and that she was straight. I told her she most definitely wasn't straight. Only to have Carla clarify that she was straight and didn't give a flying fuck what I—"

Jac put her fingers to Sasha's lips, stopping the purge of words Sasha hadn't been able to figure out how to stop on her own.

"Are you sure?" Jac whispered against her cheek, and Sasha could barely remember what the question referred to. "You said you don't want to go home tonight. Are you sure?"

Sasha nodded. She was definitely sure.

Jac picked up the handset that would let her speak to the driver without shouting and directed him to Jac's apartment block.

CHAPTER 20

JAC'S HANDS SHOOK AS SHE helped Sasha out of her coat and hung it on the peg beside her own. She turned towards the kitchen area.

"Can I get you something to drink?" She pulled a face, disgusted by her own lack of originality. *Pull it together, woman, it's not like you've never had a woman in your apartment for the purposes of sex before.* Jac frowned at the thought. The idea of using Sasha for sex seemed…unseemly. It didn't sit right with her. It wasn't that she didn't want Sasha. God, she wanted Sasha. *Need* was almost a better term for the feelings and urges coursing through her. No, want, desire weren't what made the idea of having sex with Sasha seem wrong. It was that she wanted it to be *more* than just having sex with Sasha.

For the first time she could remember, Jac wanted to touch more than just a woman's body. She wanted to touch all of Sasha. And it terrified her.

"Glass of water?" Sasha asked.

Jac nodded, having forgotten the question she'd asked until Sasha reminded her. She filled two glasses and approached Sasha shyly, handing one over.

"You okay?" Sasha frowned.

Jac nodded, unable to think of anything to say.

"You sure?"

She nodded again.

Sasha took a big gulp of her water and put the glass on the counter beside them. She took hold of Jac's free hand. "Then why do you look like Bambi's mother about to get shot?" She smiled, the kind of smile that was at once reassuring and yet somehow still alluring.

And still Jac couldn't speak.

Sasha frowned and took a step away, dropping Jac's hand. "I'm sorry, I thought…" She took a deep breath. "I didn't mean to make anything awkward. Sorry." Sasha hitched her thumb over her shoulder towards the door. "I'll see you at work on Monday." Turning on her heel, she headed towards the door. The click of her heels on the wooden floors finally penetrated Jac's brain and spurred her into motion. Placing her glass on the counter next to Sasha's, she crossed the floor in long strides, catching up to Sasha as she reached for her coat.

"Don't go," she murmured before she caught Sasha's arm and spun her around. She used the momentum to pin Sasha's back to the door and locked on to her lips with a heated kiss that stole the breath from them both. Sasha's gasp of surprise gave Jac the opportunity to slide her tongue into Sasha's mouth, to tease and explore, to dance again with Sasha's tongue in a way that promised of all the ways in which she hoped to touch Sasha.

Sasha's hands ran up her back, and her fingers delved into Jac's hair. The gentle scrape of her fingernails over Jac's scalp was driving her crazy.

She tore her mouth from Sasha's and managed to whisper in her ear, "I'm sorry I froze. I just want you so much I lost all the words I wanted to say to you." She planted her lips below Sasha's ear, then licked the skin, tasting her. Sweet and salty, and wanting.

Sasha was panting, her hands never still as they roamed Jac's back, shoulders, neck, and scalp. Jac's hands had a mind of their own as they teased the skin at the small of Sasha's back, loving the way that touch made Sasha's hips roll towards her. Jac wasn't sure if she was trying to escape it or demand more.

"What did you want to say?" Sasha asked and planted her lips on Jac's neck, licking and sucking at the skin.

Jac groaned and pressed her body closer to Sasha's. "I wanted to tell you that you're beautiful." She ran a finger up Sasha's spine until she couldn't get any higher for the door she had Sasha pressed against, so she trailed her way back down again. Gripping Sasha's backside, she pulled her flush against her body. "I wanted to tell you that I've never wanted a woman the way that I want you."

Sasha stiffened against her, and she pulled back far enough to see Sasha's eyes, already knowing she'd see self-doubt there.

"It's true." She kissed the corner of Sasha's mouth, softly, sweetly. "I know what's going through your mind. That that was a line, and that I've used that on other women, younger women. Right?"

Sasha closed her eyes and let her head fall back against the door as she nodded.

"Well, I haven't." She stepped back, took Sasha's hands in hers, and tugged her to the couch. When they were sitting side by side, Jac shifted to face Sasha. "I know this is our first real date, and that this is really, really early for this, but we've spent a lot of time together, right? I mean, with working together and dinner and everything."

Sasha nodded.

Jac took a deep breath. *Time to jump.*

"Okay, so I'm just going to lay it all out here, and I know you said you weren't looking for anything with expectations or anything like that, and I know I don't exactly have the best history when it comes to asking you to give me the benefit of the doubt but...well, there's something here, right?" She waved her hand between them. "And I don't just mean this chemistry that has me wanting to take your clothes off and lick every part of your body."

Sasha swallowed heavily.

"I mean, I do. Want to do that, I mean. But that's not all there is here, is there?"

Sasha's voice was thick and heavy with desire and emotion when she finally asked, "What do you think is here, Jac?"

Jac kissed her softly, then whispered, "Expectations." She slid her hand around the back of Sasha's neck and held her head in place as she kissed her again. "Promises." Jac traced Sasha's bottom lip with her tongue, then captured the moan Sasha could no longer contain. "All the things I've never wanted with anyone else before."

Cupping Sasha's cheeks, she worshipped her mouth, pouring everything into the kiss that she couldn't find the words to utter.

"Do you really mean that?" Sasha whispered, fingers trembling against Jac's cheeks. "Because I could really fall for you, Jac."

"I'll catch you." Jac's voice was just as quiet, just as reverent.

Sasha smiled, fingertips tracing Jac's lips. "I think I might prefer it if we fell together."

Jac kissed the tip of the finger sitting on her lower lip, then held out her hand. "Then I think I know a pretty good place for us to land." When Sasha put her hand in Jac's, she tugged her down the hall. "Together."

Jac's bedroom was lit only by the moon and the street lights shining below them, but shining through two fully glass walls, it gave them more than enough light to see. Sasha's gaze landed on the huge bed that dominated the room. Decorated in differing shades of black, grey, and white and accents of startling emerald, it looked soft, luxurious, and inviting. Just like Jac's hands in hers.

Was this really happening? Was Jac really real? Like *really* real, as in she wanted more than just a night of passion between them? Really real in that she was looking to the future with them in it? That kind of real. Did Jac really mean all those wonderful promises she'd just made?

Sasha didn't know. But as Jac let her tuxedo jacket fall from her shoulders, Sasha had the presence of mind to acknowledge one final thing before thought would be vanquished for the rest of the night. She knew herself enough to know that if Jac didn't…it was already too late to save herself from falling for Jac.

She was rooted to the spot as Jac worked the knot of her tie and pulled it from around her neck, then unfastened the button at her throat before sliding the suspenders down her arms to hang at her waist. Jac toed off her shoes and padded towards Sasha, socks brushing the plush fabric with each tentative step.

Sasha licked her lips and lifted her hands, intent on releasing the clasp that held her hair at the back of her head.

"Let me do it," Jac requested.

"Okay." Sasha let her hands fall back to her sides. Jac's hands on her shoulders gently turned her until her back was to Jac's front. Jac's lips on her neck were warm and soft, but they ignited a fire in Sasha that had only one means of control. The fingertip trailing the length of her spine, from neck to buttocks, only served to drive Sasha's temperature higher.

"Beautiful," Jac whispered before planting kiss after delicious kiss along her hairline and neck, and under her ears, finally nipping at her earlobe while her fingers continued to tease Sasha's back, her arms, and her arse.

"So beautiful," Jac breathed into her ear. "I could worship you like this all night."

Sasha whimpered and reached back, resting her hands on Jac's strong thighs. "As lovely as this is, Jac, I hope you plan to do a lot more before the night's through." She'd never heard her own voice sound as deep or hoarse as it did then, but the shudder that ran through Jac's body left her in no doubt as to the effect it had.

"God, the things your voice does to me."

Sasha smiled as Jac's hand slid up her arm and across her shoulder and neck until she took hold of Sasha's chin, tipped her head to one side and concentrated her lips about Sasha's exposed throat.

"Since the first time we spoke on the phone, I get turned on whenever you speak to me."

"Really?" Sasha asked with a soft chuckle.

"Every single time."

"Mm," she moaned when Jac found a particularly sensitive spot under her ear. "Good to know."

"Cataloguing secret weapons already, Ms Adams?" Her fingers brushed the button that fastened at the back of Sasha's neck. "May I?"

"Yes," Sasha said, her raspy voice little more than a sigh. The tension in the fabric across her chest changed when the button was released, and Jac's finger brushed the material aside and covered the newly exposed skin with her lips and tongue.

Her breath caught in her throat. "I think I need all the help I can get with you, Ms Kensington."

Jac quickly released the clasp in Sasha's hair, letting the heavy strands fall before running her fingers through them from root to tip, then she kept going, skimming Sasha's back again to the zipper at the bottom of her spine. Sasha could feel her toying with the zipper tab, lifting and lowering it over and over, seemingly intent on driving her crazy.

"Is this how this evening is going to go?"

"How's that?"

"Teasing me until you drive me insane?"

"Not at all." Jac slowly lowered the zipper, releasing one noisy tooth at a time.

"I don't believe you." Sasha moaned as the fabric finally gave way over her hips and Jac's fingers delved beneath the fabric to cup her backside and spun her around so they were face-to-face again.

"You don't?"

Sasha shook her head, reached up to grasp Jac's, and pulled her down for a searing kiss. She needed to feel Jac's body respond to her as much as she responded to Jac. The need to feel skin on skin was becoming overwhelming. Sasha ran her hands down Jac's chest, skimming over her breasts and down her stomach, tugging the shirt out of her pants.

"How much do you like this shirt?" she asked breathlessly.

"Erm, it's okay, I guess. You don't like it?"

Sasha slid her fingers between the buttons and grasped the thin material. "I'll like it a whole lot better on the floor." She pulled hard, popping the buttons and dragging it off Jac's shoulders in one swift move, then fastened her lips to Jac's neck, her shoulders, licking across her collarbone and tossing the shirt across the room. She noted a thin white line down the centre of Jac's chest, directly over her sternum, but her attention was drawn away quickly with the discovery that Jac wasn't wearing a bra. Her small breasts sat high on her chest, nipples already tight with arousal.

Jac stared at her incredulously. "Bloody hell."

"I'll sew the buttons back on in the morning."

"Forget about the buttons."

Sasha found the buttons on Jac's pants, worked them deftly, and she sighed when they slid down Jac's thighs and pooled at her feet. She stepped back far enough to ease her dress down her arms and over her hips, then stepped out of it as it hit the floor and kicked it out of her way as she stepped closer into Jac's space.

They both groaned at the sensation of skin touching skin. Lips met again in an increasingly passionate kiss that had them both desperate for more.

Jac stooped and wrapped an arm under Sasha's knees, then lifted her off the ground. Sasha wrapped her arms around Jac's shoulders and broke the kiss.

"Put me down before you hurt yourself."

Jac crossed the floor and lowered her to the bed. She stalked across her body like a hunter approaching its prey. Sasha couldn't wait to be devoured. She closed her eyes and gasped as Jac wrapped her lips around Sasha's nipple.

"Sorry, couldn't resist."

"Don't be sorry. Do it again."

Jac nuzzled between her breasts, licking the skin around each. "I will when I'm ready."

"Again with the teasing?"

Jac chuckled, and Sasha felt it through every cell in her body as much as she heard it. "You love it." Jac continued to press kisses and licks around the pliant flesh of Sasha's breasts, never getting close enough to her nipples to truly satisfy, but more than close enough to continue the tease.

Sasha did, but she wasn't about to admit that. Not right now, anyway. "It's already cost you a shirt, darlin'. What else are you prepared to sacrifice while driving me mad?"

Jac left her place at Sasha's breasts and hovered directly over her face. All trace of playfulness was gone. Instead, Jac stared at her, baring her soul. "No sacrifice. I'd gladly give you anything and everything you want."

"Oh God." Sasha slunk her arms about Jac's neck and pulled her body down on top of hers, wrapping her legs about Jac's hips so she was encased in a full-body hug. Her kiss wasn't ravenous as it had been moments before. Now Sasha was more than content to let Jac lead them this time. She trailed one hand down Jac's back and slid it inside her boxers while using the other to ease Jac's head back far enough to look into her eyes again. "Then show me madness."

Jac grinned and started to slide down her body again, licking circles around each breast until she was within a hair's breadth of Sasha's nipple.

"Just remember, Jac."

Jac looked up, her breath fanning across the top of the aching tip.

"It's my turn next."

Her grin was wicked as Jac opened her lips and pulled the taut flesh into her mouth.

"Jesus," Sasha cried and threaded her hands in Jac's hair, holding her, pulling her more firmly against her chest. She wasn't even naked yet, and she'd never been more aroused in her life. Her pussy throbbed, aching for Jac's touch. But she knew that Jac would not be rushed. Not tonight. So

Sasha tried to distract herself from her aroused body being played like an instrument in the hands of a maestro by caressing every inch of Jac she could reach. She loved the cleft at the side of her buttocks when her hips flexed. Could barely wait to run her tongue over the biceps that held Jac's weight above her, flexed as she squeezed Sasha's breasts, or gripped her thigh and pulled it higher up Jac's waist. Jac had to be able to feel how wet she was against her stomach.

Jac ran one finger along the elastic at the side of her knickers and whispered in her ear, "Think it's time for these to go yet?"

Sasha nodded, her motor functions no longer capable of producing speech.

Kneeling back between Sasha's knees, Jac shimmied out of her boxers first, then reached for Sasha's sodden underwear.

"So fucking beautiful." Jac leant forwards and kissed Sasha's knee, then hooked her hands beneath them and lifting them to wrap over her hips again. "I love feeling your legs around me like this."

Sasha hooked her heels over Jac's backside and pulled her in closer. They groaned as the wetness of Sasha's centre came into contact with Jac's abdomen as she ground against her, seeking pressure, friction, release.

"Oh no you don't. Not yet." Jac rose on her knees, and Sasha wasn't able to keep herself wrapped about Jac's body. She whimpered as she landed back on the bed and waited—impatiently—for Jac to continue with her plan.

Supporting herself on one hand and her knees, Jac used the other to pinch Sasha's nipples to tight peaks, eager for the lips that descended on them. Sasha took advantage of the slight space between their bodies to further her own explorations. Cupping Jac's breasts and twisting her nipples to attention, she tried to urge Jac up so she could get one in her mouth, but Jac was having none of it. In a lightning-fast move, she grasped Sasha's hands and held them over her head. Grasping her wrists in one hand, she used her body weight to keep them pinned in place before turning her attention back to Sasha's breasts.

"Please, Jac, let me touch you too."

"Soon," she promised. "But if you touch me now, it'll be over far too quickly." Jac looked up at her, the truth of her words shining clearly for Sasha to see.

Sasha growled but nodded her assent. "Next time, stud." Even she could hear how gravelly her voice sounded, and she felt Jac tremble.

"If you ever need a change of career, you could make a fortune as a phone-sex operator." Jac's lips covered her stomach and nibbled around her navel. Her hands slid around the back of Sasha's raised thigh and under her buttock, her fingers dipping low enough to slide through the abundant wetness she'd provoked.

"I'll bear that in mind," she said with a chuckle. Then closed her eyes at the first touch of Jac's fingers brushing so lightly across her pubic mound that she almost thought she'd imagined it.

"I have to taste you." Her breath wafted across Sasha's body, teasing the hair across her most sensitive folds. "May I?"

"God, Jac, yes. Anything. Just touch me, please."

"Yes, ma'am."

The first caress of Jac's tongue was like liquid silk gliding over her, covering fractions of the skin she wanted covered, but still engulfing her. She bit her lip to keep from crying out as Jac's fingers parted her labia and blew cool air across the burning flesh.

"Look at me, Sash. Let me see those beautiful eyes of yours."

Sasha struggled to open her eyes and stare down her body. Jac was watching her, cheeks flushed, eyes bright, lips shiny with Sasha's arousal.

"Watch me while I lick you." She dragged her tongue up the length of Sasha's slit, her gaze never leaving Sasha's. "Watch me while I make you come."

"I don't know if I can," Sasha replied honestly. The sight of Jac between her thighs, combined with the sensation, was the most erotic thing Sasha had ever experienced. "I'm so close, Jac."

Jac's lips fastened around her clit and sucked. Sasha fought hard to keep her eyes open as the muscles in her belly and thighs contracted.

"You can," Jac whispered around the mouthful of Sasha's flesh, then set to work with fervour.

Jac's lips, tongue, nose, cheeks, all worked to drive Sasha higher. Sasha's thighs clenched around Jac's head until Jac pried them open and held them wide with her elbows. With her hips bucking, reaching higher, Sasha searched for that tiny bit more friction that would let her come, that one extra ounce of pressure Jac held just out of reach. Jac pulled her clit between her lips, sucking hard as her fingers circled Sasha's opening, dipping in just enough to draw out a little more of her arousal, paint it around her clit, then suck it clean again.

Sasha clawed at the sheet beneath her hands, desperate for purchase as Jac entered her for the first time; one finger, then two, sliding in and out of her slick channel. She could feel herself trying to grip on to them, drag them in deeper, harder, longer. Needing Jac to fill her, expand her, to complete her.

The spasms began in earnest when Jac added a third finger and sucked hard on her clit, and Sasha knew she had to give in.

"Jac," she cried, reaching for her. Wanting to feel her kiss, to look into her eyes, to see *her* when she came.

Jac surged up her body, adding the weight of her thigh to each thrust of her hand, and their lips met. Sasha slid her hand down Jac's belly and rubbed barely controlled circles over her clit as orgasm took control of Sasha's body, stealing the fire from her touch, but it didn't seem to matter. Jac trembled above her, and Sasha could feel the waves of orgasm that swept over them both, like lava melting and consuming everything in its path.

Jac's strength finally gave way. She collapsed on top of Sasha as they lay panting heavily, sweating. Sasha stroked the back of Jac's head and pressed soft kisses against her forehead and cheek, loving the feel of her, the weight of her body on top of her.

Minutes passed before Jac slipped off her and positioned herself at Sasha's side, head propped up on one hand while she stroked Sasha's body with the other, tracing circles around her belly button, the contours of her ribs, the curvature of her breast.

"That was amazing." Jac's grin was infectious, and Sasha giggled at the incredibly mischievous look in her eyes.

"Yes, it was. But why do you have that naughty look on your face?"

"Naughty look? What naughty look?"

Sasha wiggled a finger in front of Jac's face. "That naughty look. What's going on in that head of yours?"

Jac wrapped her arms around Sasha and rolled over until Sasha was on top of her. Sasha slid her knees to either side of Jac's hips and braced herself on her hands.

"I'm thinking," she started and kissed Sasha's shoulder, "that I'm naked"—she kissed the other shoulder—"in bed with the most beautiful woman I've ever known." She kissed Sasha's throat. "Who is also naked." Her lips closed around Sasha's nipple.

"I'm sensing a pattern here."

Jac released her nipple. "You are?" She sucked on the other.

"Yes," she said, but it came out as more of a groan. "I definitely am." Sasha focused all her willpower and sat back. Jac's lips released her nipple with a loud pop, and Sasha's still-throbbing centre pressed firmly against Jac's belly again. Stifling her own groan, Sasha grasped Jac's reaching hands and gazed down at her. "But it's my turn now."

"I'm going to regret all that teasing now, aren't I?" Jac licked her lips.

Sasha grinned, knowing how wicked it looked when Jac swallowed hard. But she didn't say anything; she simply scooted her lower body down the bed a little and sucked one of Jac's nipples between her lips.

"Just remember, I did it for a good cause."

"Oh, I remember." Sasha bit gently on the pebbled flesh in her mouth and smirked at the longing groan she pulled from Jac's lips. Jac closed her eyes and gave in to pleasure as her head fell back. "I plan to remember every second of this night." She drew the other nipple between her lips, committing every detail to memory as she went. *For the rest of my life.*

CHAPTER 21

JAC WIGGLED HER NOSE, TRYING to move whatever was tickling her without opening her eyes. It was still there. Damn it. Her body still craved sleep, and she was bound and determined to heed it. She swatted at the tickling thing with her hand, and jumped when it spoke.

"Ow."

Jac's eyes flew open and she started to sit up, only to find she was pinned to her bed.

"You could've just asked me to move." Sasha's voice was deep and hoarse with sleep. She started to roll away from Jac, but Jac's brain finally caught up with what was going on. She caught Sasha's arm and held her in place; one arm across her stomach, one leg across her thigh.

"I was asleep but your hair was tickling my nose." She used her free hand to smooth down the offending strands, then tucked Sasha's head back against her shoulder.

"Sleep swatting? That's your excuse?"

Shrugging, Jac relaxed again. "Yeah." She kissed the top of Sasha's head. "I'm sorry. Took my brain a second there to figure it out." Jac stroked her hand over Sasha's head and down her back, luxuriating in the feel of soft skin beneath her fingertips. Sasha squirmed against her.

"Don't do that if you want to go back to sleep." The kiss Sasha planted on Jac's chest and the roll of her hips emphasised her meaning as Jac reached the small of her back.

"Sensitive back?"

"Very," Sasha said, then pulled herself out of Jac's arms and scooted out of bed.

"Where're you off to?" Jac gazed at Sasha's naked body crossing the floor, hips swaying, her bare backside tantalising in the early morning light. The desire to run her tongue all over the exposed skin on display grew with every step Sasha took.

Sasha glanced over her shoulder, smiled at her, then exaggerated the sway of her hips. Yeah, Jac's thoughts were written all over her face.

"Come back here."

"In a minute." Sasha steeped into the en suite and closed the door. That's when Jac felt the heaviness in her own bladder and decided to take advantage of the guest bathroom. *Breakfast in bed?* Jac went through a quick mental inventory of what was in her kitchen and decided she'd have to take Sasha out for breakfast if she was hungry. She decided to wait for her in the bedroom.

She was back in bed inside a minute when she heard the shower turn on…and noticed the door was open. Just a crack. But open.

Oversight? Or invitation?

Could go either way, she acknowledged. But she was pretty sure it had been fully closed when she'd left the room a few minutes ago.

Jac threw the covers off again and decided that the worst that could happen was Sasha asking her to leave while she showered. She shrugged. No big deal. And if not… Jac licked her lips and pushed the door open further.

The glass cubicle was covered in steam and water spray, and the outline of Sasha's body was silhouetted by the overhead lights. She was smoothing her hands over her head, hair wet and slicked back; hands moving slowly, like a caress. Jac moaned and stepped further into the room as Sasha turned and swiped one hand across the glass, just enough for her to see out.

Her gaze was sultry, hot, and unbelievably sexy as she curled a finger and beckoned Jac with a come-hither motion. Jac felt as if she were a puppet on a string, tugged towards Sasha and moving without conscious thought. Her feet simply had a mind of their own, and all of her wanted to be exactly where Sasha was.

Sasha opened the cubicle door and tugged her inside by her arm, then turned them so Jac was directly under the spray. "Morning," she said and placed soft kisses across Jac's collarbones, from the point of one shoulder to the other.

Jac slicked her hair back and tossed her head from side to side under the water until it was fully wet and plastered to her head. "Morning, beautiful." She leant down and captured Sasha's mouth in a slow kiss, reintroducing their mouths, lips, and tongues to each other while she curled her fingers around Sasha's hips and pulled their bodies flush together. Sasha slung her arms over Jac's shoulders and wrapped her arms about her head, pulling them closer, tighter together. Their lips parted slowly, but Jac's continued to let her hands roam Sasha's body, and Jac's need rose quickly.

Her kisses became harder, needier, and more demanding. She sought all the places she'd learnt last night that drove Sasha crazy with desire, and the escalating hitch in her breathing told Jac she hadn't been wrong. But she needed more.

She pushed Sasha back against the tiled wall, warmed a little by the hot water but still cool enough to cause Sasha to gasp.

"I need to be inside you," Jac whispered in her ear and slid her hand between their bodies. "Open up for me, baby."

Moaning, Sasha spread her legs apart, giving Jac room to work and pulling Jac's mouth back to hers. Jac let herself fall into the kiss, plunging her tongue into Sasha's mouth at the same moment she entered her; first with one finger, then two. Sasha lifted one leg and wrapped it over Jac's hip, creating a deeper angle as she worked her fingers in and out of Sasha.

Sasha tore her mouth from Jac's and leant back against the wall with a moan. "Fuck, that feels good."

"Hm," Jac hummed against her neck as she continued to move inside Sasha. "Dirty mouth."

"You seem to bring out all kinds of dirty in me."

"Oh, I like that."

"I like that too," Sasha murmured and gasped around a particularly deep thrust.

Jac grinned and worked the long, deep thrusts that made Sasha's whole body tremble against her. She kissed Sasha's neck, nibbled her ear, and whispered against it, "Come for me, beautiful." She licked the shell of her ear. "Come for me now so I can take you back to bed and fuck you like I know you want me to." She thrust again deep, and Sasha's head fell back as far as she could, a throaty, guttural cry lingering on her lips as she did as Jac demanded.

"Yeah, you want that, don't you?"

"Jac…"

Jac's arm tightened around the thigh over her hip and supported Sasha's weight by keeping her pinned to the wall. Every shudder and spasm rocked their bodies, and Sasha rolled her head from side to side as her hips bucked and thrust against Jac's hand.

"Don't you?"

When she finally opened her eyes, Sasha met Jac's gaze and nodded. She still looked a little dazed when Jac turned off the water, and slowly lowered her leg. Jac climbed out of the stall quickly, her own excitement spurring her on. She ran the towel over her own body, then Sasha's after helping her out of the cubicle before pulling her into a tight hug, gripping her backside, and lifting her up. In reflex, Sasha wrapped her arms and legs around Jac and clung on as Jac moved across the bathroom and into the bedroom.

"Put me down before you drop me," Sasha shrieked.

"I'll never drop you," Jac replied before depositing her gently on the bed. "Scoot over."

She unwound her limbs and moved towards the centre of the bed as Jac opened the drawer in the bedside table and sorted through her equipment. She pulled out her dildo and held it up for Sasha to see. "Is this okay?"

Sasha held out her hand, and Jac watched as she held it, tested the length, girth, and feel of it between her fingers. The sight of her cock in Sasha's hands turned her on more than she'd imagined possible, and she swallowed hard.

"Go slow," Sasha said as she handed it back. "It's…well, it's been a long time for me."

"We don't have to," Jac whispered, bending forwards and locking her gaze on Sasha. "I mean, if you don't want to. If this isn't something you like—"

"I do. Or should I say, I have enjoyed it previously. But Pam and I hadn't been intimate for a while before we split up, and that was five years ago. I know this isn't exactly big, but…" Sasha shrugged sheepishly.

"Don't worry," Jac said as she quickly suited up. "I'll make sure you're ready, baby."

Chuckling, Sasha shifted onto her hands and knees and crawled across the bed towards her like a panther on the prowl. She placed a kiss on Jac's belly as Jac tightened the last strap about her hips. "I know you will. But there's something else too." She wrapped her fingers around the phallus now secure between Jac's thighs.

"What?"

"Mm." She hummed as she pressed her lips to the tip of the dildo, then flicked her tongue over the bulbous head. Jac's breath caught in her throat as Sasha trailed her tongue down the length of the shaft, then back to the tip and sucked the end between her lips.

"Oh God. Erm…what?"

"I want this to take a good long time," she said and took as much of the head into her mouth as she could. Jac could feel the pull of it against her body, and while she couldn't feel the sensations Sasha would have created in actual flesh, the lewd parody of a blow job drove her desire higher in a way Jac had never before experienced.

"You do?" Jac gasped as Sasha's fist pumped the shaft back against her body, pushing the base of it against her clit.

Sasha looked up at her from under those long, dark eyelashes and nodded, the cock still in her mouth. Then she released it, still working against Jac's clit with her hand. "I really do."

"Then you should really stop doing that, or it's going to be over in like…" She closed her eyes and groaned. "Seconds. Maybe."

Sasha murmured her appreciation and ground the base hard against her before letting go and running her hand up Jac's belly, between her breasts, and sliding around her neck. When Jac opened her eyes again, Sasha was kneeling tall on the edge of the bed. Their eyes were level and Sasha's lips were moist, parted, and begging for Jac's kiss.

"Well, we wouldn't want that, would we?"

Jac shook her head and closed the distance between them. She nibbled on Sasha's lower lip before teasing it with her tongue.

"I don't know how you do it, but you manage to push me to the edge without hardly trying. You're so fucking sexy, I feel like I'm a teenaged virgin again or something around you."

"Oh, darlin'," Sasha whispered around their kisses, "there's nothing of a teenaged virgin about you." She threaded her fingers into Jac's wet hair and pulled her close. "Now show me you know what to do with that thing."

She fell back onto the bed, tugging Jac down with her.

"Yes, ma'am," she said and crawled them both to the centre of the bed. "Turn over," she whispered in Sasha's ear. She had every intention of showing Sasha that she did indeed know what she was doing, but she planned on taking her time. Not just because Sasha had requested she go slow, but because she really needed to cool down a little if she was going to be able to deliver on that particular promise. Knowing how sensitive Sasha's back was and how much every stroke, lick, and nibble along her spine turned her on, Jac decided this was the perfect place to begin.

Sasha's groan and quick compliance seemed to indicate her agreement.

It was exquisite watching and feeling Sasha writhe and moan beneath her. The way her back arched into Jac's touch. The way her hips bowed from the bed like she wanted to push herself onto her knees. The way she gripped the sheets, tearing them from their anchors in her fists. Every second Jac spent exploring Sasha's back, neck, shoulders, the tops of her arms, the curve of her buttocks, the tops of her thighs, did little to cool her ardour and everything to raise them both to the boiling point.

She could smell Sasha's arousal as she wrapped her fingers in Sasha's hair and pulled her head back, licking at the underside of her jaw.

"Are you ready?"

"I've been ready since the moment I laid eyes on you."

Jac rose on her knees, then tore open the condom packet, while Sasha looked over her shoulder at her. "Any particular position you favour?" she asked as she slid the condom down the length of the shaft.

"I want to look in your eyes while you're inside me." Sasha turned over and raised her knees, reaching out her hands to Jac.

Jac nodded but she still wasn't quite ready yet. She kissed each knee, then nibbled down Sasha's thighs, avoiding the soaked folds of her centre as she crawled up the length of Sasha's body and drew a nipple between her lips. Sasha gasped and rolled her hips towards Jac.

"Please," she whimpered. "I need you."

Jac slowly reached between their bodies to guide the phallus to Sasha's entrance. "God, you're so wet."

"All your fault."

"I'll gladly take responsibility for that." Jac grinned and eased the head in a fraction. Still mindful of Sasha's request for slow, she propped herself on her knees and elbows, sinking into her a millimetre at a time. "Slow enough for you, baby?"

Sasha licked her lips, her attention clearly focused on the sensations between her legs. "You are a master torturer." She gazed up at Jac, running her fingers through her hair again. "But, yes, this is perfect."

Loving the look of deep satisfaction that covered Sasha's face, Jac smiled when she finally accepted the full length of her and their entire bodies were pressed firmly together.

"Okay?" Jac asked softly. Sasha nodded and tugged her down for a kiss, deep and slow, and totally consuming.

Sasha finally tore her mouth away. Panting, she pulled Jac's head to her shoulder and murmured, "Now fuck me," into her ear.

Jac didn't need telling twice. She established a rhythm quickly, pulling back and thrusting in time with every counterthrust of Sasha's hips. Every movement caused a delicious friction between the base of the dildo and her clit, and when Sasha bent her head and took one of her nipples into her mouth, she couldn't stop herself. She called out Sasha's name as the first tendrils of orgasm unfurled in her belly, shooting sparks through her groin and causing her muscles to clamp tight.

Sasha's fingernails down her back, and the upwards thrust of her hips as she chased her own orgasm, fired Jac into moving as much as she could, and she felt like throwing her head back and crowing when Sasha let out a strangled gasp and bucked wildly beneath her.

"Yes," Sasha ground out, her voice gravelly and deep. Her arms wrapped around Jac's back, eyes closed, mouth open, and looking more beautiful than Jac had ever thought possible.

It could have been seconds, or it could have been hours later when Jac slowly eased out of her, unbuckled the harness, and tossed it all over the side of the bed. She pulled a boneless Sasha into her embrace, kissed the top of her head, and sighed as Sasha wrapped herself in and over Jac's body, sleep already claiming her.

Breakfast would wait.

CHAPTER 22

Sasha grabbed hold of Jac's wandering hand, placed it flat against her side, and kept it covered with her own. "I need food and fluids before you can even think about getting me turned on another time."

"Too late. I've been thinking it ever since I woke up again."

She couldn't stop herself smiling against Jac's skin. "Fine, you can think about it, but I still need something to eat and drink before anything else."

"I can do that. What do you want to eat?"

"What choice do I get?" She rolled off Jac and slowly stretched her body, the ache between her thighs reminding her off all the reasons she was so ravenous right now.

"Well, you've seen my cupboards, right?"

"Uh-huh."

"So I figured I'd take you out for something to eat."

Sasha ran a finger up and down the length of the thin white scar she'd seen last night but paid little attention to. It was clearly old and long healed. She wanted to know the story behind it, certain there had to be one.

"What happened here?"

Jac grasped her hand, kissed it, and whispered, "Another time, babe. It's getting late, and I need to get you fed."

Sasha sighed. "Fine. What time is it?"

"Almost twelve."

"Really?" Sasha sat up straight.

"Yup." Jac pointed to the clock on the nightstand. "Why?" She kissed Sasha's shoulder. "Need to get home to your girlfriend?"

"Funny," Sasha said drolly. "I don't want Mum to worry." She looked about the floor, noting her discarded dress, shoes, and underwear across the room. "Where did I leave my bag?"

"Kitchen, I think." Jac climbed off the bed. "I'll get it for you. Glass of water?"

"Yeah, thanks. That'd be great." She quickly made use of the bathroom and met Jac when she walked back into the room.

"Your bag's beeping," she said and handed it over.

"Thanks. Probably Mum wondering where I am." She fished her mobile out of the small clutch bag and squinted at the flurry of messages waiting for her.

"Is she worried?"

Sasha shook her head and sat on the edge of the bed, thumbing through the texts. "No, she wants to know when I'll be home and if I can stop at the chemist for her on the way. Her prescription's been rung through and she wants me to pick it up on the way back, that's all." Sasha looked up at Jac. "I'm probably going to regret this when Mum starts telling you embarrassing stories about me, but would you mind taking me to the chemist and then taking me home? I'd like to get changed before going anywhere to eat, and if she's asking for this, she probably needs it sooner rather than later." She bit her lip, feeling more than a little shy all of a sudden. "I mean, if you want to still spend some more time together."

Jac shuffled across the bed until they were side by side, then took Sasha's chin in her hand and kissed the corner of her mouth. "I would love nothing more than to spend the rest of the weekend with you. And the chance to see your mum again, well, that's something special all by itself. Do you want to take her out for lunch with us? Would she like that?"

"Really?" Pam had never, ever, wanted to spend time in Fleur's company. It had caused more than a few arguments between them. And while Sasha understood that Fleur could be a little full on, and a little eccentric, she was her mother. And she loved every bizarre bone in her body. The idea that Jac would not only see her in the house, but go out to lunch with her touched Sasha more deeply than she could have expected.

"Really."

"You'd really want to spend time with my crazy mother?"

"Of course. She's your mum."

"Pam didn't even like coming around to the house with me when I went to visit her." In fact, the only person in her life who had consistently spent time with her mother before had been Bobbi. Bobbi! *Shit. I was going to go around and make things up with her.* But the prospect of saying goodbye to Jac after last night... Well, that just felt wrong. And the idea of spending the day with Jac and her mother, letting them get to know each other, discovering more about Jac—that wasn't something Sasha was going to say no to. She'd catch up with Bobbi later. She swallowed down the guilt. She wasn't exactly letting Bobbi down. They hadn't made plans for today, after all. It had only been a plan in her head. Sasha would make it up to her.

"I've said it before, and I'll say it again, the woman was a freaking idiot." She kissed Sasha's shoulder again and rested her cheek against it. Sasha couldn't stop herself from kissing the top of Jac's head. Gestures of affection, not sexual seduction, or post-coital actions. And they were quickly beginning to feel like the norm.

"Give her a call and see if she wants to." Jac stood and stretched. "I'm jumping in the shower. Don't join me. I'm not going out with your mother smelling like I do right now."

"Make sure there's enough hot water left for me, then," Sasha called after her, and Jac waved her hand as she closed the door behind her. Sasha sighed and flopped back on the bed, her body aching wonderfully. She punched in her mum's number and held her phone to her ear.

"Hey, Mum."

"Honey, if you're still"—she cleared her throat—"busy, then it can wait."

Sasha rolled her eyes. "Jac asked if you'd like to come out to lunch with us this afternoon."

"Really?"

"Yup."

"I knew there was a reason I liked that one." Fleur cleared her throat again. "That would be lovely. Where are we going?"

"Tell you what, Mum, you decide. We'll be there in an hour or so. I'll just need a few minutes to change, but we can go anywhere you like."

"Hm, I'll have to come up with somewhere good that serves potpourri." Fleur's cackling laugh was infectious.

Sasha joined in the laughter. "You do that."

"How was the show?"

"Wonderful."

"And the after-show show?" Fleur asked with a snigger.

Sasha blushed, but there was little point trying to hide anything. Besides, her mother sure as shit wasn't. "Even more wonderful," she said with a sigh, feeling the warmth of memory sweep her body—just like Jac's hands had.

"Well, well, well, it's about time," Fleur cried. "I look forward to hearing all about it."

"What? No way. There's a line, Mum, and that... Well, that's like a line in another freaking country."

Fleur cackled again. "You're such a prude, fruit of my loins."

"Ew, that's such a horrible phrase. And I'm not a prude. I just don't want to talk to my mum about sex. We did that when I was twelve, and you traumatised me, and then again when I came out at eighteen. A mother shouldn't be asking her daughter for tips about oral sex."

"Well, you were the only lesbian I knew then. Who else was I going to ask? Your father wasn't exactly the font of all knowledge when it came to—"

Sasha held the phone away from her ear, wishing she could unhear most of what her mother said, waited, then tried to go back.

"—I mean I loved the man, I truly did, but he was never gonna win any prizes for his tongue—"

This time she held it away for longer.

"—listening to me, or are you holding that phone away from your ear again?"

"I'm here, Mum."

"Good. Well, since you won't give me any juicy details, maybe I'll just ask that stud you've bagged instead."

"No. Mum, just no. Please, please, don't do that."

Fleur was quiet for a moment, then came back to Sasha with the tone she'd used only a few times in Sasha's life. "You really like her, don't you?"

Sasha could barely whisper the word *yes*, but somehow she managed to get it past her lips.

"And does she feel the same?"

Did she? Sasha certainly hoped so, and Jac had certainly given her every reason to believe she did. She'd said all the right things. The sexual chemistry between them was, well, fucking electric. And she called her beautiful. And the look in her eyes when she said it certainly looked like she meant it.

"I think so."

"Then it wouldn't matter what I did say. She wouldn't be going anywhere, but if it'll make you feel better I promise I won't ask her for details about your sex life."

"Thank you."

"I'll stick to generalisations from her past, 'cos I can tell she's definitely got one of those to let me in on."

"Mum!"

"Kidding, I'm kidding. You know, it gets easier and easier to wind you up, honey. You need to start smoking some of this stuff with me or try one of my brownies. That'll chill you out."

The bathroom door opened and Jac walked out naked but for the towel she was rubbing over her head.

"I'm going now, Mum. See you in an hour or so."

Fleur sighed. "Fine. See you in an hour." Sasha hung up and propped herself up on her elbows, eyeing Jac appreciatively.

"If we're picking up your mum in an hour, you need to stop looking at me like that and go get in the shower. I'll make coffee and find you a shirt or something that you can put on over your dress." She bent down and kissed Sasha, grasped her hand, and tugged her to her feet, then pushed her towards the bathroom with a gentle tap to her bottom.

"Oh, bossy." Sasha threw her a saucy look over her shoulder. "I like that too."

The restaurant was bustling. Saturday lunchtime in any place was going to be busy, but it seemed as though everyone and their mother—literally—was out in force today. There was even a woman with a dog in a handbag on the table just three tables away. Jac almost wished she'd suggested Sasha bring Fleur to her apartment for lunch instead of going out, but Fleur was grinning and laughing so much she decided to sit back and just enjoy it for what it was. An afternoon with her girlfriend and her mother.

It was a nice place. Long, white tablecloths, polished silverware, side plates, tap water served in fancy glass bottles. The full works. Sasha frowned at her mother, but Fleur looked to be in absolute heaven. Jac hadn't seen her grin that much since, well, since the potpourri incident; so not that long ago, really. But Jac decided it was time to let go of that one.

She reached under the heavy tablecloth and took Sasha's hand, interlacing their fingers. Sasha glanced over to her and smiled, her head cocked to one side in silent question. *Are you okay?*

Jac nodded.

"So, Jac," Fleur began after they'd placed their orders with the waitress. "Where are your family?"

Jac let go of Sasha's hand, shook out her napkin, and laid it across her lap, just needing something to do. "I don't have any family. Well, except Sophie and Mags." She smiled but knew it was a poor attempt by the look of sympathy etched on Fleur's face.

"I'm sorry," Sasha said quietly beside her. When Jac finally managed to drag her gaze to meet hers, there was sympathy, yes, and empathy, but no pity. More of an understanding that Jac knew had come from Sasha losing her father years ago. That look compelled her to tell the truth. To tell them all her truth.

"There's a reason Sophie calls me Pan-pan, you know?"

"Other than your refusal to grow up, you mean?"

"Yes, other than that." She paused while the waiter deposited drinks for them all, and took a sip of the Coke she'd ordered. She cleared her throat and wondered if she'd be able to get through it all, if she'd have to before they understood everything she couldn't say. She picked up the knife that lay across the side plate and fiddled with it, wishing she had a cigarette in her hand instead. *Christ, I can't wait for that craving to finally go away.* With determination, she put the knife down and took a deep breath. *Only one way to find out.*

"Many, many years ago," she began in her best storyteller voice, "there was a woman, a beautiful young woman, who became pregnant. She was over the moon. Her husband was ecstatic when she told him. They were to be a true family. Happy and safe and secure, always." Jac took a sip of her drink and slowly turned the glass on the tablecloth, watching the condensation run down the outside and blot the white cloth. "Just days after their little girl was born, the husband died, killed in an accident, and the young woman was so lost and alone and desperate that she did the unthinkable." She swallowed. "At least that's the story I've told myself since I was a child and learnt my mother left her newborn child in a pram by the statue of Peter Pan in Kensington Gardens."

"Oh, Jac." Sasha scooted her chair closer and wrapped her arm around her shoulders. "You don't have to say anything else." Sasha kissed her cheek.

Jac studied her and smiled sadly. "I know. But I want you to know." She flicked her gaze to Fleur and waited until the woman nodded. It was a nod that conveyed her understanding of what she was giving them both, and a nod that accepted the trust she was placing in them, a trust she'd offered so few in her life. "To this day, I don't know who my parents were, what they did, where they came from, or even the simplest of things like where or when I was born. I was found on the third of October at seven thirty by a couple walking their dog in the park. I was in a pram, so clearly whoever had left me there had done some planning for my arrival. When I was older and the social workers told me about it all, they said that doctors thought I was anywhere up to a week old. But they couldn't be sure."

A waiter passing the dog table set the little thing off yapping. Might be a Chihuahua, might be a pug...or some hybrid mutt crossed between the two. Jac couldn't really tell; it was half-hidden in a checkerboard-style oversized bag. *Whole new meaning to doggy bag.* The food that set it off happened to be theirs and was set on the table before them with little fanfare. Jac couldn't be certain, but she was fairly sure they'd all lost their appetites. Maybe that's what the dog was yapping about. Detour request to drop the food off in his bag. She didn't want to continue, but she wanted Sasha to know the truth of her. All of it.

"There were no reports of missing or kidnapped children, no accidents involving new mothers, or anything like that that the authorities could point to and say, 'There, that's the woman. She's the mother.'" Jac shook her head. "All they had was the name *Jaclyn* on my baby grow. So they stuck with it. I was placed in an orphanage, and apparently they had high hopes I'd be adopted. Babies are usually the first to be adopted. But I was sickly, so I didn't get picked up. Who wants a snot-covered kid when the beautiful little blond baby looks more adorable, right?" She offered Sasha a self-deprecating grin and squeezed her hand.

"I'm sure you were far more adorable than all the others," Sasha said with a smirk, but her eyes were sad.

"Oh, they showed me one of the few pictures they had on file." Jac grimaced. "It's a wonder I didn't crack the damn camera."

She kissed Sasha's hand. She wished they were doing this at home, sitting on the sofa, or in bed, rather than in the middle of a restaurant with God only knew who was listening. But they were here now, and this was what was happening. "They didn't realise until I was a little older that I actually had a heart problem."

"Your scar?" Sasha touched her hand over Jac's sternum.

"Yes. I got a new valve, and they did a bunch of other stuff in there, and eventually I was good as new. But I was around five or six by that time. Behind at school, bit of a tearaway after finally getting to play in the sun. I spent most of my early years inside some stuffy dorm room, watching all the other kids play. Once they turned me loose, well, I had so much to make up for. Altogether, I wasn't a kid anyone wanted. I stayed in the orphanage until I was sixteen. I was lucky, though. I'd tested well in the eleven plus, so got a grammar school scholarship that led to great exam results and eventually a large scholarship at uni. I wouldn't have been able to go otherwise." She chuckled. "Still walked away with a huge amount of loans I had to pay back, but I did." She spread her hands out across the table.

"And here I am." She smiled at Fleur first, happy to see her smiling again.

When she turned back to Sasha, she could see tears shimmering her eyes and used a thumb to wipe them away as they spilled over and down her cheeks. "Hey, I'm okay. Better than okay. I'm doing great, and I did it all on my own."

"Yes, you did." She put a hand to Jac's cheek and pulled her in for a kiss, a sweet, soft, chaste kiss that whispered promises and offered comfort all at the same time. A kiss that was at once simple and complicated. Exactly as it should be between them. When she pulled away, Sasha was biting her lip like she was trying to stop herself from saying something.

Fleur cleared her throat.

"So," she said, breaking the ice, "that's where Kensington comes from, then? Where you were found?"

"Yup."

"No relation to Patsy, then?"

"Not that I know of," she said with a frown.

"I think you mean Patsy Kensit, Mum."

"Oh, yes. Not her neither?"

"Nope. Just me, myself, and I," Jac said with a chuckle.

"Lucky you." Fleur picked up her fork. "Family can be so difficult some days."

Sasha hiked up her eyebrows and turned to face her mother. "Can't they just?" Her voice dripped sarcasm.

Clearing her throat, Jac searched around for a safe topic to shift the conversation to. She didn't regret telling them her story, but she felt exposed now, like she was naked before them. And while she didn't mind being naked with Sasha, Fleur was a different story. She wanted to impress the woman. Fleur was so important to Sasha. They were obviously incredibly close, and she wasn't sure how much influence Fleur's opinion of her would have on Sasha. And she really, really wanted the older woman to like her. She was a bloody scream.

"I was wondering if you'd like to come and watch the filming one day?" Jac asked, looking over at Fleur.

Fleur grinned. "Can I shout out 'action'?"

"I think that can be arranged," Jac acquiesced.

"Can I get one of those chairs?"

Jac nodded.

"Are you sure, Mum? It'll be a long day, and you can't take any of your stuff on set."

Jac hadn't thought about that, unaware of how often Fleur needed her "medication". "We don't have to make it a full day. Just come for half a day or however long you like, and then head off whenever you need to."

"Sounds wonderful," Fleur said with her nose in the air and a superior attitude firmly attached. Jac and Sasha laughed.

The crash of a tray drew their attention away from each other. Jac stared as a waiter bearing a tray of what had been drinks was now hovering over the woman with the doggy bag. Who was dripping with whatever drinks he had been carrying. At a guess, Jac was going with orange juice, Coke, and maybe a Bloody Mary. The woman was a mess, the waiter was a mess, trying to clean her up and apologising every second. In the confusion, it seemed none of them had noticed that the doggy bag had been knocked over until the mutt of questionable breeding was scurrying around the floor, lapping up spilt drinks, then diving under tablecloths as hands stretched out for it.

"I couldn't write this shit," Sasha said. "Someone would tell me it was too farfetched."

"Not if you were writing a Will Ferrell or Adam Sandler movie."

"Or a *St Trinian's* sequel."

They glanced at each other, laughing, and losing sight of the scampering mutt.

"Someone please find my baby!" Doggy-bag Woman stood at her table, clasping her empty bag in one hand and a tomato-stained napkin in the other. Her hair was pushed back off her face but was still full of gloopy tomato juice. "Please, he's so tiny and helpless. He could get trodden on!"

"Poor woman," Fleur said. "You two should help her."

Sasha and Jac rolled their eyes but lifted the flap of their tablecloth to check under the table with Sasha muttering about "showing willing" under her breath. Jac bent to the side, her head almost in Sasha's lap so she could see under. Sasha took the opportunity to run her hand over Jac's head and slip her fingers under Jac's collar. The warmth of her hand, the gentle caress, the scent of Sasha enveloped her. Distracted her. Made her eyes flutter shut. She could have laid there all day, letting Sasha pet her like a dog.

Dog. She opened her eyes again and saw it: the bat-like ears of a French Bulldog, the huge eyes, the squat barrel body, the squashed nose of a pug, the tan colouring of a Chihuahua, and it was under the table beside Fleur, staring right at Jac, its crooked little teeth bared at her.

"Found it," she whispered. "Don't speak too loudly when you call her over. We don't want to spook it."

"It's a tiny thing, Jac. Just pick it up," Sasha implored.

"It's got teeth, and it's growling."

"Don't be a baby."

Jac tried to lower herself enough to get both shoulders under the edge of the table so she could lean forwards and grab it. She shuffled her butt cheeks to the edge of her chair and leaned a little more of her weight on Sasha's lap. She enjoyed a final stroke on her head, then lowered herself—as slowly as her thighs allowed—to her knees under the table.

"Nice puppy," she whispered. "Come 'ere, puppy." She reached out but was still too far away to touch it. It skulked away from her, cowering against Fleur's leg. It would be easy to tell Fleur to reach down and grab it. But she didn't want to scare it off and lose the little…scamp…now it was this close. "Come and see what I've got on my plate for you, you little yapper." She leant forwards again, then shrank back in horror.

It did it.

The little bug-eyed bastard cocked its leg and let loose a stream of pungent piss. All over Fleur's leg.

"Why you little—" Jac took advantage of the mutt's distraction and disadvantage on three legs and grabbed it by the scruff of the neck, hoisting it away from Fleur and holding it in front of her, away from Sasha and out from under the table, while trying to avoid the twisting head that snarled and snapped its ferocious-looking three-millimetre-long canines at her.

It was still pissing!

Jac grasped hold of its tail in an attempt to at least aim the stream of pee at the floor rather than other people…or tables…or food…but it kept going. *Is this whole dog just full of it? Surely its tiny bladder can't hold this much pee?*

Then the barking—or rather yapping—started in earnest.

"Let him go!" Doggy-bag Woman shouted. "You're hurting my baby! You don't hold a dog like that!" She ran over and snatched the now-mewling wee beastie from Jac's hands.

"You do if it's trying to gnaw your fingers off while pissing everywhere, love."

"How dare you defame my poor little Bertie's character? He would never do such a thing." She snuggled her still-tomato-smeared face against the tan fur. "Would you, my little darling? You'd never do anything like this nasty woman described." She spoke as one would to a child—if that child was a very spoiled, overindulged mutt of questionable breeding that was now giving Jac the smuggest look she'd ever had the displeasure to witness. Clearly, Bertie knew where his bread was buttered. He started licking at the mess in Doggy-bag Woman's hair. "That's right, my little prince. You help clean Mummy up after the nasty man tried to drown me with those awful drinks."

Sasha had her hands steepled in front of her nose and mouth. Her eyes shone and she was clearly trying to hold back laughter. The crying-tears kind of laughter. Fleur wasn't even trying to hide it. She was slapping the table and wiping her eyes.

Jac sat back in her seat and pointed at Fleur. "I don't know what you're laughing about. Rat Boy over there pissed all over your leg."

Fleur wiped her eyes again and tried to halt her laughing. Well, sort of tried. She reached under the table, and after a few moments, she looked like she was trying to pull her tights down.

"Mum! Don't!" Sasha shouted.

"Oh, pish." Whatever resistance Fleur was up against gave way, and she hoisted the item from under the table. "Well, so he did." Fleur held up the lower leg with a wet stain on the stocking that encased it.

Jac stared and opened her mouth to speak. "I did—but—I mean—what—it's not—" She glanced at Sasha as Fleur waved her prosthetic leg in the air.

"Oi, you, lady with the pissing machine: you owe me a new pair of tights!"

Sasha was still chuckling when they dropped Fleur back home, and she packed a bag—at Jac's suggestion—with the intention of staying with Jac for the rest of the weekend. Mr Hunt—Mr Mike Hunt—was on his way over to console Fleur on the loss of her favourite pair of tights. And Jac was still more than a little mortified. She was looking forward to soothing those ruffles later. And maybe finding out more about Jac's past.

Hearing those few details had broken her heart. Jac had tried to hide it behind the jokey story, the bluster, and her pride in her achievements. As she should be proud. But underneath it all, Sasha had seen the pain, the loneliness. And more than anything, she wanted to soothe that pain away. The little girl who had been discarded like an old newspaper, never wanted, never truly loved…Sasha had seen her hiding in Jac's eyes. And Sasha knew she wanted to spend the rest of her life trying to make the child inside Jac feel loved.

"One date and you're already in love with her." Sasha folded a blouse for Monday morning and packed it away in her bag. "Talk about a cliché."

"Oh, I don't know, honey. Sometimes when you know, you just know."

Sasha turned to face her mother as she hobbled unsteadily into Sasha's bedroom. "Was that how it was for you? With Dad?"

"Yes, I knew the first time I laid eyes on your father that I was going to marry him. That he was the one for me."

"You never told me that before." Sasha sat on the edge of her bed.

"Well, you've always been a bit more like your father than like me in these things. He took a lot more convincing." Fleur sat beside her and wrapped an arm around Sasha, encouraging her to put her head on Fleur's shoulder. "But it turns out you're more like me than I thought."

Sasha snorted a laugh. "I'm not taking your crystal."

"Good. It wouldn't work for you anyway. You need to get your own; it has to attune itself to your energy. My tarot cards, on the other hand, I'm leaving you those in my will. I'll be awaiting your call on the other side."

Chuckling, Sasha wrapped her arm around Fleur's back, her fingers grabbing on to the thick wool of the bulky jumper she was wearing. "Aren't you hot in that thing?"

"Nah, I've not made it to hell yet, darling."

She shook her head. "Mum." Sasha sighed. "I don't know what to do."

"About what?"

"Jac."

"What on earth do you mean?"

"I don't know if she feels the same way."

"Does she have to?"

Sasha pulled away enough to look in her eyes. "Of course. Would you want to be in love with someone who doesn't love you back?"

"No, of course not. I'm meaning right now. Does it matter right now if she isn't in love with you? She clearly cares about you a great deal. She clearly wants you. And she's obviously looking for more than just a roll in the hay if she's prepared to take you out with your crazy old mum." Fleur squeezed her shoulder tight as she sniggered. "You don't need to do anything but give it some time."

"But what if she never does?"

Fleur sighed and pressed Sasha's head back to her shoulder. "I don't think that will be the case, but if so, then you deal with it." She shrugged. "Life doesn't always give us what we want. I lost your father far too soon as far as I'm concerned. But I went on. You went on. We learn to adapt and deal with all the changes life throws at us, Sasha. That's what we do. It's what we always do because life is short—far too short—and it's always uncertain, my darling. Some days are good and some days a little rat dog pees on your tights."

Sasha sniggered.

"But it's all life, honey, and we deal with it and move on." She stroked Sasha's hair away from her head, combing her fingers through it just as she had when Sasha had been a child.

"Life is full of changes, full of questions, full of moments that have us wondering 'what if?', and it's never quite what we expect. Don't start this relationship with Jac wondering 'what if?'. Start it with a smile in your heart. The rest will come."

"Paraphrasing *Peter Pan* now?"

"Jac's story made me think of it."

"I know what you mean. Everything she must have gone through. I just can't imagine."

"And for that I am eternally grateful." She kissed Sasha's head. "But Jac does, and she's rather in need of all the love she can get, if you ask me." Fleur wrapped her other arm around Sasha and pulled her in for a slightly awkward sideways hug. "Now, finish packing your bags. I need a spliff, and I don't think you want me getting your girlfriend stoned." Fleur stood and hobbled towards the door.

"Are you okay?"

Fleur waved her hand. "Didn't get the sock straight after the little show in the restaurant. I need to get my leg off and lie down for a while. Nothing I can't handle, honey."

"Do you want me to help?"

"No. I want you to finish packing your bag." She turned back to Sasha, her hand on the door frame. "She makes you smile in a way I've never seen before, my darling daughter. All I've ever wanted for you is to see you happy. I told you, it's my greatest wish for you. To know there'll be someone there for you when I can't be anymore. You weren't meant to walk through life alone. No one is." There was a look in Fleur's eyes that Sasha couldn't quite make sense of. There was happiness, mirth, and joy, yes, but underneath that was something else. Something Sasha couldn't put her finger on. Sorrow, maybe? Grief? Regret? Had speaking of her dad made Fleur so sad?

"Blah, enough of this sappy shit." Fleur pointed back at the bag on the bed. "Get that bag packed, then take your girl home and fuck her brains out." She knocked on the door as she passed it, laughing.

Sasha squeezed her eyes shut and tried to erase the last five seconds form her mind. No such luck. Fleur knew exactly how to get under her skin.

CHAPTER 23

JAC TURNED THE PAGE ON the script, then flipped back, realising she hadn't been paying attention. In fact, she couldn't remember a single word she'd read. That wasn't a damning testament about the script she was reading. Sophie would have never given it to her to read if it was that bad. No, this was a testament to Jac's level of distraction. All she could think about was Sasha. The way her hair had been splayed across Jac's chest that morning when they'd woken up, limbs entwined, faces so close they were sharing the same breath.

She fiddled with her pen, flipping it between her middle and index finger, the way she used to hold a cigarette, flicking the ash from the tip. She was so distracted she found herself with the end between her lips, sucking on it. "Shit," she whispered and touched her fingertips to her lip, checking for ink.

A knock at the door startled her. She looked up to see Sophie leaning on the door frame, two coffee cups in her hands. She smiled and crossed the room, held one cup out to Jac, then took a seat in the chair opposite Jac's desk.

"Want to tell me what has you so distracted?"

Jac screwed her face up and took the coffee cup. "Do I really have to? You always said you could read me like a book."

"And I still can, my dear Pan. Did your date on Friday not go well?"

Jac couldn't stop the smile that spread across her lips. The memory of Sasha in that dress…the memory of Sasha out of that dress…made her mouth go dry and her fingers itch to do it all again. To feel her again.

"Never mind. I can see how it went. So what's all this, then? I stood in that doorway watching you for like three minutes and you didn't turn the page in all that time."

"I can't stop thinking about her."

Sophie clapped her hands. "Excellent." She rounded the desk and pulled her into a hug. "I'm so happy for you. I love seeing you all loved up."

"Hey, hang on. That's a bit—I mean, it's only been a few days, I'm not…" Jac thought back over the past weekend with Sasha. She'd shared more with her in those three days than she'd ever shared with Vanessa, or any other woman she'd been with, if she were totally honest.

"But it hasn't only been a few days, sweetie. It's been almost three months since you met her, and let's face facts here." She turned Jac's face to hers. "You started falling for her the moment you set eyes on her. Didn't you?"

Jac was frozen.

"Didn't you?" Sophie asked again and used the hand on her cheek to move Jac's head in a nod.

"I told her," Jac whispered.

"You told her what, sweetie?"

"I told her about the thing. You know, the baby thing."

Sophie's eyes opened wide. "You told her you were a foundling?"

Jac nodded.

"That's…fucking huge. I'd known you for almost three years before you told me. And you told her this weekend?"

"Her and her mum."

"And her… How the hell did that happen?"

Jac quickly filled her in on lunch, including the pissing-pooch rescue, and laughed along with her, no longer mortified at not realising Fleur was wearing a prosthetic leg.

"Stop," Sophie begged. "Now I need to pee."

Jac cackled. "I thought you were doing that Pilates class. Don't they make you exercise those muscles to stop you being incontinent?"

"I've only been to three classes. They work the muscles, not miracles." She swatted Jac's arm. "Besides, it's a genetic thing."

Sophie had been telling her—for years—about the problems her mother had with her bladder when she started menopause. She'd been convinced the same thing would happen to her too. Despite the fact Sophie had never had the six kids her mother had had. But here they were, Sophie had started with hot flashes, mood swings as crazy as the Brexit polls, and a teeny-tiny amount of weight gain that no one—not one single person—was insane enough to mention. And now the bladder issues had started. Jac was still part convinced it was only happening because Sophie had been so convinced it would.

This time, Jac, convinced silence was the better part of valour, shook her head and pushed the script on her desk further away. "Well, this isn't happening today, so let's see what other trouble I can get into."

Sophie followed her out of the room. "The dailies should be ready. Wanna go and see what the day's filming looks like?"

"That's like asking a drunk if they want a drink. Of course I do." She held her hand out before her. "Lead the way, McScruff."

"You're getting worse in your old age, Pan-pan. Maybe you should have stayed not a grown-up."

"Thou woundest me, my lady." Jac held her hand over her heart, then threaded her arm through Sophie's as they wound their way through the corridors to the editing suite. "Oh, and I invited Fleur to come and watch us filming sometime."

"You did?"

"Yeah. Why?"

"You don't normally do that kind of thing."

No, she didn't, but at the time it had seemed like the right thing to do. "I thought it would be a nice thing for Sasha and her mum to share."

"I'm sure it is. I know my mother loved it whenever she came on set and watched it all happen."

Jac smiled to herself. "I remember that time—"

"Shit," Sophie said under her breath. "Walk faster, but don't run."

"What?"

"Don't look back either. She'll see it as weakness."

"What are you talking about?" Jac tried to turn but Sophie was gripping her arm tight.

"Vanessa."

"Shit."

"Exactly. Keep going; we're nearly there."

"Jac! Wait, I need to talk to you," Vanessa shouted down the corridor.

"We can totally pull it off if we tell her you've gone deaf," Sophie continued.

"It's about the first scene for tomorrow's filming," Vanessa called.

"And she's found the jugular," Sophie whispered as she and Jac turned to face Vanessa. "You know it's gonna be totally fabricated shit, don't you?" Sophie mumbled as she spoke out of the corner of her plastered-on smile.

"Agreed. But on the million-to-one shot it isn't, I can't take the chance. The project comes first." Her own words were barely intelligible around her own fake smile. "Vanessa, what's the problem?"

Vanessa sidled up to Jac and slid an arm about her waist. "It's not a quick fix, I'm afraid. I thought it might be best if we discussed it tonight. Perhaps over dinner."

"Slapper," Sophie coughed out, and pretended to have a coughing fit. It was fairly passable. Jac wondered for a moment if Sophie was still dreaming of being on screen. *I could make that work for her.*

"What do you say? I could pick up a pizza and swing by our apartment. Say seven?"

Our apartment? Our? I think not, lady. Jac plucked at the arm around her waist and shook her head. "I'm sorry, Vanessa, but no. That isn't appropriate. *My* apartment is off limits to you. If you have something we need to talk about, we can do it right here."

Vanessa's smiley, slightly flirty expression vanished, and she turned to stare at Sophie. "I need to discuss this with Jac." Her stare became pointed. "Alone."

Sophie opened her mouth. Jac clamped her hand around Sophie's arm to keep her in check.

"Whatever you have to say to me, Vanessa, can be said in front of Sophie or Mags or Sasha or anyone else working on this film. We have a professional working relationship. Professional working matters can be discussed among the team."

Vanessa sighed heavily and put her hand on Jac's arm, clearly still not getting the message. "This is a little sensitive. I don't want to offend anyone by making this such a…public matter."

"We're all grown-ups. We can deal with a work issue." She shook Vanessa's hand off her again.

"Fine." Jac heard the door to the editing suite open behind her, and a slow smirk twisted Vanessa's lips. "It seems there've been changes made to the script, writing me out of the first scene tomorrow. I wanted to make sure you were aware that your little writer friend seems to be taking a few too many liberties with your vision, Jac."

Jac reached behind her, certain Sasha was standing there. She could smell the subtle perfume she'd sprayed in Jac's bedroom that morning when she'd got dressed. When Sasha's fingers clasped hers, she tugged until they were side by side, fingers entwined. It was time to put an end to Vanessa's game. Jac had been clear from the start. She wasn't trying to win Vanessa back; she didn't want her back. As awful as she felt admitting it, she'd barely wanted her in the first place. And it was time to make things clear to Vanessa in the only way she would understand.

"Sasha hasn't taken any liberties, Vanessa. She and I discussed the scene change before I asked her to go ahead with it. The scene doesn't need your character's input, and it will be of much greater emotional impact when the information is divulged to her later in the story." She tugged Sasha closer and wrapped her arm around Sasha's waist, waited until Sasha turned her head to look at her, and kissed her soundly on the mouth. "And she's captured the scene exactly the way I want it." She didn't take her eyes off Sasha, loving the flush that stole up her cheeks and the slightly glazed expression in her eyes.

She could see Sophie waving her hands around, hand-jive style, while shaking her booty behind Vanessa's back—stopping abruptly when Vanessa turned her head slightly.

Vanessa cleared her throat. "Well, I can't say I agree with your decision, Jac. But you are the boss. We must all do whatever you say." She looked Sasha up and down, turned her nose up, and walked away.

Sasha ran her hand over Jac's chest and behind her neck. "What made you decide to play with fire today, darlin'?"

"She was inviting herself around to *our*—as in mine and hers—apartment for dinner this evening to talk about that little script change."

Sasha's eyebrows rose. "I didn't realise she owned the—"

"The hell she does!" Sophie cried and held up her hands when they turned to face her. "Sorry, sorry. I'll just go back to watching over here, all quiet and shit." She leant against the wall, arms crossed over her chest. "Wish I had some popcorn."

Jac chuckled and waited until Sasha was looking at her again. "She doesn't own anything in my home. Nothing. Not now, not ever." She touched her forehead to Sasha's. "Nothing."

"So just another Octo-Nessa play to get you back?"

Jac nodded, heat flushing her own cheeks.

"And you chose me." Sasha's voice was the tiniest whisper. But Jac heard it, along with all the insecurities tied up inside it. She didn't blame Sasha for them. She'd admitted herself that she'd only been with younger women for years. As beautiful and wonderful as Sasha was, Jac could understand how that knowledge would be a little intimidating. How she would need reassurance. Vanessa wasn't even close to the woman Sasha was, and Jac would spend every day of the rest of her life telling Sasha that, if that's what it took.

"I will always choose you."

Sasha's lips were soft against her own. Her fingers cradled Jac's cheeks, and slowly they moved against each other, deepening the kiss. Jac wrapped her arms around Sasha's back and pressed her against the wall beside them, hands eager to explore her lover's skin, to feel her. Sasha's hands twisted into her hair in the way Jac had come to love over the past couple of days. She tugged a little, scratching her scalp and cradling her head like it was something precious to her.

"Ahem."

Their lips broke apart with an audible pop and they turned to see a grinning Sophie tapping her foot.

"Ladies, I'm always down for a hot love scene, but I might suggest we take this porno somewhere other than the corridor. Where we all work. With our staff still milling about." She twirled her finger around to indicate the half-dozen sets of eyes staring at them both. "Just saying." Sophie breezed past them and pushed open the door to the editing suite, slapping Jac on the back as she went past. "Let's take a look at the dailies, ladies. Then you can get each other home."

Sasha's cheeks flamed and she buried her face in Jac's neck. "I forgot she was there." She chuckled. "I forgot where the hell we were."

Jac held her close and walked her towards the door, still wrapped in their embrace. "Me too."

"Is this going to cause a problem?"

"What? Vanessa?"

"Yeah," Sasha spoke into the sensitive skin of her neck.

"I don't think so. Like I said, she's ambitious, and she wants this project to work. It's against her own self-interest to try and sabotage it in any way," she said confidently as she eased them apart and held a chair out for Sasha. "Let's see what we've got." Vanessa wouldn't do anything to screw with the film. She'd be an idiot to. It was Jac's company, Jac's project. Nah, there was nothing Vanessa could do to cause a problem other than maybe be moody on set.

CHAPTER 24

"Puff the Magic Dragon" blared across the sound stage. *Shit.* Sasha fished in her bag, pulled out the handset, and silenced it with a quick swipe. She winced apologetically to Jac.

"Cut, reset scene," Jac yelled across the space.

"Sorry," Sasha whispered, then put the handset to her ear. "Mum, what's wrong?"

"This ape won't let me in. Says I'm not on the list."

Sasha tried to decipher the meaning behind the words. As words, they made sense. But she couldn't for the life of her figure out what they all meant in the order they'd been delivered.

"What list? What ape? And where are you trying to get in to?"

Fleur sighed heavily. "The security ape at the front desk of your offices. He says I'm not on the visitors list, so I can't come in."

"Why are you at Reception?" She frowned as she got up from her chair and motioned to Jac that she was heading off set. Jac lifted her eyebrows in question but Sasha shook her head and held up her hand to indicate she just needed five minutes. Jac nodded, and Sasha walked quickly out the door.

"Jac invited me to come and see the place when we went to lunch the other week, remember?"

"Yes, I remember, Mum. You said you'd let us know when was a good day and we could organise it with you." She'd actually thought Fleur had forgotten, as she'd never mentioned it again.

"Well, today's a good day."

Sasha blew out a breath. It wasn't the best of days for guests on set. They were filming one of the love scenes this morning, and while it wasn't pornographically, well, graphic, it wasn't a PG-rated film either. Having her mother on set for that could get a little uncomfortable—mostly for Sasha, she admitted. But she was here now. She could hardly send her away.

"Okay, I'm almost there. Just hang on."

Then Fleur was gone. Well, she was gone from the phone. Sasha could already hear her arguing with the security guard, and there was still another set of doors to go through. Sasha pushed open the glass doors and caught the eye of the guard on duty. John Parsons was a tall man, easily six-foot-four inches of solid muscle. Conservatively speaking, he was built like a brick shithouse, and Sasha had wondered if he actually split the seams on his shirts if he flexed his arms too much—like when he picked up an envelope or something. But for all his massive size, he was full of laughter and mirth and merriment, always quick with a joke whenever she saw him. She liked John.

"Hey, sorry about this," she told him.

"Ms Adams, sorry you had to come all the way down here."

Sasha waved her hand. "Not your fault at all." She pointed at her mother with her thumb. "Jac invited my mother for a tour, but she got the wrong end of the stick and forgot to formalise the details of when said tour would go ahead." Sasha rolled her eyes and John grinned. "So she decided to turn up when she felt like it instead."

"No problem. As long as she's got ID and you can vouch for her, I'll get her name added to the visitors list for today."

Sasha wrinkled her nose. "Do I have to vouch for her?" She glared at her mother, who tossed her a little finger wave.

"Well," John started, "I could have her strip searched and X-rayed if you think she's not quite on the up and up."

Sasha contemplated it for a second, then said, "Nah, I think my mother might enjoy that a bit too much, John, and I don't want you to suffer PTSD or anything."

With a laugh John slapped the desk lightly. "You crack me up, Ms Adams."

"I wasn't joking," Sasha replied and held her hand out to her mother, who was waiting to hand over her ID.

Fleur purposefully avoided handing her bus pass to Sasha and sidled up to John. She presented it to him with all the dramatic flourish she could muster. And a saucy wink. Sasha bit her tongue to stop herself laughing as John paled, gulped, and took the ID with a slightly shaking hand.

While John got her signed in, Sasha fired off a quick text to Jac, explaining their unexpected visitor. Jac sent one back, promising to meet them at the studio doors when they finished the next take so they wouldn't disturb anyone while they were filming. The hastily-cobbled-together plan would be for Fleur to watch the rest of the morning's filming, and then she and Jac would take her on a short tour during the lunch break, before grabbing a quick bite and then continuing with the filming until Fleur got bored.

"Those are just a little gift for the cast and crew," Fleur said as John examined her bag and put a large Tupperware box on the desk. Sasha closed her eyes and barely refrained from cursing. "Homemade brownies. You can have one if you like."

Sasha's eyes opened wide, and she stepped up behind her mother. She waved her arms and mouthed, "No," with as much energy as she could muster. She motioned a finger across her throat, lolled her tongue out of her mouth, and played dead.

John's eyes were wide as he patted his belly. "Thanks, Mrs Adams, but I can't. I'm on a strict diet."

Fleur looked him up and down. "For what?"

He grinned. "Body building." He put the box back in Fleur's bag and handed it back to her. "Let me get the door for you, ladies." He walked ahead of them after giving Fleur her visitor's pass and held the heavy glass door open wide. "She a bad cook?" he whispered to Sasha as she walked past him.

"Terrible," Sasha replied with a smile. "I'm surprised I survived a childhood eating it."

John chuckled. "Enjoy your day, ladies, and please remember to leave your pass when you sign out later."

"Mum, what the hell are you doing, bringing your cakes here?"

"Relax, they're just brownies."

"Just brownies? Not hash brownies?"

"Just brownies," Fleur agreed. "I didn't have enough hash to bring a box of the good ones for the cast and crew."

Sasha looked up at the ceiling and prayed for strength as she led Fleur back to the soundstage they were filming on, but she didn't open the doors.

"So why are we waiting in the middle of the hallway? Don't you have a key or something?"

"They're filming, Mum."

"So?"

"Jac will come and let us know when they finish the take they're on and we can go in without disrupting anything and potentially ruining what they're recording."

"Oh, I see."

The door at Sasha's back opened and Jac smiled at them. She hugged Fleur. "Good to see you again, Fleur. You okay?"

Fleur smiled and wrapped her hand around Jac's arm. "I am, dearie. Now show me this kingdom of yours."

Jac led Fleur inside, explaining the scene they were set up to film. The soundstage had been dressed as a bedroom, the bed rumpled, cushions strewn across the floor, clothes scattered in various places.

"Jac!" Vanessa's voice cut across the room.

"Here we go." Sasha gritted her teeth. "What the hell is her problem now?"

Vanessa stalked towards Jac, arms swinging at her sides like a marching soldier. She pointed at Jac, stabbing her finger into Jac's chest.

Stepping closer, Sasha listened to Vanessa's latest issue.

"...don't know how you expect me to work under these conditions. I should have a body double. I'm sure that was in the contract. I always have a body double for nudity."

"Vanessa, there is no body-double clause in your contract," Jac said. "And I know for a fact you didn't have one on the last project you did. There were breast shots in that one. I remember—vividly—how you went on and on about making sure you had no visible tan lines for it."

"That was just my tits, Jac. This is full-body nudity."

Fleur leant towards Sasha and whispered, "Has your script turned into a porno?"

Sasha shook her head. "It's the scene where they're in bed together, and, yes, she's naked, but Hazaar is covering Charlie's body, so you don't see anything but her breasts. For about a second."

"Shame. You know what they say, dear?"

"What's that?"

"Sex sells."

Sasha lifted her eyebrows and sighed heavily.

"I'll do it for you, lovey," Fleur piped up, waving her hand and stepping closer to Jac.

Jac snorted and Sasha covered her mouth, biting her lip.

Vanessa's face dropped in horror.

"That'll be another tick on my bucket list. Well, I suppose it's not quite 'make my own sex tape', but it's pretty close." She pointed to Becca sitting in a chair, wrapped in a dressing gown and grinning widely at the unfolding scene. "Is that the other lady I'll be filming with?" She waved at Becca, and Becca waved back before getting to her feet and ambling over.

"Hi, I'm Becca Monterro." She held out her hand to Fleur.

"Fleur Adams. I'm Sasha's mum, and it looks like we'll be working together today."

"Nice to meet you, Fleur," Becca said and stepped to the side. She crossed one arm over her stomach and held the other over her mouth.

"Do you think I could stretch this to cover the lesbian-lover box on that list of mine too?" Without waiting for an answer, Fleur dropped her coat from her shoulders and held it up to Jac. "Be a dear and hold this for me."

Jac cleared her throat. "Of course."

"I can show you where the dressing rooms are, if you like?" Becca offered.

"I don't need one of those just to drop my clothes, dear. It's pretty warm in here."

"They turned the heating up so we wouldn't be cold while we're naked. Goosebumps aren't sexy."

"Of course."

"Jac, you can't be seriously considering this!" Vanessa shouted.

"Well, I wasn't considering anything. You were supposed to shoot your own scenes. If Fleur's happy to stand in at the last minute, it'll keep us on schedule, which will help with the budget. Fleur, how much do you charge?"

Fleur toed off her shoes. "Hm, I think a fancy dinner should cover it."

"Done."

"You're insane. She's—she's old. She can't stand in as a body double for me."

"Well, we might have to do a little bit of..." Jac turned to Fleur and looked her up and down "...creative editing in post-production."

Fleur pulled off a sock and handed it to Jac. "Don't worry, dear, my fella says I've got breasts that would make any man weep."

"What about women? The audience is likely to be mostly women," Jac said.

"Yes, I should imagine they'd work on them too."

Surely Jac will stop her before she strips entirely, right? Sasha stared, her mouth agape as Fleur pulled off her other sock and added it to the pile Jac was holding.

"You don't need any close-ups of feet or anything, do you, dear? I've not had my corns sorted recently."

Becca turned away, tears of mirth in her eyes.

"Jac! Stop her!" Vanessa demanded. "She can't pretend to be me!"

"She's offering to do us a favour. One we're in need of because of your diva attitude. So why should I ask her to stop? I need what she's offering." Jac looked around. "Can we get a wig for Fleur over here?"

Looking around, Sasha saw that Jac had asked Bobbi to find the wig, but Bobbi wasn't moving. She was staring at them from across the set with a scornful look. Surely she couldn't be that pissed at Fleur's stunt. This wasn't exactly out of character for her. But when Bobbi's gaze fell on Sasha and her eyes narrowed further, Sasha realised her stint in Bobbi's bad books was going to last a lot longer than she'd hoped.

"Bobbi!" Fleur's voice brought Sasha out of her morbid thoughts and back to the...disturbing present.

"Hey, Mrs A. I'll go find you that wig."

"Perfect." Fleur's cardigan seemed to be next on the list of items to be removed, and she worked the buttons on the thick woolly garment with a serene smile.

"Fine, I'll do it!" Vanessa capitulated. "But if there is even one microsecond's footage of my pussy in the final edit of this film, you will be slapped with a lawsuit so big you'll wish you'd never accepted this little script." She eyed Fleur up and down witheringly, then shuddered and walked away, her nose foisted haughtily in the air.

Becca and Jac bent double laughing, while Fleur buttoned up her cardigan again. Sasha walked to her mother's side.

"Sex tape? Really?"

Fleur shrugged and reached for her socks. "A girl has got to have a few achievable dreams on her bucket list." She pointed at her feet. "I really do need a visit to the chiropodist."

"Many, many years from now, when I finally get sick of you and stick you in a nursing home, if I go through your stuff and find a stash of homemade sex tapes, you realise it will scar me for the rest of my days, don't you?"

Fleur grinned. "That'll be another tick on the bucket list, then."

CHAPTER 25

THE HALLS AT KEFRAN MEDIA were empty. Jac sat reviewing the dailies at the end of the fourth week of filming. Everyone had long since left for the weekend. She pulled the box from her pocket and set it on the workbench in front of her. She'd had it in her pocket for almost two weeks now. But she still hadn't worked up the courage to give it to Sasha. Still hadn't figured out if it was too soon. Her head said it was. They'd been sleeping together for only a few weeks. That was all. Just a few weeks. But every moment apart from Sasha felt like it dragged on for hours. She wanted to wake up with Sasha in her arms every morning, fall asleep beside her every night, and know that no matter where she was, or what time it was, or what day it was, eventually Sasha would be coming home. To their home.

She pried open the lid and stared at the key on the tiny foam cushion.

It might only have been a few weeks since they slept together, but Sophie hadn't been wrong. Jac had been falling for Sasha from the moment she'd looked into those brown eyes outside Velvet. No, even before that. When she'd heard her voice on the phone, telling her she didn't have any PPI's or want any solar panels. Jac had started falling then, and it showed no signs of stopping. Not even slowing down.

She'd given keys to lovers before. Lived with more women than she really wanted to admit to. But the idea of asking them had never filled her with equal parts fear and excitement like it did with Sasha. Excitement at the wonderful idea of living with her for the rest of her life, and fear that Sasha would say no.

She hadn't even told Sasha how she felt yet. Hadn't said those three words that made Sasha so different from every other woman she'd given those keys to. So different from the women who had shared her life, her bed, but never her heart. Jac had never told anyone she loved them. Aside from Sophie and Mags, but that was different. They were the sisters she had chosen to become her family. Sasha was the woman who had stolen her beating heart from inside her chest. And Jac had gladly let her.

Did Sasha feel the same? She hadn't said it either, but Jac was pretty sure she did. She could sense it in the way Sasha looked at her, like everything in her world suddenly made sense. Like the black-and-white movie of her life had finally shifted to colour. At least that's how it felt to Jac. And what she thought she saw in Sasha's eyes when they talked, when they laughed, when they were in bed together, loving each other. It wasn't sex. It was so far beyond sex that Jac was barely able to recognise it next to every other physical encounter she'd ever had. They made love to each other. They connected, they felt each other. It wasn't about flesh meeting flesh when they touched; it was about souls meeting souls. And that couldn't just be on Jac's part. It couldn't be.

Jac didn't have that good of an imagination.

Maybe tonight would be the right time to ask Sasha. She stroked a finger over the filed grooves and ridges, then closed the lid and slid the box back into her pocket, rose from her chair, and pushed it under the editing desk before she left the room. She was almost at the door of the editing suite when she heard a voice calling her name. Jac turned and saw the slight figure of Bobbi Johnson shuffling towards her.

"Bobbi," Jac said by way of greeting. "You're here late."

Bobbi hunched her shoulders and stuffed her hands in her pockets. "I wanted to have a word with you."

Jac lifted her eyebrows in surprise. Bobbi had been avoiding her and Sasha since their first date. What did she want to say to her after three weeks?

"Can we walk and talk?"

"Sure." Jac pulled the door open and waved for Bobbi to exit ahead of her. The silence that followed them beyond the building seemed to belie Bobbi's desire to talk, so Jac decided to get the ball rolling. "What can I do for you, Bobbi?"

"Is it serious?"

225

Jac frowned. "Is what serious?"

"You and Sasha."

"Oh," Jac said, "I see." And for the first time she was absolutely certain that she did. Part of her felt sorry for Bobbi, and part of her was angry at her. Sasha was hurting because of Bobbi's behaviour. But clearly, Bobbi was hurting too. For totally different reasons. She stopped and looked over at Bobbi, then said kindly, "It's early days, but it seems to be heading in that direction."

Bobbi stopped beside her and turned to face Jac. Tears glistened in her dark eyes and she nodded. "I knew," she said quietly.

"You knew what, Bobbi?"

"That she couldn't love me. Not like that, anyway. I was always just a friend to her."

"Not just a friend, Bobbi. Her best friend. She does love you."

Bobbi's smile grew wider, yet sadder somehow. "I know. Just not the way I love her."

Jac wasn't entirely sure what to say, how to deal with this new information. Sasha had never hinted at Bobbi being in love with her, but if Jac was honest with herself, it was pretty obvious. Even over the weeks Bobbi had refused to speak to Sasha, Jac had seen her staring longingly at her. She'd just assigned the wrong motivation to that longing. She'd assumed she was missing her friend, not wishing for something Sasha could never be to her. If she could, they surely would have travelled that road before. They'd been friends for years.

"I'm sorry." It was the only thing Jac could think to say, and she was surprised to find it was the truth. Not sorry enough to even think about walking away from Sasha. But she did feel sorry for Bobbi.

"Don't. I don't want your pity."

"I don't pity you, Bobbi. I'm jealous of you in so many ways."

Bobbi snorted. "What the fuck have you got to be jealous of me for? You've got the shit-hot career, money coming out of your ears, and the most amazing woman I've ever known falling head over heels for you. You've got fucking everything, and I've got nothing."

"You've had years of being her best friend, her confidante. You know her in ways I never will. The past you share with her is something I can't ever be a part of. And I know that she misses you. She's happy, yes, but she wants to share her happiness with you too, because you're her best friend."

"I don't know if I can do that." Tears slipped down Bobbi's cheeks.

"She doesn't mean to hurt you, you know?"

"I know." She wiped them away. "But that doesn't stop it hurting." She sniffed and stuffed her hands back in her pockets. "I wish I'd never sent her script in to that stupid competition now. Everything was just fine before. Now it's all changed."

"I understand why you feel that way, but things change all the time for so many reasons. Who knows, maybe Sasha and I would've met anyway. It feels like something has drawn us together. Maybe this was meant to be."

"Then why does it feel like everything's gone to shit?"

"It hasn't. So much has happened for the better. Even for you."

"Bullshit."

"Really? You don't enjoy your new job better than the old one? You don't enjoy the pay rise or the new people you're working with? The job where you don't have to put up with racist bigots talking to you like shit?"

Bobbi shrugged, clearly not willing to admit that anything was better in any way. Even if it was the truth.

"You say you love Sasha—"

"I do."

"So be happy for her. She's got the job of a lifetime here, and she will make this her career. You and I both know that. You made that possible for her. You made it possible for her dreams to come true."

"Yes, but you're the one actually making them come true. You're the one who gets to live those dreams with her."

"She'd share them with you too, Bobbi. Any day of the week. All you have to do is let her. Stop shutting her out and be her friend."

"Do you think it's that easy? How would you feel if this was the other way around?"

Jac shook her head and put a hand on Bobbi's arm, squeezing lightly. "Far from it. I don't even want to think about it being the other way around. I don't think I'd handle it half as well as you're doing. But I do know one thing."

"What's that?"

"That being a part of Sasha's life in any way is worth it. Don't throw away the years of friendship you have with her without at least trying, Bobbi. She deserves better than that. You deserve better than that."

Bobbi stared at her, then said, "If you do anything, ever, to hurt her—"

"I won't."

"I'll hunt you down and set Fleur on you."

"That," Jac started, crossing her arms over her chest, "was just vicious, Bobbi."

Snorting a weak laugh, Bobbi turned and walked away, calling over her shoulder, "Good chat, Jac. Remember, I'm watching you."

"Think about what I said. She misses you."

Bobbi offered her a little wave of acknowledgement, and Jac wondered if this was the beginning of the two friends getting back on track. She hoped so. She hated to see Sasha unhappy. Thinking of Sasha, Jac turned and headed for her apartment, wrapping her fingers around the box in her pocket. *Maybe.*

"Oh, God, yes!" Sasha cried and gripped the headboard of Jac's bed while Jac worked her tongue between her legs. Her thighs quivered from the effort of holding herself up enough to let Jac breathe, but she wasn't sure how much longer she'd be able to stay where she was. Jac's hands roaming her backside, her breasts, and back were doing a wonderful job of ratcheting her excitement higher as her lips and tongue pushed her towards orgasm.

"Hm, so fucking hot."

The vibration of Jac's words against her clit pushed her over the edge. She arched her back, almost pulling away from Jac's lips, wrapped around her clit and sucking for all she was worth.

"Fuck!" Sasha shouted, riding the wave of ecstasy before collapsing in a boneless heap over Jac's prone body. She groaned as she lunged to the side, barely able to control her muscles and keep from squashing Jac. She lay panting, hair across her face, one arm above her head, the other flopping over the side of the bed. Her legs felt like jelly.

The bed dipped as Jac rolled towards her and brushed the hair off her face, then kissed her deeply. Sasha groaned again at the taste of herself on Jac's lips. She smiled up at her lazily when Jac pulled back. "I'm going to need a few minutes, darlin'." Eyes closed, she puckered her lips, asking for another kiss. Jac's resulting peck was quick. Too quick for Sasha's tastes, but when she opened her eyes again, Jac was smiling down at her.

"I love you."

Did she just— Am I hearing things? Did that mind-boggling orgasm induce hallucinations? Sasha was lost for words until Jac's expression began slowly slipping away.

"Did you just...?"

Jac nodded. "I know it's really quick, and I know we haven't known each other all that long really, but I do. You don't have to say it back. I just wanted you to—"

Sasha lifted her head and quieted Jac with a kiss. "I love you too," she whispered against Jac's lips. "I knew it after the first night we spent together, I just didn't...well, I didn't want you to think I was being all needy and tacky or clichéd. You know?"

"You love me too?" Jac asked, the smile slipping back onto her lips.

Tears prickled Sasha's eyes, then spilled out the corners and into her hair. "I do. I love you so much I wasn't sure how much longer I was going to be able to keep it inside." She lifted her hand and stroked Jac's cheeks, wiping the tears that gathered on her lashes.

"You don't have to." She laid her face against Sasha's neck, tightened her hold around her body, and held her. "God, I've never, ever felt like this before." She kissed Sasha's neck and shoulder before finally settling on her lips again. "I've never said that to anyone else."

"Really?"

"Yeah," Jac whispered, then amended, "Well, except for Sophie and Mags. But that's different."

Sasha's tears ran in small rivers from her eyes as she accepted the gift Jac was giving her. Her heart. Broken and patched up, and so, so fragile, and never entrusted to another soul before. Sasha reached between them and ran her finger down the scar on her chest.

She kissed Jac's lips. "I love you."

Jac's love and passion swept over her like wildfire through dry shrubs, burning away the touch of any who had come before her, searing Sasha's heart with the imprint of her own and marking her forever as Jac's. There would be no other for her. Every cell in her body was branded with one simple word, *Jac's.*

CHAPTER 26

"You're looking very pleased with yourself, honey." Fleur wiggled her finger in front of Sasha's face and smirked. "What's up?"

"Nothing." Sasha picked a blouse off the rack and held it against her body. "What do you think?"

"Black? What on earth do you want a black shirt for? With your colouring, you should go for bold colours. Bright, strong colours that will make people notice you from across the room." Fleur fingered a lock of Sasha's hair. "You got your father's colouring."

"I know." Sasha took hold of Fleur's hand, noting the dark rings under her eyes. They weren't anything new. Not really. They'd been there since her father had passed away, but they seemed to be getting bigger lately. "Are you okay? You look tired."

Fleur smiled and squeezed Sasha's hand. "I'm fine, honey. Bobbi came to see me last night."

"She did?"

Fleur nodded and moved to another rack of shirts.

"Is she okay? She hasn't spoken to me for weeks."

"I know. She's…she's struggling with all the changes, darling. But she's getting there, she just needed a little time. I've invited her for tea tonight. You need to be there. You two need to make up."

"I'll be there. What time?"

"I told her six." She swayed on her feet for a moment, then righted herself. "But perhaps a coffee break would be a good idea."

Sasha had gripped her arms as she started to sway, dropping the shirt in preparation to catch her mother should she fall. It had been quite a common thing when she'd first started getting used to her prosthesis, but it had been a long time since Sasha had felt the need to stay close to Fleur just in case.

"Are you sure you're all right? We can get you home if you'd rather go and lie down, Mum. It's okay."

Fleur shook her head. "No, I want to spend the day with you."

"We can do that at home. Takeaway, blanket over us while we watch a film on the telly. I'll make you some buttered popcorn if you like too. Then I'll cook tea before Bobbi's due to come around. What do you say?"

Fleur swayed again. Not a lot. But enough to worry Sasha.

"Mum, I really think you need to sit down for a bit, then I'm taking you home."

"Sasha, don't fuss so—"

Fleur didn't finish her sentence before her good leg gave way and she fell awkwardly. Sasha did her best to catch her and support her head as she went down, but the space between the racks made it difficult. She pushed clothes and metal stands out of the way as she held on to Fleur's tumbling body.

"Shit." Sasha quickly checked Fleur's back and neck in case she hit it on something when they landed, then shifted her into the recovery position, fingers pressed to her neck. She could feel Fleur's breath against her cheek, but her pulse was weak and way too fast. And since when had she been so skinny? Her mum had always been slender, but she was nothing but skin and bones.

"Jac!" she shouted across the store. "Jac!"

"I've called an ambulance for you," a voice said from behind Sasha's shoulder. "The dispatcher wants to know if she's breathing."

"Yes. She's unconscious, and her pulse is thready, but she is breathing." Sasha continued to run her hands over her mother's body, noting things she hadn't before. The clothes her mother was wearing deliberately hid how much weight she'd lost. There were bruises on her arms. Big, black-and-purple bruises alongside some old faded yellow-and-green ones right at the crease of her elbow. The same places where they always took blood from her.

"Any change?" the woman asked, moving to the other side of Fleur.

Sasha shook her head. "Jac!" she shouted again.

"Where are you?" Jac's voice drifted across the shop. The woman stood and waved her arms in the air. "Excuse me, let me through, please. Excuse me!" Jac's voice held the notes of anxiety and fear as she pushed her way through the crowd that had started to gather. "What happened?" Jac knelt behind Fleur's head.

"I don't know. She just collapsed."

"I've called an ambulance. They're on the way," the woman said.

"Thanks." Jac held out her hand. "I'm Jac, this is Sasha, and this is Fleur."

"Mary."

Jac looked down. "Is she breathing?"

"She is, she's just not coming around." There were other bruises she started to notice, but it was the slight yellow pallor to her mother's complexion that began to stand out to her. Sasha had long since become accustomed to her mother wearing a thicker layer of foundation. It had started when she'd battled her cancer and she'd been determined not to look "any sicker than she was". So the foundation had come out to cover up the pasty pallor that had settled on her sunken cheeks. Sasha wiped at the make-up smeared across not only her mother's face but her neck. Underneath, she was yellow. Jaundiced. She recalled the time a few months ago when she'd thought she'd seen the yellow cast to her mother's skin but had passed it off as a play of the dim light. Had it really been just that? Or had there been more? Had this been staring her in the face all this time?

"Oh God."

"What?" Jac asked.

"Why's she yellow?" Sasha's mind was racing a mile minute but shutting down in the same breath. The questions whirled through her brain, but there were no answers. "Pass me her bag." She held out her hand and Jac gave it to her.

"Could it have something to do with that?" Mary pointed to Fleur's necklace. "Isn't that one of those medical-alert thingies? What's wrong with her? The paramedics will need to know when they get here."

Sasha shook her head as she pulled the necklace free of Fleur's clothing. *Diabetes* it said on the back in big bold letters. "Mum doesn't have diabetes," Sasha whispered so quietly she was sure no one else could have possibly heard her.

Jac was going through Fleur's bag and pulled out a small black wallet. She unzipped it to display a blood-sugar monitor, strips, a syringe, a vial of insulin, and a finger-prick device.

"Maybe it's just her blood sugar." Jac held out the kit to her. "Do you know how to use this stuff to test it?"

"Mum doesn't have diabetes," she said again. Louder this time. Did she? Sasha flashed on the image of a thin plastic strip, tipped at both ends with copper; stained with blood. It was a test strip. To monitor blood sugar. *Oh God, what's going on? What has Mum been hiding?*

Jac looked at her, the kit, the necklace on Fleur's chest, and frowned. "Then why does she have all the stuff?"

"I don't know. I don't know what's going on, Jac."

Mary took the kit from Jac's hand. "My son has diabetes. It's quite simple to test." With fast, efficient hands, Mary assembled the kit, pricked Fleur's finger, and obtained a reading that she said was pretty normal. Certainly not low enough to cause Fleur's current state of unconsciousness. Jac thanked her profusely and started to put it all away as the paramedics came.

They operated with practiced ease and skill. Covered all the details they had to give and had Fleur on a trolley and en route to the ambulance before Sasha could even begin to decipher what was happening.

Before she knew it, she was in Jac's car following the ambulance to the Manchester Royal Infirmary. A ball of dread sat like a lead weight on her chest, pressing down, crushing her. Each breath she pulled into her lungs took effort, and she wasn't sure she'd make the next one.

"What's wrong with my mum, Jac?"

"I don't know, babe. But we'll find out, okay? She's going to the best place, and we'll find out."

There were worse hospitals in the world. There were better hospitals in the world. But Sasha hated them all equally. They all smelled the same no matter where they were or who was sitting next to you or how uncomfortable the bloody chairs were. They all smelled like fear, bleach, and death. *Maybe a little bit melodramatic there, Sash. You don't know anything's seriously wrong with her.* Sasha snorted to her own inner monologue. *Yes, I do.*

"Ms Adams?" A nurse stood in a doorway, holding it open behind her. Sasha stood. "That's me."

"I'm Nurse Warren. I've been treating your mother. She's stable, and okay for now. There's an ambulance on the way to take her to the hospice."

Sasha stumbled backwards into Jac's arms. They were the only things preventing her from falling. She wrapped her fingers around Jac's forearms. She needed to anchor herself, to find something to grip on to before she sank all the way down. She opened her mouth. She needed answers. She needed to know what the hell was going on. Because that sentence right there just didn't make sense. Not. One. Fucking. Bit.

But she couldn't. Not even a whimper passed her lips as she stared at the nurse. All blue scrubs and gentle smile. Understanding, piteous eyes that Sasha wanted to scratch right out along with that lying tongue.

"I'm sorry, what?" Jac asked for her. "What do you mean hospice?"

She nodded. Like one of those fucking Churchill nodding dogs, and Sasha wanted to rip off her bobbing head. But she couldn't even move.

"I'm sorry, who are you?"

"Sorry, Jac Kensington. I'm Sasha's...partner."

The nurse looked at their joined hands and smiled. "Of course. Well, yes. At this stage, I'm afraid it really is the best place for her now."

"Wh-what do you mean at this stage?" Sasha's voice sounded alien to her own ears.

"At this stage of her illness. There's nothing more we can do for her but keep her comfortable. She has a place waiting for her at St Ann's Hospice. I understand it's been arranged for some time now."

"But she—she's not ill. She beat the cancer. Years ago."

Jac's arms tightened around her body, supporting her as her knees gave way. Puzzle pieces started to click into place. The weight loss she'd been hiding with baggy clothes and heavy jumpers. The increase in weed consumption. The more frequent trips to the chemist for her prescriptions. The bruises. Diabetes. Jaundice.

"Oh God. Why didn't she tell me?"

The nurse's face dropped. Her sad, empathetic smile slid from her face, and a look of horror settled in its place. "I'm so sorry. I thought—I thought you knew."

Sasha crumpled, clinging to Jac's arms. "What kind?"

234

"I'm sorry, I think maybe you should speak to your mother."

"I will." Sasha didn't recognise the cold edge to her voice. "But right now, you're here. Now tell me what, exactly, is killing my mother."

"Sash, baby, it's okay," Jac whispered in her ear.

"No, it's not. It's not okay, Jac. It's never going to be okay. My mother's dying." She pointed behind the nurse. "She's through there, dying, and she didn't even tell me." She found strength in the anger that was boiling in her gut and used it to force herself to her feet. She clutched on to the nurse's arm. "Now you are going to tell me what's wrong with her, and then you're going to take me to see her."

"I think it might be best—"

"I don't care what you think!" Sasha shouted. "You've already dropped the ball and spilled the secret. You might as well finish the job."

A security guard stepped forwards and made to grab at Sasha's arm. Sasha glared at him, but Nurse Warren told him to back off.

"You're right." She held her hand out and indicated a room off to the side. "Let's go in there, and I'll answer your questions."

Sasha pulled her jumper down and stalked into the room. She wanted to slam the door closed, but Jac and the nurse were too close behind her. She paced back and forth in the tiny room. Two steps one way, two steps back.

"She has pancreatic cancer," the nurse began. "Looking at her notes, she was diagnosed with it about nine months ago—"

"Nine months?"

The nurse nodded. "She was offered a range of treatments, as are standard, but the cancer was already at stage four when they found it."

"Meaning?"

"Her prognosis, even with treatment, wasn't good."

"So what are they doing? What have they been doing?"

"All they could. Monitoring her condition. Prescribing pain medication. Everything she'd let them do."

"What about operating on it? Chemo? Radiation? She had all that last time."

"She refused treatment."

"Don't be stupid. No one in their right mind would refuse treatment."

"I'm sorry, at this stage I can only tell you what's in the file. We've given your mother some heavy painkillers, and it's making her drift in and out of consciousness. We thought that best until she was settled at the hospice where they can manage her pain levels best. But it says very clearly in her file that treatment was refused and she is DNR."

"DNR? DNR as in 'do not resuscitate'?"

"Yes."

Sasha covered her face with her hands, trying to physically push the tears away, to stop them falling, because she knew that once they started, they were never going to stop. Pushing them up through her hair, gripping it into her fists, she pulled at her hair until the pain outside was enough to distract her from the pain inside. If only for a second.

She's dying. She not even fighting it. And she didn't even tell me. Why? Why? Why? Why?

"How long?"

"It's difficult to say."

"You're sending her to the hospice. They don't do that if they've got months left to go. How fucking long?"

"A week. Maybe two."

Sasha collapsed to her knees and threw up. Tears streamed down her face, mingled with the vomit and the mucus running from her nose. But she didn't care. She didn't care how it looked or that it stank. On her hands and knees in the middle of the tiny relatives' room, she cried and screamed and emptied her stomach until all that was left in it was the hardening stone of grief.

CHAPTER 27

THE WALLS AT THE HOSPICE care facility were yellow. Like a reflection of the sun streaming through the open blinds that covered the window. It wasn't what Sasha had expected. There was so much light. It was everywhere. And not the horrid buzzing fluorescent light that itched behind your eyeballs and made your skin crawl. It was natural light wherever possible. Spotlights and lamps by bedsides in each individual's room. Individual. Person. Not patient. Not service user. Not dead man walking.

Sasha's mouth still tasted like vomit. It didn't seem to matter that she'd brushed her teeth and chewed gum all the way from the hospital to this place. This...the last place her mother would see.

"It's nice, isn't it?" Jac asked quietly.

Sasha didn't answer. She had too many questions she needed answers to, but Jac didn't have any of them. Only her mother did. And she was still sleeping off the painkillers they'd given her to make her comfortable for the ambulance ride.

It was just the three of them in the room. Fleur lay on the hospital bed, a thin tube in her arm, connecting her to a bag of fluids. The nurse had told Sasha they would discuss medication with Fleur when she woke up but expected they'd fix her up with a morphine pump, a device that would allow Fleur to top up her pain relief when she needed it but without allowing her to administer enough to OD on. For now, she was only receiving saline.

She looked so small. Like a child in an adult-sized bed, and it only served to emphasise even more how fragile she'd become. And Sasha hadn't even been noticing. She saw her mother every day. Every single fucking day, and she hadn't noticed when the weight had started to fall off her. She hadn't noticed when her face had started to turn yellow. Hadn't noticed when she'd developed fucking diabetes. She could scream, if only it would do any good.

But it wouldn't. It was far too late for that to help anyone now.

"Would it help if I went and packed a bag for her? Maybe brought a few of her things here. To make it a bit more personal. Would she like that?" Jac asked.

Sasha looked at her for the first time since Fleur had been wheeled into the room. She wasn't sure if Jac was offering this to get away from Sasha or to give Sasha a break from her. Either way, right then, Sasha didn't care. She wanted to speak to her mother alone, so having Jac leave would give them both some space.

"That's very thoughtful of you." She waved her hand towards her bag. "My house keys are in there. Mum keeps a wheely suitcase on top of her wardrobe. She used to use it all the time when she was coming into hospital." Sasha's voice faltered on the last words, cracking enough for some of her pain to leak out. "Sorry." She said the word. She knew she did. But no sound passed her lips. None at all.

Jac's arms were around her shoulders as the tears fell again. Jac held her, rocked her, whispered words like 'you don't need to be sorry' and 'I've got you', 'cry all you need to', 'I'm here for you, baby', and the biggest lie of all—'it'll be okay'. Jac whispered them all for her. But it wouldn't be okay. *A week. Two at most.*

Time passed. Sasha couldn't even guess at how long Jac stood behind her chair, just holding her. Minutes? An hour? Two? She'd stopped looking at the clock. It was only ticking away the time on those last days, and she prayed instead that it would stop moving. She closed her eyes and tried to remember that poem. The one she'd first heard in *Four Weddings and a Funeral*. W.H. Auden.

Stop all the clocks. That was how it started. *Stop all the clocks.* But that was all she could remember. She couldn't remember the next line, only that she wished she could follow that instruction.

When the tears dried on her cheeks, Jac kissed her, asked if she'd be okay while she went to the house.

Sasha didn't answer. She couldn't. She was still fixated on that bloody line. *"The Funeral Blues."* *The Funeral fucking Blues. She's not even dead yet, and all I can think of is The Funeral fucking Blues.*

"Why, Mum? Why didn't you tell me?" Sasha growled through gritted teeth as she swiped at tears again. She was sick of crying already.

"Because I knew you'd want me to go through it all again, baby." Fleur's voice was surprisingly strong, considering she'd supposedly just woken up.

"How long have you been awake?"

"Not that long."

Sasha stared at her.

"Go on. Ask."

"Why did you give up? Why didn't you fight?"

Fleur reached out to touch Sasha. Sasha wanted to shy away, but the need for her mother's comfort was too great. She didn't remember moving, but before she knew it, she was laid beside her mother, head on her shoulder, arm about her waist, and crying more tears.

"I'm going to be dried out like a raisin if I keep crying like this." She swiped at them, trying to catch them before they fell on Fleur's sheets.

"Doesn't matter. And I didn't give up. This battle, baby girl, was one I couldn't win."

"You don't know that. You didn't even try."

"I do know that. I know myself, Sasha. And I know what I can tolerate and what I can't. They couldn't even promise me that treatment would buy me more time, and that was the only thing that would have made it worth fighting for. More time with you, my beautiful, precious girl."

"And I've been spending all my time working on the film or with Jac." Sasha sat up and glared at her mother. "If I'd known...if you'd told me, I wouldn't have taken the damn job. I could have spent all my time with you." Her refusal to tell Sasha had robbed them of this time together. Stolen precious moments, memories Sasha would have treasured.

"The greatest gift I've had in all this is seeing you happy. Seeing you blossom and discover this new career you're embarking on. Watching you fall in love with Jac. Gaining new friends in Sophie and Mags. Knowing that when I go, you'll have people around you to help you, look after you. They'll all be there for you. Along with Bobbi."

"Does she know?"

"No. Only Mike knows. He's been helping me."

"By sleeping with you?"

"Among other things, yes."

"But I don't understand. Why start a relationship with him if you knew…?" She waved her hand up and down Fleur's body.

"That I was at death's doorstep?"

Sasha's cheeks burned but she nodded. They didn't have time to piss and arse about being delicate. Fleur had seen to that.

"I wanted to experience everything I could. At least one last time. Mike, well, he's an unusual man; I'll give him that. I'm sure you don't want all the details of how it came about, but, basically, I was high one night and was just talking. Like I do. Saying pretty much anything that came into my head. I told him I missed sex. Missed being held by a lover. I missed the closeness and intimacy. I hadn't had that since your father passed away, and I was regretting that. I was feeling my mortality and wishing I'd had a bit more fun with my life, I suppose." She sighed. "I didn't think much of it. To be honest I didn't really remember a great deal of it, but the next day, he came to me and offered his assistance in the matter."

"Even though he knew?"

"Oh, yes, I made quite sure he knew what he was signing up for before anything happened. I made him no promises but a bit of a workout, and he offered to hold me as much as I liked."

Sasha tried to wrap her head around it. In a way, it was no different to a short fling, she supposed. But it was her mother. Her dying mother.

"He gave me something I needed for a little while. And I'm very grateful to him for that."

"Do you love him?"

"I care for him, of course. But no, I don't love him. Not like I did your father, if that's what you're asking."

"I'm not sure if that makes me feel better or worse."

"Does it matter? It made me feel better for a little while."

The soft-spoken words pulled Sasha up short. She lifted her face to meet her mother's gaze. Fleur was right. In her shock, Sasha had forgotten that this wasn't about her. It wasn't about her losing her mother, it wasn't about her anger at not having all this time with Fleur. It was about Fleur. It was about her death and what she needed to do to deal with that. Sasha's emotions could be dealt with later. She'd be here to deal with them later. Fleur wouldn't.

"You're right. I'm sorry. It was such a shock that I couldn't get past the thought that you refused to tell me and that I was going to lose you. I didn't think about everything you've been dealing with all this time. I'm sorry." She laid her head back on Fleur's shoulder.

"No need to be sorry. I was planning to tell you soon. Probably this weekend. I just wanted to know you and Bobbi had things worked out first. I knew I didn't have much time left, and I know you two will need each other."

So many things began to slip into place. "You knew when you entered me into the competition, didn't you?"

"Bobbi entered you into that."

"You paid for it. Now answer the question," she spoke crossly, but there was a smile on her lips as her mother's actions began to make sense to her.

"Yes."

"Why?" Sasha suspected she knew what Fleur was going to say, but she wanted to hear it from her.

"Because I wanted you to be happy. I want you to always be happy. And if you'd still been in that crappy little job, living in our house when I go and pop me clogs, well, I wasn't sure how you'd have pulled yourself out of that rut. And you deserved so much better, my darling. I wanted so much more for you. I wanted you to be happy, and the only way for you to find that was to start you down this path."

"You could never have known I'd win it. That it was the right path for me—"

"The crystals showed me it was the right path for you, that it would lead you to your true happiness."

"Mum," she said around a heavy sigh. "You know I don't believe in all that—"

"You don't have to believe all that crap, as you like to call it. I do. I did. And it led you to Jac. It led you to this film. And that's enough for me to believe in it all for the rest of my life." She chortled. Sasha sat up and stared at her incredulously. "For the rest of my days!" Fleur cried. "Get it?"

Sasha opened her mouth to tell her off. To tell her it wasn't funny. Instead, she found herself laughing. Perched on the edge of her mother's bed, holding her frail hands, they laughed until they both cried.

"Don't think of becoming a stand-up comedienne," Sasha said when their laughter finally quieted to chuckles.

"No? I thought I'd be dead funny."

Sasha groaned. "Not funny."

"Should I try clog dancing, then? I could pop those babies anytime."

"So not funny."

"Oh, you know I'm the life and soul of every party."

"These are getting worse."

"No, they're not. They're getting better."

"You've been practicing?"

"Hell, yeah. I want everyone to see me on top form before I have left the building." She deepened her voice and shook her hips, pointing one hand in the air and giving it her best Elvis impression.

"Don't do that one again, Mum; you'll throw your back out."

That one earned her a laugh and a slap on the back. "That's my girl."

Sasha tightened her arms around Fleur's waist, determined not to cry again. Fleur had made it clear. She wasn't going out moping and lamenting the unfairness of it all. No, Sasha could do that the moment she walked out of that door. If Fleur wanted to see her laugh, she would laugh. If Fleur wanted to tell bad jokes, then she'd join in. This was about Fleur. Fleur's goodbye.

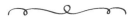

Jac let herself into Sasha and Fleur's home and flicked on the light switch. Nip wound herself around her feet and ankles, meowing loudly.

"Hey there, Miss Thing. What're you up to?" She bent down and stroked the top of her head and snatched her hand back quickly when Nip sat back on her back legs, front paws spread, claws out, and poised to catch her hand like it was an annoying fly.

"Whoa, whoa, chill. Let's get you fed and see if that settles your ninja-kitty skills out a bit." She headed for the kitchen, not sure where she'd find the cat food, but she figured Fleur's brownie tin would be on the kitchen counter if she couldn't find it. A stoned Nip was a peaceful Nip. "Sasha never told me you were some sort of guard cat."

With her cat food located and served, Nip was a happy pussy again, no brownies required. Jac made her way to Fleur's bedroom. The suitcase was right where Sasha had said it would be, but when it was opened and laid on Fleur's bed, Jac was at a loss. What do you pack for something like this? What does a person need in a hospice? She looked around the room. Fleur's room.

There were pictures on top of the bedside table, on the chest of drawers, all over the walls. Pictures of her and a man who looked a lot like Sasha. Pictures of Fleur and Sasha. Pictures of Sasha with her dad. Pictures of just Sasha. Ones Jac hadn't seen before. A little girl missing her front tooth, and a teen with a dreadful perm, neon socks, and pink-and-purple eyeshadow. It was truly scary, but Jac loved it. Looking at where it was on the wall, right opposite the bed, she guessed that Fleur did too. She imagined it appealing to the quirky woman, probably mostly because it would embarrass Sasha. She took it from the wall and put it in the suitcase. The one beside the bed, a family picture of the three of them, with a twenty-something-year-old Sasha grinning into the camera, went in next.

Yes, Fleur would need nightclothes, underwear, toiletries. But she'd need more than that, right? She'd need it to feel like her space. Jac would in her place. Maybe. Or would that make it harder? Seeing the pictures of happy times? Jac didn't know. She sat on the bed like pins had been pulled from her knees.

She couldn't imagine what Fleur or Sasha would be feeling right now. Well, she knew Sasha was in shock. But that would wear off, and then what? What emotion would be lying underneath it all?

Would she feel lost? Like Jac had when she'd figured out no one was ever going to come for her like they had for the other kids. Would she feel anger at the unfairness of it? Or would the grief and sorrow supersede it all? No way to know until the shock wore off. All Jac could do was be there. Hold her. Let her cry and vent and shout and scream, and cry some more. Whatever she needed.

"You better be fucking ready for this, Kensington, because she is going to need all the help she can get."

But Jac wasn't ready. She'd known Fleur hardly any time at all, and the thought of the vibrant, wonderful, quirky woman not being around anymore to make them all shudder at her sex life, her giant spliffs, or her waxing lyrical about her latest pot-filled brownie recipe just didn't compute. She wanted a cigarette, but she'd quit. She wanted a drink, but she needed to be able to drive, to function, to do whatever Sasha needed her to do. She wanted to go back to yesterday when it was all perfect. But there was no going back, only going forwards. She pulled her phone from her pocket and dialled.

"This better be good, Pan-pan. I was about to get my freak on with my wife."

"Sasha's mum collapsed while we were out this afternoon. She's just been admitted to St Ann's Hospice."

Silence.

Jac carried on. "Pancreatic cancer. The nurse said she's got a couple of weeks, tops."

Sophie still didn't say anything.

"I'm trying to pack some stuff for Fleur now. Sasha's there with her. Sasha didn't even know. Fleur never said anything to her. She's known for nine months and she never said anything. And I don't know what to pack, Soph. There's a suitcase here, but I don't—I put in these two pictures because I thought that might make it feel more like home, you know? But what if she doesn't want that? What if that's the wrong thing to do and it upsets her? Or upsets Sasha? What will she want, Soph? Please, tell me what to pack."

Sophie's voice was thick and raspy. "Give me the address." Jac reeled it off the top of her head. "I'll be there in twenty minutes, Jac. Just hold on, okay?"

Jac nodded, then remembered she couldn't see her. "Okay."

When Sophie hung up, Jac dropped the phone on the bed and looked at the rest of the pictures. The story of Fleur and Sasha's lives was played out across the walls of the room, from the ubiquitous baby-on-a-rug picture to school pictures. Holiday snapshots of a toddler on a beach with a nappy halfway down her legs, grinning atop a donkey with Blackpool Tower in the background. Sasha's little face scowling at the camera, arms folded over her chest and a definite bowl cut to her lovely hair. Jac wondered if the cut had caused the scowl or something else. She made a mental note to ask about it later.

When the doorbell sounded, Jac answered, expecting it to be Sophie, but found Mike Hunt looking up at her.

"Oh, hello," he said. "Fleur about?"

"I'm sorry, no."

"Oh, do you know when she'll be back?" Jac was torn. She didn't want to go blabbing Fleur's personal business, but at the same time this guy was her...boyfriend...and it wasn't like she'd be able to hide what was going on for long.

Jac took a deep breath. "She's not very well, Mr Hunt."

He held his hand up. "Mike, please. So it's happened, then? The hospice?"

"You knew?"

He nodded.

"Wow. How come you knew but Sasha didn't?"

"Well, women are a funny breed. Happen you know what I mean, hey, lass?"

Jac almost wanted to point out that she was a woman, but it looked like he had more to say, and she wanted to hear it. If what he had to say could help her to help Sasha later, well, then it was worth listening to his outdated ideas. It wasn't the first time someone had assumed her to be "the man" in the relationship when they saw her. Hell, even one or two of her exes had.

"When I asked Fleur that very question, she said it were all about them bloody crystal things she uses. Said they told her that she had to get Sasha settled on't right path before she started pushing up't daisies."

"The crystals? That's what you're telling me?"

"Aye, that's what I thought n'all. Load a bloody codswallop. But she said that all't crystals told her was that this competition thing was the way to go. She believed that the universe would take care of't rest for her. She said she'd asked for nowt all her life; now her dying wish were that Sasha were sorted before she were measured up for that there wooden box, like."

"That still doesn't explain why she didn't tell Sasha."

"Aye, it do. She knew Sasha would wait on her hand and foot if she knew. Poor lass'd never leave her mam's side if she'd known how ill she were.

She'd have never gone and chased those big dreams of hers." He inclined his head at Jac. "She'd have never have met you."

"You're telling me the bloody crystals brought me and Sasha together? The same crystals I've seen Fleur wave over a plate of hash brownies to decide which one she's going to eat? Those crystals?"

Mike grinned. "Nah, I said that's what Fleur said." He stuffed his hands in his pockets. "I think 'im upstairs 'as a plan myself. But I'm guessing you're not the sort sitting in his camp either, are ya?"

Jac shook her head. "Never been much of a fan of religion."

"Didn't think so. So you call it what you like, lass. Fate, serendipity, karma, universe, crystals, or just one bloody stubborn and pig-headed woman trying to do what she thought was the right thing. Don't matter none to me. All I know is that Fleur enjoyed every second she could, right up till she couldn't no more. She has a daughter she loves more than life itself, and she's had a good life, a life she's loved and one she wanted to say goodbye to on her own terms." He licked his lips. "I think we all have to respect that. Whether we agree with it or not."

Sophie's car pulled into the street, slowing as she sought out a parking space.

"I'll be heading back there in a little while. Do you want to come with me?"

Mike shook his head. "That was one of Fleur's rules to our little arrangement. Once she left this house, I wasn't to see her again." He smiled sadly. "She said she wanted me to remember her as she was here. Not as she'll be in there."

Jac's eyes watered. Fleur certainly had thought of everything. "I think I can understand that request, Mr Hunt."

"Aye, she planned everything. All paid for too. Wanted to make it as easy on Sasha as she could. When't time's right, I've got a folder with everything in." He pointed over his shoulder as Sophie pushed open the gate. "Just knock on when you're ready." He reached out and squeezed her forearm. "Give Sasha my best, would you? She's a lovely girl."

"I will."

With a final nod, he turned and walked away. Sophie hiked up her eyebrows in question and indicated her head in Mr Hunt's direction.

"Fleur's boyfriend."

"Oh, that's the fella?"

"Yup. Sorry I interrupted your freak."

"Yeah, well, when I said it'd better be good, I was hoping for actual good, not just blow your whole fucking world apart, you know?" She wrapped her arms around Jac's waist and squeezed as tight as she could.

Jac sighed and clung on like a drowning woman to a life preserver, terrified she'd drown the second she let go. "Yeah. Been one of those days, Soph."

"I called Mags on the way over. She's going to review the filming schedule and see what wiggle room Dock 10 has. See if we can shuffle things back."

"I don't think they can. We were a slot-in, if memory serves."

"Well, she's gonna try. So don't even worry about it."

Jac shook her head. "We've got about a week's worth of shooting left to do. We'll have to do it without Sasha, but we'll figure it out. We're too far in to call anything to a stop now."

"I've seen where you're taking the direction. Vanessa's cooled off. I'll cover as much of the shooting for you as I can if Mags can't move things."

"But you hate directing."

"Yeah, well, doesn't mean I can't do it. You can swing by when you can to make sure we're on track. We'll make it work."

"Thank you."

"No need. I know you'd do it for me, Pan-pan."

"I so would, but then, I love directing."

Sophie snickered. "Come on, then. Let's go take a look and see what Fleur might want with her." She backed out of the embrace but kept her arm around Jac's waist and led them into the house.

The attack was silent.

Until Sophie screamed, at least.

Nip launched herself from the shelf above the coat pegs, the one Fleur kept her collection of hats on. Only now the hats were scattered as Sophie ran down the corridor with Nip on top of her head, clinging on, front paws stretched down around Sophie's jaw, the back ones gripped onto her coat where it lay across her shoulders.

"Get it off me!"

"Stop running, then!"

Nip clung on like it was her first time on a roller coaster. Jac somehow doubted it. The move seemed far too practiced, the cat far too ninja-kitty and far too comfortable-looking in her cat-hat position. Oh no. She'd done this before.

"Get this fucking thing off me!"

Sasha stared at her phone, Bobbi's contact details on the screen, her finger hovering over the Connect Call button, as tears ran down her cheeks. She swiped at them angrily and hit the green button, just hoping Bobbi would answer this time. She didn't want to have to say something like this in a message. She couldn't do that to Bobbi. Bobbi loved Fleur too.

As the phone rang for the sixth time, she was about to disconnect when Bobbi's voice crept through the handset.

"Sasha?"

Sasha smiled, so glad to hear Bobbi's voice, even as more tears slid down her cheeks. "I have a confession to make."

Bobbi snorted quietly. "Do we need bail money?"

"Not this time."

"Need my car to run Vanessa over?"

Sasha choked back a sob. "Maybe tomorrow."

"Sasha? What's wrong?" The worry in Bobbi's voice echoed in Sasha's ears.

"Maybe I should have said, 'My mum has a confession to make.'"

"Okay," Bobbi said. "Is she pregnant?"

Sasha laughed through her tears and held a tissue to her nose. "Not this time." Her voice cracked. "She's...she's sick, Bobbi."

Silence stretched between them. "How sick?"

"She doesn't have long."

"What do you mean 'she doesn't have long'? This is your mum we're talking about."

"The nurse said she's got a week, maybe two left."

Bobbi was silent.

Sasha held the phone away from her ear to check they were still connected. They were. "Bobbi? You still there?"

"No fucking way," Bobbi whispered. "It's your mum. Mrs A's invincible. She's even bionic now."

"The cancer's come back. It's spread. All they can do is keep her comfortable until...until she's gone."

"This isn't funny, Sasha."

"It isn't a joke."

Silence again.

"I really need my best friend right now," Sasha whispered brokenly. "I really need you, Bobbi."

"I'm on my way."

"Jac," Fleur said as she opened her arms in welcome, "what d'you think of my new digs, then?" She waved her hands to indicate the room.

"Very nice."

"Oh, pish. But they'll do till I move on to the big house in the sky, hey?" She cackled, then stopped laughing when Jac stared at her. "Not funny?" Jac shook her head, and Fleur sucked on her teeth. "I'll have to keep working on my material." She pointed to the case in Jac's hand. "What've you got there?"

"I brought you some stuff from home. I wasn't sure exactly what you'd want, so I just—well, I just grabbed a bunch of stuff. I can take back anything you don't want."

"Been rifling through my drawers, 'ave you?" The gleam in Fleur's eye was wicked. "Don't let Sasha know you've a thing for my undercrackers. She's the jealous type, that one."

"Not jealous of you, you old harpy," Sasha said as she stepped out of the bathroom. "I like to drink my fluids, not have them drip-fed to me."

Jac stared at her. She'd been expecting tears when she got back. Maybe arguing. Anger. Not...banter. Not shit jokes about death and a repartee that sounded almost normal between them.

"Harpy." Fleur chuckled. "I like it. The maid brought my undercrackers, dear."

"So I heard." Sasha crossed the room, took the case from Jac's hand, and stretched up to kiss her cheek. "You okay?" she asked quietly, then stepped back to watch her eyes.

Jac nodded dumbly, and Sasha mouthed, "I'll explain later," before stepping away and hoisting the case onto the bed. "Did you have space in here for more than one pair of Mum's giant granny pants?"

"Just you wait, young lady. You'll be getting your own before you know it."

Sasha's hands worked quickly to unpack the clothes Sophie had picked out and folded neatly—after she'd recovered from the cat-hat attack—but they were shaking. Jac could see the effort Sasha was putting in to maintaining this façade. It was etched in the lines that were pulling at the corners of her eyes, the edges of her mouth. And Jac wanted to kiss each one away. But there was an explanation to be had, and until then, she would follow Sasha's lead.

The conversation was inane. Words with no meaning passed between the three of them as Sasha worked, all of them seemingly in need of something—anything—to do.

Underwear and thick socks were folded neatly into one drawer, nightgowns another. The dressing gown Sophie had insisted upon found a home on the back of the bathroom door, and a pair of slippers were tucked under the bed, just below Fleur's bottom. Exactly where her feet would be when she swivelled on the bed to stand. When Sasha got to the photo frames, she paused. Her lip trembled and she bit it, blinking rapidly. Jac had no doubt she was forcing back tears. She ran a finger over the picture and swallowed before she held it out to Fleur.

The one of the three of them together. Jac recognised the frame.

"Ah, my Bert." Fleur smiled and whispered, "Not long now, my love."

A strangled cry rasped out of Sasha's throat. But she had turned and fled the room before Jac could even stand and go to her.

"Give her a minute, love," Fleur said. "Just give her a minute."

Jac sat back down in the padded, vinyl-covered chair and stared at the door.

"Did she ever tell you how we met? Her father and I?"

"No."

"I was stepping out with another fella. Nice chap. He was working on the Gas, about as interesting as white on bread. But, like I said, nice chap, just not for me. Anyway, this chap, John, he was called. He took me to the Plaza one night. Dancing. Well, he had two left feet, and one of them wasn't for keeping in time with the other, and there I was in my finery. It was 1962, and I was wearing a midcalf maxi dress made out of a pair of old curtains. I thought I looked fabulous. But truly, it was hideous. I burnt it after we got married." Fleur cackled, but her eyes looked so very far away.

Jac waited, wondering who would come back first, Fleur from her mental wanderings or Sasha from her physical flight.

"So, anyway, after I'd had my feet trodden on more times than I could count, Bert came over and tapped John on the shoulder. Asked if he could cut in, you know?" She stroked a finger down the picture. Jac assumed it was down Bert's face. "No one had ever done anything like that for me before. And I looked up into those big brown eyes—just like Sasha's—and that was it. I was a goner." She smiled over at Jac. "Much like you were, I imagine."

Jac snorted a quick laugh. "Pretty much." She stared at the door again. "The voice doesn't hurt either."

"Ah." Fleur lifted her head knowingly. "That husky, raspy, sounds like she has a forty-a-day habit does it for you, does it?"

Jac shook her head. "You are something else, lady."

"Who're you calling a lady?" Fleur was indignant. "Never been so insulted in all my life."

"Sorry, my mistake." Jac held up her hands. "Why's she pretending nothing's wrong?"

"Because I asked her to."

"Why?"

It was Fleur's turn to stare at the door now. "Because I don't want her last memories of me to be morbid and riddled with nothing but tears." She smiled sadly. "There'll be plenty of time for those after I'm gone. But while it's in my power to do so, I want her to see me smiling. I want her to shout at me for telling stupid jokes. She needs to know I'm still me." She reached out, and Jac rose slowly to come to the bed. Fleur's grip was strong. "And she needs to remember I love her." She swallowed. "More than anything. Will you tell her that for me when she forgets?"

Jac nodded, unable to say anything around the lump in her throat.

"Promise me."

"I-I promise," Jac managed to stammer out.

Fleur snatched back her hand and blotted her cheeks. She flapped a hand at Jac's face. "Wipe them away before she comes back. No tears in this room. Not while I'm in here."

"Jesus, you're hard-nosed, aren't you?"

"When it comes to my little girl, I always have been. Always will be." She blew her nose. "Remember that after I'm gone. I'll have access to lightning bolts and shit once I'm up there."

"Who says you're headed up there?"

Fleur cackled. "That's better. And if I'm headed down there, then I've got flaming pitchforks and the Devil himself on my side. So you better watch your pasty-white arse." She winked. "As lovely as it might be."

Jac stepped back. "Say what?"

"Oh, Mother, stop flirting with my girlfriend. You'll scare her off." Sasha breezed back into the room and laced her fingers with Jac's. "Need me to protect you?" she asked with a wink. Her eyes were puffy and red-rimmed, all traces of her make-up were gone, and the tip of her nose was red from blowing. But Sasha still looked beautiful to her.

"Not much of a girlfriend if she needs you to protect her," Fleur butted in.

Sasha rolled her eyes and opened her mouth to speak, but Jac got there first.

"I'm happy to fight my own battles, and who says the Devil would be on your side? I may or may not have already sold him my soul." Jac tugged her towards the pair of chairs beside the bed, pulled them side by side, and wrapped her arm around Sasha's shoulders when they sat down.

"Excellent. I'll look forward to company, then."

Sasha's phone pinged with a text message. She glanced at the screen quickly.

I'm outside in the car park. Can we talk for a minute before I come in? B xoxo

"I'll be back in a minute," Sasha said as she stood and strode to the door. "Don't go running off before I get back."

Jac caught her arm as she pulled open the door. "Everything okay?" The worry and questions in her eyes shone through as clearly as her love did.

"Fine." Sasha leant forwards and kissed her cheek. "Bobbi's outside. She wants to talk before she comes in."

"Want me to come with you?"

"Thanks, but no. You keep the old trout company for me," she said loud enough for Fleur to hear.

"Less of the old, young lady," Fleur shouted. Sasha offered Jac a quick wink, a smile, and let the door close behind her.

Bobbi was leant against her car, the grey hood of her hoodie pulled up over her head, and she looked smaller than Sasha could ever remember her looking. She looked defeated, beaten, and so, so lost. Sasha didn't even think; she trotted over and wrapped her arms around Bobbi's shoulders.

"I'm sorry," Bobbi said into her neck.

"Doesn't matter now."

"It does." Bobbi pulled back so she could see Sasha's face. "I shouldn't have said the things I did to you. I was being selfish."

"It's fine. I shouldn't have forgotten about—"

"Sasha, I was only throwing the stupid party to get you to spend time with me. Thought it would be a bit more exciting than another *Friends* fest and popcorn."

"I love our *Friends* fests and popcorn."

"I know. I was just scared."

"Of what?"

"Of losing you."

"Bobbi—"

"No, please, Sasha, let me say this, and then we can move on, okay?"

"Okay," Sasha agreed, but she still wasn't sure she wanted to hear what Bobbi was going to say.

"I was scared of losing you when I realised how much everything was changing. I think you know how I feel about you, don't you?"

Sasha's cheeks burned but she nodded. This wasn't a time for modesty or trying to hide behind the charade they'd carried on for years.

Bobbi mimicked her movement. "Okay, right. So you know, and while I can't say I'm over the moon to know you're with Jac now, I knew we'd only ever be friends."

"It still hurts you, though."

"Yes, but not because you're in love with someone else. I always knew that would happen one day. That makes me sad, but I truly want you to be happy, Sasha."

"I don't understand, then."

"I'm hurt and scared because I lost my friend. That part I didn't count on."

"Oh, Bobbi. You haven't lost me. I told you, I'll always be your best friend."

"So much was changing, Sash. So much still is. The jobs, Jac, your mum. It felt like you didn't have any time for me anymore. And we were always together. Always. And it's not like I could spend time with your mum either. She was seeing Mike Hunt all the time."

"Please don't use his full name like that. It's too easy to get it wrong, and I don't want the alternative ringing in my ears."

Bobbi snorted. "Sorry."

Sasha squeezed her tighter in her arms. "I'm sorry I abandoned you."

"You didn't. Not really. I mean, you got me the job, so we were working in the same place. It just… I just felt like I couldn't compete with all the exciting new stuff you had going on. I should have realised how much everything would change when you won this competition, but I didn't. I just thought it would be something cool. We'd go see your film at the cinema and I'd shout out to everyone there that you wrote that shit. You. My best mate, Sasha Adams, wrote the film they'd all just paid to see. I thought it was going to be fucking awesome."

"We'll still do that."

"Fuck off. I want a front-row seat at the red-carpet premiere for this shit now."

Sasha chuckled. "You got it, honey."

Bobbi grinned. "And my name in the credits."

"Already done."

"Really?"

"Really. Production assistant, Bobbi Johnson."

"Awesome."

"I promise I'll make more time for us."

"And I promise I won't be so needy." Bobbi squeezed her arms tighter around Sasha's waist.

"Are we okay now?"

"Better than okay. We're besties."

"Well then, bestie," Sasha started, then smiled and kissed Bobbi's cheek, "let's get inside and see if my mother's come up with any more crappy jokes."

Bobbi frowned as they walked towards the doors, arms still slung around each other's waists. "Your mum's telling jokes?"

Sighing, Sasha pulled open the door. "It's like this…"

CHAPTER 28

SASHA STARED OUT OF THE window as Jac drove them home. She'd offered to take her back to her house but Sasha couldn't face it. At that particular moment, she wasn't sure she'd ever be able to face it again. But that was something she'd think about tomorrow. Maybe. Right now she wanted to forget. She wanted it all to be a dream—a nightmare—that she'd wake up from in the morning, safe and secure in Jac's arms.

But that wasn't going to happen.

Part of her had wanted to pull her coat over her shoulders and try for the impossible. To sleep. It would make no difference if she was in the chair at Fleur's bedside or in a bed. She knew sleep was about as likely as her winning the lottery that night. But neither her mother nor Jac were going to let her get away with staying where she was. So she'd shrugged into her coat and followed Jac out to the car. The sun that had shone earlier had long since given way to the weather norm: drizzle.

The door beside her opened and Jac held out a hand. Sasha hadn't even realised they'd stopped driving. "Sorry," she said, taking Jac's hand and climbing out of the car. "Miles away."

"I'd be surprised if you weren't right now, babe." She wrapped her arm about Sasha's shoulders, and Sasha snaked hers about Jac's waist, snuggling into her warmth.

This all would be so much harder without Jac. As new as their relationship still was, Sasha knew it to be true. She couldn't explain it. Frankly, she was too damn tired and heart-weary at that moment to even try. She just knew that Jac's presence brought her a sense of peace she hadn't expected to find when she'd been on her hands and knees throwing up at the hospital. In those few minutes, her whole world had turned upside down, but Jac had scooped her hair back from her face, pulled a tissue from somewhere, and held it out to her. Bought her a toothbrush and toothpaste from the hospital shop and a packet of chewing gum. She didn't say a word. There was nothing she could have said, and they both knew it. Instead, she simply did everything she could.

"Sophie said she was cooking a stew earlier. Said she'd bring around some for us to pop in the microwave to heat it up. Fancy it?"

Sasha shook her head.

"You have to eat, Sash. You won't be any good to her if you make yourself ill not eating."

"I know. Doesn't mean I fancy the stew, though."

"Then what do you fancy?"

"Truthfully?"

"Always."

"Bacon butty."

"Well, it just so happens we have some of that bacon left from breakfast yesterday. So that is a wish I can accommodate." She kissed the side of Sasha's head. "How about you go jump in a bath while I rustle us up some bacon butties, and then we can stare blindly at some shit TV until you're ready to go to sleep?"

"Are you saying I stink?"

"*Stink* is a strong word, babe."

"Smell, then?"

"Well, you did spend a good portion of the afternoon chucking up. And I know a bath always makes me feel better when I feel like crap, so... Forget it. It was a stupid—"

"It's a perfect idea. Sorry, I think I need to switch into a different frame of mind or something. I feel like I'm still back there with Mum, having to tell stupid jokes and take the piss all the time."

Jac led them into the lift and punched the button before pulling Sasha into her arms. "You don't have to apologise. This has been one fuckfest of a day, and we're both reeling. All I want is to help you feel a bit better. If taking the piss will help you do that, then you go right ahead. If the bath helps, I'll fill kettles with water if need be. If you want oysters, or hot dogs, or pizza, I'll go to the shops. If you need a little time alone, it's yours. Whatever you need. All you have to do is let me know."

"What if I want to punch something?"

"I'll buy you a gym membership."

"Scream?"

"Go right ahead." She stuck her fingers in her ears.

Sasha chuckled sadly and wrapped her arms even tighter around Jac's waist. "Are you always like this in a crisis?"

"Like what?"

"Oh, I don't know. Brilliant? Accommodating? Understanding?" She looked up and whispered, "Perfect?"

"Only for you." The kiss Jac placed on her lips was soft and chaste, and it made Sasha want to burrow inside it. To hide there in Jac's arms and block out everything else. She buried her face in Jac's shoulder and followed when Jac opened the door to the apartment.

"Why don't you go start that bath? Bacon butties might take me a while." Jac frowned in the direction of the kitchen.

"Want me to cook? You can go run the bath. I'll get in after we eat."

"No, no. I'm spoiling you tonight." Jac waved her off. "It's only a bacon butty. How hard can it be?"

Sasha sniggered and walked away. "Okay, let me know if you change your mind."

"Do I wrap it in foil before I put it in the microwave?" Jac asked over her shoulder.

"No!" Sasha spun around, hands held out before her like a shield. "God, don't put foil in—you're such a shit, Jac Kensington." She slapped Jac's belly when she saw her chuckling and then walked out of the room, shaking her head. "Remember not to play with any of the knives. You might cut yourself," she called through the apartment as she entered the bathroom.

"Funny. How will I butter the bread, then, genius?"

"Use a spoon." She turned on the water, poured in some of the bubble bath on the side, and left the tub to fill. She could have the sandwiches done and eaten by the time the bath was run.

"Sarcasm doesn't become you."

"Wasn't being sarcastic. Trick of the trade, darlin'. Caterers always use a spoon rather than a knife to butter bread. It covers a wider surface area so you get each slice done faster. When half a second counts because you're buttering half a dozen loaves at a time, it all adds up." She bumped Jac out of the way and grabbed the frying pan from the cupboard beside the stove.

"Hm. Okay, I'll believe you."

"Pass me the bacon out of the fridge. I'll cook it; you can butter the bread."

"What about me spoiling you? What about your bath?"

"The bath is running, and I think I'd rather share all of this evening with you. Is that okay?"

"Whatever you want." Jack kissed her again softly, then turned back to buttering the bread. "This spoon trick really works."

"Told you." Sasha put the bacon in the pan and rummaged through the cutlery drawer for a pair of tongs.

Bread buttered, Jac turned around. "I'll just go check the bath's not overflowing. Won't be a minute."

"Okay, the bacon's nearly done, so don't be long."

The sandwiches were made up and cut in half to make triangles—just like Fleur had always made them—and sat on the chopping board on the island counter when Jac came back. Sasha was pouring two glasses of wine and sat on the stool beside Jac. They ate and drank in silence, lost in thought. When they'd finished, Sasha took Jac's hand and tugged her into the bathroom with her, where she slowly divested her of her clothes and covered her skin with delicate kisses—kisses not meant to ignite passion but just to connect, to feel.

"I should do the dishes," Jac said.

"They can wait." She pulled her jumper over her head and tossed it on the floor before removing her jeans. "Please stay with me." She pointed to the bath. Jac merely nodded, removed her underwear, climbed into the tub, and spread her legs wide to make space for Sasha between them.

Sasha finished undressing and stepped in. The hot water swirled around her legs, easing the aching in her muscles that she hadn't even realised she was feeling. The scent of lavender and jasmine hung in the air, and candles Jac must have lit earlier flickered and sputtered around the bathroom.

With the door closed, the steam rising, and the light so gentle, it was easy to forget for a few minutes that the world outside was still turning. That time was still counting down, and that the darkest of days was coming.

As she settled back against Jac's chest, stroking her hands down Jac's knees, calves, and thighs, she could forget. When Jac reached for the scrubby, loaded it up with liquid soap, and started to rub it across Sasha's chest, belly, and arms, Sasha sighed. A feeling of peace displaced the ball of grief that had settled in her gut. When Jac lifted her hands out of the water and spent countless minutes cleaning each digit, rubbing the scrubby over her palms, the backs of her hands, then down her wrists, Sasha's heart began to thaw, the ice that had settled in her chest warming, melting under Jac's loving attention.

She turned her head and kissed the underside of Jac's jaw. "Thank you," she whispered hoarsely. "I love you."

"I love you too, Sasha." Jac sloshed water across her torso with long, slow sweeps of her hands, and after a while, Jac whispered in her ear, "You okay?"

"Not even a little bit," Sasha answered truthfully. "I don't know what I'm supposed to do, Jac. I don't know how I'm supposed to feel right now."

"I don't think there's a right or wrong way, babe. Today has been a huge shock for you. That takes time to process."

"But I don't have time. You heard what the nurse said. A week. Two at most. That doesn't give me any time."

"I know. But you need to give yourself time to do what you need to, to think what you need to, or you'll drive yourself nuts."

"You don't think I should be just thinking about Mum and—and what she's going through?"

"You have been. You've been doing that all day. You've done everything she asked you to do in that room. You told bad jokes, berated her for hers, held your tears and your fears in check. And I am so damn proud of you." Jac wrapped her arms around Sasha and pulled her tight against her body. "But Fleur isn't the only one going through this. You are too. We are too. And we need to be able to do what's right for us outside of your mum's room. If that's sitting in a bath together while we wash each other, then so be it. If there's something else you need, well, I'm here. Just tell me, and I will do everything I can to make it happen."

Sasha turned her head to look at her, her eyes itching with tears. "Right now, I feel like I want to forget."

"I'm not sure there's anything wrong with that either, babe." Jac smoothed her hair back. "Not for a little while, at least." She turned Sasha around so she could see her eyes clearly. Sasha was grateful Jac seemed happy to talk about how Sasha felt. It made her feel even more connected to her. More understood than she had ever felt possible. In fact, Jac was helping her understand herself more.

"Everyone deals with shock and grief differently, and when it's as extreme as this is, I'm guessing your feelings and emotions can change in a flash. Don't fight that. Don't try and force yourself to feel or think or do what you think other people expect you to. Just do what you need to, Sash. Just be you."

Sasha nodded and allowed herself to enjoy Jac's hands on her as she continued to stroke her hair gently.

"Thank you." Sasha smiled at her. She truly appreciated Jac's words, her understanding, but she needed to lighten the mood again. She couldn't deal with heavy discussions any more. Not tonight. "So if I told you I wanted to make mad passionate love all night, you wouldn't think I was some sort of crazed nymphomaniac, then?"

"Well, maybe." Jac smirked. "But it might just be a genetic thing, this nymphomania. I mean, have you seen Mike Hunt recently? Poor bloke looks worn out to me." She deliberately dropped the *H* and let the words roll together.

Sasha laughed and splashed water at her. "That's it. After putting mental images like that in my mind, you've just scuppered your chances."

"I'm crushed," Jac deadpanned, and pulled Sasha back into her arms, laying back against the tub. She continued to trail her fingers over Sasha's body, lacing their fingers together and tracing the fine bones, muscles, and tendons through her hands as the water cooled and they both began to shiver. "Time to get out, beautiful." She tapped Sasha's hip.

When they were both out, dried, and wrapped only in towels, Sasha grabbed Jac's hand and pulled her in close. "Thank you."

"You keep thanking me, but there truly is no need. If it were the other way around, I know you'd be doing the same, if not more, for me. Wouldn't you?"

"I would."

Jac leant forwards and captured her lips in a slow, tender kiss that almost made Sasha weep.

When they lay in bed, Jac tucked around Sasha's body, protectively spooning her. It brought back a warmth that had fled when she'd seen her mother collapse to the floor. Jac's loving touch, her protective embrace, and her gentle kisses slowly but surely began to melt the shards of ice that had tried to form around her heart.

As they melted, the tears came. Not the gut-wrenching sobs of earlier. Now it was a steady stream of tears flowing down her cheeks that seemed to have no end. Tears for her pain, tears to cleanse.

Jac's spicy, musky scent made her feel grounded, and the love in her eyes gave her hope and strength, and something else she couldn't find the words for. Not yet.

CHAPTER 29

Jac yawned and pushed the Rewind button. Four days of running backwards and forwards to the hospice, of comforting Sasha through the night, and of going over scenes with Sophie on the phone had left her drained. She'd lost track of the number of hours she'd spent with Sasha and Fleur. She'd seen a gag gift in the garage when she was filling up with petrol, a 'world's worst joke' book. They'd take turns reading it out.

Well, they did when Fleur wasn't sleeping, something that was happening more and more as the days ticked by. The pained look on her face would grow sharp, then they'd hear the click, a soft whir of machinery, and see the tell-tale slackness on Fleur's face when the morphine from the drip machine kicked in.

Jac rubbed at her eyes, hoping she could rub the images away at the same time. No such luck. She needed to get this review of the dailies done. Tomorrow was the last day of filming, and if anything needed to be reshot, Sophie needed to know tonight. Not only was it the last day of filming tomorrow, but from Saturday on, the crew on a show scheduled to begin filming on Monday would have to build up the new sets. Kefran would simply have no other chance to do this again.

Shaking her head, she rewound the scene again. Sophie was right: this one wasn't working. She made a note on the master script for Sophie and moved on to the next scene. Her eyes itched and she rubbed at them tiredly.

She heard the door open but didn't take her hand from her eyes. "I'm sorry, Soph. I'm only about halfway through."

"Sophie left a while ago."

At the sound of Vanessa's voice, Jac eyed her warily. Vanessa dropped into the seat next to her and pointed to the screen. "How're they looking?"

"Pretty good." Jac turned back to the screen and continued to review the scenes. "Only one scene to reshoot so far."

"I have to admit, I was sceptical when Sophie said she was filling in as director on Monday, but she's been okay."

"I'll pass that on to her," Jac said with a chuckle. Sophie and Vanessa had always mixed like oil and water.

"Please don't. I'd never live it down."

Jac squinted at the screen, noting a continuity error that needed to be fixed. "Your secret's safe with me."

"Thanks. How are you doing?"

"I'm okay, thanks." She wasn't; she was exhausted and hurting, and she felt helpless almost all the time. But Vanessa didn't need to know that.

"I could always tell when you were lying, Jac." She put her hand on Jac's arm where it rested on the table. "Don't lie to me now. We might not be together anymore, but we meant more to each other than that."

Jac took a deep breath. Vanessa had a point, as much as she hated to admit it. And they hadn't parted on bad terms. If she was willing to be friendly, there was no reason Jac couldn't be too.

"No, you're right, I'm not. It's all shit right now, but there's nothing we can really do about it except get through it all." She shrugged. "It is what it is, you know?" She wiped at the tears that had gathered in her eyes. She wanted Vanessa to go, to leave her alone so she could cry in peace. Maybe that would let her clear her mind a little bit. Enough to finish going through this bloody footage anyway.

Vanessa nodded, but Jac knew she'd never been through anything like this and she simply couldn't relate to what they were going through. She'd never lost anyone she cared about like this.

"I hope you know I'm here for you. If you need anything, shoulder to cry on, someone to talk to, you know where I am."

"Thanks, I'll bear that in mind."

"Please don't dismiss my offer. I know you think I'm shallow, and maybe I am. But I know you're hurting, Jac, and I'm here. Not Sasha or Sophie, or Mags. Me." She knelt beside Jac's chair. "Doesn't that mean something to you?"

"Sure, I'm very grateful, thanks." She pointed back at the screen. "I need to finish going over these scenes, though. I have to get back to pick Sasha up in a little while." She swiped at yet another tear at the thought of Sasha sitting at Fleur's bedside—alone—while her mother slept. Both of them waiting. All of them waiting.

The nurse's timeline just counting down for them all. A week. Maybe two. They were four days into it. How much longer did they have before that clock ran out? Three days? Ten? Jac put her head in her hands and couldn't stop the sob that shook her body.

She felt hands on her shoulders, tugging her into an embrace. Comforting words were whispered in her ear, soothing rubs and pats covered her back. But they weren't the arms she wanted to hold her. It wasn't the voice she wanted to hear. She'd rather cry alone than have Vanessa witness her pain.

She forced her tears away and pulled out of Vanessa's arms, offering her what she hoped was a grateful smile. "Thanks, but I really should get on with this." She tipped her head towards the screen.

Vanessa smirked widely at her. "You know where I am if you need a shoulder to cry on again. I'm here for you, Jac. Anytime."

"Yeah," Jac's voice was flat even to her own ears. "Thanks."

"No, I'm not doing it."

Sasha paused with her had on the doorknob, about to enter Fleur's room. Bobbi's voice was strong and adamant, and Sasha wondered what the hell her mother wanted of her now. So she waited…and listened.

"If you loved me you would."

"I do love you, Mrs A. But I can't do that."

"Why not?"

"Sasha would kill me."

"I'm the mother, not Sasha."

"Yeah, but right now she's stronger than you are, and she'd kill me."

"I'll haunt you."

Sasha sniggered and put her other hand to her mouth to smother it. What the hell did Fleur want?

"I don't believe in ghosts," Bobbi said, but she didn't sound anywhere near as confident as she was before.

"Yes, you do. I'll haunt you if you don't do this for me. I'm an old woman, and I'm dying. This is the least you can do for me."

Bobbi groaned. "You can't pull the dying card, Mrs A. That's a low blow."

"Okay, okay. I'll make it worth your while, then."

Sasha frowned but still couldn't bring herself to open the door and walk in.

"Keep talking." Bobbi sounded a lot more interested.

"I'll give you the directions to my emergency stash."

"Pft. I can get weed anywhere."

"Not this much you can't."

"How much are we…no forget it. I'm not a dealer. And if I smoked that much, I'd get sacked."

"I'll throw in my recipe book too."

"With that latest recipe in it?"

"Yup."

Bobbi whimpered. "Sasha will kill me when she finds out."

"Well, hurry up and get on with it. Then she won't."

"Fine. Don't move, and I'll be back as soon as I— Oh, hey, Sasha. Didn't see you there." Bobbi grinned as she pulled open the door and stared up at Sasha. Well, sort of.

Sasha lifted her eyebrows. "What, exactly, am I going to kill you for?"

"Erm, nothing. Nothing at all. I haven't done anything." Bobbi's smile looked more like a grimace.

"Yet." Sasha turned to her mother. "If you're going to try your hand at bribery and corruption, you should keep your voice down a bit." She crossed the room and deposited the box of chocolates and magazine she'd been dispatched for on Fleur's table. "So, spill. What do you want now?"

"I want to see Nip."

Sasha narrowed her eyes in frustration. "Mum, we already asked. They can't let her in here. There are too many people with lung issues, and the cat dander could make their conditions worse. I'm sorry."

"I know. That's why I wanted Bobbi to bring her to the gardens and then take me out to sit on that bench for a little while." She pointed out of her window to the memorial bench in the grounds that overlooked the small pond. Her grin turned conspiratorial. "Where there's a will, there's a way, dear. Remember that."

"Mum, it's November. It's cold out there. You need to stay warm—"

"Staying warm won't change anything, Sasha. I want to see my poor little kitty. I want to stroke her again. Cuddle her. It's not a lot to ask, honey."

It wasn't. It really wasn't. But the simplest of things wore Fleur out. Just going to the bathroom wore her out. The look in Fleur's eyes, though, told Sasha she would get her way come hell or high water. She was going to see her cat again.

"Fine." Sasha turned to Bobbi. "Do you know where the cat carrier is?"

"In the cupboard under the stairs, right?"

"Yes. You know she's going to claw you to bits, right?"

"There's a fire gauntlet in the carrier, sweetheart," Fleur said. "Use that when you get hold of her."

"I will."

"And make sure you close all the bedroom and living room doors so she can't hide under the furniture."

"Got it."

"I used to find that you could lure her in there with a little bit of ham in the back of the carrier," Sasha said.

"Got it." Bobbi nodded like she was adding items to a list. "Bribery, locked doors, gauntlet, then run."

"Call me when you're in the car on your way back." Sasha pointed at her. "I'll start helping Mum get ready then and meet you in the gardens."

"Will do." Bobbi started for the door.

"Don't forget," Fleur added, holding up a hand.

"I won't forget the other bit, either." Bobbi pulled open the door and was gone.

"What other bit?" Sasha asked.

"You'll see."

"You've not asked her to bring you a joint or something, have you?" Fleur tapped her nose.

"Mum, you'll get kicked out of here."

"Oh, pish. The only way I'm going out of here is feet first, and we both know it. Now tell me what's going on with this film of yours?"

"Well, if you like, I'll show you some of it."

Fleur rubbed her hands together in excitement as Sasha reached for her laptop case. Jac had given her a DVD of some of the scenes cut together in the order they would play in the final film. It was rough, the edits nowhere near finished, and one or two of the scenes needed to be reshot, but they both knew this would be the only way Fleur would ever see some of Sasha's work come to fruition. After all Fleur's meddling to put this into motion… it felt right.

"Now," Sasha said around a lump in her throat, "if you tell anyone about what you see here, I'll have to kill you."

Throwing her head back, Fleur laughed as Sasha blinked away her tears. "Perfect, honey. That one was perfect." Fleur grasped her hand and squeezed as Sasha set the laptop on the table and wheeled it to hover over the bed. Fleur scooted over and patted the space beside her. Sasha climbed on and settled against her mother.

"Shame we haven't got any popcorn."

"I'll bring it next time, Mum." She stretched towards the Play button. "Now, there aren't any opening credits or anything, and there are more scenes still to film, but the story is mostly here now. It's just some of the stuff Becca needs to film tomorrow to add to the emotional intensity of the scenes where she's imprisoned."

"Understood. I remember from the script. Now press Play. I want to see what you've created, my clever, clever girl." Fleur kissed the hand she was holding and motioned for Sasha to start it playing. So she did.

The shot opened with Vanessa bouncing around in a jeep, as she "sped" through the CGI-created desert towards a ramshackle Pakistani village on the edge of the Peshawar Plain. Fleur's eyes were open wide as she pointed.

"That's exactly how I imagined it when I read it."

"Me too." She laced their fingers together and snuggled in beside her, just like she had done as a child when they'd watched *Bambi*. "Now be quiet and watch my film."

She felt the kiss Fleur pressed to the top of her head. "So bossy. Where do you get that from?"

There were only ten minutes left of the film when Sasha's phone chimed. It was a text from Bobbi, informing her that she and the holy terror were en route, but traffic was awful. In other words, don't rush. So Sasha let the clips finish and passed Fleur a tissue when the screen went blank.

"Amazing. Absolutely amazing. You did that, honey. You."

Sasha shook her head. "It took an awful lot of people to do that."

"Without you, they wouldn't have had anything to start with." Fleur hugged her tight. "I'm so proud of you."

"I'm glad you got to see it. Even though it's not finished yet."

"Me too." She pushed Sasha away from her a little. "Was that Bobbi?"

"Yep. She's on her way but traffic's awful. It's gonna take her some time. Do you need the bathroom?"

Fleur shook her head. "I thought I told you earlier."

"Told me what?"

"They put in a catheter last night." She tapped the edge of the bed, and Sasha leaned over to see the collection bag.

"Nice. Something else to drag around with you."

"Indeed. But it's a little more comfortable than those terrible grampers pads," she said referring to the awful, thick incontinence pads that were the alternative. "They made my arse look huge. And I've got standards to maintain."

Sasha decided to let that one go. "Fine, I'll go and find a wheelchair, then. Back in a few."

Before she could get off the bed, Fleur had hold of her hand again. She turned to face her.

"I am so proud of you, baby girl."

Sasha fought the tears. "I know, Mum."

"I love you."

"I love you too," Sasha whispered, her lip trembling. She wasn't sure how much longer she could keep her tears at bay.

"Thank you."

"What for?"

"For being my daughter."

"Shouldn't I be thanking you for that? For making me who I am. For being my mother?"

"No, honey. We've made a good team over the years, and we've had a lot of fun. And for that, I'm truly grateful. Many women have daughters. But how many women are best friends with theirs too? I look at you and know without a shred of doubt that I played a hand in shaping a truly wonderful, beautiful, generous, kind, and loving woman. One that I am more than proud to call mine." She wiped the tears on Sasha's cheeks. "I know you're angry and hurting, and you will feel pain, but remember I love you more than life itself. You're my baby girl, and I will always, always be here for you." She wiped more tears away. Sasha couldn't make them stop. "Even after I'm gone, I'll still be here for you." She put one bony hand over Sasha's heart. "Remember that, okay?"

All Sasha could do was nod. She couldn't speak. There were no words left for her to say. And even if there had been, she had no voice left with which to speak them. Fleur put her hands on Sasha cheeks, tugged her down and placed a kiss on her forehead.

"Now go and find me a chair. I want one with flames down the sides and spikes on the wheels, like a Roman gladiator chariot."

Sasha chuckled as she wiped her face with a tissue and climbed off the bed. "I'll see what I can do." Then she scurried out of the door. She needed a moment to try to collect herself. To find herself again in the sea of emotion that threatened to engulf her, to wash over her, and drown her again and again and again. Relentlessly tossed upon the waves of loss, horror, anguish, despair, pain, and the gut-wrenching, soul-twisting laughter of the gallows humour Fleur doled out.

She leant heavily against the wall, bent at the waist, and sobbed, casting aside the anchors and stays that had held her fast for the past few days. She allowed herself to feel the true depth of all she was losing. Fleur. Her mum.

How do you stay strong in the midst of that? How do you stay afloat and not drown? How do you—

"Hey, babe, what's happened?" Jac's hands on her shoulders lifted her until she was standing. Wrapped in her strong embrace, she let herself slowly come back to reality. She let the questions go and absorbed the scent and warmth of the future. The spicy aroma of sandalwood, musk, and citrus. The heat of Jac's body. The solid feel of her arms, anchoring her back to the real world. Sheltering her from the crashing waves and keeping her afloat when despair tried to pull her down.

"Is she—"

"She's okay. Needs a wheelchair. Wants to go into the gardens."

"But it's dark out there. It's freezing."

Sasha took a deep breath and managed to get herself together enough to make herself speak. "She wants to see Nip. She bribed Bobbi into going to get her in the cat carrier. Obviously, Nip isn't allowed in here, so she wants to go outside to see her."

Jac nodded.

"Well, we needed to go and get Nip and bring her back to the apartment. She shouldn't be alone at your mum's house. We can just take her home with us tonight."

"You want to take mum's cat back to your place?"

"Well, you're hardly ever at home and you sleep at my place most nights. It…well, it makes sense, right? Nip's probably missing your mum too."

"You'd really do that?"

"Of course. She's part of the family."

Tears welled in Sasha's eyes again and she waved a hand in front of her face. "You'll make me cry again."

Jac held her tight again, then pointed to the bathroom door. "Why don't you go and tidy yourself up a bit, and I'll go and find your mum a wheelchair?"

"Thanks." She moved out of Jac's arms. "She wants one that looks like a cross between a Roman chariot and greased lightning."

Jac's eyebrows rose. "She does, huh?"

"Yup."

"Oh, damn." Jac patted her pockets. "Looks like I left my crayons in my other clothes."

Sasha sniggered.

"I'll try and get one that goes in straight lines and doesn't have a wonky wheel."

"Perfect." Sasha kissed her cheek and stepped into the bathroom. She pointed at the mirror. "That's not quite so perfect." She ran cold water and splashed it over her face, dabbed the back of her neck, and hung her face over the sink, letting water drip from her nose, chin, and eyebrows. She counted the drops, trying to let her mind go blank. To let the overwhelming emotions just drip away.

By the time she returned to Fleur's room, Jac had her sitting in the wheelchair, just a regular wheelchair, and wrapped with blankets. She was kneeling at her feet and forcing a second pair of the thick fluffy socks onto Fleur's foot.

"I'm telling you, it's freezing out there. If you don't wrap up warm you'll catch your death."

Fleur chortled loudly and Jac froze, seeming to realise what she'd said. She looked up, and Fleur's chuckle deepened and broke into a full-belly laugh. She patted Jac's flaming cheek.

"You'll do, Jac Kensington. You'll do."

Jac frowned and Sasha pushed her way into the room.

"Ready?" Sasha asked. "Bobbi texted a couple of minutes ago. She's at the bench, waiting. She doesn't want to let Nip out before you get there in case she runs off."

Patting the arms of her chair, Fleur cried, "Let's blow this joint!" She clicked her fingers. The sound she made was so small, like she didn't have the strength to create enough pressure to truly make it. "Driver," she said to Jac and pointed to the door. "Onwards, Parker."

"Yes, milady." Jac gave her best impression of the put-upon driver from *Thunderbirds* and wheeled her forwards. "I'll need directions, milady."

At Fleur's cackle, Sasha grabbed her coat and followed behind them. Bobbi was sitting there, waiting, shivering. Sasha could hear her teeth chattering from ten feet away. Jac pushed Fleur so she was at right angles to the bench and snapped on the brakes.

"Don't want you rolling down that hill and into the pond, do we?" Jac asked.

"Nah, then I really would catch my death, wouldn't I?" Fleur chuckled again and pulled the hat Jac had stuck on her head lower over her ears. "So where's my baby, then?" Fleur held her hands out as Bobbi opened the mesh door to the cat carrier. Nip mewled indignantly, clawed at Bobbi for good measure, then sprang across the space to Fleur. She paced back and forth across her lap, complaining about her mistreatment and abuse all the while. Sasha and Jac sat next to Bobbi on the bench, Sasha closest to her mum, Jac in the middle with her arm about Sasha's shoulders. Bobbi held up a sleeping bag, Fleur's old yoga mat, and a couple of blankets.

"I grabbed these from the house, Sash. I hope you don't mind."

"God, not at all. Good thinking." They spread the yoga mat across the cold bench, opened the double sleeping bag, and stood in it before sitting down, the three of them giggling at the close quarters to get all of them inside and the bag pulled up to their waists. Then spread the blankets across their shoulders.

"Well don't you all look cosy," Fleur said. Nip had finally settled into her usual position on Fleur's arm, throwing her minion-of-darkness glare at them all and meowing lazily...perhaps slightly threateningly...as she eyed the cat carrier with disgust. "Bobbi, did you bring the other thing I asked you for?"

"Yup."

"Mum, I told you, no weed. You're on morphine now."

"She didn't want me to bring any weed." Bobbi frowned over at Fleur and asked, "Did you?"

"No. I want my hot chocolate."

Bobbi held up a thermos flask and some plastic camping beakers. "That I did bring." Bobbi poured them all a cup and handed them down the line.

Inhaling the sweet-smelling steam as it rose out of the cup, Sasha smiled. Then she caught the other aroma. "How much Bailey's is in this?" She pointed at Jac and Bobbi. "You two have both got to drive tonight."

"Erm... One cup won't put us over the limit." Bobbi sipped, and her eyes widened a little. "Probably."

Jac sniggered and poured a quarter of her cup into Sasha's and another quarter into Fleur's. "Just enough to take the chill off." She tapped her cup to everyone else's and held it aloft. "To Nip." They all followed the toast and sipped on their drinks.

Sasha tipped her head back and stared at the night sky. There was barely a cloud overhead, just the twinkle of stars glittered against the inky blackness of the universe. She reached over with her free hand and interlaced her fingers with her mum's. Jac's arm tightened around her shoulders, and for a moment—just a moment—she could forget.

So Sasha did. She sipped her drink and enjoyed the peace and quiet with her family.

CHAPTER 30

ANOTHER BREATH RATTLED OUT OF her mother's chest and Sasha held her own. Waiting, hoping, that Fleur had the strength to pull in another. She couldn't believe how quickly she had deteriorated. Six days. It had only been six days since she'd been admitted to the hospice, and the nurse had already warned Sasha that Fleur was unlikely to make it through the night.

Jac sat beside her, hand clasped in Sasha's, watching with equal parts dread and hope on her face. Dread and hope for the same exact thing: Fleur's last breath. Dread, because no one wanted the end to come, but hope, because they'd all seen Fleur's pain, and death now was the only release she'd truly find.

When Fleur gasped in another breath, they both breathed with her, each strangled lungful the new marker of time. Each one fought for. Each battle taking more from Fleur than simple breathing should. And each one was slower to come than the last.

A chill ran down her back, and Sasha needed to be closer. She let go of Jac's hand and sat on the edge of the bed. Grasping Fleur's hand inside her own, she pulled it to her chest and bent to kiss her mother's head.

"I love you, Mum."

Fleur's eyes fluttered open, and her lips twitched. It wasn't a smile, but it was meant to be.

Tears dripped from her cheeks and splashed on Fleur's face. She started to pull her hand away, to wipe the tears away, but Fleur gripped her with more strength than Sasha knew she had left.

"You know the place between sleep and awake?" Her voice was tiny, a whisper, "The place where you can still remember dreaming?"

Oh God, no. Please no. Not this.

"D—don't quote me *Peter Pan*, Mum." Sasha could barely get the words out around the bands constricting her chest.

Fleur's gaze never wavered, and her eyes were the clearest Sasha had seen them in days. "Then you tell me, baby girl."

Why? Sasha wanted to scream. Instead, she sniffed back her pain and gave her mother what she asked for. Her throat was thick with every unshed tear as she managed to whisper, "That's…that's where I'll always love you." She couldn't say any more. She couldn't form the words. Sasha couldn't draw enough breath into her lungs to force even a sigh from her lips.

Fleur drew in a rattling, scratchy-sounding breath. "That's where I'll be waiting," she said as she let the breath go. Her eyes closed.

And Sasha waited.

She waited for that next scratchy breath. She waited for that next inhalation that signalled her mother was still there. Still fighting for those few more precious moments they could have together.

But it didn't come. Ten seconds turned to thirty. Thirty to a minute. A minute became two, and finally it started to sink in.

Fleur was gone.

CHAPTER 31

Jac held on to Sasha's hand as they sat in the front pew. The past week had been a blur of meetings with funeral directors, confirming Mike Hunt had been telling the truth. Fleur had indeed made all her own arrangements, meeting with the vicar who would conduct the service at the crematorium. Fleur had picked the music she wanted—right down to her refusal of hymns in favour of her own...personal choices. Jac still couldn't make up her mind how she felt about the choices Fleur had made for the service. But she'd been clear. Concise. And Sasha was determined this was to be a reflection of the woman her mother had always been. Quirky. Unconventional. And damn well unforgettable.

The vicar smiled sadly as he welcomed the huge crowd, and spoke soft words about the woman they'd all known. Jac expected Sasha to cry, but she didn't. She stood with her head held high, staring at the picture of a laughing Fleur that sat on top of the casket. She was dressed in a hula skirt, long grey hair flowing and covering her chest and what Jac hoped was some sort of bikini top on under there. The flowery lei and hair obscured it, though. She had a coconut shell in one hand, a straw and umbrella sticking out of it, and she was clearly having a ball.

When the first song choice blasted out of the speakers, Jac was startled back into the present. She closed her eyes but she could hear the titters of laughter starting further back in the chapel. Bon Jovi. "Blaze of Glory". An epic choice only someone like Fleur could get away with.

Prayers were swapped out for poems, Bible readings exchanged for anecdotes from friends. When the vicar looked at Sasha and held out his hand in invitation, Jac was still surprised to see her dry eyes.

Sasha stood up at the podium and cleared her throat. "Thank you, everyone, for coming today. Mum would be very pleased to see the turnout." She paused a beat while she looked at the coffin. "Of course, she'd accuse you all of only being here for the spread afterwards. But she'd still be pleased."

Low chuckles ran through the crowd, and Jac knew immediately why Sasha hadn't cried. If she allowed herself to let go, she'd never make it through this. This was her chance to say all the things to her mother that she hadn't had the chance to say before. And she intended to make it count.

"We all have our own memories of Mum. Some of you from long before I came along and ruined her life and figure, apparently. And afterwards, I look forward to hearing every single one of them. There was more than enough of Fleur Adams to go around, but I must admit, I have the urge to collect and hoard all those bits she's spread around over the years.

"Mum was more than just Mum to me. She was my best friend, my confidante, my protector. She always had been, and she did that right up to the very end. And I still haven't decided if I'm more grateful or angry for that. Because she never gave me the chance to be all those things for her too." Sasha's voice cracked, and Jac wished she could step forwards and hold her hand, offer her support in some way. When Sasha's gaze locked on to her, she realised that where she was in the chapel didn't matter. She was giving Sasha what she needed simply by being there.

"This last week, we've done nothing but talk. Going over all those old memories that we'd built over a lifetime. The time I almost burnt the house down when I was making her breakfast in bed. I blame my father. I mean, who lets a five-year-old fry bacon while he's outside smoking?"

"Good old Bert, that's who!" a voice chimed up from the back.

"You got that right, Uncle Eddie. But it started the whole ball rolling about things I remember most about Mum. And I don't just mean recent stuff. I mean when I was little and she told me not to throw a punch at a boy because he was being mean to me. No, not my mum. She taught me it was much more effective to knee him in the groin when he got close enough."

Jac sniggered, as did Sophie sitting next to her, but Jac could see some of the blokes in the crowd shifting uncomfortably in their seats. "Good old Fleur," Sophie whispered. Jac couldn't agree more.

"There was also the time she spent a Sunday afternoon teaching me how to forge her signature. She said if I was going to do something, I was going to do it properly. Then she grounded me for a week when I used it to get out of PE. Apparently doing something properly didn't excuse you from the consequences when found out."

"Must have been a riot growing up with her," Sophie muttered again.

"I'm sure it was."

"But what I remember most was when I came out to her. The day I told her I was gay was probably the scariest of my life. I was so worried that I'd be a disappointment to her. That she'd be upset, or that she'd take it badly. I was afraid to lose her, you see?" Her voice cracked again. She sniffed, and Jac worried for a moment that she wouldn't be able to continue. Then Sasha glanced at the picture on the coffin again.

"Instead, she told me about a girl she worked with who was, in her words at the time, 'one of those' and said she'd set me up on a date. She took me to my first Manchester Gay Pride parade that summer, and she went with me every year after that."

Applause shuffled around the room, alongside a few cheers.

"I'm sad to say she often got hit on more than I did." Sasha rolled her eyes and chuckled. "Mum had such an energy about her. It drew people to her. People just wanted to be near her because you never knew what was going to happen. She was so exciting, so full of life." The tears Jac had been waiting for broke free and slid down Sasha's cheeks, but she continued to smile to the crowd.

"One of my most treasured memories is of her reading to me as a child. Oh, the adventures we went on in my bedroom. We sailed the seven seas, explored entire universes, travelled infinite galaxies, and fell in love with a little boy called Peter." Sasha took a moment to wipe her face and swallow. Jac could hear how difficult it was becoming for her to finish her eulogy. Everyone could. Tears and open sobbing were becoming increasingly noisy throughout the chapel.

"We read those stories over and over again, and I'd like to leave you with a line from Peter himself, and one I know Mum would want us all to bear in mind as we let—let her go." Sasha sniffed and wiped her nose with a tissue, then stepped down from the podium and took the picture off the casket. Cradling it to her chest, she faced everyone and said, "'To die would be an awfully big adventure.'"

The tears and sobs began in earnest, and from somewhere in the back, the cue for Fleur's final goodbye was recognised. The opening haunting chords began to filter through the speakers as Jac stepped from the pew and wrapped her arms around Sasha's sobbing form. As Freddie Mercury demanded to know, "Who wants to live forever," Jac led Sasha out of the chapel and into the cold autumn air. Leaves of red and gold danced in the wind, and grey clouds gathered overhead. And as the crowd filtered out slowly behind them, weeping their own grief and whispering their own memories of the woman Fleur had been to them, Freddie sang on.

Jac glanced up at the sky and wondered if she was looking down at them, singing along, and laughing at the stories they were all swapping. Memories of the life she'd lived. *Enjoy the adventure, Fleur. May it be all you ever dreamed it would be.*

Sasha hadn't really realised just how many people her mother knew and it was strange to see so many of the different facets of her mother's life come together. To see them all in the same place. The hall her mother had wanted them to use for the wake was huge. And it needed to be. There were literally hundreds of people there. Nurses from the hospice and from before. Ones who had treated her original cancer, helped her through her rehab. Sasha even recognised one of the doctors from the GP's surgery they went to. Mike Hunt was there, chatting to a few of her mother's friends from bingo. Fleur's friends from her "crystals" group were gathered around a table, swinging their own crystals over plates of sandwiches and pork pies. They'd refused the chicken drumsticks, just in case. She wasn't sure "just in case" of what. Salmonella? E. Coli? Botulism?

Dante and the rest of the street thugs sat around a table at the back. All drinking the hard stuff—Cokes all round, full fat, none of that diet crap. Jude behind the bar knew none of them were over eighteen, and he wasn't risking his license for anyone. Every few minutes, one of them would hold up their glass and start another toast to her mother. So far, she'd heard them toast to her adventures, to her advice on women, to her "career" advice, to her gardening tips—Sasha didn't want to even think about that—and to her willingness to buy them cheap booze every now and then from the offie. No wonder they looked out for Sasha if they were trying to keep her mother sweet.

Maria and a few of the other girls from the salon sat at one of the other tables. They'd all shown up, piling out of Maria's car like they were trying to break a Guinness World Record.

Bobbi herself was wandering around, helping Sophie and Mags. But every now and then she'd stop and just stand there in the middle of the room looking lost. Like some unexpected memory or thought had just occurred to her and she wanted to share it with Fleur but she couldn't. Just like Sasha felt. Sasha found it hardest to look at her. She had so many shared memories of Bobbi and her mother that they were the hardest to push away, to get through the rest of the day when she saw the tears on Bobbi's cheeks.

There were friends there who she hadn't seen in years. People who Fleur had said were on "Christmas-card only" terms, others who were "once a month" mates—as in they spoke on the phone once a month—and there were close friends. Those she'd see on the way to or from the shops whenever she ventured out. Close friends she'd known many years, and some she hadn't known that long but had gone through her cancer battle or rehab with.

Every one of them knew and loved Fleur. Well, almost all of them.

Sasha stared at the small group of people who had come from Kefran Media. People who were there to help her and Jac, support them throughout the day. Sophie and Mags were working tirelessly, bringing out plates of sandwiches, tearing through cling-film wrappings, and helping the bar staff by clearing empties off the tables. They never seemed to stop. And they seemed to understand Bobbi's need to help as much as she needed their understanding when she lost what she was doing. Sasha had seen Sophie rescue a tray of sandwiches Bobbi was about to drop on the floor, then wrap her in her arms and hold her while she cried. Mags had gently shifted her from the middle of a walkway to a quieter corner where Bobbi could stand without being run over by the crowd stampeding the buffet line. And when Bobbi's tears had run down her cheeks, one or the other of them had been there with a napkin or a tissue for her. Sasha was glad. Because she wasn't sure she had it in her to offer Bobbi comfort herself. Not today.

Sophie and Mags's presence was truly a comfort, and everything they were doing let Sasha stop worrying about the details of the day. The nitty-gritty stuff she'd been so worried about. They took care of it all. She wasn't sure how she was going to be able to repay them. But she was truly grateful for everything they were doing. But most of all, she understood why they were there. They were there for her and for Jac. To make the day easier for them. Not because they knew and loved Fleur; though Sasha knew they did like her, they simply hadn't known her long enough to form the kind of bond with her that others in the room had. But what Sasha couldn't understand was why Vanessa had come with them.

Since walking in, supposedly under the pretext that she was there to work with them to help, she'd done nothing but stand at the bar, staring daggers at Sasha and drinking steadily. Sasha knew this because she had wanted to go over and get a drink several times but hadn't wanted to go near her. She didn't have to work with the woman anymore, so Sasha had no reason to try to be polite. Neither did she want any drama. Today was difficult enough. Today was Fleur's day. And Sasha didn't want to get drawn into a conversation with Vanessa that might in any way detract from that.

She felt Jac's hand on the small of her back and turned to look at her. Jac's eyes were red-rimmed and puffy, her smile as tight and weak as her own. "You okay?" Sasha asked.

"I was going to ask you the same thing."

"I'm fine, love. Wouldn't mind a drink, but I don't want to tempt the barfly into conversation."

Jac looked over her head and scowled. "She might as well not have bothered coming. She's not done anything to help Sophie or Mags or Bobbi."

"I know. But I don't want any drama." She rubbed a hand over Jac's belly, drawing her attention back to her. "Not today."

"No, not today. I'll go and get you a drink, babe." She bent forwards and kissed her lips. "What do you want?"

Sasha inhaled deeply. "Brandy, neat."

"You sure?"

"God, yes. Make it a double."

Jac tipped her head to the side but didn't argue as she said, "One double brandy coming up." They wandered to the other end of the twenty-foot-long bar to where Vanessa was propping it up.

"I can't believe there are so many people here," Sophie said, appearing at Sasha's side.

Sasha nodded but kept her eyes locked on Vanessa as she began to teeter over to Jac. "Mum was a popular lady. It always seemed like she knew everyone whenever we went anywhere." She pointed to where Octo-Nessa had just clamped her hand over Jac's arm while she waited to get the bartender's attention. "What do you think it will take for her to get the message that Jac isn't interested anymore?"

"I don't know," Sophie said, "lightning bolt from above?" She looked skyward. "Think your mum's broke into the heavenly stash yet?"

"Wouldn't put it past her. But just in case she's been held up with red tape or something, let's go and get Jac out of there." She sighed heavily. "Why did she have to turn up today? I just don't want to have to deal with her shit today."

"I'll go. You stay here. Maybe go and get something to eat."

"No, Jac's got my drink anyway." Sasha set off to the bar. It wasn't too far away. Maybe only twenty feet or so, and as they neared, Sasha could hear Vanessa's whiny voice as she ran her hand up and down Jac's arm.

"...Look I just want you to know I'm here for you, Jac. Anytime. Just like I was the other night. Holding you in my arms again was magical. I know it meant something to you too. You've never let go and cried like that before."

"Vanessa, get over yourself," Jac hissed. "I was upset. I wasn't letting go with you. I was just...upset. Now just leave me alone. If you aren't going to make yourself useful today, maybe you should think about leaving." Jac turned around, drinks in hand, and stopped as soon as she saw Sasha. She held out the brandy snifter. "Hey, babe. One double brandy as requested."

Sasha took the glass but didn't say anything. She wasn't sure what to say, to be honest. She was sure there was some innocent explanation to what Vanessa had said. Of course there was. Jac had been her rock, Jac loved her, Jac was not now, nor ever would be again, interested in Vanessa. But Vanessa just wasn't getting the hint, for fuck's sake. Today? Today she was supposed to deal with her mother, with saying goodbye to her mother, not Vanessa's petty, stupid fucking drama.

"What was she talking about, Jac?" Sophie demanded as Sasha continued to stand there, still deciding if she actually wanted to deal with it all right then.

Vanessa stumbled closer and wrapped a hand around Jac's elbow. "Sorry, you weren't meant to hear that. I didn't mean to make things awkward."

Jac whirled around to face her. The expression on her face totally stunned. "What the fuck are you talking about? You're making something out of nothing! You—you—" Jac tore her arm from Vanessa's grasp, knocking Sasha's drink out of her hand and spilling her own as she did. "I was upset and crying in the editing suite." She turned to face Sasha. "She hugged me while I cried. That's it. She's making it sound—"

Holding up her hand, Sasha cut her off. "Fine. Please, just get her out of here, Jac. I can't deal with this right now." She brushed past them, intent on getting another brandy from the bar. Instead of one, she ordered two. Suddenly, the urge to get totally and utterly fucking pissed was climbing high up her to-do list.

She heard the scuffle of bodies behind her as she knocked back the first glass of brandy, the alcohol burning her gullet before it warmed her belly. She hadn't realised how cold she'd felt. No, *cold* wasn't the right word. *Numb.* That was a better one. Angry whispers, and eventually the slamming of the door accompanied the second glass's journey to join its predecessor, and Sasha felt herself begin to relax—just a little—for the first time in days.

"Another?" Sophie asked.

"Oh yeah."

"Maybe take a little water with this one."

"Nah."

"Then sip it, at least."

She picked up the glass as soon as the bartender set it in front of her, nodded her thanks to him, and turned to lean her back against the wood. "I'll think about it." She held the glass under her nose.

"Jac wouldn't have done anything—"

"I know. I trust her." She took a sip and savoured the warmth in her mouth. "I don't trust Octo-Nessa, but I trust Jac. I'm sure she was upset; she has every right to be. She's been so strong for me that she's been holding all her own emotions in. I'm glad she was able to find a time to let go when she needed to." She shrugged. "I'd have preferred it had been with you or Mags…or just about anyone else in the world, if I'm totally honest. But I don't believe for a second it was anything other than Jac letting go of some of what we've been dealing with." She smiled at Sophie. "Like I said earlier, I just can't deal with Vanessa and her crap today. Not today. You know?"

Sophie clinked her glass to Sasha's. "Won't have to anymore. The film's done, and we can just get on with everything else life's decided to throw at us."

Sasha snorted. "Right."

Sophie knocked back the rest of what looked and smelled like a shot of vodka and said, "You gonna be okay while I go and make sure Jac isn't being arrested for murder?"

Sasha nodded. "I know I should go out there with you but—"

"I know, hon. Not today. Today, let me go and bury the body."

"Thanks." Sasha hugged her tight. "You're a really, really good friend, Soph."

"Remember that when I need bail money."

Sasha tittered and let her go. "Promise."

"What the fuck were you thinking?" Jac shouted at Vanessa when they exited the hall. "I mean seriously? She's just buried her mother and you're trying to do what? Split us up?"

Vanessa had her arms folded over her chest. "I was just trying to be your friend, Jac. I was trying to offer you support like you needed the other night. That's it. That's all I said."

Jac heard footsteps behind her and turned to see Sophie and Mags step up to her side. "That might be what you said, but the way you said it—the implication you gave it—you were trying to make it sound like I'd done something wrong."

"Seeking the comfort of another woman's arms during a difficult time could be construed that way, Jac. If you're the jealous type like Sasha seems to be."

Jac stepped towards her, balling her hands into fists at her sides. "I did not seek you out. You came looking for me. You have been trying to needle your way back in since we started rehearsals. And I told you, from the very start, it wasn't going to happen. I told you I wasn't interested. I told you I was with someone else. But it didn't stop. I avoided you, and you sought me out. You've tried to come between us, and now look what you've done!" She towered over Vanessa, spittle gathering at the corners of her mouth, but she didn't care. "This is probably the second worst day of her life, and she's in there dealing with it—alone—because you are a selfish little bitch who can't take a hint."

Jac closed her eyes to block out the picture of Sasha's dejected face when she'd told her to leave. Told her to take Vanessa and get out. She wanted to march right back in there and explain everything to her. To tell her word for word what had been said, and more importantly how she'd felt. Maybe there was still CCTV footage from the editing suite that she could find. If she could show Sasha that Vanessa was just full of shit, then maybe everything would be okay still. She just had to show her.

She balled up her fear of losing Sasha, twisting it into more anger than she ever remembered feeling, and let loose on Vanessa.

"So let me make this perfectly clear." She grabbed Vanessa's shoulders and shook her. "Are you listening?"

"Jac, stop it. You're hurting me."

"Not as much as you've tried to hurt me today. Not as much as you've hurt Sasha. So I'll ask you again. Are you listening to me?"

Vanessa nodded, and Jac could see a sliver of fear in her eyes.

"Good. I do not want to be with you. I do not love you. I will never love you. Whether or not I am with Sasha, it makes no difference. I will never take you back. I have zero interest in sleeping with you, of being in a relationship with you, or even working with you again. Have I made myself clear?"

Vanessa's eyes were watering, but Jac refused to allow herself to feel sorry for her. Not now, not ever again.

"Are you under any illusion that you and I have any kind of future together?"

Vanessa shook her head, tears falling down her cheeks. "You don't have to be so mean, Jac."

"Apparently, I do. I tried being nice to you. I tried being friends, against my better judgement. I tried working with you. But you still pulled this!"

She sniffed. "I love you."

Jac laughed harshly. "Bullshit."

"I do!"

"Lady, the only person you're capable of loving is yourself. You loved the idea of what I could do for your career. You loved the money and the prestige you seem to think comes with me. You never loved me."

"You don't know anything. You don't know me." She pointed to the building behind Jac. "You fucking deserve the shrivelled-up bitch. See how much good she does your career, towing around an ugly old…bitch like that at parties. She won't help you woo investors."

"That's all crap, but even if it wasn't, I still wouldn't care. I love her. Her. Not her body, not the way she looks on my arm, or what I think she can help me gain at a fucking party. I love every single thing about her."

Vanessa snorted. "Yeah, and when you get fed up of her saggy old tits, don't bother to come looking for me. I won't stand for anyone treating me like this." She pulled herself from Jac's grip and stumbled away.

"I'd rather grow old by her side and watch that happen than live with those fake lumps you have on your chest."

Vanessa's back straightened and she almost lost her balance.

"Shit," Jac said under her breath. "I shouldn't have said that." She started after Vanessa. She didn't want the woman to fall and hurt herself, and she was clearly the wrong side of sober.

Mags put a hand on her arm. "I'll make sure she gets home okay. I've already called a taxi to come and get her."

"Thanks, Mags," she called after her as Mags quickly caught up to Vanessa.

Jac turned back towards the hall and stared up at it. "Shit."

"Yup," Sophie said and clapped her hand over Jac's shoulder. "Glad that's over with." She tugged Jac's arm, trying to head her back towards the door. "Come on. Better get back in there or you might have to carry Sasha home. She was on her third double brandy when I came out here. God knows how many she's had by now."

Jac's feet stubbornly refused to move. "She told me to get out of there."

"What're you talking about?"

"She threw me out. She told me to get out of there."

Sophie rolled her eyes. "Have you been drinking too?"

"No. That's what she said. She said she couldn't deal with this."

"Yes, she did say that. She told you to get Vanessa out of there because she didn't want to deal with her melodramatics today. It's her mother's funeral, after all."

"She pushed me away."

"Don't do this, Jac."

"Don't do what?"

"Don't hear things she didn't say, don't run because you think she's pushing, don't leave because you're afraid to lose what you've got."

Jac stared at her.

"She did not tell you to leave. She asked you to help her by taking care of a problem. Do you know what she said to me when she was busy chugging back brandy?"

"What?"

"She told me she trusts you. That she was glad you'd found some way to deal with the emotions you were going through too, because you'd been her rock through all of this. She did wish it had been me or Mags you'd cried on, but she didn't begrudge you a meltdown. And she didn't for a second think it was anything more than that. She's in there, waiting for you to come back after taking out the trash." She ran a hand over Jac's back. "I heard you accuse Vanessa of making something out of nothing. Don't you go and do the same."

"But—"

"No, no buts. You love her, yes?"

"Yeah," Jac whispered.

"She loves you. And I know that alone scares the crap out of you. You've never had what everyone else has. You've never had something you could trust before. Something you could believe in. Someone you could believe in." She pointed towards the door. "She's right in there. You can believe in her, because she believes in you."

The doors loomed before her. Jac hadn't realised just how scared she was. All her life she'd ached for someone to belong to, someone who would hold her heart as tenderly as she would hold theirs. And now she'd found her, she was terrified of losing her. The past two weeks of watching Sasha lose her mother had struck that chord of fear in her with increasing resonance as every tick of the second hand on the clock over Fleur's bed had gone by.

"She won't abandon you, Pan-pan."

"You can't know that," Jac whispered.

"Yeah, I do." Sophie chuckled. "But more importantly, deep down, so do you. Don't you?"

Jac shook her head but whispered, "Yes." As though she believed but still couldn't quite bring herself to believe that she did. As though the whole notion was still just a little too incredible for her to wrap her head around.

"So get back in there and save her from the hangover she's working on."

Jac stuck her hands in her pockets and felt the velvet cover of the box she'd carried around with her for weeks. She pulled it out and pried open the lid, then ran her finger over the grooves and notches of the key.

"Yep, I think that would be the perfect pick-me-up for her today." She shoved Jac forwards. "Now go and give it to her."

She didn't remember her feet moving or making the decision to walk back into the hall. She didn't remember looking for Sasha in the crowd of mourners. What she did remember was the slightly glassy look in Sasha's eyes when she stood beside her at the bar and the sloppy way she was holding her brandy glass. The grin that played over her lips when she wound her arms around Jac's waist and the trickle of liquid down the back of her shirt before Sophie plucked the glass from Sasha's hand and deposited it on the bar.

"Hey," Jac said quietly and wrapped her arms around Sasha's back.

"Hey," Sasha slurred back.

"She gone?" Bobbi asked from the other side of Sasha, a pint glass in her hand that seemed like it was as big as her head. She, too, looked glassy-eyed, but more from crying than alcohol.

"Yeah. Mags is putting her in a taxi."

"Good." Bobbi took a drink, the foamy head creating a white moustache over her lip before she licked it away. "We don't need that kind of crap today."

"Agreed."

Bobbi nodded and turned back to the bar, picking up a packet of nuts and shaking a few into her mouth, seemingly content to let Jac take over comforting Sasha.

Sasha leant in close and rested her head on Jac's chest. "Can you cry with Sophie or Mags next time, babe? Octo-Nessa'll only try to take advantage again."

Tightened her hold around Sasha, she chuckled at how foolish she felt for questioning this. "Promise."

"I think I'm a little bit pissed."

"Yeah." Jac rested her cheek on top of Sasha's head. "Little bit. Did you have anything to eat?"

Sasha shook her head.

"Want something?"

Sasha shook her head again, then turned to press her forehead onto Jac's sternum. "The world's spinning."

"I'll get her a couple of sandwiches," Sophie said from Jac's side.

"Don't want anything," Sasha protested.

"It'll stop the world spinning," Jac added to quiet her protests. *And maybe you from puking.*

"Fibber."

"Maybe." She stroked her hands up Sasha's back. "But you love me anyway, right?"

Sasha tipped her head back and gazed up at her. "With all my heart."

She pulled the box from her pocket and held it up so Sasha could see. "I have something for you. I was waiting for the right time, but then I realised it was always the right time when I'm with you, so…?" She pried open the lid and picked out the key, then held it up between them. "What do you think? Will you move in with me?"

Sasha didn't say anything. She plucked the key from Jac's hand and stretched up, capturing Jac's lips in a deep kiss. Her tongue fought for dominance, and her fingers drove into Jac's hair in that way that made Jac moan and deepen the kiss further. They searched and explored each other, Jac aware the whole while that people around them were probably staring and wondering just how drunk Sasha was. Was she planning to stop this anytime soon? Exhibitionism hadn't been something Jac had thought would be Sasha's cup of tea, but she certainly seemed not to care—

"I'm gonna be sick." Sasha tore herself away from Jac, bent at the waist, and let loose.

Everyone around jumped back, but pant legs were splattered and shoes were covered as Sasha returned her brandy deposits with interest, crying and apologising the whole time. Jac scooped her hair back and smiled sheepishly to the gathered crowd.

"Sorry. She doesn't normally react like this when she kisses me," she said to the barman as he sent someone off for a bucket, handed Jac a small towel, and waved off her apology.

"Love, if ya can't get pissed till ya chuck ya guts up when ya bury yer mam, when can ya?"

"She's a really good kisser." Sasha's voice was small and smothered a little by her position, talking to the floor as she was. "She makes my belly flop, but in a good way."

Jac grinned rakishly when the barman threw back his head and laughed.

Sophie arrived with a paper plate filled with a selection of triangular-cut sandwiches. She eyed them, then Sasha's still-bent-over body, then Jac, still holding Sasha's hair. She shrugged and picked up one of the little triangles, then finished off an egg and cress in three giant bites.

"What?" she asked around a mouthful. "She's not gonna eat 'em now."

CHAPTER 32

"Are you sure about this?" Bobbi asked for the hundredth, possibly thousandth, time.

Sasha slapped the back of her shoulder as Bobbi walked past her, carrying an armful of cardboard boxes that needed to be taped together. "I'm positive. We've been over this. I'm moving in with Jac." She looked about the home she'd shared for so many years with her mother. "Being here's too painful right now, but at the same time it's where I grew up. I'm not ready to let go of it yet either. Having you rent it from me is the perfect solution."

"Yeah, but you could get yourself a nice little nest egg together if you sold it."

"I'm not ready to sell it. Mum and Dad bought this house when she was pregnant with me. Part of me still can't imagine not seeing Mum here, but I can't bear to see someone in here that I don't know either." She shrugged. "I know it doesn't make sense, but it's how I feel, and as for the nest egg, well, there's no mortgage on this place. Mum signed it over to me when I first moved back, so there's no inheritance tax for me to pay on it. Literally the only thing I have to cover out of the rent you pay me is landlord's insurance. I honestly feel bad asking you to pay me."

"You're asking me to pay a fraction more for a whole house than what I've been paying for a room in a scummy houseshare with a billion students. I'd gladly pay double." She dumped the boxes on the kitchen table and reached for the packing tape. "Not that I could afford double, but if I could, I'd gladly pay it."

Sasha took the box from her when she finished securing the bottom so it wouldn't fall through. She jumped when a hand pinched her bottom. She turned her head with a grin and was met by Jac's lips. "About time you got here."

"Be nice." Jac held up a couple of large paper bags and jiggled them. "Or you won't get the breakfast I so lovingly made for you. Hey, Bobbi."

"Hiya, Jac." Bobbi barely looked up from her task

"You do do a fantastic drive-thru run, baby." She kissed her again and put the box down by her mum's old Welsh dresser. It was full of ornaments and knick-knacks that needed to be sorted and packed away. This had been a task Sasha had managed to avoid for the past month. Staying with Jac, bringing over Nip, her clothes, and her personal belongings a bit at a time had been easy. Coming back to her house whenever she needed something had been the hard part.

Over time, she had got used to walking through the door in which she still expected to see her mum lounging on the sofa, smoking a joint, or eating one of her brownies, stroking Nip like she was some kind of Bond villain with her minion of darkness on her lap. But the moment was here. Not time to let go. As she'd told Bobbi, she wasn't ready for that. But it was time for her to take the next step and fully move in with Jac.

Renting out the house had been Jac's suggestion if she didn't want to sell it. And the off-the-cuff remark had sparked the idea of Bobbi taking the place on. No-brainer, really. It also meant she didn't have to figure out what to do with most of the furniture, as Bobbi only had enough to fill her small room. She was more than grateful to have Sasha leave the dining table, chairs, sofa, and everything else. They could sort out the details in time, when Bobbi was ready to invest in her own furniture.

Removal men were coming tomorrow morning to pick up the boxes they were packing up, boxes that would be filled with books, pictures, clothes, ornaments, and knick-knacks, boxes that would be filled with a life lived and lost.

The front door swung open, and Mags and Sophie wandered in, Mags carting some more collapsed boxes, and Sophie waving a tape dispenser around like a gun. As she stepped into the kitchen, she struck a pose.

"I'm totally feeling all Farrah Fawcett today." She primped her hair, still holding the dispenser like a gun, then pointed to her feet. "I used to have such awesome bell bottoms and platform boots. Good times." She sighed and reached for the breakfast sandwich Jac held out to her. "Thanks, Pan-pan."

They all ate quickly, eager to get on with the task at hand—or rather eager to be *done* with the task in hand.

"Where do you want to start?" Mags asked when they'd all balled up their greaseproof paper and stuffed them back into the bag.

"Good question." Sasha had been trying to decide what would be the best way to set about the task since they'd committed to doing it. There were so many aspects of it all that were so personal; she wanted to be a part of it, to know what parts of her mother were being boxed up and packed to move or packed to go to the charity shop. "I've already taken most of my personal stuff, so my room won't take me long to sort. The bathroom just needs boxing up for rubbish. I don't really think half a bottle of mum's shampoo or her old mascara is going to be much use to anyone." She didn't mention she'd already packed a half-used bottle of Fleur's perfume and her old hairbrush and taken them to Jac's a couple of weeks ago.

"I'll do that," Mags said. "Do you want me to give it a scrub while I'm there?"

"If you wouldn't mind," Sasha said.

"No!" Bobbi said at the same time. "No. You don't need to clean. I'm more than capable of doing that once everything's packed up."

"I don't mind. Really," Mags told her.

Bobbi sighed. "Thank you, but I'd only go and do it again. I'm the same whenever I move in somewhere new. I have to clean it from top to bottom. Even if it was sparkling when I got there. Peace-of-mind thing. OCD thing." She shrugged. "I don't know. But I do, so you might as well leave it for me to do tomorrow afternoon."

Mags clapped her on the shoulder. "Well, it's gonna be your place, so I guess we'll go with that then, my friend." She grabbed a black bin liner and headed up the stairs.

"Want me to start on the books?" Sophie suggested. "I'll go through the house and box up any I find. Then you can decide what to do with them later."

"That would be great. I'll want to keep some, but others I was going to donate to the library."

"I know you're leaving the crockery and stuff, but do you want me to start on your mum's china?" Bobbi pointed to the glass display case they could just see through the open door in the living room. It was stuffed full of crystal glasses, the fine bone-china crockery Fleur and Bert had received as a wedding gift. Sasha could only remember it being used at Christmas or special occasions, like…well, she couldn't remember it being used except at Christmas.

"Please." She looked at the ceiling. "I guess I'll start in her bedroom." She grabbed a box and started for the stairs.

Jac picked up a roll of tape and a handful of collapsed boxes. "I'll come with you."

A wave of relief swept through Sasha. She hadn't been relishing any of the tasks, but the idea of deciding which of her mum's clothes she wanted to keep and which she was donating was…well, daunting didn't even start to describe how she felt about it. Overwhelmed? Maybe. She was a writer. Words were her thing. They gave her comfort at times when she needed it. Not being able to find the ones she needed sucked. But, quite frankly, the whole experience had her lost for words. And she hated it.

She kept one box aside for things she wanted to keep and shook open a heavy-duty black bag for items she would donate. She pulled open the wardrobe door and pointed to the hangers on the rail. "Okay, anything in tie-dye can go to charity."

"Surely not." Sarcasm dripped from each word as Jac picked up the first item, a long skirt of many, many layers, and held it up for inspection.

"I'm sorry, babe, but it's just not your colour."

"Nope, it's every colour." Into the bag it went, as did all the others. Sasha set to work on the drawers. There were a few things she wanted. An old cardigan that had been so comfy just to lounge around in. Sasha held it to her nose and sniffed, tears coming to her eyes. It still smelled like her. That hideous eau de toilet she insisted on wearing, the slightly stale odour of old weed smoke, and the scent underneath it all that was just Mum. She folded it and put it in the box labelled *keep*.

On top of the dresser was an old jar she didn't remember noticing there, but she remembered it, nonetheless. It was an old jam jar filled with seashells. There was scrap of paper taped across the front of it. Both were yellowed with age, the writing long since faded, but it had read, *Happy*

Mother's Day, to the best mum in the whole wide world. The apostrophe had been the wrong way round and the comma had looked more like a full stop, but she'd written it in her best five-year-old handwriting. It was the year they'd been on holiday over Mother's Day. She'd spent all day scouring Morecambe Beach for the prettiest shells she could find. As she turned the jar, she could see some of the shells were chipped, others still perfectly intact. Fleur had gushed over the simple gift when she'd given it to her. Alongside the obligatory burnt piece of toast, half a spilt glass of orange juice, and the cup of tea Dad had carried up to save Sasha from scalding herself. Forty years. Her mother had kept it for forty years.

Sasha wiped her eyes and wrapped the jar in the cardigan that was already in her *keep* box.

"Sasha?" Jac turned to her, staring at something in her hand.

"Yeah?"

"Why does your mum have a calendar of Spam in her wardrobe?" Jac frowned, then turned the wire-bound pages to show her.

Sasha grinned, then held her hand over her mouth as she started laughing. "I can't believe she still has that." She crossed the room and took it from her before sitting on the bed.

"What is it?"

"A calendar. From about ten years ago now."

"I gathered that with all those little dates on it. But why does she still have it?"

"It was a gag Christmas gift." She pointed to the picture of a tin of Spam on a makeshift raft—a piece of driftwood—sitting in a puddle beside a road. The caption underneath read, *The Adventures of the Travelling Spam.* Sasha giggled. "When I was little, Mum and Dad took me on holiday with them. Abroad, no less."

"Ooo. Fancy."

"I know."

"Where did you all go?"

"Benidorm."

"And what does Spam have to do with that?"

"Mum wasn't convinced we'd be able to eat the foreign food, so she insisted on packing some staples, just in case." She tapped the picture. "A tin of that gelatinous chunk of stuff was her idea of a saviour, if the worst came to the worst."

"Did you all eat it?"

"God no, the food was lovely. But it became a bit of a family joke. And wherever we went on holiday after that, Mum or Dad would hide a tin in the other's suitcase. For years they carried on doing that. When I got a bit older, I joined in the fun and started trying to get them to have their picture taken with it. Like it was a member of the family, enjoying the holiday with us. I'm almost convinced it was the same tin of Spam every year as well." She flicked through the pages. Spam at Blackpool Tower. Spam outside Buckingham Palace. Spam on a train. Spam on a deck chair on a beach next to her dad, fast asleep. Her dad that was, not the Spam. Spam on a lilo with her mum. Every picture brought back a memory that she shared with Jac until they were crying with laughter.

"So you made this up for her?"

"Yeah. I guess you had to be there, but when you know the memories each one is a part of, it, well, it made it special. You know?"

"Clearly she loved and treasured it."

Sasha closed it up and slid it into the *keeps* box.

"And clearly you're just as crazy as your mother was."

"Yeah," she conceded, "probably."

They finished emptying out the clothes, laughing as often as they cried at some of the things Fleur had stuffed in her wardrobe. A few more things found their way into the *keeps* box. Fleur's jewellery box—including the wedding ring Bert had given her almost fifty years ago. Sasha couldn't remember her mum taking it off, but she hadn't been wearing it in the hospice. When she'd asked about it, Fleur had simply told her it was too precious to risk it getting misplaced in a place like this. That it was safe at home.

On the bedside table a reflection caught her eye. Fleur's crystal. The one that had "chosen" which scone would taste the best, "chosen" to send Sasha down the "right path", and given Fleur a focus and comfort in the final months of her life. As much as Sasha had been annoyed by the way her mother had waved the thing around, crying its power to anyone who would listen to her, Sasha couldn't bear the thought of getting rid of it now. She picked it up and slipped it over her head.

"Oh no, don't tell me you're going to start asking your 'higher self' what you should eat for tea, are you?" Jac asked, wrapping her arms around Sasha's waist from behind.

"God, no." Sasha chuckled. "I just...it just feels like it was a part of her for a long time, and I can't—"

Jac kissed her cheek. "I get it. I told you before, we've got plenty of space in the apartment, and if there is too much, we'll get a storage facility. Honestly, it's no problem."

"No, I don't want to keep everything. Then it would all just blend into the background." She tapped the box. "We've only done one room so far. There'll be loads more stuff to clutter up our house before I'm done."

"I'm looking forward to it." Jac grinned and tipped her head towards the wardrobe. "I, erm, found something else in there." Jac handed her an old shoe box, the lid covered in her mother's handwriting that read, *Only open this if I'm actually dead.*

"What is it?"

"Open it," Jac said, her voice cracking with barely supressed laughter. Sasha stared at her questioningly, but Jac held up her hands in surrender. "Oh no, I'm not making the shout on this one." She pointed. "Open it."

Sasha lifted the lid. There were half a dozen VHS cassettes inside. Each one bearing a sticky label with Fleur's distinctive cursive. She picked one out and squinted a little through tired eyes to read it, then screamed as she threw it and the box on the floor.

Jac laughed and bent to scoop up the box and the items.

"Burn them!" Sasha shouted as she heard footsteps coming up the stairs.

"We heard screaming," Mags said from the doorway.

"What's up?" Sophie barged past Mags and into the room.

"It's nothing. Just a bit of a fright," Sasha said, trying to get the tapes back in the box and covered with the lid. "You, stop laughing," Sasha hissed at Jac. "It's not funny."

Sophie and Bobbi managed to snag escaped tapes before Sasha could get a hold on them. Sophie started laughing too. "Your mother was fucking priceless."

Bobbi held her stomach and dropped heavily onto the bed. "Wonder who filmed them?"

"Wonder who the co-star is?" Sophie bantered back.

Sasha held out the box, not wanting to touch the actual tapes if she didn't have to. "Put the contraband back in the box for destruction."

"That's not contraband, Sash. Your mother said it was on her bucket list." Sophie sniggered but tossed the tape into the box.

"This is so not funny."

"Sasha, other than, like D- to Z-list celebs, how many other people can say their mother made sex tapes?" Sophie shook her head. "At our age, I mean."

"There's a reason for that, Sophie. A very good, very big reason."

"And what is that?"

"I can't think of it right now, but there is, I'm sure of it."

Sophie laughed louder. "That woman was fucking awesome."

"How would you feel if it were your mother making sex tapes?"

"I doubt my mother ever had sex."

They all laughed harder. "Hate to break it to you, love, but how do you think you and your five siblings got here?" Mags asked her.

Sophie waved her hand back and forth, then said, "Okay, she had sex a maximum of six times, all of which I blame on my father. But I'm certain she never had an orgasm. So there is no way on God's green earth she would even know what a sex tape was, never mind make one."

"Exactly. No one wants to know about their parents and this stuff. It's just..." Sasha shuddered and waved the box at Bobbi, still holding on to the tape she'd picked up.

Bobbi dropped it in. Jac had slid off the bed, she was laughing so hard, but she managed to angle the lid so they could all read it. *Gotcha* was printed in huge black letters across the inside.

Sasha closed her eyes and put a hand over her chest.

"They're fake?" Bobbi asked.

"Evil." Sophie chortled and dropped down on the bed. "That woman was so evil. I wanna be Fleur when I grow up."

"You're well on your way," Sasha quipped and stared at the box again.

"Is this what she meant when she said she'd haunt us all?" Bobbi asked.

"Probably," Sophie said. "Who knows what else she planned for us?"

"Wonder what really is on there?" Mags asked.

Sasha shrugged. "I've no idea. We don't even have a VHS player anymore."

"We have equipment back at the office we can use. Put it on a disc if you want? I can check if it's nothing first, of course."

"You'd do that for me?" Sasha asked.

"Sure." Mags beamed. "Come on, we'll put it with the stuff in the Duster." They carried the last few to-donate items downstairs together and put them into the boot of Mags's large car.

Boxes of to-keep stuff were stacked and neatly labelled in each room, and there were only the personal knick-knacks left to pack away by the time Sasha and Jac made it back into the living room. They worked their way through, laughing as Sasha and Bobbi told stories until the sun had long since set and the need for food drove them to order in pizza.

"Guess what I found?" Bobbi asked when they'd all finished eating and were lounging around, bemoaning bloated stomachs.

"Winning lottery ticket?" Mags asked.

"Fleur's vibrator?" Sophie guessed. Everyone stared at her in shock, except for Sasha who bent double, laughing.

Bobbi pulled a box from behind her back, looking like she'd just lost a tenner and found a penny. "Erm, no. Just this."

"Ooo, mum's Monopoly set." Sasha held her hands out for it. "Right, let's do it." She started pushing away the empty pizza boxes and setting up the board.

"I also found these." Bobbi held up a set of shot glasses. Each one had on it a slogan from the famous "Keep Calm" range that had blown into fashion.

Sasha smirked and pointed at the board. "Fleur's house rules?"

"Oh, yeah, gotta be done," Bobbi said.

"Erm," Jac started, "what are these rules?"

"Whenever you land on a Chance card, you have to take a shot," Bobbi started and lifted up a bottle of vodka.

"You pass Go and collect two hundred pounds, and take a shot," Sasha continued. "If you land on a property that's got a hotel on it, you get a shot too. Because Mum always said she couldn't sleep in a hotel without a little assistance."

Bobbi grinned wickedly. "You up for it, ladies?" She held up the shot glasses.

"Hell, yeah." Sophie said, pulling her phone out of her bag. "I'll just let the wife know I'll be home in a state."

"Me too," Mags said.

Text messages were fired off as Bobbi set the shot glasses in front of them all. Jac picked up her glass and grinned as she read out her slogan. "Keep calm and stay not a grown-up." Nodding, she added, "Oh, that is so me." She looked at Mags. "Come on, what's yours say?"

"Keep calm and put the kettle on." She sniffed. "Bit boring, that one." She looked at Bobbi. "What's yours say?"

"Keep calm and eat the brownie." Bobbi grinned and looked at Sasha. "Any left about the place?"

"If there was, I wouldn't recommend eating them now. It'd have been there for weeks. You'd likely be getting a mushroom ride to go along with the hash." Sasha held hers up to read: "Keep calm and dance like nobody's watching." She grinned. "Nice. What've you got, Soph?"

"Keep calm and wait for the other shoe to drop."

"That was Mum's favourite. After her op," Sasha said.

"She was so twisted. I love her."

"Me too." Sasha knew her smile was sad when the faces that smiled back at her looked like they were fighting back tears. She shook her head and held out her glass for Bobbi to fill with vodka. Everyone else followed suit and watched Sasha.

"To Mum. There'll never be another like her." She swallowed the shot as the group around her toasted to Fleur, drank their shots, and set up the game.

Laughter rang around the walls as they recounted tales of Fleur's stoner antics, picked their markers, and the five of them played long into the night.

"Wish you were here to see this, Mum," she said under her breath as she passed Go for the third time, collected her cash, and downed her shot.

She was more than a little merry as she shuffled over to Jac and cuddled into her side, Jac's arm about her shoulders.

From somewhere in the universe, Sasha felt Fleur answer, *"I am."*

ABOUT ANDREA BRAMHALL

Andrea Bramhall wrote her first novel at the age of six and three-quarters. It was seven pages long and held together with a pink ribbon. Her Gran still has it in the attic. Since then she has progressed a little bit and now has a number of published works held together with glue, not ribbons, an Alice B. Lavender certificate, a Lambda Literary award, and a Golden Crown award cluttering up her book shelves.

She studied music and all things arty at Manchester Metropolitan University, graduating in 2002 with a BA in contemporary arts. She is certain it will prove useful someday…maybe.

When she isn't busy running a campsite in the Lake District, Bramhall can be found hunched over her laptop scribbling down the stories that won't let her sleep. She can also be found reading, walking the dogs up mountains while taking a few thousand photos, scuba diving while taking a few thousand photos, swimming, kayaking, playing the saxophone, or cycling.

OTHER BOOKS FROM
YLVA PUBLISHING

www.ylva-publishing.com

JUST MY LUCK
Andrea Bramhall

ISBN: 978-3-95533-702-5
Length: 306 pages (80,500 words)

Genna Collins works a dead end job, loves her family, her girlfriend, and her friends. When she wins the biggest Euromillions jackpot on record, everything changes…and not always for the best.

When Abi Kitson fell in love she always knew it would go unrequited. The woman of her dreams was so close yet seemingly untouchable for so many reasons. Reasons like - they are best friends, or the big age gap, or the 'other' woman, nevermind Abi's own baggage. And even when those reasons crumble it seems luck just isn't on her side.

It's a learning curve for both of them. But what if money really can't buy you everything you want? What if the answers aren't hidden in a big, fat bank balance? What if happiness is right in front of them? They just have to reach out…

A WORK IN PROGRESS
L.T. Smith

ISBN: 978-3-95533-850-3
Length: 121 pages (37,000 words)

Writer Brynn Morgan has been in love with her best friend and muse, Gillian Parker forever. She's the only one who can fill the emptiness in Brynn's life, ease the ache in her chest, and get her writing juices flowing again. The problem is Gillian is straight. And she's more focused on enlisting Brynn to see whether her doctor fiancé is a cheat. No matter what Brynn turns up, what should she tell Gillian?

This UK rom-com, part of the Window Shopping Collection, proves that the path to true love has more than a few bumps in it.

UP ON THE ROOF
A.L. Brooks

ISBN: 978-3-95533-988-3
Length: 245 pages (88,000 words)

Book-loving Lena likes order, cleanliness, peace, and quiet. When Megan, a loud and clumsy young woman, moves into the flat below hers, chaos ensues, and Lena's already-high anxiety rockets. It gets even worse when a devastating storm leaves Lena needing a place to live.

Against her better judgment, Megan offers her a spare room, and they both know it's a terrible idea. After all, they've clashed from the first moment they met. It can surely only end in disaster.

As time passes, Lena and Megan realise that, underneath their differences, there's an inexplicable pull between them that seems hard to resist. Can they learn to deal with their clashing personalities and let the attraction blossom? Or will what divides them be too much to overcome?

A fun, awkward, and sweet British romance about the power of opposites attracting.

FALLING INTO PLACE
Sheryn Munir

ISBN: 978-3-95533-972-2
Length: 228 pages (56,000 words)

Romance is not for Tara. Embittered after a college fling, she vows to never fall in love again—especially since she believes there's no future for same-sex love in her home in urban India. Then, one rain-drenched evening, an insane decision brings the bubbly Sameen into her life and everything changes. Sameen is beautiful, a breath of fresh air…and almost certainly straight. All Tara's carefully built-up defences start to crumble, one after the other. But is this relationship doomed before it can even start?

Lost for Words
© 2018 by Andrea Bramhall

ISBN: 978-3-96324-062-1

Also available as e-book.

Published by Ylva Publishing, legal entity of Ylva Verlag, e.Kfr.

Ylva Verlag, e.Kfr.
Owner: Astrid Ohletz
Am Kirschgarten 2
65830 Kriftel
Germany

www.ylva-publishing.com

First edition: 2018

Credits
Edited by Michelle Aguilar and JoSelle
Cover Design and Print Layout by Streetlight Graphics

Printed in Great Britain
by Amazon

56599426R00187